Also by John Calvin Batchelor

The Birth of the People's Republic of Antarctica *(1983)*

American Falls *(1985)*

Thunder in the Dust: Images of Western Movies,
by John R. Hamilton; text by John Calvin Batchelor (1987)

Gordon Liddy Is My Muse,
by Tommy "Tip" Paine *(1990)*

Walking the Cat, by Tommy "Tip" Paine:
Gordon Liddy Is My Muse II *(1991)*

Peter Nevsky and the True Story of the
Russian Moon Landing *(1993)*

Father's Day *(1994)*

The Further Adventures
of Halley's Comet

The Further Adventures of Halley's Comet

A Novel

John Calvin Batchelor

An Owl Book

Henry Holt and Company
New York

Henry Holt and Company, Inc.
Publishers since 1866
115 West 18th Street
New York, New York 10011

Henry Holt® is a registered trademark
of Henry Holt and Company, Inc.

Published in Canada by Fitzhenry & Whiteside Ltd.,
195 Allstate Parkway, Markham, Ontario L3R 4T8.

Library of Congress Cataloging-in-Publication Data
Batchelor, John Calvin.
The further adventures of Halley's Comet : a novel /
John Calvin Batchelor. — 1st Owl book ed.
p.   cm.
"An Owl book."
I. Title.
PS3552.A8268F8   1995   94-49338
813'.54—dc20   CIP

ISBN 0-8050-3788-8 (An Owl Book: pbk.)

Henry Holt books are available for special promotions
and premiums. For details contact: Director, Special Markets.

First published in hardcover in 1980 by Congdon & Lattès, Inc.

First Owl Book Edition—1995

Illustration by Gary Carson

Printed in the United States of America
All first editions are printed on acid-free paper.∞

10   9   8   7   6   5   4   3   2   1

Excerpts from "So You Want to Be a Rock 'n' Roll Star,' by Robert McGuinn and
Chris Hillman, copyright © 1966, Tickson Music, BMI. All rights reserved. Used
by permission.

Excerpts from "I Won't Get Fooled Again," by Peter Townshend, copyright ©
1971, Towser Tunes Inc. All rights reserved. Used by permission.

The author wishes to acknowledge NASA's Comet Halley Science Working Group, its chairman, Michael J. S. Belton, and two of its participants, Ray L. Newburn, Jr., and D. K. Yeomans, whose work proved useful in the conceptualization of this fiction.

Contents

The Further Adventures
of Halley's Comet

Prologue

Wherein We Survey
the Comet Kingdom

Cosmetological Calendar

HELLO, Your Majesty, Cain-raising kind of comet, riding your celestial flare anew for a midheaven rendezvous, long about the chill of the Year of Our Lord 2062, with direful Mother Earth impatiently awaiting you, her chivalrous star, as she's done so oft before.

Yes, Your Majesty, Cain-raising kind of comet, as when you and yours came:

Before the Christ, e.g.,

to convince Cheops the pin-headed to launch a yahoo yacht to follow the Bright (Ra) One, like you do: alas, it leaked into the dark Nile River, as did the Old Kingdom, but then their gross habit of proto-sodomy while watching you race round Ra meant too much sarcasm, not enough orgasm, and not nearly enough smarts to finish the pyramid at Gizeh with chambers meant just for you (Executive Hairy Star Lounge); or to trouble the Harappan Witches' Cabal by the rude Indus River, when they sought to evoke

Aryan demons by eating the placenta of
comet-crossed births while chanting,
"Don't come!" (which eventually worked,
as the empire crashed mysteriously,
c. 1500 B.C.); or to scourge the Shang
Dynasty by the crooked Huang Ho River
of its Gang of Erections grown snippity in
their "Great Sperm Domain," and how the
yellow ones never forgave you—calling
you "Broom Star"—as they marked your
apparitions perspicaciously, waiting for you
to make that inevitable slip into the pit; or,
tellingly—these pagans skittishly
superstitious and not a little clumsy at
self-abuse (which idiot-savant was it who
first proposed Spill-a-Seed-for-Hairy-Star?)
—to advise the terrible Assyrian King
Assurbanipal, literally "Assyrian
Ejaculator," in his last surly year between
the tepid Tigris and the cold Euphrates, to
forget about Egypt's treachery at Thebes,
to forget about his brother's treachery at
Babylon, and to bury deep that clay tablet
copy of an enchanted urban guerrilla text,
the very one ripped from the broken hands
of the aide-de-camp (why did he ever
write it down? It was the only secret
worth keeping!) to the Babylonian
Underground's mysterious Chief of
Operations, Mar'zi'pan.

    And, yes, yes, Your Majesty,
Cain-raising kind of comet, as when you
and yours came:

In the Year of Our Lord 66

(having cursed Foul Rome thrice,
316 B.C., 240 B.C., 187 B.C., and the
vainglorious Octavian family twice, 87 B.C.
and 11 B.C., calling young Julius Caesar a
venal clod and leaving his spermatozoa to
their monstrous ends, and calling Caesar
Augustus a pious fool and leaving his
spermatozoa to their monstrous ends), to
urge the restless in Jerusalem to heed
troublemaker James and his Zealots as they
cried, "Come the Revolution (of the
comet)!" which it did: Palestine a pack of
Jewish punks gone grim with their pool
cues laying open Roman heads till the Pig
Legion laid open a swathe through heady
history that left Jerusalem a charnel house,
that left the Temple a towering inferno
kicking cinders up toward All Vengeance
Himself, that left the bards enough
material for two millennia of bitching—let
there be no doubt that Foul Rome made
only one irreparable mistake, and that was
to alienate those self-elected
revolutionaries, called Cretins by some,
Jews by others, but Street-Fighting Men
by reputation and design, as you
witnessed:

In the Year of Our Lord 141,

with your quiet (7-degree tail)
pilgrimage to Simon Bar "Son of Hairy

4

Star" Kochba's mass grave to say a few
consoling words to the ravaged children of
revolution—"Are you an angel?" they
asked—with fire in their hearts to burn
beacons to guide future insurrections, such
as:

In the Year of Our Lord 218,

when you stopped over in Foul
Rome to pay off the Assassin Emperor
Caracalla's assassins, then, just for fun
(how Foul Rome adored the Barrack Room
emperors with their locker-room tastes for
pederasty and impermanence), decided also
to pay off the Assassin Emperor
Macrinius's assassins—your thirty pieces
go further when you bank at the
Tiber-No-Trust—and what a lark:

In the Year of Our Lord 295,

to take a vacation, Foul Rome all but
forgotten, its disasters (bad stars) certain
now, and so boating to balmy Teotihuacán
to bide with the Mayans, who called you
"Agent Provocateur," but, inexplicably,
refused to take bids on a comet pyramid;
you shrugged, better to let the Bright One
and the Moon take the praise as well as
the blame, because it freed you up
(freewill, a delicately philosophical
concept) for temperamental mischief,
speaking of which:

In the Year of Our Lord 374,

there was plenty about, for faithless
Valens in the East had drifted into the
accursed Arian camp (if Jesus was just a
man, that made you just one too),
necessitating some fancy talking on your
part with those ambivalent but pliably
superstitious Visigoths, who really had no
interest in making a stand at Adrianople in
378, but then, they were
Up-Against-the-Western-Wall, same as
you:

In the Year of Our Lord 451,

when you nearly had to slit
Honoria's (Valentinian's hot-to-knot sister)
throat to keep her from humping Hun-y
Attila into a dowry-domestic bliss that
would've not only slant-eyed all Gaul but
also would've seriously complicated your
well-laid plans to send Foul Rome into the
pit, phew (!):

In the Year of Our Lord 530,

when you visited (incognito) Athens
to unearth Aristotle's secret "Hairy Star
Notes" (for Alexander), wherein he had
proposed an eerie correlation between
hairy star apparitions ("atmospheric
perturbations") and mutinous doings in the

Macedonian Empire—a dangerous
document you carefully rerolled and
carefully consigned to a small campfire
you'd treated yourself to on your long
walk north to Byzantium, where that pup
Justinian was even then mishandling the
rabble into an open revolt (hee hee) that,
but for that nervy whore Theodora,
fellatician-to-the-stars, might've pulled
down the Hippodrome as well as the
Palaces of Byzance in 532—but *nondum,* so
you turned your attention:

In the Year of Our Lord 607,

to a walking tour in sylvan Britain,
passing through abandoned Roman camps,
over the Prescell (Cambrian) Mountains,
making inquiries as to this local ruffian
named Arthur you'd heard talk of in
Londinium, until you came to a smoky
copse by the River Towy, where you sat
up all night exchanging pleasantries with a
lanky lad calling himself Mordred the
Wronged, as you assured him he was
(wronged), spinning a starry tale of
revelation, defiance, and retribution that
left him howling for King Arthur's blood
and yourself noting that this scenario had
that certain feel of the eternally
melodramatic, as you also found:

In the Year of Our Lord 684,

in Mecca, where one day the Grand
Mosque would be built around the black
rocks of the Kaaba (a cornerstone of which
is a piece of a hairy star), and where you
took rooms above the open bazaar in order
to flip through notes you'd taken on this
new covered bizarre, the Koran (Mahomet
none of your doing, that was certain,
though he smacked of heavenly
handiwork), and how typical of this
martial metaphysics called Islam to think
of you as scimitar-shaped, more
broadsword-shaped really, as you certainly
appeared over the West:

In the Year of Our Lord 760,

brighter, fiercer than you'd been
since Attila's frustration at Chalons (451),
though this time your mission was subtler
—chatting with Pepin the Short's chubby
son Charles, who thought you a mad
pilgrim, so he wouldn't listen as you tried
to dissuade him from his predilection for
cosmic abandon (slaughter while the Bright
One ran red), you leaving Gallic court
politics behind, disgusted, in order:

In the Year of Our Lord 837,

to begin a two-century-long
adventure with the Northmen, so dear to

your heart, for their incendiary iconoclasm
knew no bounds as they scourged Europe
from Seville to the Dnieper, smashing,
burning, desecrating, and only incidentally
killing whatever they touched in their
metaphorical boats:

> From the fury of the Northmen
> Spare us, good God,
> From the great hairy star
> Good God, redeem us!

that first grand time behind rough'n'ready
Rollo, when you and twenty more fell
upon a monastery's vineyard at Arnhem,
the priests screaming as you crucified
them, "Come the Revolution (of the
comet)!" and again:

In the Year of Our Lord 912,

with old rough'n'ready Rollo's line
now in ascendancy in Normandy—growing
fat on a deal forced upon Charlemagne's
wasted spermatozoa—you shipping out
with five boatloads of berserkers to
rampage right up to the golden gates of
the Omayyad Court at Córdoba, on the
Guadalquivir River, only just sparing
effete Abdu-r-Rahman's invincible
reputation: what enchanted revolutionaries,
these Northmen, to whom you returned:

In the Year of Our Lord 989,

to counsel the natty Swede Olaf to
ally himself with that sloppy Dane Sweyn,
to avenge themselves on Wessex for a
century of defiance: and neither quarter
nor mercy was shown from Margate to
Land's End, you quietly pleased when you
had to leave them that the Northmen had
raped their coming well into the loins of a
land that would one day, by chance, eight
centuries on, pay you your true due, but
beforehand there was else to do:

In the Year of Our Lord 1066,

stalwart by William throughout:
first, to urge him across the Channel, since
he was rough'n'ready Rollo's seed but not
his mettle; second, to urge him to damn
the wizard's charts, to take the spectacular
hairy star for what it seemed, and to
attack (!), because the Saxons would not
stand at Hastings, which they didn't,
Wessex now more Viking than ever (and
wasn't Queen Matilda's tapestry, later at
Bayeux, a nice gesture?) as you held your
pose for two months in the western sky,
half as large as Luna, never more
vainglorious, never more ominous,
sweeping your bushy tail to rain comet
dust on them all so that:

In the Year of Our Lord 1145,

you needed a retreat, some research
in the Holy Land (notice how your early
work in Jerusalem was coming together
with your middle-period work in Mecca
and your later work in the North Sea) a
sound idea, and so passively observing as
pious Nurredin, Sultan of Syria, heaved
those cocky First Crusaders out, knowing
their cockier spermatozoa would come
wriggling back again and again, crying,
"Come the Revolution (of the comet)!" so
you purposefully kept a low profile, never
more than a 10-degree tail, not like:

In the Year of Our Lord 1222,

when you frightened them all
profoundly, a first-magnitude star scooting
out of Taurus, warning them to get serious
or else this yellow chap, Genghis Khan by
name, Numb Nuts by reputation, was
going to reduce the Holy Roman Empire to
so many potsherds in the pit: and what
irrational reaction from them—an
Inquisition instead of an inquiry; the
Teutonic Knights scrapping with Alexander
Nevski instead of with the Infidels grown
mean in the Egyptian disaster (bad stars)—
yet such was Christianity's way of
avoiding external defeat with internal
victory, as it continued:

In the Year of Our Lord 1301,

yet it was no longer of any real
concern to you, lighting up the European
sky as far north as Ultima Thule and as far
south as the Sahara, a 70-degree tail, as if
to augur your new fascination in the
remnant of Foul Rome, where you
sojourned, to prideful Florence, to invest in
some few books, then to search out an
engaging portraitist named Giotto, whom
you liked, and a suspicious, overserious
poet named Dante Alighieri, whom you
didn't like, so sulking, and then:

In the Year of Our Lord 1378,

unnerving them with a six-week
stay, because you weren't sure this
Reawakening in the remnant of Foul Rome
was the good idea it had first seemed,
them and their foppish excesses, seeking
Beauty rather than Truth, vouchsafing
Order rather than Justice, making
iconography rather than iconoclasm—bah!
—so you shook them into some healthy
philosophizing:

In the Year of Our Lord 1456,

when you, posing as Papal Archivist
Platina, wrote, "A hairy and fiery comet
made its appearance for several days, [and]
as the mathematicians declared that there

would follow a grievous pestilence, dearth, and some great calamity, [Pope] Calixtus [III]—to avert the wrath of God—ordered processions that if evil were impending for the human race, He would turn all upon the Turks, the enemies of the Christian name; he likewise ordered, to move God by continual entreaty, that notice should be given by the bells to all the faithful, at midday, to aid by their prayers those engaged in Battle with the Turk . . ." (?): sneaky doings, really, since you cared not who won what battle, were only interested in forever goofing up the Holy Catholic Church's records with bullshit declaring, "LORD SAVE US FROM THE DEVIL, THE TURK, AND THE COMET," which they were still snickering about:

In the Year of Our Lord 1531

(well after the Lisbon disaster), when you casually (7-degree tail) chanced upon a charmingly scruffy medical student named François Rabelais, whom you encouraged to write down, merely for his own amusement, some thoughts on the Great Malfeasance (ah, Rabelais, Rabelais, if only John Calvin had gone that away): you unaware that as you and Franny chuckled, certain keen observers—puzzling as to why you always kept your face to the Bright One, your long and silky hair swept away from the Bright One—were noting what would soon be taken as your Inclination to the Ecliptic, 18 degrees; your Longitude of the Ascending Node, 49 degrees; your Longitude of the Perihelion, 301 degrees; your Perihelion Distance, 0.57 A.U.; and your Motion, Retrograde: such intimacies, they guessing you were supra-lunar after all, thus shattering forevermore Rennie Descartes's silly Doctrine of Celestial Vortices, as you did again:

In the Year of Our Lord 1607,

with the great Johnny Kepler Himself writing in his "Comprehensive Report on the Hairy Star Which Appeared in 1607," "Longitude of the Node, 50 degrees; Longitude of the Perihelion, 302 degrees; Inclination to the Ecliptic, 17 degrees; Distance at Perihelion, 0.59 A.U.; Motion, Retrograde," and so forth, you realizing it was now only a matter of machinery (the telescope out of a Dutchman you chatted up while in the North Country) and mathematics (Kepler's Big Three, of course, especially the one that states planetary orbits are elliptical with the Bright One as one of the foci, though Johnny Kepler mysteriously failed to apply this insight to you, thinking you riding a straight line) before these men of science—that Polish monk Copernicus; that Danish hermit Tycho Brahe; that Italian metaphysician Galileo Galilei; and, of course, that English alchemist Isaac Newton—caught on to your game, which you played to the end:

In the Year of Our Lord 1682,

when you hiked to Cambridge, posing as a Puritan witch-burner, to reassure pious but self-persecuted Zack Newton that Rennie Descartes's Doctrine of Celestial Vortices explained nothing because it itself was unexplained; to urge pious but self-persecuted Zack Newton to pursue Robbie Hooke's suggestion, following Kepler, that particles orbiting the Bright One with a force, varying inversely as to the square of their distance from the Bright One, would describe an ellipse (!), with the Bright One as one of the foci; and finally, to mention to pious but self-persecuted Zack Newton that a certain youngster named Ed Halley (rhymes with Yalie) might someday soon (prodded by a note from you) come calling, asking after Zack's health, and did Zack have some few computations that might, by chance, change the face of Creation (*Philisophiae naturalis principia mathematica,* 1687); but even while you did your best to calm Zack Newton's epileptic-tocs, their telescopes tracked you keenly as before: Inclination to the Ecliptic, 18 degrees; Longitude of the Ascending Node, 51 degrees; Longitude of

the Perihelion, 302 degrees; Perihelion
Distance, 0.59 A.U.; and Motion,
Retrograde: can't you picture the
moment(?): Ed Halley (also rhymes with
Red River Valley)—now Savilian Professor
of Geometry at Oxford, thanks, in large
part, to that note from you—gathering
together statistics on two dozen hairy stars
and mumbling to himself, "Aha! Gotcha!"
then making his sanguine prediction in his
Astronomiae cometicae synopsis, 1705 (using
Zack's doodles, it incredibly never having
occurred to anyone before that comets
follow elliptical as well as parabolic orbits),
that you would return:

In the Year of Our Lord 1759,

which you did, first spied by a
Saxony peasant (your proletarian
sympathies emerging as the proletariat
submerged) on Merry Christmas Day
1758, though not reaching perihelion until
March 1759, visible five months, leaving
you plenty of time to investigate the
intriguing new doings across the Atlantic
in the so-called New World—perhaps
they'd name a city for you (Hairy
Starville?), but no, instead they named you
for Ed Halley (and has been known to
rhyme with creepy-crawley), so that when
you came again:

16

In the Year of Our Lord 1835

—well-pleased with the Scientific
Revolution, the Industrial Revolution, the
American Revolution, the French
Revolution, the Romantic Revolution,
those barks of "Come the Revolution (of
the comet)!" celestial music to your ears—
you decided to take the monicker *Voluntas
Hallei* (Freewill of Halley) as an apt
description of what you'd wrought these
past two millennia in the Lord-God-
Almighty-Maker-of-Heaven-and-Earth-
(and-Hairy-Stars)'s Christian West, sigh,
Mother Earth grown so thorny: you
reading *La Caricature*'s censored headlines in
the Parisian Latin Quarter, where you'd
stopped to chat with the proto-socialist
Honoré Daumier, it now clear that these
Rational Men no longer trembled at your
coming, grieved at your going, yet they
still needed your doing, Revolutionary
Comet, as you said:

In the Year of Our Lord 1910,

when you highballed it out of
Taurus, coloring the spring sky with a
betimes 140-degree tail, they thinking you
were only for young lovers (playing an old
game: Come-Uh!-with-the-Comet) and old
stargazers (measuring your nucleus, coma,
and tail, analyzing your spectrum), but you
knowing there was much to be done, with

the Czar in the Hermitage reminding you
of Foul Rome, with the President in the
White House reminding you of Foul Rome,
with the Kaiser in the Palace reminding
you of Foul Rome, with the Prime
Minister in Downing Street reminding you
of Foul Rome; was this it, then, did you
have to tinker anew(?)—best to start
modestly (though poisoning the lot with
your tail dust of cyanogen gas—"LA FIN DU
MONDE!"—was a droll, if silly, yellow-press
concept), concentrating on reigning in
these quasi-exempt Ltds., Incs., and Corps.,
with taxes (was the Sixteenth Amendment
your idea?), for this energetic, crowded
twentieth century would endure many
revolutions before your eccentric one
(seventy-four years to seventy-nine years,
depending upon the giants Jupiter and
Saturn and, of course, the Dark One—
sshh!) came again:

In the Year of Our Lord 1986,

in order to fight for your very life,
for the life of your loyal subjects
everywhere (true swords and
revolutionaries all), and for the life of an
entire planet—two planets!—oh, what a
heroic struggle, Cain-raising kind of comet,
and oh, what a fearsome noise,
Iconocomet, and oh, what a romantic tale,
Comet-of-a-Thousand-Appearances, when
you . . . but hold! . . . better to tell this at

18

length, for many cousins don't yet know what went down when you came down, in the spring of 1986, fiery-headed and bushy-tailed, for yet another splendiferous coming, doing, and going in the further adventures of Halley's Comet, that is, His Majesty, *Voluntas Hallei*, Comet Incarnate.

Coming

"Revolution eats its children."
—Abel

Book I

Wherein the Dishomed
Returns from the Holy Wars

The Manhattan Island

IT WAS late September 1985, and the hippies had long since left law school. Two such graduates, Swinyard & Schleppend, finished their work day at 7 P.M., filing out of their offices to board the express elevator for the long drop from the 100th floor of the Great Monolith Southeast, a partially owned auxiliary of modern capitalism's most monolithic superduchy, the Proto Industrial Trust (PIT).

These were modern times. These were not modern times. These were feudal times. These were not feudal times. Swinyard & Schleppend, Attorneys-at-Law, performed legal tricks on the 100th floor of the Great Monolith Southeast for Cedric Broadsword & Sons, Ltd. Cedric Broadsword & Sons, Ltd., performed investment tricks on the 125th floor of the Great Monolith Southeast for the Means Corporation. The Means Corporation performed conglomerate tricks on the 150th floor of the Great Monolith Southeast for the Proto Industrial Trust (PIT). The Proto Industrial Trust (PIT) just tricked Creationwide for Capitalism Itself. Though it had been 209 years since certain long-haired (Gk: cometic) terrorists secretly convened in a drafty hall by the Delaware River had monickered that Declaration of Independence, the superdukes and their well-armed vassals still held absolute sway over the Phantom of Liberty yet burning for a better day in the Manhattan Island's wasted harbor.

Still, anarchy notwithstanding, two SDSers (ret.), Swinyard & Schleppend, had brains enough to reserve half of their expensive briefcases for the rock'n'roll LPs they'd ripped off that afternoon by slipping them between the pages of *Kong Weekly*. Beefy, balding Swinyard, a fair, sentimental, sloppy man even in his expensive, pin-striped attire, toked extra deep on his joint anticipating this here plastic music for this here Friday evening. They were going to a party. They were going to get wasted. They were going to let it all hang out. But they were going to keep their shirts tucked in. It was late September (last weekend of summer) 1985, recall, and the hippies had long since left law school.

"What's happening, Herr Schleppend?" said Swinyard.

"What's happening, Herr Swinyard," said Schleppend, a neat, sarcastic, clownish pothead, with a Levantine nose that was easily the biggest thing about him, "is that I am air-sick."

"Think boogie," said Swinyard. "Is that sharp-eyed Yella Kissl getting down with us tonight?"

"I have no comment whatsoever," said Schleppend, grumpy.

"Chairman Means got to you today, didn't he?" said Swinyard. They exited the complex through a bank of airlocks that whooshed as they hit the street. They turned away from the tangle surrounding the sedan chair line on Liberty Street. Before them squatted the lower Manhattan Island, all angles, broken lines, spires, lopsided ovals, and every so often, through incinerator haze, infernal ozone, and opaque clouds wafting up from the loins of the inmates, a genuine pyramid. The Bright One dipping toward the outer wall's parapets colored the Manhattan Island's gray geometry with unnaturally gay pinks and purples, yet only the bleached shrubbery in the various copsewoods suggested that airborne inorganics were not the best sort of prism. It seemed a fine, busy Friday night of many erections, a few destructions, even more accidental constructions, as Swinyard & Schleppend rejoined the energetic herd.

"No more than Prexy Means," said Schleppend. "Whatcha think this will come to? This 'Macho Project'? The traffic is up ferocious. Did you see the ball today?"

"What I saw, I have forgotten," said Swinyard. "My advice to you is the same. As for the 'Macho Project,' I wouldn't know, if I knew."

"That scary, huh?" said Schleppend.

"As our roomie used to say, 'Believe it!' " said Swinyard. "One shudders. Broadsword's likely to lose another son. Did you see the look they gave him? Young Abbott Broadsword's a nosy fool. Those Means people even sound like trouble. Rasp. Rasp. Oh, God, Herr Schleppend, what did Peace of Mind close at?"

They turned up Broadway, past Cortlandt Street's gambling dens, past Dey Street's whaling taverns, dodging the ambulatory lepers at the curb. They paused behind a newsstand at the corner of Fulton and Broadway in order to allow a snake dance of syphilitic flagellants to wend past.

"I heard twenty and a quarter. Bad biz that," said Schleppend, reaching down to rip off a *New York Crimes* with a banner headline reading:

COMET COMES!
PIT PEAK CONFIRMS SIGHTING
COLLISION UNLIKELY
(photos p. 3)

and flipping to the closing prices on the Exchange. There it was: Peace of Mind at twenty and one-quarter. That was down over ten points in one week. The bottom was falling out of the hallucinogenics industry. All that remained now was the bottomless pit. Or so the lackeys joked at the Great Monolith Southeast whenever the inspector generals descended from the Means Corporation with directives said to have descended from PIT Central, wherever that was (the rumor mentioned a mobile air unit).

"I won't sell! My mama gave 'em to me," said Swin-yard.

"The times are not sentimental," said Schleppend. "This talk of highs and lows. Shall we flick out? There's a devastating double Errol Flynn on Canal Street. Eh? No? Yer too down for that high? Supper then? Gorge your blues? Shall we proceed on foot to SoHo? It's hours yet till boogie time."

"Let me check with her," said Swinyard, breaking off to move to a booth, shoveling in gobs of corrupted copper and punching the seven-digit code. He hugged the booth while he waited for the machine to connect with Lyra, kinky blond fantasy of his love life. Through the cracked plastic, he watched a sedan chair screech to a halt before a self-service bodega. An officer in the Cardinal's Guard hopped out, drawing his weapon. This looked like crime control. The officer charged into the bodega. Swinyard heard the clash of steel as his connection was made.

"Identify," said Lyra's machine.

"The man, very junior," said Swinyard.

"Oh," said Lyra's machine.

"Can she make it early for eats?" said Swinyard.

"No way," said Lyra's machine.

"Please?" said Swinyard.

"No way," said Lyra herself. "I'm not near high enough for the street. Don't you want me high and tight for the bash? You say Broadsword's loosening the bankroll, yeah?"

"Yeah, yeah," said Swinyard.

"I love you for asking," said Lyra, click.

"I love you for refusing," said Swinyard, click.

"So?" said Schleppend, watching for the officer in the Cardinal's Guard to emerge from the bodega with his score.

"So we eat stag," said Swinyard.

"Fish for me. That muscle reminds me where I am," said Schleppend.

"You're Jewish," said Swinyard.

"And still moving," said Schleppend.

They skirted the self-service bodega to West Broadway, turning north again past the groves of dying elms and coloring oaks, past the heaps of minor monoliths and surly shibboleths, past the noses for scandal and the hands of fate, all of which shaded the rapid transit paths of the various indigents of the Manhattan Island as they staggered home at the end of what had seemed, in this walled city at the very crossroads of the Old World to the New World, of the old metaphysics to the new natural physics, just another trouble-behind week.

Trouble Ahead

THAT MERCURY in the vacuum tube had dropped a full inch by the time Swinyard & Schleppend sneaked out on their supper check. They cursed their planning to have walked so far out of their way, Broadsword Hall being a good league to the southeast of SoHo. They'd be dodging alley rats and broken drain cascades if this low burst within the hour. Toking up for smoother gamboling, they hit the street in earnest just as a caravan of opulent sedan chairs—chrome-covered, mink-upholstered, powerfully cylindered—purred to a halt before them at the corner of King and Knave streets.

"Envy and so forth," said Swinyard, tugging Schleppend's attention to these beautiful wheels.

"Eh?" said Schleppend, looking up. He felt the vibes miss a three-quarter beat. He squinted through the bulletproof tinted glass of the lead sedan chair. There could be no mistake. Here they were, in the bathed, perfumed, and powdered flesh, the Twin Sisters Means, two of the most compellingly beautiful women ever to perambulate reinforced-concrete Creation: Justine, on the left, haughty and harrowing, with her white-golden locks combed back to highlight her delicately sculptured face, her strobe-light blue, no, more azure, eyes; and Christine, on the right, a mirror reflection save for what personality does to a face, looking indifferently sympathetic and adorable, her equally white-golden curls piled high to accent her high forehead, her deep azure eyes, her wide, wet mouth, her long, pale neck. He'd never before been this close to them. But the highbrow gossip *(Crimes* and *Kong)* had it right. These two seemed incubus's succubi. More, these two seemed otherworldly architecture, embodiments of the whole number 2 that divides the ineffable sum atop the mathematical symbol of mystical perfection, the Golden Mean itself, $(1 + \sqrt{5})/2$. Certainly, these two seemed worth the degrading anxiety of the Gross National Product. Schleppend forced himself to stare the more, his eyes burning from the fiery imagery of the Twin Sisters Means. Was he there too?

Yes, of course, by the far window, the white-golden boy himself, Torrance Means VIII, younger brother to the Twin Sisters Means, heir apparent to the Means Family Empire, and President of the Means Corporation. Torrance VIII, no less pretty than his sisters, though markedly stranger for the eerie vacuousness in his azure eyes, for the deep lines of regret and crooked scars of conceit in his countenance, was the very Means whom Schleppend had earlier called "Prexy." The "Chairman" was Torrance VII, Chairman of the Board of the Means Corporation, member of the Board of Governors of the Proto Industrial Trust (PIT), and, hardly incidentally, patriarch of the great American family Means.

Schleppend scrupulously cataloged this fairy-tale scene for future daydreaming. Justine was dressed in elegant party wear—a dark, ethereal sheath with a deep neckline revealing too much (for Schleppend) of two supple breasts firm with the quintessence itself. Christine was wrapped

29

more conservatively—in a black pajama suit—as befitted a mother of one, Torrance IX, bastard by birth, but also, by birth, future heir apparent to the Means Family Empire. Schleppend didn't think Christine's white-gold nosering tacky jewelry for a woman her age (thirty-nine). She wore it proudly. It was said to have been given her by her father on the occasion of her giving birth seven years before, an occasion which also marked her retirement from the urban guerrilla cadre she and Justine had once so ostentatiously led. But that, as they confab, was a long story—which Schleppend knew. What was their name for it? thought Schleppend, saying:

"The Straw People."

"What of 'em?" said Swinyard. "Counterrevolutionary lot that they were."

"The former fearless leaders of the Straw People park their unthinkable derrières in yonder," said Schleppend.

"You mean Means?" said Swinyard. His eyesight was poor, his vanity rich, so without his pince-nez he couldn't match Schleppend's reconnaissance. Still, he could see three patrician figures in the rear of the lead sedan chair. And he could see, now that he knew to look for it, the Means Family crest—a five-towered, pentagonal castle atop a sinister plateau encircled with Latin*

*By All Means By All Means By All Means

—tastefully embossed on the side of the lead sedan chair and the two following vehicles. In the second sedan chair he spied four handmaidens, two wispy Caribbean girls, two dainty Oriental girls. The third sedan chair held a grim contingent of black-suited, burly bodyguards, two of whose number also served as chauffeurs for the first two sedan chairs. Swinyard had heard enough of the Means' private guard—martial arts experts, small weapons experts, demolition experts, Bad Company—to take a quick step back from the curb when he saw them, and another quick step when he saw the chauffeur of the lead sedan chair stick his head out, yelling:

"Hey, you two!"

"Ignore him," said Swinyard.

"C'mere, will ya?" said the chauffeur.

"Yes?" said Schleppend, stepping down between the gutter rubbish to move within a yard of the chauffeur's window. Swinyard followed, keeping watch on the third sedan chair.

"Forgive me, but is that you, Schleppend?" said a heretofore unnoticed figure on the far side of the front seat. It was Aaron Verbunko, Senior Vice-President of the Means Corporation, the de facto chief counselor of the Means Family Empire. Verbunko was regarded by his inferiors as a genius. Ultimately, he was Swinyard & Schleppend's absolute boss, though he appeared anything but an absolute man. He was a thin, gray, moustached, middle-aged Swiss—now a naturalized American citizen—said to have left a Dominican monastery to serve several years in an overseas branch of the Means Corporation before making the jump to the Manhattan Island. More, Verbunko was said never to have said a careless word about anyone. Verbunko was said to have lost his faith, no longer fearing God or the Devil. Verbunko was said to work for anyone who'd pay him his thirty pieces with bonuses. Verbunko was said to impress no one and to intimidate everyone. He certainly frightened Swinyard & Schleppend. Verbunko was an heroically eloquent rhetorician. Verbunko was a Western legal scholar of the first rank. And Verbunko was a corporate law wizard, which was why he sat as Senior Vice-President of the Means Corporation, and was also why he sat in the front right seat of this sedan chair. Torrance VII had long let it be known that he'd like Verbunko (never wed) to wed into his family. Also of interest was that Aaron Verbunko was rumored to have been deeply in love with Justine Means for too many years to account.

"Yes, sir, Mr. Verbunko, Schleppend here," said Schleppend.

"What luck! Hello, Justine, one of the boys from the office. Is that Swinyard with you? What luck. And just when we'd thought we were up against it," said Verbunko in an insincere fashion.

"How can I be of assistance, sir?" said Schleppend.

"We've gotten turned around," said Verbunko. "We're trying for Broadsword Hall. It's around here somewhere. Never been there myself. We were just discussing what a grand gesture it is for Cedric Broadsword to give a grand ball for his ward. Great horsewoman and all."

"Aaron, hurry, please," said Justine. Schleppend gasped. He'd never heard either of them, since they shunned talking-head land. Justine surprised him. She sounded passionate, presumptive, and powerful. She also sounded dangerous. Schleppend dared a glance. She sat there like a Hellenistic goddess. She spoke like a regicidal priestess. Studying that face, a man could forget to breathe, truly, thought Schleppend, remembering, breathing, saying:

"Broadsword Hall? You're close. Not much farther. Let me think." He straightened up, trying to clear his mind of Justine.

"I'll tell him," said Swinyard nervously, bending down to face Verbunko. He glanced once at the Twin Sisters Means. His pothead reeled. Better not to look into those four identical eyes for long. Swinyard concentrated on Verbunko's neat, weasely face, saying, "Keep on Knave till Finn Square. Pick up West Broadway south till you hit Vesey. Go

32

left till Broadway, another right, south till you come to the sunken cross at the Wall Street crossroads. Go left, right to the river. You can't miss it. The pennants have the Broadsword crest."

"Uh," said the chauffeur, dizzy.

"Really, Swinyard," said Verbunko.

"Are you surrounded by idiots, Verbunko?" shot Torrance VIII. He was short-tempered—at his worst, impetuously cruel.

"It's how it's done," said Swinyard.

"Any trouble here, sir?" said a martial voice. Two of the burly bodyguards towered over Swinyard and flanked Schleppend. There was a pause, and then, for reasons having to do with the rebel deeply nurtured in sentimental, sloppy men, Swinyard lost his cool. The pigs! he thought. Who did they think they were, treating us like rabble? The pigs! He dropped his expensive briefcase, rolled his copy of the *New York Crimes* into a blunt instrument, and stood upright to battle this slavish foe. He was high, chubby, and outnumbered, but he wasn't going to take this bullying.

"Now, now, there, there," said Schleppend, stepping into his partner's arms, whispering, "Stay loose, old friend."

"Uh," said Swinyard.

"My companion didn't mean to confuse you, Mr. Verbunko, Mr. Means," said Schleppend. "He's not that familiar with the neighboring quarters. If you'll proceed south here till Spring. Go left on Spring till Broadway. South again on Broadway until you reach the sunken cross at the Wall Street crossroads. Turn right to the river. Broadsword Hall will loom."

"Very well, Schleppend," said Verbunko. The caravan of three opulent sedan chairs glided off smoothly, the bodyguards rejoining their vehicle on the run. Schleppend handed Swinyard his briefcase.

"Herr Schleppend, you told 'em wrong," said Swinyard.

"Believe it!" said Schleppend, taking his partner's arm

33

as they pressed on beneath a blackening, billowing sky to Broadsword Hall, a good league to the southeast.

"Graceless," said Torrance VIII.

"Tory, be more giving," said Justine.

"They set it right in the end," said Verbunko.

"This best be worth it. Horsewoman, indeed," said Torrance VIII.

"The best for five years running at the decade," said Verbunko.

"Says who?" said Torrance VIII.

"Aaron's correct," said Justine. "I recall her at the Garden one year. Magnificent on all mounts. A striking presence. Remember, Christy?"

"Barely in your class, Justy," said Christine.

"Thank you, sister," said Justine.

"Will she have her mounts tonight?" said Torrance VIII.

"Hush, Tory. She's nearly retired, now," said Justine. "I understand the last Mediterranean tour was a disappointment. Seems she refused to perform twice."

"How's this?" said Verbunko. "The legendary Grace Thyme not performing?"

"Some personal problems," said Justine. "She's a drunk."

"Oh, fine. You drag me into this plague-ridden metropolis after hours to meet an athlete gone fuzzy," said Torrance VIII.

"It is unattractive of her. But she was stunning in the saddle. Sexy," said Justine.

"Not again," said Torrance VIII.

"You have your fun," said Justine.

"And then some," said Christine.

"Reproach? With your heaps of discarded suitors?" said Torrance VIII.

"Not heaps," said Christine.

"You must be on your guard," said Justine. "No

lunging at the virginal Miss Thyme. Old Cedric covets her more even than his name. He waves pistols at any man who flirts."

"This improves," said Torrance VIII. "Could be worth an effort."

"Speaking of whom," said Justine.

"What's that, Justine?" said Verbunko.

"Don't jump, Aaron dear. I was being coy. Telling my baby brother that old Cedric gets irrational when Miss Thyme is concerned. He drove away his older son because of her."

"Delicious," said Christine.

"The hippie freak? The draft-dodging felon? The radical fool?" said Torrance VIII.

"Effert Broadsword," said Justine, "dishomed because of the virginal Grace Thyme. Thirteen years ago, I do believe."

"You've been studying. What gossip," said Torrance VIII. "This is a setup. All right, I surrender. What?"

"The sentimental usual. Young lovers star-crossed by fate," said Justine. "She was twenty-two and romantic. A dope and empathy Smithie. He was twenty-four and self-possessed. A Yalie dropout, recently indicted for pouring goat's blood on a senator. She discovered his desperado zipper. He discovered her cowgirl snaps."

"Mmh," said Torrance VIII.

"Abortion soon followed, though not as you might suppose," said Justine. "She was thrown from a horse. No one knew she was pregnant until she started bleeding on her breeches. There was melodrama at Mass. General. All-night floor-pacing. The baby died. The mother lived. Cedric threatened to hang Effert on sight. Exit Effert, posthaste."

"So our virgin's no virgin. I never realized Effert had left for any reason but idiocy," said Torrance VIII. "Are you sure?"

"Tory," said Justine. "And think, once smitten, twice shy. I'll wager the only thing she's mounted for thirteen years has four legs. It explains the drinking."

"Is this a challenge? Do we have a wager?" said Torrance VIII.

"We have a wager," said Justine. "Now, what do I really, really want?"

"Redemption," said Verbunko.

"Release," said Torrance VIII.

"Revenge," said Christine.

"A weighty list," said Justine. "But for now—myself against one absolute obedience. I'll take your word for the deed."

"Done," said Torrance VIII.

"Incest?" said Verbunko.

"Tradition," said Justine.

"To rule, one must be shameless," said Torrance VIII.

"And, brother dear," said Justine, "you'll have to work. Old Cedric has his own ideas. He has another son."

"Adopted," said Verbunko.

"Heir and successor, nonetheless," said Justine.

"The pious Abbott Broadsword, seminarian turned usurer," said Verbunko.

"Your language, Aaron," said Justine. "Yet a man to confront."

"Here's Wall Street," said Verbunko abruptly. He claimed they were to turn right. The chauffeur respectfully submitted that Broadsword Hall was said to overlook the East River, which was left. The caravan of three opulent sedan chairs purred to a halt at the Wall Street crossroads, which opened, to the left, onto the now deserted cavern of stone, steel, and strange temptations that was the very spinal cord of Capitalism Itself. The slit through the sheer gray walls was narrow, but wide enough, while the Bright One shone, to feed the captains of industry to the titans of finance to the fates of men to buy low, sell high, and split the difference with the Lord God Almighty Maker of Heaven and Earth (and Hairy Stars).

To move the debate, Verbunko recalled that there was supposed to be a sunken cross. The chauffeur could see no sunken cross, just, to the right, a darkened spire that was Trinity Church, well-known Anglican coffer. Suddenly, two burly bodyguards approached the sedan chair from either side to indicate that there was a body over there in the churchyard, above ground, if not moving. They were told to fetch the body. They moved heavily into the graveyard, weaving in and out of antique headstones, to a genuine sunken cross of stone which marked the last resting place of

WILLIAM KIDD
1645–1701
Hanged for Capitalism
R.I.P.

against which lay a man's long body. They poked. He was already awake, bounding to his feet, pocketing a tattered paperback of H. G. Wells's *In the Days of the Comet*, assuming a defiant posture, reaching to his waist as one might reach for a sword. Fortunately for the burly bodyguards, this man was neither Kidd reincarnated nor armed with a sword. He was, however, hostile, tall, broad, bearded, hairy, and covered by a ratty, dark, ankle-length foul-weather coat and an equally ratty, dark foul-weather cap. He carried a nondescript satchel on his back. Overall, he seemed a brutal, if self-abused, figure. The bodyguards grunted to him that he was to move to the sedan chairs. He obliged cautiously.

"Forgive me, pilgrim, could you help us?" said Verbunko. "We're trying for Broadsword Hall. Do you know it? No, I suppose not." Verbunko sighed, because he could see, as the pilgrim passed the headlights, he was more Bowery bum than informed traveler. Everything about him seemed worn and foreign. The pilgrim slumped to within five yards of Verbunko, then straightened to well over six feet. At least he didn't look underfed.

"Broadsword Hall?" said the pilgrim.

"Do you know it?" said Verbunko.

"Aye," said the pilgrim.

"Then tell us how to get there!" shot Torrance VIII.

"It would be better if I showed you," said the pilgrim.

"I see," said Verbunko, turning to Torrance VIII for a decision. Torrance VIII looked a torturer. Christine looked a cipher. Justine nodded approval, however, indicating the pilgrim should sit up front.

But before Verbunko could say as much, the pilgrim had mounted the running board and bowed briefly to communicate instructions. The journey was not long. The pilgrim guided them via Wall Street into the quarter of the island once known as the South Street Seaport. They maneuvered hazy avenues, some lined with ominous structures embellished with undergarments, hopelessness, and video glow; others scarred by craters, fences, mounds of discarded metal. They proceeded on to Water Street, over once-reclaimed river land which, through the years, was slowly returning to the river, so that it had the odor of marshland about it, as if reptiles, vapors, and exitless mazes awaited the unschooled. They avoided a fork at Fulton Street, skirted a mossy, snake-covered mound, regained Water Street, and glided up to the Peck Slip crossroads, nearly lost beneath the gold-paved highways-in-the-sky that had bypassed the seaport many decades before.

Before them now, as promised, loomed Broadsword Hall, lit grandly in the midst of what could very well have been, once upon a time, a treacherous swamp. The Broadsword pennant flew high above the five-story structure, a brick and timber construction of uncertain architectural style, but clearly meant to be economically defended. Its main gate, opening into a central courtyard, was iron and closed.

The lead sedan chair again purred to a halt, just as the first big drops of what would soon be a heavy downpour splashed on the caravan.

"Hey there! Stranger," said Justine to the pilgrim, surprising everyone in the sedan chair, "who are you?"

"A poor boy," said the pilgrim, dismounting, walking backwards from the caravan. "Returned from the Holy Wars. Originally from this quarter. Most honored to have been of service to the Means. To the lovely ladies Means."

"What's that?" said Verbunko, but the pilgrim was gone in the storm which just then broke mercilessly. The chauffeur sounded the sedan chair's horn. The main gate swung open.

Broadsword Hall

WHAT IS it with me? I'm thirty-five years old! I'm a grown-up lady! I've got two Olympic golds! I've been Woman Athlete of the Year! Beatles have courted me! A king once goosed me! I get the best stalls every Atlantic crossing! So what is it with me!? Why am I such a mess?" said Grace Thyme, sprawled casually, wine-glass in hand, in an overstuffed armchair before an empty fireplace, which, when lit, was meant to provide charm to this memento-cluttered apartment on the fifth floor of Broadsword Hall. She was half-dressed for a ball, wearing a crème-colored chemise and enough powder to coat one of her pet Shetland ponies. She also wore her long left arm in a surgical sling (separated shoulder) and her long neck in a surgical brace (strained vertebrae). She was not talking to herself. She addressed a red setter so ancient only the blinking of his long lashes indicated he was not himself— proud, patient, all-knowing—as stuffed as his armchair.

"Oh, Landrover, you're so smart. You must know," continued Gracie. "Is it because I'm ugly? I am, you know. No, none of that slick city-dog manner. I'm ugly. Well, at least I'm not attractive. I was never even half those Means girls. Too much nose, see? Not enough mouth, see? I have my strengths, but they aren't looks. I read you what that magazine man wrote. That 'the legendary Grace Thyme' was difficult to picture apart from her horse. You get it. They think I'm part horse! Do I cry every time they tell me that?

39

You betcha. In my lonely hotel room, Grace Thyme, heroine to millions of eager girls hoping against puberty to ride in the Olympic trials, I bawl my heart out! Wouldn't you, Landrover, if somebody wrote it was difficult to picture you apart from your leash? Ashes, it's all ashes now, Landrover. Fleeting fame. Fickle fortune. All I ever got out of it was mythical confusion with equus. That's horse. Like that damn paperback writer said, 'All that equinity in femininity.' I shoulda never read my own clips. Never let them talk me into celebrityhood. Hooked me on my own vanity. 'Sexgoddess amount' indeed. Horseshit! That's what it's been. It's true. I know you're familiar with dogshit, but how many stalls have you ever mucked out? Let me tell you, being famous never exempted me from mucking stalls. Some might say that I never had to do a man's laundry, never had to swish a toilet bowl, produce short-order dinners, and they'd be right. Instead, famous Grace, she got to muck out horseshit. Mountain ranges of the stuff after all these years. You think I enjoy it? No! Well, maybe no. After all, what else do I know how to do? Do I know how to rock a baby to sleep? Do I know how to wait up for a man? Do I even know how to do that oral sex? No! Only what I've read in *Vogue,* no more, saith Thyme. I'm a sassy, uppity old maid who gets roses four times a year from her guardian, dear old Uncle Cedric. That's it. The only man who ever sent me a blossom, and the only thing he wants is obedience. Where are my divorce proceedings? My estranged lovers? I've fallen behind my sisters. I've never even been abandoned! Unless you count Effert, and you wouldn't, would you, Landrover? He abandoned you. He forgot me. All right, Gracie is feeling sorry for herself. Why not? I'm ugly, bitchy, and old. I'm old! And I'm too proud to make myself do anything about it except accept their praise and reject my reproductive organs. It awaits me, that. And do you know how they deal with my depression? Do you know what they do when they know I'm cuddling with a claret every night? When they know I fall off horses on purpose? They throw a ball to celebrate my return! Who're they fooling? Everybody knows Gracie's finished. And alone. Oh, God, alone. Who cares if alone is lonely? It's alone. The only man I ever loved was so romantic he ascended directly into fantasy to sit on the right hand of the Faerie Queene. The only job I could ever do is now so boring I'm transforming it into kinky sex. Yes, that's why I fall. I'm ashamed of myself, but it's true. And the only child I'll ever bear is thirteen years dead and gone, without a name, a mother, a fate. Oh, God! Oh, Landrover! I'm pathetic. And now I'm supposed to go down there and meet those beautiful people in this contraption. Sure, it's funny-looking. I fell off another horse. Sure, I'm drunk. I deserve it. Sure, nobody cares about the trouble I've caused. So what? What is it with me? Who will deliver me from this terrible pleasure?"

Gracie paused, startled by a horn blast below her bay windows. What time? she thought. Gone past nine, she saw. The guests gathered. Yet the guest of honor remained anything but together. She brushed her burning cheeks. There were no tears. She'd given this monologue in too many silent, empty rooms, in too many silent, empty world capitals, for her to weep while she wailed. It was true. It was false. It was self-criticism, and only her God and a red setter had heard. God would do what He would, she knew. Landrover, however, would only love her the more for lavishing energy on a dog forgotten in his own home for thirteen years. As Grace Thyme had been Effert Broadsword's devoted woman, Landrover had been his devoted hound. When Effert had gone missing, he'd not only broken Gracie's heart, nursing from a miscarriage in Boston, he'd also broken the heart of a lovesick puppy fending for himself on the Manhattan Island. For thirteen years, the only time Landrover emerged from his sulk through the damp corridors of Broadsword Hall was when Gracie visited during the National Horse Show. Otherwise, Landrover mourned. Now fifteen years old, he was dying of heroic patience. When Gracie had run to greet Landrover the week before, she'd realized he couldn't survive another winter. Her last sentimental hold on Effert was slipping from her. So, in part, her wordy self-pity was compensation for her speechlessness before so profoundly sad an event as the death of a deserted dog.

Landrover lowered himself carefully from his perch, padding across to Gracie, lost in her doubts. He raised his right front paw just high enough to run her pantyhose at the ankle. Then he nuzzled into the back of her knee. Gracie broke her thoughts to lean forward and smooth back his graying ears. At least something male ran her hose. She worked sleep crust from Landrover's eyes. He wagged his tail, then stopped, as if to protect his heart. He was very old, but he was also a crafty dog with a mission. He'd vowed (one can suppose) to live until the day Effert returned to him to apologize for being absent without leave for thirteen years.

"Not alone?" said Gracie. "Is that what you say? You're here. Yes, you are, you old sweetie. And I love you, I love you!"

"*Allora?*" said the Contessa Bianca Stupefacenta Capricciosa, sweeping into the room from the far doors with the determined agility that, aside from her dark beauty, was her most striking quality. "Not dressed? Gracie! *Madonna mia!*"

"*Madonna mia* is right, Bee. Gracie's not dressed. She's sloshed," said Gracie, waving her empty wineglass.

"Gracie, not again. Are you going to be sick this time? I have just washed my hands," said Bianca, rushing to Gracie, brushing Landrover back, pulling Gracie upright. As they teetered before the mantel, they made a study in how remarkable contrasts make for remarkable friendships. Whereas Grace Thyme was tall, broad, muscular, and all-American WASPish, the Contessa Bianca Stupefacenta Capricciosa was short, petite, firm, and Continental Jewish. And whereas Gracie's features were regular and fair, Bianca's were exotic and olive. Gracie wore her flaxen hair pulled back in a bun to give her womanly figure the contradiction of a girlish countenance. Bianca wore her black hair long and full, with several strands twisted fancifully on either side of her face, held together with gold clasps, giving her girlish figure the contradiction of a mature, lofty countenance. What is more, Gracie was, at her best, handsome and charming. Bianca was always and only a musky Mediterranean beauty who would keep her figure and her admirers as long as they kept her attention. Her black eyes were for worship. Her full lips were for seduction. Her elegant hands were for priceless gems. And her aristocratic manner was blended with a passionate temperament that communicated to the men who paused to love her that she would be as much trouble when pleased as when aroused.

Bianca already had two husbands to attest to that truth, though one could only do so from the grave, the other from a prison colony, both ruined by their irrational jealousy of a wife neither of them had ever felt comfortable possessing. Bianca, at thirty-nine, was Bianca's. She radiated an unrelenting will which, when turned upon something or someone, would not be denied. She was said to have the energy and finesse, if not the politics, of her Eurocommunist mother, the famous Florentine commissar, Europa Stupefacenta. She was also said to have the wealth of kings, thanks to her first husband's intestate will and her second husband's guilt-ridden generosity. Combining all these assets, Bianca was the embodiment of luxurious, loving whimsy.

Her current charity was "the legendary Grace Thyme," whom Bianca had befriended and befunded years before, as patroness to the arts and the stables, but had only recently returned to during Count Nazzareno Capricciosa's trial for murdering, in a pistol duel, an alleged gigolo keeping an alleged rendezvous with Bianca.

Gracie had balked from her performance at the Neapolitan Horse Show at about the same time Bianca had balked from her performance (in Nazzareno's defense) in a Neapolitan courtroom. Romance being what it is, Bianca had rushed to the airship in order to accompany Gracie: first, to a Florentine Horse Show, where Gracie had balked again; then, to Bianca's Parisian suite to dry out Gracie's innards; then, to Bianca's Sardinian villa to dry out Gracie's head; and, finally, back to America to construct an act for the rest of Gracie's life. Gracie's practical solution to Gracie's existential dilemma had been fine wine. Bianca's practical solution to Gracie's existential dilemma was masculine.

Bianca helped Gracie into the bathroom, leaning her against the sink, leaving her there to vomit or not to vomit. Bianca rushed about the apartment gathering Gracie's turquoise ball gown, slippers, and jewelry. Bianca herself wore a wine-red gown, without any jewelry, save for those gold clasps in her thick black hair.

"Bee!" said Gracie. "I'm not going to be sick. I won't."

"That is right, Gracie. You are not to be sick. You must dress now," called Bianca.

"You're so nice, Bee. Is there any hope?" said Gracie.

"There are men. There are many men," said Bianca.

One hundred years before, when the merchants reigned along the South Street Seaport, Broadsword Hall had been an exclusive warehouse for precious cargo. With the passing of the seaport facilities, Broadsword Hall had been renovated by Cedric Broadsword's grandfather, Wilfred, into a damp estate befitting a stolid family which gradually called itself investment bankers.

The introduction of the income tax in 1913 (the Sixteenth Amendment a suspiciously cosmic idea) not only forever ended certain aspects of capitalistic treasure-burying, but also forever necessitated certain types of piratical capitalism. Hoarding was out. Making your swag work for you was in. The Broadsword family, first from their base in the Hall, later from offices off Wall Street, and now from their office in the Great Monolith Southeast, had become middle managers for the fabulously wealthy family empires. Only modestly endowed itself, the Broadsword family, as currently represented by Cedric Broadsword & Sons, Ltd., acquired its ponderous prestige (though only qualified power) by running paper errands for the superdukes. Accordingly, masculine prestige seemed everything to Cedric Broadsword. What is more, Broadsword Hall had been without a woman's hand for over three decades, and it showed to its monomaniacal advantage.

The courtyard was crowded with broad oaks, draping their gnarled limbs over the cobblestone drive. The four inner walls were covered with ivy (Yale cuttings) that twisted up over jutting gargoyles to the smoke-blackened roof. At the side of the courtyard was a towering bronze statue—in the mannered Academy style of the late nineteenth century—of Elijah Broadsword, eighteenth-century patriarch of the Broadsword family in the Americas. The Hall's main entrance was at the center of the east gallery. Inside, the dimly lit atmosphere hung with manly reticence. The bare brick walls were hung with portraits of sea captains. They were a stern, Protestant-looking gang, precisely the sort of men who might have owned the trappings that now filled Broadsword Hall. For the Hall was, more than anything else, a museum of naval furniture and the kind of cargo abandoned in obsolesced sailing ships long before sold for taxes or just consigned to scrap. The Hall seemed a late-twentieth-century testimony to the capriciously acquisitive nature of free enterprise. Effert Broadsword (until he'd gone missing) had called it what it seemed, "Broadsword's haul!"

But that had been Effert's troublesome manner. Certainly, the Broadsword bounty had not been meanly weighed this particular September's eve. The ball celebrating Grace Thyme's return from her Mediterranean tour was set in the north gallery's ballroom, sumptuously lit and decorated for the occasion. Here, at the foot of the steps down from the hallway, stood the lord of the Hall himself, Cedric Broadsword. Beside him stood his adopted son,

Abbott Broadsword. And at the exact moment when Gracie, five floors above, announced to Bianca that she wasn't going to be sick, Abbott turned to Cedric to announce in a loud whisper (the dancing already begun), "Here they come," meaning the Means—Aaron Verbunko escorting Justine, Torrance VIII escorting Christine.

Feast of Swords

AYE, AYE, I see," said Cedric Broadsword gruffly, as impatient as he was bearlike a man. He stood well over six feet, all of it broad and fleshy—a tremendous organism with iron hair, a bold snout, a surly squint, and a leathery face, wide and jowled. Cedric Broadsword was said to have once growled the stock market up a point by closing. If not literally true, the anecdote communicated that this quick-tempered, prideful, grudge-bearing sexagenarian (sixty-seven) was capable of sweeping aside his family's foes with a backhand stroke. He'd once killed a man with a single thrust of that paw, though the man had been a felon, and though there were those who claimed his death could actually be attributed to the leap he'd made from the balcony onto the floor of the Exchange attempting to escape Cedric's wrath. Still, fellow bankers afterward talked of "that thane Broadsword" in the respectful tones one associates with discussions of marauding grizzlies. Yet his reputation was also Cedric's curse, for he was regarded only as a limited (Ltd.) commander, not as a corporate (Corp.) player. Cedric's temperament suited a self-possessed lord husbanding a portion of his ruler's sylvan land; it did not suit a privy councillor supposedly husbanding a portion of his ruler's paper empire. Cedric was not only regarded by Torrance VII and Torrance VIII (his overlords) as an aging, indiscreet tyrant, but he was also regarded by the corporation players

(Verbunko and et cetera), who knew how to compromise, betray, and survive, as a naive (because honorable) vassal to be used, abused, and discarded.

"Shall I see what's keeping her?" said Abbott.

"Grace will be along when she is along," said Cedric, reaching out to move Abbott back a step from his line of sight to the Means party. Not that Abbott blocked much of Cedric's bulk, being boyishly slender for a man said to be near six feet. That he was Cedric's adopted son was self-evident, for no even miscreant seed of Cedric's could have produced so wiry and dapper a man, his brown hair coiffed stylishly, his tinted shades level on a comely clean-shaven, lightly tanned (weekends on the Long Island) face, his long neck flowing into a supple, firm body with narrow hips, a shapely ass, and long, loose legs. Abbott was an excellent racquet ball player, an excellent gourmet, and an excellent host. He was also a mild disappointment to Cedric. Abbott had the looks of a California dandy, the intelligence of a Presbyterian diplomat, and the morality of an off-shore banker. Cedric had found an able successor in Abbott, but not a cock who'd fight.

"So good of you to have us, Cedric," said Verbunko.

"My pleasure, sir, for you to have come to my home, finally," said Cedric.

"And may I introduce Miss Justine Means. Or have you met?" said Verbunko.

"Not for too many years," said Cedric. "You were younger. So was I. Your father has spoken of your beauty many times, Miss Means. I see now how words can fail."

"Thank you, Mr. Broadsword. How gallant," said Justine.

"This is my son, Abbott, Miss Means," said Cedric.

"Your gown excites me," said Abbott.

"No need for that," said Cedric.

"Oh, I like it," said Justine.

"Please enjoy yourselves," said Cedric. "Abbott tells me this noise and these lights are for dancing. I've not danced since Bess passed on. She liked to dance. I regret our

47

guest of honor's been detained. There are many young people here from the corporation. I'm sure you'll find your friends. There's Szell from BP, Mr. Verbunko. And Ranke from Txc, Tsky from Mbl. And there's Ystorm, Miss Means, your cousin, I believe, from Grimmen Aircraft. Just written up in the *Journal*."

"What *Journal* is that?" said Justine.

"Why, uh, what?" said Cedric.

"You are sweet, as Daddy says. Be sure to introduce me to Grace Thyme when she joins us," said Justine.

"Me too," said Torrance VIII.

"Good evening, Mr. Means," said Abbott.

"Mmh?" said Torrance VIII.

"Abbott Broadsword, sir, junior partner to . . ."

"Yes, nice to, uh, Christine?" said Torrance VIII.

"A joy," said Abbott. "More beautiful than perhaps even . . ."

"Identical, Mr. Broadsword," said Christine.

"Welcome to Broadsword Hall, Torrance," said Cedric. "I'll want to escort you about later on. Show the heirlooms."

"No need for that, Cedric," said Torrance. "I'm told you lock away the best."

"I don't know what you mean," said Cedric.

"Easy, just a jibe. You look panic-stricken. Though you must have locked away Grace Thyme. I don't see her, do I?"

"No, not yet," said Cedric. "And you are correct. She is my treasure. She's not locked away, but she's well guarded. There won't be any question about that, will there, Torrance? Is there a stronger way I can say this and not flag the party spirit? Should I raise my voice? Grace Thyme is my treasure."

"If you'd like to say it again, please," said Torrance VIII.

"I said that Grace Thyme is dear to me. She is my heart's delight. I would die for her. Only one other woman would I say that for, and the Lord took her from me long ago.

Grace is my blessing. If anyone were to bother Grace, I would damage that person. I promise sincerely, Torrance. Damage."

"You're not the same man who works below me, are you?"

"I am Cedric Broadsword. Son of Hobart, grandson of Wilfred. This is my home. I know your father knows what this means. I trust so does his only son. Nothing is more important to me than Grace Thyme. Not my name, not my livelihood, not my property."

"Nor a son?" said Torrance VIII.

"Nothing," said Cedric.

"Damage? What's this of damage?" said Christine.

"My sister, Christine," said Torrance VIII.

"An honor, Miss Means," said Cedric.

"Very dear. What damage, Tory?" said Christine.

"We were discussing family business," said Torrance VIII.

"No, we weren't," said Cedric.

"Oh," said Christine. "Where's Grace Thyme?"

"She's slightly detained," said Cedric.

"You promise to introduce me?" said Christine.

"I keep my promises. I promise," said Cedric.

"And your threats?" said Torrance VIII.

"Come on, Tory," said Christine, pulling her baby brother away from his purposeless confrontation in order to confront purposefully the swirling lights, the swishing gowns, and the deafening dance music on the ballroom floor. The cavernous room was packed. The cacophonous company was high (some organics). The collective mood was higher (much inorganics). Christine danced her baby brother as far away from Cedric Broadsword as possible. She favored vanity in men, not vainglory—an old, tragic bias. Christine danced her baby brother beneath the seven-piece band to drown out his pique with the noisy elegance of modern rock. The big green these days was in a form of rock'n'roll that skulked under so many disguises that no musician could be sure he or she was making it until his or

49

her LP had mounted the charts, fallen off the charts, and then been resurrected by *Kong Weekly* at year's end as a misrepresented masterpiece that'd nearly bankrupted its label. Most rockers couldn't stomach the anxiety (called the "rock shits"), so they turned to making ballroom oriented rock (BOR-ing) for high society. It was trite, but in America, land of the *instant riche,* it was steady.

Perhaps because of the frustration of being a true son of rock, yet self-condemned to a fate worse than spinning the top 40 playlist, the band leader just then grabbed himself savagely in the groin and bellowed forth an inhuman wail that reverberated through the ballroom with the help of amps, dials, gadgets, and wires, sounding something like

Yeaaaaaaaaaaaaaaaah . . .
Meet the new boss!
Same as the old boss!

"What was that about, Tory?" said Justine.

"Please, Justine, I can't dance alone," said Verbunko.

"Here, Christy, trade partners with me," said Justine.

"He upped the stakes on our wager," said Torrance VIII.

"Too exciting! What did he say? It's the damsel, not the beast, you're after," said Justine.

"We stand to gain more than we'd thought," said Torrance VIII. "His name, job, home, and maybe his son, though he got strange there. Senile old man. You were right about the Thyme woman. He covets her. Something of the lecher, I suspect. Young maiden reminds him of dead maiden. The forever mourned Bess."

"You can back out now, if you want," said Justine.

"No time limit?" said Torrance VIII.

"Time itself, ha ha," said Justine.

"Mmh, you're not afraid of losing something worth keeping?"

"Not to you," said Justine.

"Come here, Justy," said Christine. "You boys

circulate. Listen, Justy. I've figured out something about that pilgrim."

"A secret?" said Justine.

"It just came to me. Seeing old Cedric," said Christine.

"What took you so long?" said Justine.

"I'm hysterical," said Christine, "and look."

Across the ballroom, Cedric straightened pridefully, turned to the staircase, and beamed a smile to melt the heart of any little girl who ever dreamed of a sugar daddy. Here came Gracie, on Abbott's arm. She wobbled slightly, her surgical brace removed at Bianca's insistence, her surgical sling covered by Bianca's careful draping of the gown.

Gracie bucked as she sniffed the hallucinogenic odor of a ballroom full of boisterous well-being. Give a big smile to Uncle Cedric, she thought, but hold your head still— ouch! Smarting, Gracie's heart went out to this energetically patriarchal man who'd struggled to be her father, mother, and knight-errant these past thirteen years. Not that he hadn't done so before. But with the retiring of Effert from the lists, Cedric had redoubled his effort.

"You look a dream, my Grace," said Cedric.

"I'm in a dream, Uncle Cedric," said Gracie.

"For you, all for you, our heroine. I should have done this years ago," said Cedric. "Everyone wants to meet you, from the richest to the prettiest, yet none are as rich as me for having so pretty a ward as you."

"I wish I were what you think I am," said Gracie.

"I love you, Grace. I will never let anything harm you," said Cedric, "as God is my witness and judge."

"I love you, too," said Gracie.

"None of that," said Cedric. "Abbott, your handkerchief."

"Thank you, sniff, Abbott," said Gracie.

"Your hose is run," said Abbott.

"Isn't it neat? Landrover did it, the cutie," said Gracie.

"Filthy beast," said Abbott.

"Not to worry, Bee let him out, I think. Where is Bee?"

"What's that?" said Cedric.

"Sir," said a servant.

"Father, there's a crasher at the door," said Abbott.

"Where's the Contessa, Abbott?" said Gracie.

"No running away, now, my Grace," said Cedric. "Here are the Means. Justine and Christine and so forth."

"Neigh-hey-hey," said Gracie, bracing up, taking Cedric's thick arm, prepared to do her championship best in this, an arena fashioned just for her, "the legendary Grace Thyme," sans mount.

The Passing of Landrover

ENCHANTED ball whirled and straightened locks curled until the midnight hour, when the band took a break for the sake of a candelabra-lit buffet supper served in the adjoining dining hall. Outside the wall of windows, the storm also took a break. The heartier dancers strolled in the drizzle along the terrace. The more winded flopped on the chairs at the long tables inside. Here, the talk turned on finer things, such as post-coital lust and Proto Industrial Trust. It was agreed that the band was creditably prurient, that the atmosphere of the Hall was romantically decadent, and that the crowd was athletically loose, considering that the males spent their days with their manicured fingers stuck in their orifices and that the females spent their days, their ovum, their daddy's swag, and anything else that might be considered negotiable. These were not the good people of Creation. These were not the bad people of Creation. These were the best people of Creation.

Being best, none had ears to hear, or eyes to see, or wits to turn and be amazed by the spectacle of the pilgrim from the sunken cross slipping into the dining hall from a rarely used passage, edging along the bank of fireplaces, ducking behind a bus station heaped with untouched sweetmeats, and climbing four steps to a mantel that provided a well-concealed (in shadows) command of the hall. The pilgrim unharnessed his satchel—hooking it on a peg—and tucked his legs beneath him. He rubbed his hands vigorously, his foul-weather coat having failed to fend off most of the foul weather. He then produced the sweetmeats he'd snatched. Before beginning his meal, he doffed his foul-weather cap, revealing a healthy countenance with a straight nose, a toothy mouth, and self-righteous eyes. The face above the beard was deeply tanned, but not as if he'd just come from a timeless resort, rather as if he'd just passed a long time of no shelter. He had the look of a careless, ineffective wanderer who'd tired of a sudden, now indulging his most otherworldly illusions. He pulled forth his tattered H. G. Wells, but was soon distracted by the chatter at the four tables below him.

At the first table, to the pilgrim's near left, another pilgrim, this one sixtyish and female, dined with vigor as she scolded in Italian the Contessa Bianca Stupefacenta Capricciosa seated across from her. Bianca no longer seemed the proud beauty, rather the juvenile delinquent, enduring another lecture from her mother. Which was the exact case. How could you have abandoned your husband? asked the sixtyish female, who was, incognito (lest she be detained for questioning by the state for her part in the Mbl scandals of the mid-seventies in Italy), the famous Florentine commissar Europa Stupefacenta. Don't tell me he murdered your lover, continued Europa. Your husband, whose name I've sworn never to speak, is a degenerate monster who should be hanged by his heels until his eyes come out to see what he and his kind have done to our people, but, nonetheless, he is your husband! You must comfort him and suffer for him! You are a disgrace, my child, but you are my only child, and I raised you to respect your vows. You must come home with me to stand by your man, convicted murderer that he is. If you do not, I shall disown you. I will have no daughter. Don't tell me you are a mother of a child! Don't shame my grandchild so! You haven't mentioned her for a decade! You have become as full of straw as these Americans. I can forgive you your first husband, that musician, who was mad, but not this. I leave tomorrow. Be at the aerodrome with me or no longer be a Stupefacenta!

At the very next table, to the pilgrim's far left, Schleppend paused to consider this Italian anguish. He spied an old woman stern enough to stop Panzer tanks lecturing a young woman fetching enough to stop Mercedes limos. They were obviously profoundly related. This was a family affair. My, she's beautiful, he thought, getting an elbow for his trouble from his supper companion, the sharp-eyed Yella Kissl, who at one time might've been called a Jewish American Princess, but was now better described as a demythologized, double-divorced roadie for the Department of Energy. Yella Kissl reminded Schleppend that she was all the trouble he could handle. Swinyard, across the table, laughed. Lyra, seated next to Swinyard, said that she hoped, pause, that Swinyard was laughing at Schleppend and not at her sister, Yella Kissl, or at her two Italian sisters. Swinyard put his head on the table. Lyra also said, pulling at her blond afro, toying with her clavicle, that her astrologer, Mazda Maxim, had told her that very afternoon that this comet might change *everything,* perhaps even the quality of her orgasms. Swinyard raised his head to offer a toast to the patron saint of ballroom intercourse, saying, "Hear! Hear! Saint Non Sequitur!"

At the very next table, to the pilgrim's far right, Aaron Verbunko agreed with the toast. Seated next to Justine Means, he felt the non sequitur. Justine was surrounded by admirers jerking at her every nuance like wind-up dolls. Justine sipped her wine and fealty. There was Bardder, the Xxn buttonman, talking gems. There was Lwoff, the Glf bagman, talking St. Moritz, how flat it seemed without Justine's mound of Venus. Verbunko, disgusted but resigned, turned to see a near duplicate to this scene at the far end of the table. Of course, Christine seemed to attract half-men,

54

wounded men, quasi-men. There was the left-armless Doppeln, the Citibank plastics man, inquiring after one of Christine's slippers. There was the blind LeCraw, a Tsx mouthpiece, offering a ride on his space shuttle, customed by Grimmen no less. Verbunko, who had no tolerance for other men's self-degradation, turned away again, accidentally catching the eye of Abbott Broadsword across from him. Abbott spoke up, asking if Verbunko was enjoying himself and, by the way, what did today's Means directive mean about diverting funds to a "Mr. Harold Starr," or was "Harold Starr" a person? Aaron Verbunko darkened, reaching into his breast pocket for a notepad, scratching a thought as he asked Abbott if he considered it discreet to discuss confidential corporation business at a social gathering. Abbott choked on his carrot. Verbunko ignored him, thinking he'd best press this. He called across to Cedric Broadsword, asking him if he had any questions about today's directive involving cash-diversion? Cedric, concentrating on something in the distance, ignored him. Abbott shook his father's arm. Cedric turned to demand what? But before Verbunko could speak up, Justine interrupted to ask him if he'd be a dear and go ask Tory the dates of next spring's doings at Means Manor, for Daddy's birthday. Verbunko hesitated. Justine stared till he bounded up. She told the assembled that they were all, of course, invited to the "Rites of Spring." Yes, thank you, from everyone but Cedric, who quibbled. And Grace Thyme, too, of course, said Christine, you'll have fun. Cedric humphed, saying that he'd ask Grace later, turning away.

For at the very next table, to the pilgrim's near right, Torrance VIII huddled with Gracie. They'd been talking since Cedric had introduced them. Cedric had tried to break them up at first sentence, but Abbott had insisted he come away to deal with a crasher, who was no crasher, but the Contessa's mother—a striking foreign woman whom Cedric momentarily thought he'd seen before, a long time back, could it have been Italy at war's end? He couldn't be sure. Yet he was sure, once he'd returned to the ball, that Torrance

VIII wasn't about to let Cedric get Gracie back, dancing her away each time he'd approached. Gracie hadn't objected either, had indeed seemed blissful. Bother! thought Cedric. He was just a pretty face, nothing as significant as his father. What could they be talking about like that? Look at the way he's rubbing her! Look at the way she's nuzzling him! Cedric might have done something rash, if Verbunko hadn't just then interrupted Torrance VIII to ask Justine's question. Torrance VIII barked that he didn't know and didn't care, turning back to Gracie, who, as high on bubbly as she was on this beautiful man's attention, asked what "fete" was that? Torrance VIII said it was his stepmother's idea of the "Rites of Spring"—idlers making fools of themselves for three days. He stopped, saying, uh, you'll be there, of course? There's jousting. And a cross-country horse race that Justine and I win every year. It would be amusing to see you beat Justine. Gracie stuttered that she wasn't doing as much riding as she used to, on doctor's orders. Torrance VIII beamed his most winning facade, and Gracie surrendered, saying she didn't know about winning a horse race, but she'd love to come along. Where? Means Manor, said Torrance VIII, at the "sex" of the Long Island, impossible to miss, taking Gracie's hand, whispering it was even harder to miss than he was. Gracie blushed, but didn't pull her hand away. Damn it, thought Gracie, it's been too damn long since any man did anything so wonderfully crude with me. God forgive me, I like it, she thought, wishing she could offer to hold his sex with both her hands, but, alas, the surgical sling wasn't that flexible. It was an intriguingly large sex, thought Gracie, pressing slightly with her index finger on a bulbous ridge. She tried to lower her gaze to see how bumpy the cloth was, but her neck twinged—ouch! Gracie thought to conceal her embarrassment by saying, "Gosh." Torrance VIII replied that it was a shame he'd be away all winter on company business in Africa, but that he and Gracie would pursue this evening's pleasure at the "Rites of Spring." "I'll miss you very much," said Gracie, forgetting every defense, forgetting her horse sense as well, as she crossed her long legs the tighter. She wished she had a horse to fall off of right now, though if Torrance VIII got much larger against her hand she could fall off him, gulp. There I come, thought Gracie, "Ohhhhhhh! Oh! Oh."

"What happened? Grace! Are you ill?" said Cedric.

"Huh?" said Gracie. "Oh, Uncle Cedric."

"Leave us alone, Cedric," said Torrance VIII.

"This is my home," said Cedric.

"Gentlemen, the party must go on," said Verbunko.

"Father, please, everyone's staring," said Abbott.

"I'll not be dismissed in my own home," said Cedric.

"Go get him, Tory," said Justine.

"Don't, Justine. They're quite drunk," said Verbunko.

"What's he say?" said Christine.

"Cedric called Tory out," said Justine.

"Grace? Are you well? You looked flushed," said Cedric.

"Fine, really, just woozy. See? Oops," said Gracie.

"What have you done to her?" said Cedric.

"Meddling old fool," said Torrance VIII.

"Father, come away, it's not what you think," said Abbott.

"Delicious, delicious," said Christine.

"Is it what I think?" said Justine.

"Let's settle this amicably," said Verbunko.

"Right. He can swing first," said Cedric.

"Oh, for pity's sake, Uncle Cedric, stop!" said Gracie.

"Get her some coffee, Abbott," said Cedric.

"She needs more than that," said Abbott.

"Take my coat, Verbunko," said Cedric.

"And my cigarette," said Torrance VIII.

"Backing down, then, boy?" said Cedric.

"I don't scuffle with men as old as my father," said Torrance VIII.

"Hit him once, Tory," said Justine.

"Justy!" said Christine.

"Gracie, what happens?" said Bianca.

"Oh, Bee, they don't care about me," said Gracie.

57

"Is she ill, Contessa?" said Cedric.

"No, *Padrone,* not as you mean," said Bianca.

"Satisfied now?" said Torrance VIII.

"I still don't like your tone," said Cedric.

"Nor I yours," said Torrance VIII.

"What's a party without a good fight?" said Justine.

"Please, let's all sit quietly. A misunderstanding," said Verbunko. "More wine. Sit, everyone. More wine!"

"Mama, this is my dear friend, Grace Thyme," said Bianca in Italian.

"Your mother? Here? Bee!" said Gracie.

"Very nice to meet you," said Europa in Italian.

"She's pretty, Bee. You never told me your mother was pretty," said Gracie. "Everyone, isn't Bee's mother pretty?"

"Christy, isn't that her?" said Justine.

"It couldn't be another commissar," said Christine. "Does Tory know?"

"God, I'm smashed, Bee," said Gracie. "Isn't it dangerous, her being here? You know, what you told me?"

"Ssshh," said Bianca.

"This is better, yes?" said Verbunko. "The music's begun again. Why don't we return to the dancing? Justine?"

"You've popped another bubble, Aaron," said Justine.

"And Miss Means, might I have the honor?" said Abbott.

"Will you dance with me, *Padrone?*" said Bianca.

"Go ahead, Uncle Cedric, she's sweet on you," said Gracie.

"An honor, Contessa. Excuse me, one moment. See here, young man, mind your manners with my ward. I think I have made myself clear as to how far I'm willing to go to protect her happiness," said Cedric.

"Aye," said the pilgrim of a sudden, stopping everyone in midmotion. They spun back to the table, looking for that mysterious voice: Verbunko to the left; Abbott to the right; Cedric to the rear; Torrance VIII to the fireplace. Justine and Christine knew where to look, however, up, up, on the mantel, in the shadow of the great stone chimney. Bianca saw the eyes of the golden twins fix on a dark lump and pointed out as much to Gracie, who turned to squint.

"What's Landrover doing up there?" said Gracie, spotting a familiar wagging tail drooped down from the mantel.

"Landrover?" said Bianca.

"Who are you?" demanded Abbott Broadsword.

"A comrade to Effert Broadsword," said the pilgrim.

"What!" said Gracie.

"Come forward and show yourself," said Cedric.

"I'm not fit for your company, sir," said the pilgrim, moving forward on his perch to display his once again capped head in the firelight. "I've been on the road a long time. With a message from Effert Broadsword to his family."

"I'll thank you not to speak that name in this house," said Cedric. "I've forbidden it."

"What message?" said Gracie.

"Do you believe this?" said Justine.

"Delicious," said Christine.

"Your son sends his greetings, Mr. Broadsword. He asked me to say to you that he begs your forgiveness for his misconduct and disrespect," said the pilgrim.

"Aye," said Cedric.

"He's alive, isn't he? Not sick or dead?" said Gracie.

"When I left him," said the pilgrim.

"Father, I don't like this," said Abbott.

"He sends greetings to you also, Abbott Broadsword," said the pilgrim.

"How do you know so much? Where's Effert?" said Abbott.

"Delayed in his return from the Holy Wars," said the pilgrim.

"How do we know you know my son?" said Cedric.

"I do," said the pilgrim.

"I see. Then when can we expect him? Did he say, Mr., uh, what is your name, sir?" said Cedric.

59

"I've taken a vow not to use my name until I've completed a quest," said the pilgrim.

"A quest?" said Justine.

"A quest?" said Christine.

"Of course, I understand," said Cedric. "Have you eaten? May we offer you a room for the night?"

"He's guessed," said Justine.

"Perhaps," said Christine.

"No, wait!" said Gracie. "Can't you tell us more about Effert?"

"Still running away from responsibility?" said Torrance VIII.

"Tory, don't," said Christine.

"You must be Torrance Means the Eighth," said the pilgrim.

"What of it?" said Torrance VIII.

"Nothing of it," said the pilgrim.

"See to our visitor's needs, Abbott," said Cedric.

"But—" said Abbott.

"Now this is settled, shall we rejoin the ball?" said Cedric, "Contessa, I believe I have this dance?"

"Pardon me, sir," said Verbunko, stepping genteelly between Cedric's bulk and Bianca, "I'm hoping I might have this dance with the Contessa, that is, if you'll introduce us?"

"Why, uh, yes, of course. Contessa," said Cedric, puzzled, "may I introduce Aaron Verbunko, Senior Vice-President of the Means Corporation. Mr. Verbunko, the Contessa Capricciosa."

"A rare pleasure," said Verbunko.

"Yes," said Bianca. "Mama, come with us."

"Well, you get to dance with me," said Justine.

"An honor, Miss Means," said Cedric.

"Come on, Tory," said Gracie, "I have to freshen up."

"Mmh," said Tory.

Leaving Abbott alone with the pilgrim, who still perched atop the mantel, stroking Landrover's gray-red mane. Abbott paused to collect himself, since his father's conduct with regard this vagabond puzzled him. Just then, the pilgrim stiffened. He bent over to put his ear to Land-rover's breast. He sat up again, reaching a hand underneath Landrover's chest, pressing his fingers against the pulmonary artery. He bowed his head, returning to stroking Landrover's gray-red mane. He straightened his cap, leaned back resignedly against the stone wall. He whispered from *Julius Ceasar,* ". . . but the heavens themselves blaze forth the death of princes." Slowly, then, and ever so sadly, he squatted on the mantel, saddled up his satchel, and turned back to Landrover's body. He reached forward, sliding both arms underneath the torso, lifting Landrover. He descended the four steps, halting several feet from a curious Abbott Broadsword.

"Landrover's gone," said the pilgrim.

"Oh?" said Abbott.

"A broken heart," the pilgrim said.

Wavy Rufus

PEAKED HAT askew, masquerade mask drawn across his sightless orbs, white beard scraggly down over his billowing black robes, only ten cracked fingernails visible from his cavernous sleeves, ancient Rufus Broadsword, called "Wavy Rufus" for too many decades to recount, balanced precariously atop his sorcerer's stool, grooving on a favorite tune, coming his way courtesy of WHIP-FM, Metromaniacal Radio:

> *So you want to be a rock'n'roll star?*
> *Then listen now to what I say.*
> *Just get an electric guitar,*
> *Then take some time and learn how to play.*

And when your hair's combed right,
And your pants fit tight,
It's gonna be all right.
Then it's time to go downtown,
Where the agent man won't let you down.
Sell your soul to the company,
Who are waiting there to sell plastic ware.
And in a week or two, if you make the charts,
The girls'll tear you apart!

Wavy Rufus rocked back on the fantasy of it all. Not the part about being torn asunder by rutting females, of course, since, at 107 years old, Wavy Rufus enjoyed nature's reward for those who bust a century—sublime dispassion. No, what moved Wavy Rufus about the Byrds' track was the fantasy of star-becoming—any sort of star, rock'n'roll, or great red giant, or tiny white dwarf. Stars in all masses, colors, and ages, from all parts of the Hertzsprung-Russell diagram of stellar evolution, all such, filled Wavy Rufus's imagination. The man saw stars, and only stars, since he was physically blind. Wavy Rufus was a star groupie, which is jargon for saying that Wavy Rufus was also the twentieth century's oldest living cosmologist. Twenty billion years old, the cosmos, according to cosmologist Wavy Rufus, was always and only stars, that is, star-becoming, star-being, or star-passing. And perhaps one should consider also that Wavy Rufus's fascination for stars was his peculiar way of concerning himself with human nature. We are all of us, Wavy Rufus might insist, star-made, star-f——ed, star-dead, and star-reborn. At ten billion years, that G-type star swinging overhead each day is, at least, a second-generation thermonuclear ball since the Big Ball that began it all. Molecular us, we carry the very atoms of that Imponderable Beginning. It's not so much dust to dust, Wavy Rufus might say, as stardust to stardust, and again.

Still, Wavy Rufus's concern seemed beyond total obsession. He seemed a mad old coot. Cedric Broadsword said that his granduncle, Rufus, had lost more than his vision that fated day in midcentury when he had telescope-tracked a comet straight down into the horizon, zap, here comes the Bright One's corona, and there goes Wavy Rufus's coronae. And, to be fair to Cedric, who'd never been fair to Wavy Rufus (the Broadsword family's single contribution to logical positivism during its two-hundred-years-plus residence in the land that logical positivism built), Wavy Rufus was not demonstrably sane—too starry-eyed for that.

Following his blinding vision, Wavy Rufus had withdrawn to his self-styled hermitage atop the tower centering Broadsword Hall's east gallery, situating his thinking on what came to be called, with the advances of astronomy, the right and left side of the electromagnetic spectrum's 1-micron (visible light) wavelength, from where Wavy Rufus came not at all. He'd been there ever since, a silent, serious listener, plugged into the cosmos only to the extent that he heard its "waves." Wavy Rufus waved himself out, and he seemed all the more content for having done so, opening his observatory skylight every night and, instead of "looking" at the dome of the sky, "listening" to the dome of the sky. In over thirty years, he'd granted audiences rarely, and then only to his great-grandnephew, Effert, who cherished Wavy Rufus deeply, and to his great-granddaughter, Gracie, who cherished Effert's cherishing of Wavy Rufus deeply.

It had been Effert who had informed Wavy Rufus of the expanding beauty of the airwaves, that is, as close to the music of the spheres as most ears are likely to come: the inauguration of the FM band in the mid-1960s, which eventually led to the cosmic triumph of rock'n'roll. And, given the fact that Wavy Rufus realized he'd never be able to enjoy what the cosmos must sound like to those modern cosmologists equipped with radio telescopes, microwave antennas, satellite observatories, and germanium-bearing balloons reading gamma ray rates, Wavy Rufus had allowed Effert to install the necessary amps, preamps, tuners, and speakers so that Wavy Rufus could tune in rock'n'roll, which Wavy Rufus soon came to adore as a philosopher's helpmate. Wavy Rufus found that whenever a problem seemed too much for him—say, the Missing Mass Muddle, which eluded him as it did all sighted, expensively equipped cosmologists, that is, where's the mass needed to recollapse, according to the Eternal Law of Gravity, the cosmos for another cycle (?)—all he needed to set his mind at ease was to switch on the FM radio, turn it up loud, and groove along those elliptical tracks.

In his dotage, then—if that's what 107 is—Wavy Rufus was a rock'n'roll groupie as well as a star groupie. These two juxtaposed passions, of the very pop, and of the very First Pop, might have been the secret to Wavy Rufus's longevity. This wasn't so. His real secret to long life was that he awaited a certain coming.

"Hail, Wavy Rufus!" called the pilgrim from the landing below the observatory.

"Who?" said Wavy Rufus.

"Wavy Rufus! You're alive!" said the pilgrim, carrying a foul-weather lamp.

"Please, yes," said Wavy Rufus. It was Effert, his great-grandnephew.

"Wavy Rufus, I never thought . . . well, you're here. Oh, Wavy Rufus, how are you? You look the same as ever, great!" said the pilgrim, who, incontrovertibly identified by Wavy Rufus, shall henceforth be called Effert Broadsword, dishomed son, returned from the Holy Wars after thirteen years. Effert respectfully doffed his foul-weather cap, unfastened his foul-weather coat, unharnessed his satchel, and dropped everything on the floor. He was dressed in Nam surplus, scratches here, patches there, an ersatz cold war warrior just emerged from the bush in which all derring-doers dwell.

"Where've you been, Effert? It's been some time, hasn't it? A war? Who won?" said Wavy Rufus.

"Aye, Wavy Rufus, aye," said Effert, flopping on an armchair, putting his feet up on a lab table. "In the service of His Majesty. I feel as if it was just this morning we last talked. Remember? I've missed you. How's the Missing Mass Muddle? The Dark One?"

"Hush!" said Wavy Rufus, clapping his hands the way one supposes even more ancient metaphysicians (cosmology is not merely natural physics, is it?) might once have invoked spells.

"Sorry," said Effert. "Where I've been, they don't know what it is to have a man about who's in touch with the ineffable. Being with you, I can relax."

"What troubles you?" said Wavy Rufus.

"Landrover's gone," said Effert.

"God rest his soul, a fine old friend," said Wavy Rufus.

"Do you remember him? He was my dog," said Effert.

"I remember them all. God rest all their souls," said Wavy Rufus, "such fine, old friends."

"You got it. God, I'm tired," said Effert, who fell magically into a deep sleep. He might have dreamed— those next few hours while Wavy Rufus sat still as night on the sorcerer's stool awaiting his great-grandnephew to awaken to continue their discussion—that he'd come home to Gracie, lace- and flower-bedecked, sighing for him at the doorstep of Broadsword Hall, saying, "Oh, Effert, my brave Effert, you've come home to me as I knew you would, for I love you more than life and want to be your wife." He might even have dreamed that he'd agreed to such a fabulous proposition. But he didn't dream anything like this, and that was that. At most, he suffered the fitful sleep a personal, irrecoverable loss engenders. He dreamed he'd forgotten how to get home again. Where was that map, or was it a map? Something important at the subsurface of his awakening, crying out, "Mar'zi'pan!"

"Effert!" called Wavy Rufus.

"Uh?" said Effert, awake immediately.

"You said 'Mar'zi'pan,' " said Wavy Rufus, clutching his chest. "Have you found it, then? Is that where you've been? Pass it here, boy."

"Right, right," said Effert, reaching across to his satchel to pull forth a long rectangular, weighty package. It was far too heavy to hand up to Wavy Rufus. He shifted his body to lay it out on the lab table.

"This is it, then?" said Wavy Rufus, turning on his sorcerer's stool.

"Can't say for sure until you agree," said Effert. "It wasn't where you thought. In fact, it was far enough away to cost me five years' scratching. There's an oil field there now, you know. It was near the southeastern wall, about two hundred yards off the Adad Gate. Finding it was guess-work. Last year, I just burrowed where this crew chief said they'd found some burial sites. Odd thing was that when I found it, I knew I'd found it. Magic, huh?"

"More than that," said Wavy Rufus, slitting up the leather wrapping, flipping it out, smoothing aside the oilskin until he hit clay. Once the wrappings were off, Wavy Rufus paused to apply his scientific self. Tape recorder humming, he began, "A clay tablet, approximately sixteen inches high and nine inches across. Badly beaten. Broken at the bottom." And so forth, until he'd detailed its physical condition. Then he turned to identification, feeling the speckling, as one might read Braille, save for the fact this was Babylonian cuneiform, the inscription at the top reading:

MAR'ZI'PAN DECLARES . . .

which was all Wavy Rufus needed to say "Yes."

"I've done it?" said Effert. "This really is Mar'zi'pan's text?" Effert jumped up to dance a jig, for he'd brought home the goods, that is, the clay tablet Assurbanipal (liter-ally, Assyrian Ejaculator) himself had pondered smashing into bits, but could not, because of his superstitious respect for the written word. And, knowing (thanks to the advice of a mysterious mathematician at his side) that he shouldn't take it home to his grand library at Nineveh along with the rest of the booty from his scourging of his brother's Babylo-nian uprising, he'd ordered it buried deep with the corpses of the fallen rebels. Now, twenty-six centuries later, this same clay tablet had been unearthed (in part) by a pure-at-heart iconoclast. Effert Broadsword had found, several yards beneath the saline soil of proud, purple Babylon, the top half of the enchanted urban guerrilla text ripped from the broken hands of the aide-de-camp to the Babylonian Underground's mysterious Chief-of-Operations, Mar'zi'pan. And he'd brought it home to his great-granduncle, Wavy Rufus, the only man alive who understood the novel truth of the matter: there was such a doing as a Comet Incarnate.

"Hear me now, Effert," said Wavy Rufus. "Do you know what this means?"

"That we can still expect His Majesty in the spring?" said Effert. "I still believe."

"Yes. I do, too. If only I could be certain we're doing right," said Wavy Rufus. "Should we even know about Mar'zi'pan? Can our knowledge harm His Majesty? Ah, but you've done well, Effert. Perhaps it's best you give me time with this."

"Sure. Back in the morning. I've some chums to see. Swinyard and Schleppend, my old roomies, do you remember them?" said Effert, spinning away as he saw Wavy Rufus's attention move into Thought. Effert maneuvered back down into the dark junk-filled halls, then stopped as he heard a scraping up ahead—no, more the swish of a skirt. He pressed against a shadow, capping and coating again.

"There you are!" said Bianca.

"What?" said Effert, impressed. This was the Italian beauty Gracie called Bee, and she could either see in the dark or, more worrisome, was fey.

"Come with me," said Bianca, leading Effert down the passageway, the steps, the hall, that led to Gracie's rooms. They were inside Gracie's sitting room before Effert could freeze, less from the chill of the September storm out there than from the melancholy of his own inconsolable past in here. Gracie hadn't altered the room in thirteen years. There were hundreds of horse show ribbons tacked neatly along the cornices, the windowsills, the backs of the closet doors, the bases of the window seats. Their dates—from 1955, when Gracie had first ridden in a lead line class atop her eight-hand Shetland pony, Dog, to 1968, when Gracie had given up parochial showing in order to ride with the Olympic téam for the first time—marked the sine curve of an athletic love affair. There seemed a ribbon here for every pile of fresh-mown hay Effert had ever heaved Gracie atop before leaping atop her, boots and jodhpurs flying—teenage lust. What a joy it'd been horsing among the horses. To date, whenever Effert sniffed animal sweat, horseshit, hay, and leather, he was transported to the good-natured frustration of his youth, trying to get Gracie to ride him bareback. And whenever he heard a horse whinnying, he was transported to the good-natured realization of his early manhood, trying to get Gracie not to ride him bareback quite so rough, for Gracie had learned to whinny in her orgasmic arch. Forgive me, Gracie, thought Effert, making fists, bowing his head; and yet how unforgivable, how cruel I was to leave you. No apology could be adequate. I'm best dead to you. And why didn't you ever marry—make à wife, have a life, seed in the summer and breed in the spring?

Then Effert's other self spoke up—the one capable of misanthropy, misogyny, misogamy, misology, and not to forget, missing the obvious. This troublesome, willful self, the conscience of a draft-dodging dropout, said in Effert's head, "Come the Revolution . . ."

"Of the comet!" chanted Effert aloud.

"Psst!" said Bianca from the doors leading to the bedroom, waving Effert to approach, ushering him into Gracie's supine presence. Gracie did not look well, propped up against her pillows, in the dead drunk center of her canopied, toy-animal-covered, lace-draped bed. She'd exchanged her ball gown for a toy-animal-covered dressing gown. She'd also slipped back into her surgical neck brace. She looked to be innocence wrecked by the colossal accident that is unrequited love. Effert's huge heart went out to her. His visceral reaction was to take charge of such a pathetic scene. Whoa, there, boy blue, he thought. He took his heart back, slipping into the shadows of the room.

"Come closer," said Gracie softly.

"Aye," said Effert, not moving. Did she know?

"Thank you for coming," said Gracie.

"Sure," said Effert. No, she didn't know.

"I'm hoping you can tell us more of Effert Broadsword," said Gracie. "Where did you meet him?"

"Uh, on the road," said Effert.

"What's that?" said Gracie.

"Around," said Effert.

"When? I mean, why, that is, when?" said Gracie.

"Back some. We holed up together for a while," said Effert.

"Why? You were hurt? Was he?" said Gracie.

"Naw. He's fine. Better shape than me," said Effert.

"Is he older?" said Gracie.

"Married! Is he married?" said Bianca, annoyed by Gracie's reticence before a man she suspected knew more than he said.

"I don't know," said Effert. "We never discussed it."

"Oh, Bee!" said Gracie.

"Don't be foolish, Gracie," said Bianca. "Ask him."

"I can't! I just can't," said Gracie. "You do it."

Madonna mia! said Bianca, sitting next to Gracie, taking Gracie's shaking hand. "Does Effert Broadsword speak of a woman named Grace Thyme?"

"Well," said Effert.

"See, Bee. See!" said Gracie, near hysteria.

"Sometimes," said Effert.

"Oh, God, oh, God!" said Gracie.

"Sometimes? Does he? Doesn't he? How well do you know him?" said Bianca.

"Uh," said Effert. This Bee was not to be crossed.

"He said sometimes, Bee. Don't be hard," said Gracie.

"Men!" said Bianca.

"I remember once," said Effert, before he could stop himself, "he said he hoped this girl, Grace, he hoped she'd forgotten him. I mean forgiven him."

"Oh! Bee!" said Gracie, weeping in Bianca's arms.

69

"What'd I say?" said Effert.

"Gracie, Gracie, ssshhh," said Bianca. "He's not worth it."

Well, I'll be truckin'," said Effert—in form—dropping out when confronted with adult decisions. He did not wait for a fare-thee-well, sprinting from this sobbing, on the run, faster, faster, hurtling the doorjamb, grabbing a banister to catapult down the stairwell, throwing his long person through a service door, crashing to a rest in the familiar clutter of a long-unused linen closet that Effert, as a very young miscreant, had used as a hideaway. Wow, thought Effert, for nothing he'd seen once around the world frightened him so totally as female passion. Here, among his childhood fantasies, he regrouped his adult ones. There was his collection of plastic soldiers. There was his telescope. There was his globe. There was one of Gracie's bras transformed into a slingshot. There was a Yale banner. And so forth, all here, untouched for thirteen years, boy blue growing up heroic. Oh to be little boy blue again, thought Effert (once of the Yale Blue, always of the Yale Blue), when all there was to fear was Cedric's temper, ha ha, none of the truly terrifying in the shape of genuine Otherness sentimentally aroused. Oh, Gracie, thought Effert, grabbing his chest to monitor his heart. He still loved her, which surprised him. Yet, stop in the name of love, for he had to keep mind and heart and other parts on his find (clay tablet several yards beneath the saline soil of proud, purple Babylon) and off his own kind. Effert also knew, or at least believed, that he was a man who had no right to his own destiny until he'd completed the quest set him by Wavy Rufus, and by romance. Effert hauled himself erect, and was about to rejoin the game when he halted, hearing voices in the hall.

"Anything?" said one martial voice.

"No," said another.

"She's up here somewhere," said a third.

"How many places can an old bag hide?"

"That old bag is a Commie with a big reward on her head."

"Stupefacenta? A big reward? Yeah? Means tell you that for sure?"

"He told me he wants her. What's that mean to you?"

"Yeah, you're right."

Effert waited until well after their torchlight had stopped dancing along the wall. Crude lot, he thought, knowing they were Means pros. What could they want with that old Italian woman? Resolved, Effert ordered his immediate future: first, Swinyard & Schleppend; then, sadly, Landrover; then, Wavy Rufus; finally, a rescue and an escape. He loved this hero act, saying, "Believe it!"

"Gracie! Wake up!" said Bianca, shaking Gracie hard enough to knock her from the side of her bed. Gracie, in the midst of a ferocious dreaming, climaxed as she hit the floor, thinking she'd just fallen off a mount.

"Ohhhh!" said Gracie, curling her toes, a lush little orgasm, nothing Yale-banner-waving about it, but nonetheless that made two in twelve hours' time. Her sex life was improving.

"Gracie!" said Bianca, diving over the edge of the bed to support herself on the edge of the mattress. "Mama!"

"What is it?" said Gracie on the floor in afterglow.

"Mama! I went to her room! She's gone!" said Bianca in Italian.

"Hey, Bee, slower," said Gracie. "What time is it? Oh, Lordie, it's daytime."

"Mama! Look!" said Bianca, shoving a sheaf of stationery at Gracie, who, once she'd focused, read, *"Mia carissima Bianca,"* and no more. It was in Italian. "I can't read this," said Gracie.

"Okay," said Bianca, who translated:

My dearest Bianca,
I must go without you. A comrade has come to say
that I will be arrested if I do not go with him
immediately. I pray for you. He also tells me

71

disturbing news that could affect the Party. He says you and your friend, Grace, must go to "Wavy Rufus." Wavy Rufus will explain. I understand now what I did not before. Forgive me my intolerance. These are ominous days.

I kiss you,
Europa

"Wavy Rufus?" said Gracie, sitting up to take the note from Bianca. Yep, it said "Wavy Rufus."

"Isn't that . . . ?" began Bianca.

"My great-grandfather," said Gracie.

"I do not understand, do you?" said Bianca.

"Nope," said Gracie.

Book II

Wherein We Survey the Last Four Apparitions of Halley's Comet

(AS TOLD BY WAVY RUFUS)

Spring 1910

AT SEA, aboard H.M.S. *John D. Rockefeller:* steaming north through the Persian Gulf, on their way to their final observation station, the distinguished passengers, cometologists all, annoyed each other with fashionable politics. Expectedly, given the international makeup of the team, sides were taken, men learned to hate just as if their hate mattered. An Italian technician was heard baiting a German technician, screaming, "Long live anarchy!" each time *Rockefeller* took a heavy wave across her bow. One of the French lectured about the moral fiber of the revolutionary syndicalists until a Swiss journalist was moved to interrupt, screaming, "F—— the CGT!" A fistfight ensued in which everyone lost but the large Spanish mathematician, Pissaro, who was said to be a socialist saint because of his stance in the Barcelona riots the summer before.

Finally, the leader of the expedition, the Florentine nobleman Arturo Cassinni, let it be known at dinner two days out of Abadan (at the mouths of the Tigris and Euphrates), that if this bickering continued, the troublemakers would be dismissed at first landfall of a civilized country.

This only exacerbated the tension. These were astronomers, not diplomats, certainly not adults. They'd spent their lives bickering with students, colleagues, and women. They knew nothing of teamwork. Astronomy was a lone eagle discipline. Cooperation was beyond them. Even if it hadn't been true that every major astronomical discovery in two centuries had been stolen twice before it had been published, they still would have distrusted each other. Discuss my work with that fool? Are you joking? And so they discussed newspaper headlines,

THE KING IS DEAD (London)
MARK TWAIN IS DEAD (New York)

or they discussed dirigibles. They discussed anything but their work. If anyone had been so foolish as to use the word "comet" at dinner, he would've been poisoned by breakfast.

The only agreeable man on board, in Cassinni's opinion, was the single American, Rufus Broadsword. And he was only on board, and a member of the team, because Cassinni had thought it queer that a scientific expedition of this magnitude should have a British ship and crew, a predominantly Italian and French team, and yet be totally funded by an American philanthropist. When Cassinni had first been approached two years before, he'd mentioned that he hoped chauvinism could be kept out of the selection process. The Rockefeller family representatives—a surly group of Viennese lawyers—had replied, matter-of-factly, that Mr. Rockefeller wanted quality, not equality. If Cassinni had so ordained, he could've chosen a team of Macedonian Slavs.

Still, an American had seemed a safe idea. Cassinni had written Lowell at the Harvard Observatory, asking for names. Lowell had proposed half a dozen geniuses, all impossible for Cassinni. He didn't want a reputable American astronomer, for that would be dangerous beyond speculation. The Americans he'd met at conferences were continually trying to embarrass the European astronomers with unglued theories. A Mount Wilson man would give a paper declaring the Milky Way finite. Then, in the same colloquium, a Yale man would give a paper declaring the Milky Way infinite. Cassinni knew that the Americans would try to argue a comet as famous as Halley's into some sort of secret to the cosmos. No, the Harvard list was out. So Cassinni had written Wimperwitch at Greenwich Observatory, asking that he recommend an American student—some idle rich boy dabbling in astronomy. Wimperwitch had sent back the name Rufus Broadsword, cautioning Cassinni that not only was the man a former artist—one of those Parisiantype watercolorists—but also that he was a complete layabout, rich enough to afford the best equipment, but not serious enough to advance independent theories. Broadsword seemed content to stare at the heavens, to say nothing extraordinary. The best that could be said for him, Wimperwitch had concluded, was that he would "toe the line." Cassinni liked English expressions like "toe the line." He'd written Broadsword in Soho immediately.

("Why do they want *you?*" Pamela had asked, mid-December 1909, upon Rufus's receipt of the invitation to the expedition. She was unsure whether she should admire Rufus the more for being a sought-after scientist, or should suspect him the more for securing a clever way to escape her ardor. She loved him. Admittedly, he had a family back in America. Yet he hadn't mentioned New York since she'd first seduced him. He was her man now—a wild and sexy American dilettante. So what expedition threatened her?

"Everybody wants me," said Rufus, pulling her down on the divan beside him, setting at her buttons and bows.

"But why you? You told me they think you're thick," said Pamela, slapping his left hand away as his right hand slipped under her hem.

"End of the world, Pam," said Rufus. "They want me along to paint the end of the world. See the giant cloud of poisonous gas approach the undefended planet. See the planet covered with deadly effluvium. See the masses choking as the bourgeoisie purchases safety in specially equipped rooms of pure oxygen. 'LA FIN DU MONDE!' by Halley's Comet, as captured by Rufus Broadsword. Want to see?" He abandoned her thighs to lope across his studio to a large canvas covered with a dropcloth. He toyed with the skylight in an attempt to arrange the midday sun the better, then said, "Voilà!" hoisting the dropcloth.

"Rufus!" cried Pamela. "When did you do that?"

"Like it? It came to me last night, after getting Cassinni's letter," said Rufus, stepping back to admire his inspiration. It was a watercolor of a large globe spinning in deep space, half-bathed in sunlight. But something was obviously wrong. A pall hung over the globe. Upon closer examination, one could see a shimmering film emanating from the upper reaches of the canvas. There was no evidence of a comet.

"It's the most horrible thing you've ever done," said Pamela. She thought it terrifying in its banality—a God's-eye view of Mother Earth, dying.

"You really think it's horrible?" said Rufus.

"Horrible," said Pamela, who also thought it was erotic, this casual watercolor of Creation's oblivion arousing her Protestant soul: some will be damned, so make love while the sun yet shines.

"Just the tail, you understand, supposed to consist of cyanogen gas," said Rufus. "The comet would be too far away to get in a picture of this scale. Though we're to pass within ten million miles next May. That's a near miss in astronomical terms."

"Come to me, Rufus," said Pamela, hoisting her skirts. She had only half an hour before she was due at the gallery.

"No reason to be scared, of course," said Rufus. "The poison gas talk is nonsense. Surprising the papers would mention it. Journalistic license. Typical French genius for the popularly stupid. At the most, there'll be a heat."

"Here's some heat," said Pamela, hunching up on the

divan, shaking what she had to shake as her dropcloth came away.

"You think the coming of the comet does this?" said Rufus, approaching the divan hurriedly. "Or are you women sensitive to cosmic visitations?"

"Gad, Rufus," said Pamela, groaning at his touch, "you ask dumb questions of a girl.")

And now, after five months at sea bouncing from observation station to observatory, from the Bay of Biscay to the Persian Gulf, Cassinni had to admit that of all the folk on board *Rockefeller,* Rufus Broadsword was the only one who'd done nothing but "toe the line." Broadsword did his work in silence. Broadsword never complained about the cooking. Broadsword never discussed politics. Broadsword even had nice things to say about the demimondaines the French brought on board.

Dinner the very night before docking at Abadan seemed an excellent example to Cassinni of how agreeable Broadsword could be.

"I tell you," said Pooeff, a French solar expert and foot fetishist, winner of an Academy medal for his papers on sunspots. "It's the Jews. It's always been the Jews."

"I agree," said Broadsword.

"Don't listen to him, Broadsword," said Freneticci, a Milanese anarchist turned stargazer after he'd lost his left arm in the '98 uprising, "the Socialists want it all."

"I agree," said Broadsword.

"What do you know of socialism, comrade?" said the Russian, Lopov, whose youngest sister had once been seduced by Peter Kropotkin's correspondence secretary and who therefore had personal reasons to hate the anarchists, whom he still regarded as socialists, despite their expulsion from the Second International twenty years before. "Only with strong men making strong decisions can Europe survive. We must have leaders with imagination and nerve. Not heritage or sentiment."

"I agree," said Broadsword, twisting his dapper moustache. He thought them all unfathomably mad.

After dinner and brandy, Rufus took his cigar up on deck, just escaping Cassinni's summons to a bridge game. Rufus had other ideas. He wanted to work tonight, leaning back to consider the comet splashed across the dome of the night sky. He tossed his cigar into the sea foam sudsing away from *Rockefeller* steaming steadily north. He walked quickly to the quarterdeck, where the Captain had permitted him to store his easel and paints in a locker.

Up above, in the dimly lit wheelhouse, Rufus could see the officers of the watch eyeing the sky. Rufus had taken to studying, without their knowledge, other men's ways of looking at the comet. Some gazed openly, their heads back until their necks cracked. Others shot a glance up, then looked away, preferring to concentrate on where they were walking, none of this cosmic abandon. Still others—especially the educated but melancholy ones who'd dazzled their mothers and sweethearts with their precocious promise, but then had made bad tradesmen, worse professional men, and dissolute parents—sat in their lawn chairs to watch the comet as if it were a vision of their unattainable ambitions. Which is how the comet seemed to Rufus. Once it had been New Year 1910, and his life had seemed pleasant but directionless. Then it had been March, and the comet had come out of the western sky, visible to the naked eye by April, growing brighter each evening, growing a tail each morning before sunrise. Suddenly, for Rufus, there was something in Creation with which he could compare Creation, and how miserable mankind seemed when considered before this exotic spectacle. The comet had thrown Rufus into a cosmic crisis. He had done the religious thing. He had attached his mind and body to the comet. His pleasure was now the comet's. His direction was now the comet's.

Am I going mad? Rufus had thought. Is this not grand, this heavenly pilgrim? Why doesn't history alter its course before so great a presence?

The petty politics of his colleagues had seemed all the

more appalling to Rufus in that they had continued *as if the comet had not come.* For all its wisdom, in Rufus's opinion, Western Europe failed to match lesser lands' responses to the comet.

From China, for example, had come reports of riots in the large cities, Sun Yat-sen's Republicans using the comet's apparition to stir the rabble into insurrection against the Open Door Empire. Look up, they'd cry, and know that the Revolution is come! The authorities had been hard-pressed to quell the rumors, perhaps because they half-believed. Their solution to the "comet riots," as the papers called them, was to distribute a handbill with a sketch of the comet, a list of its previous apparitions back to A.D. 1066, and a statement to the effect that nothing awful had happened then, so why should it now?

Yet in the American Southland, according to the papers, the people called Baptists had not been so easily calmed. Mass prayer meetings filled the dark forest night with hymns of supplication. There had been an epidemic of speaking in tongues in Mississippi. There were reports of mass baptisms in Georgia. Whole towns in the Carolinas gathered in the square to pray beneath the comet.

Rufus knew he wasn't afraid of the comet. His feelings were more complicated—awe, apprehension, curiosity, humility, but not fear. He saw himself as a chronicler, painting watercolors of the comet for posterity. Perhaps, in the distant future, men would have the means to interpret Halley's Comet.

Rufus reached the quarterdeck, setting up his equipment quickly, beginning his work quickly. He did the nucleus first, brighter than Venus tonight at its center. Then he did the coma surrounding the nucleus, half as large as the moon tonight, just brushing Gemini, 5 degrees above the western horizon. The tail was more difficult with the quarter moon coming up. The tail stretched like a head of hair nearly 110 degrees across the night sky, nearly to Jupiter. Directly overhead, of course, the tail was lost in the brilliance of the Milky Way. Yet even this detail added to the legend of the comet, as if to remind one that the comet itself, inexplicable visitor from distant aphelion, was no equal for the mysterious imperative of even more distant phenomenon. A comet was a hairy star—though the neat Orientals said "Broom Star" and the martial ancients had said "Sword Star"—and not a genuine star. Its nature was subordinate to the wonder of the cosmos.

Rufus began again. He widened the tail, from 5 degrees to 10 degrees. He changed the shape of the coma, splitting it subtly into a forkbeard shape. On some nights, Rufus thought he could actually watch the comet change shape. The oddest configuration had been a pentagonal star, on 11 May, the night after perihelion. The last eight nights, the coma had seemed more a triangle. But tonight, for variety, Rufus tried a forkbeard. Not that he was being unfaithful to the comet. He had come to understand that each man could see exactly what he wanted to see in the comet. If Rufus wanted to see Pamela's face, for instance, he could see it. But Rufus didn't want to see Pamela's face. He began again. He painted the coma into the shape of Pamela's vulva. The tail became the heat waves emanating from between her legs. He colored in the rest of her body, on her back, waiting for him. What a fine, randy idea, thought Rufus—comet as cunt.

"Evening, sir," said the ship's second officer, Buys.

"Oh, hello," said Rufus, looking up to realize Buys had been standing behind him silently, studying Pamela's parts.

"Beautiful she is," said Buys.

"Yes," said Rufus, unsure if he meant Pam or the comet.

"Been meaning to ask you, sir," said Buys. "Some of the other officers, and myself, we've wondered what you're to do with these pretty pictures."

"Do?" said Rufus.

"Are they for Mr. Rockefeller, sir, or for you?" said Buys.

"I hadn't thought. I might send him one," said Rufus.

81

"But they aren't for sale, Mr. Buys, if that's what you mean. I'd be happy to give you one. Here, with my thanks for your patronage." He handed him forkbeard.

"Glad, sir, very glad," said Buys.

"I'd appreciate it if you kept this to yourself," said Rufus.

"Quite right, sir, and thank you kindly," said Buys, who could not, or did not, comply. Rufus had three notes at breakfast from ship's officers requesting audiences. He should have been flattered, but he wasn't. This meant trouble with his colleagues. With his new status in the crew's eyes, they were sure to be less amused by his self-deprecating passivity. Worse, even Cassinni glowered over his grapefruit—the American had stolen the show after all.

So it was no surprise to Rufus when, after the docking at Abadan's iron-age harbor, he found he'd been left off the shore party list, as if he were ill. Rufus considered marching into Cassinni's cabin to tell him what a jealous fop he was, but abandoned this idea as tiresome. Let them go, he thought, watching them from the quarterdeck as they assembled the caravan of carts in a sudden rainstorm. At least they'd left the women on board. Rufus decided he wouldn't ask the Frenchmen first, he'd just choose. The one called Julienne was said to like angry young men.

"It makes me very sad, Monsieur Rufus," said Julienne, passing the opium pipe, pulling up the bedclothes.

"Why? Isn't the comet beautiful?" said Rufus.

"Because it won't come again until I am dead. Because it just comes and comes. I am here once," said Julienne. "I don't know. It's hard to explain. I don't know."

"Yes, you do," said Rufus, leaning forward to kiss her on the brow. "Is it different than the sun, the moon, an eclipse of the sun or moon? The stars?"

"It's a comet," said Julienne, puzzled.

"True, but it's also only an astronomical event, as when the moon is full. Nothing different, is it?" said Rufus.

82

"You're making fun of me," said Julienne, slipping completely under the bedclothes.

"No, I'm not," said Rufus. "I want you to tell me. We've measured, photographed, debated, and recorded. We know that this comet travels in an elliptical orbit, that it is not an asteroid, that a comet like Halley's has special properties we call the nucleus, the coma, and the tail. We know that the coma—that blur about the center—consists of frozen gases being evaporated as the comet approaches the heat of the sun. We know the reason the tail always points away from the sun is that the sun's light exerts pressure, like a wind. And we know, or at least we suppose, that the nucleus of the comet consists of dust and gravel held together by those frozen gases. Some say frozen oxygen, or frozen hydrogen, or frozen helium. We even know enough about Halley's Comet to be able to predict its return in 1986 within hours of the event. We've done our scientific work. Yet, my dearest Julienne, we've not asked 'What?' about this heavenly event. We're scientists, logical positivists, and that might mean we're more constrained in our adventures than the most superstitious heathen. So tell me, trust me, what is it that you see, when you see Halley's Comet?"

"Oh, Monsieur Rufus, you're so smart. What can I know? Don't you want to play some more?" said Julienne.

"Not just yet. Tell me," said Rufus.

"Like a wedding? A party? A celebration in the square? Like a battle we've won. How is that?" said Julienne.

"In other words, the comet signals some historical correlative. It marks time for you. You attach loose phenomena to it, like a war, a plague, a birth?" said Rufus.

"I think so," said Julienne.

"The usual mass hysteria. I was hoping for more," said Rufus.

"How's this? Me on top?" said Julienne.

"Ouch! Watch it. Ouch!" said Rufus.

"There," said Julienne. "How's this? This is a comet for me. This. And this. Ooooh."

"What?" said Rufus.

"Oh!" said Julienne.

"You women seem sensitive to something," said Rufus.

"Oh!" said Julienne.

"What could I be missing?" said Rufus.

"Oh! Monsieur Rufus," said Julienne, collapsing. "Nice."

"Did you see the comet just then? Is that it?" said Rufus.

"Are you making fun of me again? I saw stars." said Julienne. "I always see stars."

"Many or just one? Did it have a tail?" said Rufus.

"Like a comet?" said Julienne.

"Yes! A comet! Is that where we've seen comets before? We see comets when we climax. We come with the comet!" said Rufus, bouncing up.

"I don't understand. I didn't see a comet," said Julienne.

"No? You're sure? Not just one little comet in the middle of all those stars?" said Rufus.

"Not even one. Are you all right?" said Julienne.

"Yes, yes, I thought we were on the brink of a major scientific discovery. The primal comet vision. I would have shared the Nobel with you, of course. Too bad," said Rufus.

"Money too?" said Julienne.

"Baskets of the stuff. More importantly, our names on plaques in the Royal Society. Would you like that?" said Rufus.

"The Academy of Science, too?" said Julienne.

"Why not?" said Rufus. "What do you know of the Academy?"

"My family," said Julienne.

"Your family?" said Rufus, interrupted by a knock.

"Excuse me, Mr. Broadsword, sir," said Buys through the door's vents. "Might I come in? A delicate matter."

"Come ahead, man. Cover yourself, Julienne," said Rufus.

"Sorry to disturb you, sir, but the Captain and Number One are ashore, leaving me in charge. There's a problem. Oh, sorry, sir, I didn't know you had company. Miss Julienne, ma'am, my apologies."

"No, stay, what's this trouble?" said Rufus.

Buys explained that there was a party of Arab astrologers at quayside, demanding to board *Rockefeller* to visit with "Pasha Rockefeller." Buys explained that when he'd told them there was no one on board who could help them, a large crowd had gathered, despite the storm, staring in adoration at the Arab astrologers, chanting bizarre, Infidel phrases, and growing restless that their holy men should be so shunned. Buys explained that if the situation collapsed into a riot, he would be held responsible by the Captain, the British legation to the Ottoman Empire at Istanbul, and the Rockefeller family in America. Buys concluded by asking if Mr. Broadsword, being the only member of the expedition on board who seemed a "good sort," could perhaps receive the party of Arab astrologers as if he were "Pasha Rockefeller."

Rufus listened without comment. This was what he'd been waiting for. This made the adventure worthwhile. Perhaps these Arab astrologers could tell Rufus what he wanted to know about the comet. Rufus laughed, saying, "Of course!"

Buys spun away. Shortly, he tapped on Rufus's door again. Julienne squealed, burying herself beneath the covers. Rufus lit up his cigar, straightened his smoking jacket, saying, *"Entrez!"*

Three men in dark desert robes emerged. One was as huge as a camel, and half as broad, with arms to his knees. One was as small as a chimpanzee, with normal-sized trunk and head, but short, muscular arms and legs. And one was of average height and build, but with a grace to his movements which reminded Rufus of the King's Birthday. Their faces were mostly covered with their robes, but Rufus could see they were heavily bearded.

"Peace to you," said the dwarf astrologer in excellent French, tinged slightly, it seemed to Rufus, with a vague Eastern European accent—Polish?

"Yes," said Rufus in English. "I speak no Arabic or Turkish."

"And we speak no English worth pretending," said the dwarf.

"A dilemma, then. Can we converse in French like this?" said Rufus in French.

"We can. But perhaps another language is possible with so enriched a host," said the dwarf, turning respectfully to the graceful astrologer, whispering, turning back, and bowing deeply with a courtliness that impressed Rufus. "Do you know the Roman tongue?" asked the dwarf.

"Very little Italian," said Rufus.

"I mean Latin," said the dwarf.

"Greetings to you, Pasha Rockefeller. I am called Freewill. It is most generous of you to entertain us today," said the graceful astrologer in exquisite Ciceronian Latin.

"My God," said Rufus, who knew enough Latin to know that he'd just heard Latin spoken as it had not been for at least two millennia—full of clipped vowels, delicate consonants. The astrologer's name seemed most unusual, "Freewill," but then Rufus knew Arabs were wanderers enough to be named anything. He attempted a reply, "And greetings to you, Freewill . . ." but fell short. He felt foolish.

"Not possible, then?" said the dwarf.

"No, sorry. Who are you?" said Rufus, in French again.

"We are pilgrims," said the dwarf.

"You've come about the comet, though, Halley's Comet?" said Rufus.

"This also concerns us," said the dwarf, conferring again with the graceful astrologer. The giant stood silent.

"Are you frightened of the comet?" said Rufus.

"Indeed not, Lord," said the dwarf. Was that amusement? The dwarf continued, "Could you tell us, please, what is the true nature of capitalism?"

86

"Capitalism, as in money capitalism?" said Rufus.

"Capitalism as you practice it. In recent discussions with a Mr. Twain of the State of Connecticut—who sends his regards—we have learned that you are a capitalist of the first rank. Mr. Twain of the State of Connecticut emphasizes 'rank,' " said the dwarf.

"Twain?" said Rufus. "But he's . . . oh, yes, a jest, of course. Capitalism? I'll wager Mark Twain gave you an earful about capitalism, eh? Don't you believe that old fox. He's mad, you know, pristinely mad. Do you understand me? He predicted his own, uh, passing. Said he'd come in with Halley's Comet and would go out with it. And he did, by God! Ha! ha! Oh, yes, I see, yes, capitalism, sorry . . ."

"No need to apologize, Lord," said the dwarf. "We did not know this about Mr. Twain. He was a superior host. He bade us farewell, saying, 'Now I have seen everything.' But . . ."

"Capitalism is private ownership and private investment," said Rufus. "You work for money so that your money will work for you. How is that?"

"Less than illuminating," said the dwarf. "Would you characterize it philosophically?"

"It does not have a philosophical basis," said Rufus.

"So?" said the dwarf, whispering, nodding. "And the true nature of nationalism?"

"Is this a puzzle? All right," said Rufus. "Nationalism is a function of man's limitless need to delimit space. Farce."

"This is instructive, though unexpected," said the dwarf. "Could you tell us now the true nature of revolution?"

"Revolution? Political revolution?" said Rufus.

"Whatever you say, Lord," said the dwarf.

"Revolution is replacing one gang of fools with another equally foolish gang," said Rufus.

"Aphelion? Perihelion?" said the dwarf.

"I would agree. Aphelion. Perihelion. No difference whatsoever. What goes up must come down. Man's politics subordinate to the eternal laws of gravitation," said Rufus.

"And the comet, Lord. What is the purpose of this expedition?" said the dwarf.

"Purpose? Hadn't thought of that. Why, to study the comet, of course. Science is the purpose," said Rufus.

"Thank you, Lord," said the dwarf, turning to the graceful astrologer. Rufus waited, sucking on his cigar. Why did he feel ignorant? He added:

"Say, now. I've answered your questions, haven't I? Who are you? What is it that you want? I don't think you really are Arab astrologers. Who are you?"

"And you are not Pasha Rockefeller, are you?" said the dwarf slowly, turning back to Rufus.

"My name is Rufus Broadsword, from New York City, in the United States of America," said Rufus.

"And your companion?" said the dwarf.

"Oh, this is Julienne, uh, Julienne," said Rufus, reaching over to pat her. "Introduce yourself, Julienne."

"Yes, Monsieur Rufus," said Julienne, peeking from beneath the bedclothes. "My name is Julienne Thyme."

The three pilgrims—for they were not Arab astrologers after all—left without another word, shutting the door softly behind them. Rufus rolled out of bed, nervous, unsettled, sweaty. He threw his cigar through the portal. He noticed a small package by the door, quickly discovering it was a paper-wrapped bottle of claret, dated 1835. They'd left behind them a comet vintage—a Halley's Comet wine. Rufus opened it with his penknife and sniffed an excellent bouquet: not sophisticated, but magical, transporting. Rufus poured two glasses and moved to nudge Julienne out of her hiding place to hand her one. They drank one glassful, two, and sipped a third before speaking. Rufus felt that something was profoundly wrong. He asked Julienne if she'd ever heard of anything so queer as those men. He'd meant his question rhetorically. Julienne understood it as a sincere inquiry. She said, yes, she had, once upon a time.

Fall 1835

MICHEL Thyme left Honoré's studio just before nightfall. Though he'd been up all the night before—the
fourth time this week—Michel hadn't been able to
sleep. There was too much excitement at the Observatory.
He found it more refreshing to busy his days with his
friend's concerns, of which Honoré Daumier had an abundance. Yesterday, for example, according to Honoré, three
men had followed him home from the printer's in St.-Ger-
main. Honoré said they'd looked like secret police, Michel
had no reason to believe, given current Parisian intrigues,
that they weren't. He wondered if he were being followed
as well.

But why should they follow a junior astronomer? It
was one thing to shadow a former illustrator for the banned
La Caricature, a subversive publication, certainly. It was another to shadow his school friend, especially when this
school friend had great expectations of becoming the best
astronomer in France. Nevertheless, thought Michel, should
I mention this to the Professor? Would the Professor be
sympathetic, or would he panic, removing my name from
the privileged at the Paris Observatory? Who knew whom
you could trust in such affairs? There was no predicting how
petty the Palace of Justice might be about politics among
faculty. It was getting as ugly as it had ever been under the
Bourbon's Villele. This Louis Philippe—so-called Citizen
King—was not what they said he was, thought Michel, having trouble, because he was stubby and unathletic, stepping
over a vagrant in Honoré's studio's entranceway. Poor
wretch, thought Michel, who'd inherited his dead father's
sympathies, if not his Babeufian politics. The vagrant had no
legs, just a wooden trolley on which to shove himself along.

"Sous for *La Garde?*" said the vagrant, shoving his gnarled right hand up Michel's pant leg.

"Get away!" cried Michel.

"Sous for *La Garde?*" said the vagrant, holding out his left hand, fingers worn away from years of dragging himself along cobblestone alleys.

"Yes, yes, my father," said Michel, collecting himself, reaching into his waistcoat, handing down a note to the vagrant. It hardly mattered if the man told true. He might be a Waterloo veteran. He might not be. He was legless, in pain, and wretched. "Here, my father."

"Bless you, sir, true son of the Revolution," said the vagrant, looking up.

Michel reeled away from the man's eyes. There was unspeakable sorrow. There was also bitterness, madness, forgetfulness. There were all the dark passions the poets had learned to bury beneath lyricism. There was Hell there, indeed, two sockets to the depths of the pit. May the heavens burst, thought Michel, how horrible that he lives. How tough men are to kill when they want not to die, for how else could this half-man have survived twenty years of begging? What sort of nation-state abandoned its wounded veterans to wooden trolleys? More important, for there seemed to Michel more at issue here than war and peace: what did it mean about a nation's character that it permitted men like this on every corner, in every doorway, filthy and hopeless?

Michel walked away quickly. Michel couldn't deal with suffering, which is why he'd chosen natural physics many years before, none of those imponderable metaphysics. Let Honoré address the matter in his way, drawing pictures of people so horribly broken that words failed before them. Best of all worlds, thought Michel, to keep one's mind not on this world at all, but on the heavens.

The heavens had been filled with wonder this past month. Halley's Comet had returned, on schedule, amid bustle and celebration at the Observatory. For a full five weeks, across the dome of the night sky, the comet had

moved toward perihelion in mid-November. And each night
the comet's tail had grown, from almost nothing on 1 October, to almost 40 degrees last night, 30 October. Michel had
spent the week sketching the coma of the comet as it
changed shape, from an egg, to a star, to a forkbeard, to a
near parallelogram. Tonight, Allhallows Eve, Michel was on
duty again. That was why he'd needed especially to visit
Honoré, to pick up another of his excellent sketchpads.

Twenty meters past Honoré's doorway, Michel
paused at the corner of Rue St.-Jacques to watch a caravan
of carriages pass by, filled with early evening merrymakers.
Here was the bourgeoisie that so enraged Honoré. Oh,
Honoré, thought Michel, admiring the powdered girls, then
looking back toward Honoré's entranceway as if addressing
him in person, why is it that the bourgeoisie seems acceptable to every class but the sons and daughters of the bourgeoisie? Not even he, thought Michel, meaning the vagrant
still seemingly asleep in Honoré's entranceway, not even he
would reject the bourgeoisie with the fervor you do,
Honoré.

What was that? Michel jumped back, bumping an
apple cart. Those dark figures there, lingering in the alley
across from Honoré's entranceway. Yes! Honoré was being
watched! Yet, he thought, how far would they go? Have
they written my name down already? Will they tell the
Professor that I frequently visit a known subversive? But I
have seen him only a dozen times since summer! What to do,
thought Michel, spinning away from the apple cart. I'm a
simple scientist. These politics are not for me! Yet, I should
rush back to Honoré to warn him. I should act the hero,
assert myself, confront those dark figures in the name of
justice, liberty, and reason. I should sacrifice myself, as my
father, as Gracchus Babeuf on the guillotine, as all "true sons
of the Revolution."

No! No! I can't do it, thought Michel. I couldn't
survive those jails. I'm not as strong as Honoré. They'd
break me, and I'd never recover. And any accusation, any
detention, any trial—innocent or guilty—will finish me at

the Observatory. I might as well be dead then. No, I can't go back to warn Honoré. I am ashamed, but I cannot.

Michel shivered as he hurried on. It wasn't just the evening's chill. He shivered in his soul. His father had taught him well. He knew what true cowardice was—when one ignored principles rather than renouncing them. When one made a decision by refusing to make a decision. What difference now, Michel, he asked himself, between Simon Peter's betrayal of the Savior the night of His arrest and your own abandonment of Honoré to those dark figures? None whatsoever! Before the Revolutionary Court, Michel Thyme, you stand accused, convicted, and condemned.

Michel bent into the gusts as he passed the Val de Grace. Perhaps, once, a man such as he might have rushed into the Val de Grace at such a moment to confess his sins, to seek penitence. But no more—these were modern times. Michel Thyme, like many of his colleagues at the world-famous Paris Observatory (zero degrees longitude for a goodly part of the non-Anglo world since 1667), was embarrassed to admit to a faith in a Power Beyond the Zero, that is, Michel was embarrassed to admit to a faith in God. Michel was eager, however, to admit to a faith in the Eternal Laws of the Universe, such as Gravity.

Michel left one sort of faith behind him in the Val de Grace then, as he hurried on to another sort of faith up the road, at the corner of Rue Cassinni and Rue St.-Jacques— Colbert's grand vision—the Paris Observatory, its four walls perfectly arranged north, south, east, and west, its occupants perfectly smug in their inhumane positivism.

"Tell me quickly, Etienne. No time to waste. The midnight conference," said Michel, rushing up the spiral staircase to the Observatory terrace to do his first sketches of the comet just then coming up over the western horizon.

"That's the thing, Monsieur Docteur," said Etienne, one of the university students permitted to do the bidding of the Observatory staff. "At the midnight conference. The King!"

"Where?" said Michel half-heartedly, looking over the terrace balcony to see if Louis Philippe's well-lit carriage and caravan could be seen on the Boulevard de Port Royal below.

"No, Monsieur Docteur," said Etienne, hugging the wall, for the continual rush of the updrafts frightened him. "The King is coming here tonight. For the midnight conference. The Professor says the King is especially interested in the Observatory, and that the King has mentioned to his ministers that the Observatory is due for expansion. The Professor says the King has asked his architects about designing a dome!"

"Has the Professor said anything of the staff being investigated by the King's ministers?" said Michel.

"Why, no, Monsieur Docteur," said Etienne. "Investigated? Oh! You mean investigated as to which member the Professor should recommend for the new chair."

"What new chair?" said Michel. Etienne must have his ear to every door in the Observatory.

"Haven't you heard?" said Etienne. "The Professor has received a letter from an anonymous nobleman, said by some to be a Pole, by others to be a Frenchman living in Poland. This letter promises to fund a Halley's Comet Chair of Cosmology at the Sorbonne. A plum, yes?"

"Don't you mean an Edmund Halley Chair of Cosmology?" asked Michel, already hungry for such a fruit.

"No," said Etienne, deciding to retreat, "a Halley's Comet Chair. Don't forget. The King at the midnight conference. Shall I fetch your good linen for you?"

"Yes, Etienne, how thoughtful," said Michel, handing Etienne his flat key. Michel decided he'd have to reward Etienne more fully for his information and service, even if the boy was afraid of heights. But that was for tomorrow. Tonight, Michel lost himself in the comet, sketching it again and again the next few hours as it rose toward the Milky

Way, its tail a lengthy 40 degrees. That tail was the subject of a lively debate in the community.

One school held that the tail was caused by the comet rushing through the heavens' "resisting medium," as the world-famous cometologist Herr Professor Franz Encke characterized it. What this "resisting medium" consisted of was not certain. Some, following Descartes, said the heavens were filled with an ether of uniform substance which held celestial bodies in orbit as much as did gravity. Others argued, more daringly, that the heavens were not filled with a uniform ether at all, but instead with atoms of many different substances, distributed randomly in "seas." This "atomic" explanation meant that the comet's tail changed lengths because the comet pushed through seas of atoms of varying densities.

Worrisomely, the "resisting medium" theory, while it seemed to explain why some comet orbits shrank with each revolution around the sun (friction), could not explain why the comet's tail always pointed away from the sun. If the tail was the wake of the comet as, say, a ship through water leaves a wake behind it, then why didn't this comet wake remain directly behind the comet as it traveled? Why did it, instead, always point away from the sun, regardless of the direction of the comet's movement?

Michel rejected the "resisting medium" theory, with all due respect to Herr Professor Encke. Michel believed that the answer to the comet's tail lay not in the nature of the medium through which the comet passed, but in the nature of the comet itself. The important question for Michel was, what is a comet made of?

If it was made of ice, for example, then the tail could be evaporated ice—steam—rushing from the comet's center, in the same manner as smoke poured off a burning coal launched through the air. Of course, the steam would increase as the comet neared the sun's heat, and decrease as it moved away from the sun's heat. In addition, Michel's "Iceball Theory," as he called it, explained why the comet's orbit was not regular, why comet orbits had been observed to shrink with each revolution. As the comet's ice evaporated, the mass of the comet changed, and with the mass change, the orbit changed, following Newton et al.

Most of his colleagues regarded Michel's "Iceball Theory" as inadequate. How can you explain the brightness of the comet, they asked—light reflected off of ice? Foolishness, since Halley's Comet was as bright as Venus. Moreover, they said, how is it that a comet doesn't simply evaporate as it reaches perihelion, since what sort of ice can withstand the sun's heat at .58 A.U.?

Michel admitted he couldn't answer these questions. And, annoyingly, his "Iceball Theory" also could not explain the same problem that Herr Professor Encke's "resisting medium" school could not explain, that is, why does the comet's tail always point away from the sun?

Nevertheless, Michel believed that his approach—analyzing the nature of the object and not of the medium—was superior. But, more importantly, Michel's theory set him apart. It might not be thorough, but it was novel. It made Michel a local authority in cometology, which had, ever since Edmund Halley inaugurated it as a legitimate pursuit of natural physics in 1705 (with his prediction of the return of the comet now called Halley's in 1759), concentrated on calculating comet orbits and not on the composition of comets.

Michel had come to understand that calculating orbits, while useful, was best left to geometrist drudges. He saw himself as addressing deeper problems, a cometologist cum cosmologist, which is why, as he sketched Halley's Comet on the evening of 31 October 1835, from the terrace of the Paris Observatory, he was nearly breathless for the dreaming of that Halley's Comet Chair of Cosmology.

"Dong, dong, dong, dong," went the Observatory clock, interrupting Michel's marriage plans, townhouse plans, château plans, "dong, dong, dong, dong," interrupting Michel's European Lecture Circuit plans, "dong, dong, dong, dong," interrupting Michel's election to the Academy of Science plans. It was midnight! I'm late, panicked Michel, late, late, pounding down the spiral staircase, realizing he'd no time to change his linen. He tucked his sketchpad under his arm, stuffed his pencils in his waistcoat, straightened his pince-nez, fluffed his beard, brushed the lint from his suit, the crumbs from his cravat. He looked shabby, but intense, grimacing as he approached the closed doors to the conference room. They'd started the meeting on time for once. Perhaps they wouldn't notice his entrance. He tossed his hat on a bench, took a big breath, and opened the door as quietly as he could. The room was warm and bright, filled with noble fellows, fellow nobles, not a few heavily scented, stunningly gowned ladies of the Court, and, of course, the "Citizen King," Louis Philippe, hefting his umbrella.

"There you are!" said the Professor.

"Oh," said Michel.

"This is the lad I was telling you about, Your Highness," said the Professor. "One of my young champions, Docteur Michel Thyme."

"The one who studies Halley's Comet?" said Louis Philippe.

"Come forward. So shy, Michel?" said the Professor.

"You are the one who knows about the comet, then," said Louis Philippe. "I'm told that it does not mean war or famine or pestilence. What does it mean, Monsieur Docteur?"

"Your Highness honors me with so profound a question," said Michel with a slight bow. "It is true that Halley's Comet has been associated in the past with unhappy occasions, such as the burning of the Temple of Solomon in the first century. Or such as the assassination of the Emperor Caracalla in the third century, or, more historically pertinent, such as the victory of William the Conqueror over Harold of England at Hastings in the eleventh century, a matter that has led to so intemperate a people as the English."

"You worry me," said Louis Philippe.

"Ah, but Your Highness need recall that Halley's Comet has also been associated with bounty, such as the victory over the infidel Attila in the fifth century, and the victory over the Turk in . . ."

"All blood and death," said Louis Philippe. "It seems a violent sign."

"There is the birth of our Lord Jesus," said Michel slowly.

"Halley's Comet was the Star of Bethlehem?" burst Louis Philippe.

"It is not impossible," said Michel, shifting his feet, because he knew he was playing loose and dangerous with his dating here; but his point had carried the moment. Louis Philippe was delighted. Michel decided to press on—ignoring the thought of the German theologians who would someday groan at Louis Philippe's misinformation—and say, "I conclude that Halley's Comet means long life and great glory for Your Highness."

"Hear! Hear!" said the Professor, the noble fellows of the Observatory staff, and the fellow nobles of the Court.

"Psst! Psst!" said the heavily scented, stunningly gowned ladies of the Court.

"Well and good," said Louis Philippe. "Yet I had hoped you could tell me more scientifically. Victor tells me that if a comet like this struck Paris, God forbid, it would pound it into ashes. Is this true? Is there a chance of this?"

"A very small chance, Your Highness," said Michel. "So small it need not concern Your Highness. And might I add, though I am an astronomer, and familiar only with celestial catastrophe, I believe it impossible that any comet, no matter how famous or large or ominous, could ever reduce Paris to ashes."

"Yes, well said, but," said Louis Philippe, "aren't these shooting stars already striking the earth? Isn't it the comet which brings these shooting stars? Aren't they pieces of the comet? Couldn't the comet strike as well?"

"Once again, Your Highness," said Michel, "in astronomy, there is no certainty. There are those who argue that these shooting stars, or meteors, are closely associated with the comet. But if I might extend a personal opinion, I am not convinced that meteors have a strict relation to a comet, or 'hairy star,' as ancient scholars called it. The meteor showers we have witnessed this month are a recurring event which we call the Orionids, because they seem to descend from the constellation Orion. Certainly, this meteor shower would have occurred without the apparition of the comet."

"That's a relief!" said Louis Philippe, pausing while the various flatterers around him laughed heartily and insincerely. "You have set me at ease, Monsieur Docteur. This is a good fellow, Professor. I trust he will be rewarded for his diligence."

"But of course, Your Highness," said the Professor.

"What's that you have there?" said Louis Philippe.

"Merely some sketches, Your Highness," said Michel.

"Of this comet?" said Louis Philippe.

"Show us," said the Professor.

"Well, uh, yes," said Michel.

"I see, very nice. Here's Montmartre. There's Val de Grace. And the Boulevard St.-Michel," said Louis Philippe. "These are lovely. See how the comet moves across the sky, Elise? Victor?"

"Your Highness would honor the Observatory if he would accept one of these drawings for his renowned collection," said the Professor. "Wouldn't he, Michel?"

"Why, uh, yes, honor," said Michel. "Please, Your Highness, all of them, if you will. They are just rough, but please."

"How very generous," said Louis Philippe. "The entire pad? Won't Adolphe be envious? And you've signed it already. Oh!"

"Yes, well, that's not my signature," said Michel.

"I can see that," said Louis Philippe. "Victor? Isn't this that fellow? Yes, I thought so."

"You see, Your Highness, I, uh, borrowed this for, uh," said Michel.

"Is there something amiss?" said the Professor.

"Do you know this Daumier, Monsieur Docteur?" said the King.

"Honoré Daumier? The subversive?" said the Professor.

"It's just a casual thing," said Michel.

"What else do you have to show us tonight, Monsieur Professeur?" said Louis Philippe, plopping the pad down on the conference table, turning away from Michel as if he weren't there. The Professor caught the flow of the politics and turned away with the King, leaving Michel, his head bowed in utter despair. How close he'd come to his Halley's Comet Chair of Cosmology. How completely he'd lost an opportunity to attain so lofty a position in Louis Philippe's France. If Michel was a "true son of the Revolution," as that legless vagrant had said, then surely he'd meant the Revolution of '89, and not the July Revolution of '30 that had birthed Louis Philippe and his bourgeois imperative. The noble fellows, fellow nobles, and heavily scented, stunningly gowned ladies of the Court surrounding Michel in the conference room were the true heirs of the July Revolution—rich, practical, hypocritical, and devoted to the status quo with a carnivorous ferocity. These were the folk who would reap more than they sowed as long as Louis Philippe remained on the throne.

Without fully considering his helpless position in this room full of trendy power brokers, without fully comprehending the condescending stares of the Royal Court about him, without fully remembering his dead father's advice that it was not brave for a revolutionary to sacrifice himself to the ruling class's bottomless appetite for melodramatic martyrs, Michel raised his head again and proclaimed, loudly, passionately, "Honoré Daumier is my friend."

Hatless beneath the sudden rainstorm, soaked through his clothes, clutching his sketchpad as if it were his last hold on his destiny, Michel Thyme barreled up Rue St.-Jacques, past

Val de Grace with its early morning worshipers preparing in the pre-dawn dark for their spiritual ordeal this All Saints Day, past more worshipers grouping before St.-Jacques du Haut Pas, wherein was buried Giovanni Domenico Cassinni, founder of the Paris Observatory (Michel pausing, puffing, to bow—an old superstition), past Rue Soufflot opening onto the Pantheon, wherein was buried the hero of these new, so-called socialists, Jean-Jacques Rousseau, and wherein was buried the hero of true revolutionaries everywhere, François Marie Arouet de Voltaire. Michel staggered as he reached the confines of the University. He was winded, aching, but he must push on. He must confess his earlier shame to Honoré, so that he might explain how he'd redeemed himself, in part, by sabotaging his own career before the King of France. Michel hoped Honoré would understand. Michel hoped Honoré was not arrested.

Michel tripped over something warm and dense in Honoré's dark entranceway. It was the vagrant. Michel apologized with a swallow of air, half-crawling up Honoré's stairs, pounding on the door, crying, "Honoré! I've done it! I'm no longer afraid of them! I'm free!"

But there was no response. There was no one home. Michel collapsed before the door, weeping, not for himself, for though his ambitions were done in Paris, there were other observatories (perhaps with Herr Professor Encke in Berlin, where Michel's shaky politics would be of no concern), and not for Honoré, whose career could only improve as his ability to caricature the middle class sharpened. No, Michel wept for the stupidity of this situation. If Honoré was arrested, it was Michel's fault. And though Honoré could probably endure another imprisonment, might even profit by it, Michel had had an opportunity to be heroic, to be a true friend, and he'd missed it. It made his defiance before the King all the more absurd. It made him pathetic, not Romantic, and for this he wept.

"Sous for *La Garde?*" said the vagrant.

"Anything, my father," said Michel, handing over his money clip without looking up.

"You're his friend?" said the vagrant, taking the money, examining the clip, pocketing it as well.

"They've taken him!" said Michel.

"Follow," said the vagrant, walking down the stairs on his hands, depositing his torso atop his wooden trolley, turning to call to Michel again, "Follow."

Michel stood, wiping the rain from his brow. What was this? Perhaps this beggar knew where they'd taken Honoré. Perhaps there was still something Michel could do.

They followed a bizarre route. The vagrant, on his trolley, rattling along the cobblestones, seemed to know every treacherous alley and filthy close in the Latin Quarter. He led Michel on a path only a man reduced to legless locomotion could know, avoiding major avenues lest he be run down by carriages, avoiding well-lit squares lest he be booted away by shopowners, avoiding even the usual roads lined with poor refugees from the provinces come to Paris for unclear reasons in order to make their livelihood or to perish slowly, by starvation or disease, it hardly mattered. As the light improved with the approaching dawn—somewhere up there above the rain clouds—Michel realized he had no idea where they'd been, where they were. He kept his eyes to the ground, following the sound of the trolley. Michel suffered the sight of the tragedies they passed— families huddled together in doorways, derelicts laid out prone in gutters, so still and wasted that the Angel of Death could hardly surprise them should it tap them and say, "Follow."

Finally, they reached a close more awful than any they'd traversed before. The odor was gagging. The sounds were worse, however, for among the crying, sobbing, heaving, mewing, gasping, choking, spitting, moaning, and mumbling was the immediately recognizable sound of the death rattle. Michel trembled when he felt a hand at his ankle. Then he felt another hand on his knee. He hurried on, high-stepping, following the trolley to a basement entrance way.

Why would the secret police bring Honoré here?

thought Michel. Only if they intended to do more than interrogate—torture.

"No!" cried Michel. The vagrant barely paused. He catapulted himself from his trolley, walked down the steps on his hands. The door opened, admitting the vagrant, and remained open. Michel padded down the steps to peek in. The air was bad, the light worse; but at least it was dry, smelling of human sweat, none of the odors of the close. Michel walked in, squinting. He heard a shuffle up ahead— the vagrant, hand-walking. Michel stepped across the earthen floor toward the noise, his eyes adjusting to the shadows. Other eyes stared back at him. That rasping sound was breathing.

"Identify yourself!" came a deep voice.

"Trooper Ragan, of the First *Lanciers de la Garde!*" said the vagrant.

"State your business," said the deep voice.

"This cousin, for the artist," said the vagrant, now identified as Trooper Ragan of the First *Lanciers de la Garde,* who'd ridden to their grand doom on the plateau of Mont St.-Jean twenty years before, behind Marshal Ney and Milhaud's Fourth Cavalry Corps—that vainglorious first cavalry charge on the Allied center, which, failing, had served to signal for the first time that day, 18 June 1815, that this was the closest Emperor Napoleon Bonaparte would ever get to that inconsequential Belgian town up the road a few kilometers, the headquarters of the Duke of Wellington, Waterloo. The vagrant turned to Michel again to say, "Follow."

This couldn't be the secret police, thought Michel— trundling ahead, down more steps—yet who could these people be? There seemed to be hundreds of them, hanging from every rafter, seated quietly along every ledge. Michel had heard fancy stories of the Parisian "Den of Thieves," but these folks didn't seem felons.

Then all Michel's questions were answered with one vision. He paused in a doorway to look in on an alcove, where, hanging on a stone wall above dozens of burning candles, were two portraits of unmistakable personage. Here was Romance. Here was Marshal Michel Ney, the Prince of Moscow, executed for his desertion to Bonaparte in '15. And here was the Emperor Himself, as charismatic as ever, just as if he wasn't dead and buried some fourteen years now, thousands of miles from the country that still loved him, on the inconsequential English island, St. Helena.

So, thought Michel, these men are patriots, Bonapartists, the survivors of Waterloo who had been, for whatever reason, too bitter to rejoin permanently a French society anxious to put the Hundred Days behind. Worse, many of these men, Michel realized, were broken like Trooper Ragan. Michel wondered if they lived here, or just came here to tell tales of happier days—the Italian Campaign, the Spanish Campaign, the Polish Campaign, the Russian Campaign. This place was an underground city of vanquished revolutionaries.

"Here," said Trooper Ragan, nodding to a passageway. Michel ducked through to a room brighter than the others because it had windows on the street above. A gray light poured through the casements along with rainwater.

"Michel!" said Honoré Daumier, stepping back from his easel. "How did you find me?"

"Honoré! Oh, Honoré!" said Michel. "You're not arrested!"

"Of course not," said Honoré.

"I thought you were arrested. Trooper Ragan. In your entrance way," said Michel, stuttering in his excitement.

"I see. Ragan," said Honoré. "He must trust you a great deal to bring you here. Secrets, you know. Something wrong?"

"Well, yes! I mean, no, no longer," said Michel, collapsing on a bench, realizing they weren't alone. There were three men standing on the other side of the room, watching him work. Honoré was painting a portrait of a riotously decrepit old soldier, seated before the easel, dressed in a tattered Hussar uniform. "Everything is fine now, Honoré," added Michel. "I thought you'd been arrested by those secret agents."

"Arrested? Not this time," said Honoré, putting down his palette and brush, moving over to Michel. His naturally jovial, ruddy face took on a conspiratorial shape. "Listen, Michel, I was wrong about those agents. They're over there."

"What!" said Michel.

"No, calmly, my friend," said Honoré. "They aren't secret police. Merely pilgrims, or so they say. With the most curious questions. It's fortuitous that you've come. We've been chatting about the comet, among other matters. I told them about you. They said they wanted to meet you. They seem pleasant. The little one, there, he does the talking. He's Polish, I think, speaks French, though his accent is very odd —old, somehow. The huge one doesn't talk. The third one, he seems their leader. He doesn't speak any French. Just Latin."

"Latin?" said Michel, looking over. They were heavily bearded and all but hidden in their damp religious cowls.

"Odd, isn't it?" said Honoré. "Come on, I'll introduce you. I don't know their names, though I think the dwarf called their leader 'Majesty.' And I think the leader introduced himself to me as, uh, 'Freewill'?"

"Majesty?" said Michel. "Freewill?"

"There now!" said Honoré, leading Michel by the arm over to the three pilgrims. "This, gentlemen, is my dear friend, Michel Thyme. The fellow from the Observatory whom I mentioned. The cometologist."

"Cometologist! How happy it is that you've come," said the dwarf pilgrim.

"I understand you're interested in the comet?" said Michel.

"Indeed we are," said the dwarf pilgrim. "But we have other inquiries as well, if you would be so kind?"

"How can I be of assistance, my father?" said Michel, charmed by the dwarf. And though the average-sized one hadn't said a word to him—just whispering with the dwarf —he impressed Michel as deserving of courtly deference, certainly a most regal and graceful presence, as men such as Louis Philippe could never hope to be.

"See what I told you?" whispered Honoré to Michel.

"We're hoping you can tell us the true nature of socialism," said the dwarf pilgrim.

"Socialism?" said Michel, amused. "That's more Honoré's expertise. He and his 'Social Gospel.' I'm a scientist."

"Socialism, gentlemen," began Honoré, "is a term recently proposed to describe a utopian state of human affairs wherein everyone in a community shares not only the bounty of the community but also in the making of the bounty."

"Utopian?" said the dwarf.

"Utopian," said Honoré.

"And what is the true nature of nihilism?" said the dwarf.

"Ho!" said Honoré. "Nihilism is also a utopian state of human affairs based upon the premise that it is possible to reject all legal, moral, and spiritual authority."

"Utopian again?" said the dwarf.

"Utopian," said Honoré.

"And what is the true nature of revolution?" said the dwarf.

"You deal with this one," said Honoré.

"Why, er, revolution, gentlemen, is replacing one position with another. A reversal in human affairs," said Michel.

"Aphelion? Perihelion?" said the dwarf.

"Aphelion? Perihelion?" said Michel. "Yes, that's about it. That is it! Like the Eternal Law of Gravity."

"Really, Michel, none of your deism," said Honoré.

"He asked," said Michel lamely.

The dwarf pilgrim turned again to the regal pilgrim, whispering to him. The regal pilgrim nodded. They seem

magnificently serious, thought Michel, amused by the senti-
mentality of his life—how so tragic a night of events could
have come to this, so comic a morning of events.

The dwarf faced Michel again, this time with a bottle
of claret, offering it to Michel with a smile. Michel inspected
it, showing it to Honoré. It was dated 1759, a comet vintage
—a Halley's Comet wine. Michel opened it with a palette
knife and poured a bit in a paint cup. It was excellent: not
so sophisticated, but magical, transporting. Michel laughed
as he poured the cupful, and another for Honoré, and three
for the pilgrims, and a large amount for the ancient Hussar.

"Tell us, please, about the comet," said the dwarf.

Michel drew up a stool, suggesting to Honoré with a
broad gesture that he should return to his easel, since this
would take some time. Michel then handed his damp
sketchbook over to the three pilgrims. He began his lecture
with "Once upon a time."

Spring 1759

THE DECISION to leave his farm on the Borders, at the
last, had been easy for Eli. There was nothing left for
him after Meg had left him in the typhus of '51. She'd
buried their three children while he'd rotted in the King's jail
in York. After the general amnesty, he'd made his way home
to find only a shell of his one great love. Eli had suspected
that if it hadn't been the typhus, it would have been melancholy that took her. Meg had been dead for years in spirit.
Her body had just taken longer to succumb to the despair
of being a "treasonous dog's" woman—an outcast in her
village, her family, her country.

And so Elijah Broadsword, formerly a promising

career officer in His Majesty's Coldstream Guards, and then, because of his Jacobite sympathies, a broken felon condemned to ten years' hard labor for his treason in the '45, had buried sweet Margaret (née Shaw) Broadsword by the River Eden in Cumberland County:

Here Lies
Margaret Broadsword
(1726–1751)
Beloved, Mourned

Eli had made his way south, prepared to follow whatever fate was left him. He'd chanced upon a regimental recruiter in Liverpool, who'd said he had no prejudice against Jacobites. Eli had enlisted as a common trooper. Because of his military experience, however, and perhaps because he'd left his innocence behind by the River Eden, he rose through the ranks quickly. By '56, when Lord Pitt's brand of imperialism moved to post Eli's new regiment to the American colonies to combat French expansionism, Elijah Broadsword, at thirty-four, once again found himself a commissioned officer in the Royal Army.

Still, he remained an embittered Jacobite beneath his dispassion. His fellow battalion officers, mostly younger men, came to calling him "Gray Eli" for the cloud that seemed to hang over him. They respected him, but they puzzled about him and his "secret melancholy," as the poet among them dubbed it. In '58, at Louisbourgh on the Acadian coast, where the battalion landed just in time to mop up after the fall of the French fort, "Gray Eli" was seen fraternizing with some of the captured French officers. It was said they'd discussed the afterlife and other such weighty themes. Even General Amherst was said to gossip about "Gray Eli's" funk. One of his aides said that the General preferred "Gray Eli" at his table to any of the learned but depressing Moravian Brethren who continually appeared out of the wilderness to proselytize among the captured heathen.

After Louisbourgh, Eli's regiment removed to New

York for the winter. Rumor had it that there'd be a new campaign in the spring of '59. Some said all signs—entrails, inn, cosmic—pointed toward a march to the northwest for a siege on the French fort Niagara, along Lake Ontario. Others said all signs—entrails, inn, cosmic—pointed to the sea again, for sieges on the French forts St. John and Port Royal, in Acadia. Still others, understanding that Montreal was the key to Lord Jeffrey Amherst's grand strategy, said all signs—entrails, inn, cosmic—pointed due north, up the Hudson River Valley to His Majesty's forts Edward and Anne, from which the British could stage a campaign against the French forts Ticonderoga and Crown Point, along Lake Champlain. The last were correct, of course, but it hardly mattered. All the signs—entrails, inn, cosmic—agreed in pointing toward more war, regardless of the direction of tactics. For look! Isn't that what the comet means?

The garrison commander at Fort Edward was a Forbes—of the Royalist Forbes of Culloden, whose Laird forever shamed his family by turning from his true sovereign, Bonnie Prince Charlie, in '45—and that was reason enough for Eli to dislike the man. But he had sound military reasons as well. Fort Edward stood along the Hudson River shore of a vast virgin forest, not on a rolling, heather-patched plain. Yet Forbes conducted himself as if his fort commanded uninhabited vistas. For instance, rather than post picket lines along the two main trails running from Lake George to the very gates of Fort Edward (at the bend in the Hudson), Forbes was content to maintain sentries only atop the fort's lookout tower. An enemy party could move within eyesight of the walls before giving itself away.

But yesterday morning, Forbes had shown himself to be worse than a pigheaded second-rater. He'd ordered out a patrol to investigate two "signal" fires to the northeast. It was obvious to Eli those hadn't been "signal" fires, but fires lit by the heathen to burn through the spring ice for fishing. And they were most likely hostile heathen—Iroquois, or

"Mingos," as they were called colloquially—in the employ of the French to maintain a distant watch on the British forces gathering at Fort Edward. Eli knew those men would never return. Eli knew those men's "scalps," as they were called (actually the longer locks attached by a thin layer of the scalp's skin), would decorate some heathen's pouch by nightfall. And Eli knew why the General had made it clear in his orders that Eli's battalion was not under the direct command of Lieutenant Colonel Forbes, but was, instead, an advance force of Royal regiments moving piecemeal up the Hudson to mass for a summer campaign. The General also knew Forbes to be an idiot.

Nevertheless, Forbes's obtuseness forced Eli to a rash position. Forbes claimed ignorance of the enemy's strength up the lakesides to Ticonderoga, claiming also that he was garrison commander, his first responsibility to the settlers down the valley, his responsibility ending with the security of the fort. This "campaign" was none of his affair. If General Amherst wanted glory in the north, so be it, but Lieutenant Colonel Forbes wasn't about to weaken his command by doing Amherst's reconnaissance for him. If Major Broadsword—well known as one of Amherst's protégés, since the General had given Broadsword a battalion after Louisbourgh despite the well-known fact that Broadsword was an ex-convict—wanted information about the French strength at Ticonderoga and Crown Point, then he should go get it, with his own men.

Eli felt that Forbes's opinion was not only inferentially cowardice, but was also the sort of military myopia that had led to the loss of Fort William Henry, at the southern tip of Lake George, to the Marquis de Montcalm in '56, following which Montcalm had retreated north again, reinforcing Ticonderoga at the northern reach of Lake George along Lake Champlain. It was Ticonderoga that Amherst must now have.

Dressing, the morning after the doomed patrol had gone chasing after those "signal" fires, Eli was at peace with his resolve to take independent action. He had his orderly lay out his warmest underclothing and his field pistols.

"Sergeant!" called Eli.

"Yes, sir!" called Sergeant MacDonell, of the Mac-Donells of Keppoch, ever a warlike clan and the first to strike against the Hanoverian tyrant in the '45. MacDonell strode into Eli's bedchamber.

"Talk to me, Sergeant," said Eli, raising his foot for his orderly to shove on his boot.

"Yes, sir!" called MacDonell. "A fine, clear morning, sir! Ice flowing freely on the river, sir! No news of the patrol, sir! Captain Chisholm sends his compliments, sir!"

"Has the Captain located those wilderness men?" said Eli. "Jessie, hand me my buckskin tunic."

"Yes, sir!" called MacDonell. "They're here, a colonial and a red man, sir! In the officer's mess for you now, sir!"

"Very well, and I'll have my map case, if you please," said Eli, pulling on the remainder of his harness, inspecting himself in the looking glass he'd had his orderly lug up the Hudson. Elijah Broadsword was correct, sharp, and vainglorious. "Oh, Sergeant," continued Eli, "that's a colonial and a red man?"

"Good morning, sir," interrupted Lieutenant Oliphant, crashing into the small room. Oliphant was an awkward pup, but his father had fallen at the side of Alexander MacGillivray himself, who commanded the Clan Chattan regiment that wiped out the left of the Hanoverian line at Culloden (God rest all their souls, but especially those attainted in the eyes of the Hanoverian King, George, but forever ennobled in the eyes of true revolutionaries). For his father's gallantry alone, Eli loved Davie Oliphant. Oliphant had already returned Eli's trust by becoming one of the best mapmakers in the regiment. During the stopover at Albany, Oliphant had busied himself correcting several army maps hopelessly outdated by overgrown trails and changing river channels, endearing himself to Amherst as well as to one of the Schuyler women.

(It is worth mentioning here that Elijah Broadsword,

once he'd gained command of the battalion after Louisbourgh, had set out to fill his commissioned and noncom-
missioned officer posts with the blood of Jacobite clans.
Their despair for what might have been, Eli believed, knitted
them into a ferocious fighting unit. Aside from that, Eli was
an eighteenth-century man to the extent that he believed in
"right-thinking.")

"What's the word from him?" said Eli, meaning
Forbes.

"He'll have none of it. Bit daft, sir," said Oliphant.

"D—— the man," said Eli. "We'll be quit of him soon.
Oh, and Sergeant? Those volunteers?"

"Yes, sir!" called MacDonell. "Ready and able, sir!"

"Who's my squad leader?" said Eli.

"Why, Sergeant MacDonell, sir!" called MacDonell.

"Very well," said Eli, turning to go, "let's see those
wilderness men, then." They proceeded out, across the
battalion yard, direct to the officers' mess.

"Attention!" cried Captain Chisholm (whose maternal uncle had led Bonnie Prince Charlie to safety after Culloden) as Eli entered the room. Eli's dozen officers shot up.

"Now, Captain," said Eli, taking a mug of coffee from
his orderly. "You've apprised them of the situation? You are
to avoid Forbes while I'm gone. There are orders for you on
my desk, as contingency. All understood, then?"

"Yes, sir," said Chisholm. "Your scouts, sir."

Eli walked toward Chisholm. Yes, here they were,
behind Chisolm, along the wall. They seemed to blend into
the room. The white man was hard-looking, angular, with
open, darkly complected features. He was dressed in greasy
animal skins—a trapper's style, not a settler's. He hefted a
beautifully carved powder horn, a bedroll slung over his
shoulder like a bandolier, and an unusually long musket that
seemed much used, unlike the shiny, shorter, newer muskets
carried by Eli's troopers. The white man's companion was
equally hard-looking, though, being a red man, he had
blunter features and a stockier build, covered not quite as
completely in animal skin. He wore his black, greasy hair

111

longer. He had several scars running this way and that on his brow, his forearms, and his torso. He also hefted a powder horn, a bedroll, and a musket. There was a mean hatchet on his belt as well, and a belt pouch with some black strands of hair poking through.

Undeniably, both of them held themselves nobly, self-assuredly, in the manner the Court pundits liked to philosophize—new men in a new land, bold and unencumbered. Eli was reminded of a biblical passage, but let it go. The American colonies might be the New Jerusalem, and these might be citizens of the New Jerusalem, but, for the moment, the King's business was at hand, and the French enemy slept in great number to the north.

"I'm Major Broadsword," said Eli to the white man.

"This one is called the Pathfinder, sir," said Chisholm.

"That I am called by the troopers of His Sacred Majesty," said Pathfinder, standing to greet Eli with a self-effacing nod. The man seemed without guile. Paradoxical nature, thought Eli, for a woodsman.

"You have other names, do you?" said Eli, amused.

"That I have," said Pathfinder. "By the Frenchers I am called *La Longue Carabine,* for my Killdeer here. By sartain redmen called the Mohicans, what's left of 'em, I am called the Hawk Eye. From what I've learned of your need of me, from the Captain here, it's the Pathfinder you need."

"You do have a Christian name?" said Eli.

"I have not been Christianized by the Moravians, like so many of the Delaware, it is true," said Pathfinder. "But I was born of woman, and truth is my Pole Star. I have a Christian name, Major, and if it please you to know it, I tell you it is Natty Bumpo. My companion here also has names to suit our friends and foes. He is a red man, sartain, but it please me if you'll remember each color has its gifts, its laws, and its traditions, and one of his is not to condemn another because he does not exactly comprehend him. This is a man of the Delawares, and as brave a friend you'll never find. He has a chiefly, Mohican name, but is best called, as I do, Big Sarpent."

"Very well," said Eli. The man's reputation as a scout was impeccable, but he hadn't been told of the man's talents as a rhetorician. "I'm pleased to have you with us."

"Gen'rous of you, Major," said Pathfinder.

"Yes, now, has Captain Chisholm told you what I have in mind to do?" said Eli, waving to Oliphant to lay out the maps of Lake George.

"That he has, direct," said Pathfinder.

"And your opinion?" said Eli.

"It can be done, but not in the time you allow."

"Can you show me how we'll go, how long it will take?"

"I can, but it wouldn't mean much," said Pathfinder. "Only way to know how long is to count up the days we've passed when we get there. And them trails are likely to be filled with Mingos. We will go as we go. A column will have an oncommon difficult time."

"Not a column. Myself and volunteers, traveling as light as yourself," said Eli.

"Not a column?" said Pathfinder. "Good. I have conversed with Sarpent, and his son Uncas, afore he fell, on the disagreeable natur' of a column of them fancy redcoats trying to travel unnoticed."

"My men and I will be outfitted as yourself—buckskin, I do believe. Does it suit you, Pathfinder?" said Eli, folding up the maps.

"Sartain, Major," said Pathfinder. "Me and the Sarpent will lead you to Ticonderoga, and then lead you back. A soldier's calling is honorable, provided he has fit only on the side of right. As the Frenchers are always wrong, and His Sacred Majesty and these colonies always right, I take it you and your men have quiet consciences as well as good characters. I have never slept more comfortably than when I fit the Mingos, though it is law with me to fight always as a white man and never as an Indian. The Sarpent here has his fashions and I mine. And yet we have fit side by side these many years, without either thinking a hard thought consarning the other's ways. I tell him there is but one Heaven and one Hell, notwithstanding his traditions, though there are many trails to both. Does that suit you, Major?"

"Indeed it does, Pathfinder," said Eli.

The second morning out of the fort, they came upon remains of the doomed patrol. After conferring with Big Sarpent, Pathfinder told Eli that the main body of the patrol had been ambushed here, in the glen, but the Mingos hadn't pressed their advantage. The survivors had fled down the glen into that frozen stream. The Mingos paused to take scalps, rob the bodies, and perform other heathen acts of victory. Pathfinder reasoned that this meant the Mingos didn't have a French officer with them, since any military man would have insisted upon the chase. He also advised against breaking off their march to pursue the survivors, saying:

"Only thing you'll find that way, Major, is more buryin'. Them troopers fled into high country. Either froze, or was took by Mingos."

Eli agreed, sending back a lone runner to inform the fort of the tragedy. They continued over the hillsides, the climbing made more difficult by the general thaw. Somehow, though, Pathfinder usually led on firm snow or frozen ground. They emerged from the low hills that evening, pausing before the beauty of Lake George at sunset—vast under a crystalline ice sheet, limpid blue at the center, where the ice was breaking up. Eli ordered camp made by the earthen redoubts of the destroyed fort. All that remained of Fort William Henry now, three years after the inexplicable massacre of the garrison and settlers by Montcalm's Indians (some said drunkenness caused it, others a woman's honor), were charred superstructures beneath a light snow covering. Eli walked around the graveyard after supper.

"It was a terrible thing to see," said Pathfinder, noting Eli's somber expression upon his return to the campfire.

"You saw it?" said Eli.

"Me and Big Sarpent and Uncas, afore he fell. Terrible. It was very still like, so we knew something was wrong.

We came in easy. Still, we waited. We looked in one of those blockhouses. Enough to bring any nonbeliever to his knees. It was a terrible thing. It was avenged."

"Was it you who avenged it?" said Eli.

"I was among those who did," said Pathfinder.

"Thank God for your justice," said Oliphant, seated across from Pathfinder, map book in hand. Oliphant marveled at Pathfinder and didn't care who knew it.

"Why is it that the Frenchers employ them, then, if they can't control them better?" said Eli, getting comfortable, waiting for MacDonell to report all's well for the night.

"Can't say I know for sure, Major," said Pathfinder, "but Sarpent tells me it's more the Mingo that employ the Frenchers. Frenchers don't want to settle, like the colonials. Just trap. Mingos don't mind that."

"That's the way you'd like it as well, isn't it?" said Oliphant, sketching quickly by the firelight.

"That towns and settlements lead to sin, I will allow," said Pathfinder. "Out by our lakes, bordered by our forests, one is every day called upon to worship God. Although, that man is not always at his best in the wilderness, I also admit. But that men are better suited to the wilderness than they are to towns, I've often thought. The difference between a settlement man and a wilderness man is as plain to be seen as the difference between a Mohican and a Mingo. Or between the moon and that hairy star there."

"No churchman ever made as much sense to me," said Eli, impressed by Pathfinder's colloquial dissertation. In fact, Eli was impressed by all that Pathfinder represented. His logic seemed pristine. This was the first time Eli had been this alone in the wilderness since leaving Britain. And though he'd once thought forts like Edward to be free of civilization's constraints, he now realized that not until this moment—tired, warm, and expectant, in the company of good men and true—had he glimpsed the profound nature of the New World. One had to hike out here, camp amid the dense pine forest, beneath the starlight of imponderable reaches, to understand that what had been appropriate for a European man could never be appropriate for an American man. The Americas approximated amnesty for the soul. Here, it didn't matter that he'd been a Jacobite, a traitor, a convict, a widower. It only mattered that he was healthy, clear-witted, and ambitious. If Eli wanted to fashion a new life, then he should, discarding this "Gray Eli" persona, ceasing his brooding about the failure he'd made of his life in Cumberland, about the life he'd buried by the River Eden. Green was the American color, and so it should become Eli's —verdure and hopefulness.

Eli lay back to consider the "hairy star" overhead, just emerging now over the western treeline, as bright as Venus tonight, its head half as large as the moon, with a tail slightly shorter than it had been last night. It had been a month since its closest passage to the sun, or "perihelion," as Oliphant called it. The comet had seemed to shrink each night since its farthest reach a fortnight before: nearly 110 degrees, they'd said in the mess. When it had first appeared, out of the constellation Taurus, in February, there had been heated debate in New York City's East Ward taverns over what it meant. The salts had told wild tales of great waves rising from Hell, crashing over to splinter His Majesty's ships. The burghers spoke of how restless the comet made their wives, their stock, and their hold on the corn exchange. Fellow officers, whose fathers had seen service on the Continent against the Dutch, spoke of a comet like this one that had passed over Copenhagen in '28, a week before Copenhagen was destroyed by fire. Then there was loose talk of plague, famine, and earth tremors. Eli had listened with an ear opened the more by good rum, but had not taken the matter to heart. The only tale that had interested him was spun by an idle gentleman said to have been sent down from Cambridge for fraud and general bad form, exiled to the colonies by his family. He had given his name alternately as the Bard of Craven Castle, the Duke of Malmsey, or Torrance Means, Esquire. Despite his drunken manner, he impressed Eli as educated and sly. He had astonished them all by claiming that this comet was the same one the late Sir Edmund

Halley, of the Royal Society, had predicted would return in 1759. He'd gone on to claim that this comet, which he called "Halley's Comet," was a revolutionary comet, meaning that it circled the sun in a great ellipse much the way the earth circled the sun. It was fantastic, and all too much for Eli, a simple soldier of the King, but he'd asked Oliphant afterward—since Oliphant had been at university in Edinburgh—if there was anything to what this Means fellow had said. Oliphant had replied that Eli hadn't heard the half of it, for this Means also told a wild tale about his maternal granduncle, alternately called the Bard of Craven Castle, the Duke of Malmsey, or Francis Colquhuon Craven, Esquire, who was said to have been at Cambridge at the time of the great Sir Isaac Newton.

Eli had suspended his opinion of the comet talk at the time, because he thought discussions of portents immaterial to a man as ill-fated as himself. But now, with Pathfinder, here in the wilderness, he had reason to reconsider. Perhaps the comet's coming meant war, as they said, and perhaps it meant scientific things, as they said. And perhaps the comet meant what one would. Eli decided he wanted the comet to mean bounty ahead for Elijah Broadsword, Major commanding a second-class infantry battalion under Lord Jeffrey Amherst.

A question came to Eli, so he asked it. "What do you make of the comet, Pathfinder?"

"I fear I might become foolhardy if I answer that direct as I should, Major," said Pathfinder. "I love to speak of my scoutings, and of my marches, and other adventures, with Sarpent and his son Uncas, afore he fell. But my mind wanders from me when I speak of the Lord's mysterious ways. It is better, I declare, to tell you what Sarpent has told me of hairy stars—comets, as you say. The mighty Delaware have roamed far, and met all men on honorable terms. In return, those that have dealt fairly have told the Delaware of ancient Indian legends, from the West, where a white man has yet to settle, though Frenchers are said to have walked there in pursuit of beaver and bear. These legends speak of hairy stars, though they have a different name for 'em. The Indian name would mean little to you that don't speak the language."

"Can you approximate it?" said Oliphant.

"Every creatur' has his gifts, Leftenant," said Pathfinder, "and book-learning is not one of mine. But if I had to say, I'd say it was Chief-Who-Walks-in-Rain."

"Beggin' your pardon, sir!" called MacDonell of a sudden. "Sentries set for the night, sir! Your orders, sir!"

"Wake the men a half-hour before sunrise," said Eli. "We'll make good time on the ice, won't we, Pathfinder?"

"Sartain, Major," said Pathfinder, who indeed led a good and grueling pace the next day, and for three days after that as well, up the west bank of Lake George, alternately along the trail through the treeline and upon the ice still solid along the shoreline. They met neither friend nor foe, though the Big Serpent reported regularly to Pathfinder signs of Mingo parties. The weather had been warm when they'd left their camp at the ruined fort, and it turned warmer still as they neared the northern shore of Lake George. They finally had to abandon the ice and trudge along soft trails, veering away from the lake just below the riverlet that connected Lake George to Lake Champlain. They circled to the west, intending to approach Fort Ticonderoga from a west-southwest direction. Toward evening of the sixth day, a wind came up, threatening a heavy spring storm before nightfall. Eli halted his party to have Pathfinder and Big Serpent scout ahead for a good camp for the night, one that could be easily defended should a patrol from the fort chance upon them in the early morning. The morrow's march would bring them within sight of Fort Ticonderoga's watchtower. While they waited, it began to rain, slowly at first, but quickly building with big gusts from the surrounding hills. Eli huddled with Oliphant under a pine grove, discussing the maps, hearing thunderclaps from the far west.

"Runner coming in, sir!" called MacDonell.

"Down then!" called Eli, the men flattening in the bush.

"Oncommon ahead," said Pathfinder, suddenly beside Eli, having crossed behind the patrol, without being seen, to overtake Eli from the rear. "Sarpent says a party of Mingos up ahead with prisoners. Redcoats with 'em, Major, and others."

"What do you make of it?" said Eli.

"A roundup. Mingos bring in prisoners to trade for goods. The Frenchers are known to put bounty on redcoats."

"The Devil you say!" said Eli. He decided immediately. Those men might be the remnant of that doomed patrol, and they might be poor wretches from elsewhere—no matter, for Eli owed it to those butchered men he'd buried to ignore military procedure, to risk combat on reconnaissance, to rescue those men. Enlisting Pathfinder's experience, since Eli had never commanded an ambush before—it being most ungentlemanly in the clockwork Old World, but strangely fitting in the timeless New World—Eli ordered his men at the quick. They secured a position well ahead of the Mingo party coming in from the south. Pathfinder said knives and bayonets only, for even in the rain, they were too close to the fort's outer pickets for gunfire. Eli agreed unhappily. They lay like serpents in the mud, with five men sent aloft in the boughs of pines.

In the failing light, the gusting storm—sometimes a hard downpour, other times slackening to drizzle—made visibility extremely difficult. Eli puzzled if they'd missed the Mingos. No, for then he heard shuffling, different from the swishing of the pines. (He heard a twig break.) He dared expose himself for a look, spotting immediately, ten yards off, the fierce, ugly face of the lead Mingo, moving quickly, as fast as a trooper at double time, and straight at Eli. Eli counted five Mingos leading the party, followed by several troopers tethered like dogs. Then there appeared several more Mingos leading three more tethered white men, or so they seemed, though their faces were hidden by cowls. Eli was reminded of Moravian Brethren, but their overall disposition seemed wrong: the first was as short as a dwarf; the second was of average height but with an extremely proud bearing; and the third was a giant among men, towering over the Mingos bringing up the rear.

The lead Mingo turned sharply to his right, not ten feet from Eli, but without seeing him in the rain. The rest of the party followed.

"Aheeee!" cried Pathfinder and Big Serpent, leaping atop the lead Mingos, signaling the patrol to do likewise.

"Bloody work!" cried MacDonell from the rear.

"Pathfinder!" cried Oliphant, who'd chosen the largest Mingo for himself, and had quickly been overwhelmed.

"Ah's me!" cried Pathfinder, straightening up to launch a hatchet across the trail, striking the big Mingo squarely.

"Major!" cried a voice from the side, alerting Eli that a buck had deserted the scene to escape into the bush, perhaps to warn the fort. Eli booted a falling Mingo out of his way and skipped after the buck. The Mingo was inhumanly quick, but Eli used geometry, cutting him off, tackling him from the rear into a pine-needle-covered clearing. The Mingo was instantly to his feet, swooping down upon Eli with a war whoop, bringing his hatchet from the side toward Eli's breast. Eli reflexively drew his pistol but, remembering no shots here, used it only to fend off the blow. The hatchet ripped into Eli's hand, bouncing away. Eli jerked with the pain, but kicked out before the shock befuddled him. The buck went down. Eli rolled sideways atop him, muscling him flat, kneeing him in the stomach. The buck raised up once, then seemed to lose his strength. He resigned. Eli finished the job with his knife.

"Are you able, Major?" called MacDonell, suddenly there beside him. Eli rolled off the corpse, sat up, wiped the buck's blood from his face and beard, and tried to collect himself. His left hand throbbed. He must stop the bleeding.

"Report," snapped Eli.

"Success, sir! No serious casualties, sir! The lads that was prisoners are bad, sir! They'll improve now, sir!"

"Where's Pathfinder?" said Eli.

"Be along, sir! That Serpent one's taking scalps, sir!"

"Yes, yes," said Eli.

"Your hand, sir!" called MacDonell.

"Yes, yes," said Eli, who fainted straightaway, not to awaken for several hours, not until after camp had been made, sentries posted, rescued troopers cared for, and the comet presumably risen again above the storm clouds.

Eli emerged slowly from his daze. He registered that he was alive, on his back, reasonably comfortable, warm on one side, toward a fire, cold on the other, away from the fire, and damp—but not soaked. He wanted to open his eyes, but could not. He supposed they'd rigged a lean-to over him and the fire, for he could still hear the rain falling. He checked his other senses. He could smell burned meat. He could feel the pain in his hand. He could taste his own vomit. There were voices. He wanted to talk, to wake up completely, to take command, but he could not, so he listened. There was Oliphant. There was Pathfinder, unmistakable. And there was an unknown voice, speaking excellent French with a slight accent. Who could that be? There was Oliphant again, his Scots tongue flattening his French. Suddenly, another unknown voice spoke out in as beautiful a Latin as Eli had ever heard—polished, immediate, charismatic, as if the speaker was voicing not a second tongue but his native language. Eli heard Oliphant stumble in his translation of the Latin to Pathfinder. The accented French voice (was that a Polish accent?) picked up the translation in French. Eli smiled. Could these two be the Moravian Brethren?

"Tell us then, for we want to hear," said the French-Polish voice, "what is the true nature of colonialism?"

"He asks what is the true nature of colonialism, Pathfinder," said Oliphant.

"These are strange questions to ask of men more used to the company of the forest creatures than of their own kind," said Pathfinder, "but if you will tell the little fellow that I mean him no disrespect, seeing he is a man of God, I will answer that to be a colonial is to be a free soul in the wilderness, beholden first to your own destiny, then to the God that made us all, and third to His Sacred Majesty, George." Oliphant translated freely.

"First, to his own destiny? Second to his God? And third to his King?" said the French-Polish voice.

"Yes, that's it," said Oliphant.

"What is it that you are saying, Leftenant? Have I offended the little fellow by speaking out so completely my understanding of these colonies?" said Pathfinder.

"Not in the least," said Oliphant. "I'm not sure where this is going. It is odd that they don't speak English, being Moravians."

"Frin'ship comes in divers ways in my experience," said Pathfinder. "'Twould be onfair if I were not to answer him direct. He and his companion convarse agree-able like, tho' with the tongue of the Frenchers and others, that is sartain."

"And what is the true nature of republicanism?" said the French-Polish voice.

Oliphant translated for Pathfinder, who began his remarks with a grunt, as if he was thinking intensely:

"I have fought side by side the soldiers of the King for many years, which means, if not exactly side by side, then a little ahead, as becomes a scout. I have passed many a hard-fit and bloody day, like when we delivered you men of God from those Mingos. And it's the way of skirmishers to think little of the fight when the rifle has done cracking." Pathfinder paused to allow Oliphant to catch up in his translation. "At night," continued Pathfinder, "around our campfires, on our marches, we talk of the things we love. I do allow that of the things I love, the Delaware are first, for I am a friend of the Delaware, and have been so from my boyhood. But my feelings for them, or for the best of them, are not the same as those I got for this wilderness and the folk that settle it with reverence for its plenty. I'm sometimes afeared it isn't wholesome for one who is occupied in a manly calling, like that of guide or soldier, to form strong feelings toward a community of men and women—settlers in particular—as this seems to lessen his love of enterprise and to turn his feelings away from his gifts and natural occupations." Pathfinder stopped abruptly. Oliphant overtook Pathfinder's discourse.

"This is an honest man," said the French-Polish voice.

"Thank you, friend," said Pathfinder, who knew enough French for this, continuing again, "I would like to return your kindness by telling you what you asked. A republic is what I love. A community in this wilderness with faith in itself, just as I have faith in myself. For the wilderness has taught me that no one man knows the future better than another, and that all men should be allowed opinions equal, if they have faith. In this wilderness, great faith means great works. If I seem to speak disrespectfully of the proper ways of government, or of the Creator and His church, then I am thinking that must be the way it seems."

Oliphant finished it. They sat in ponderous silence, save for some whisperings in Latin. Eli thought that must be the end of the most elaborate political discussion he'd witnessed since first he'd been approached by the Jacobite recruiter in '45. But no, there was another item—one that much occupied Eli's thoughts as he composed his military memoirs thirty years later in New York City, long after he'd forgotten many of the particulars of his successful reconnaissance from Fort Edward to Fort Ticonderoga and his return with Lieutenant Oliphant (disabled, as a Major, out of His Majesty's Army in '75 at Ticonderoga, when Ethan Allen and his Green Mountain Boys, along with Benedict Arnold, captured the then-British fort for the patriot cause, so Oliphant journeyed to Albany, having wed a Schuyler niece, enlisted in Washington's Continental Army, and when last seen by the good burgher Eli in '89 was on his way to a meeting at Mount Vernon, Virginia), and Sergeant Mac-Donell (retired from active service in '65 to a Boston tavern-keeper's life which obliged him to join in thick with the so-called Sons of Liberty and led him to a certain local notoriety by the time of his grandfatherly death in '80), and of course, Pathfinder and Big Serpent (disappeared into improbable myth over the Appalachians, as far as Eli could determine).

"And lastly," said the French-Polish voice, "what is the true nature of revolution?"

Oliphant asked Pathfinder if he might address this matter. Pathfinder answered him that this would be generous, given that Pathfinder had no decent thoughts on the subject.

"Revolution is a radical act, whereby one group of just men seek to overturn another group of unjust men who, by their tyranny and deceit, have usurped the true and divine rule of the land," said Oliphant with a voice that might have been his dead father's.

"Overturn?" said the French-Polish voice. "As in a wheel rotating?"

"Why, yes, like that," said Oliphant, "though that seems a queer way to picture it."

"Are you familiar with the natural physics taught at your universities of Oxford and Cambridge and Edinburgh and Glasgow?" asked the French-Polish voice.

"I have some passing knowledge," said Oliphant.

"Aphelion and perihelion, then?" said the French-Polish voice.

"Revolution like the comet? Ho! Why, that's bloody neat," said Oliphant. "I never thought of it that way. Makes it seem mechanical. Unavoidable, too."

"You know of the comet?" said the French-Polish voice.

"Only what I've heard in town, from a traveler," said Oliphant.

"He wants to speak of the 'hairy star' we spoke of?" said Pathfinder, hearing *"la comète."*

"Yes, I think so," said Oliphant.

"Your associate knows of the comet also? He speaks of 'hairy star,' does he not?" said the French-Polish voice excitedly, chewing over the English "hairy star." Eli heard the pop of a wine cork.

"Yes, though he knows more of heathen legend than

of science," said Oliphant. "This comet is the one they are calling in London 'Halley's Comet,' if that's what interests you."

"All of it interests us, friend. If you will share our wine? All of it interests us more than I can express," said the French-Polish voice. There was a pause, Eli hearing wine being poured. Then the French-Polish voice said, "Tell us especially of this 'Halley's Comet.' Is that the mathematician Edmund Halley? My, my, please, whatever you know of the comet."

Oliphant laughed, as if gay with wine, and said, "Once upon a time."

Fall 1682

As a Third Assistant to His Majesty's Secret Agent at Cambridge, young Francis Colquhoun Craven, Esquire's, responsibilities included the daily examination of correspondence addressed to and posted by the more suspect luminaries of the University. This was high-born politics, of course, and no especial besmirchment of Francis Colquhoun Craven's character. His family in Lincolnshire was too well fixed with the Restoration infrastructure, via his now-deceased uncle, Sir John Colquhoun, for all but gross calumny by the second son to damage Craven ties to Charles II's rule. In addition, his Third Assistantship provided Francis Colquhoun Craven—a sloppy scholar at Trinity College but a stout gambler at Bile of Bat tavern—with a handsome yearly retainer: not thirty pieces, true, but a healthy percentage of same.

All this, because it had come to pass in the turbulent land where Francis Colquhoun Craven, Esquire, was birthed, bred, and burdened with sinful tasks, that good King Charles II, true heir to Clan Stuart's Regency, suffered the sort of nocturnal phantasms common to sons of Beheaded Monarchs. He was overcautious and oversuspicious. Charles might have lost a few relatives to Parliamentarian regicide, might have lost a few battles to Oliver Cromwell himself, might have lost a few subjects to London's Great Plague and Great Fire, might have lost a few ships to the feisty Dutch, might have lost a few in-fights to Whig and Tory Parliaments, and might have lost a few gametes to Barbara Villiers, Louise de Keroualle, Nell Gwyn, and Catherine Peg; but he wasn't about to lose his gamey head to any bureaucratic fox-hunt. Legitimate sons he had none. Scruples he had few. Years left him in Creation he had less. But he had lots of under-the-table coins to purchase men's souls, to transform them into his exclusive Secret Agents, and to loose them upon their fellows' sneaky doings.

Who is so joyous, Charles's deputies had asked Francis Colquhoun Craven in the initial recruiting interview, as a man who spies upon another? Recall your Greek passions, they'd said. Voyeurism surpasses even that most sublime form of eroticism, narcissism, for one doesn't have to admit to one's impaired humanity (hearts and parts, polluted by sin) in order to study the sensual intercourse of mirror-refracted humanity. The King's most distinguished scholars, they'd continued, even now apply their scientific talents to assist us in our espionage; for all at Court know that the Royal Society's recently acquired understanding of reflected light through specially ground lenses (which increase the eye's ability to see over distances) is most correctly employed not to examine the eternal heavens—the Lord's most perfect Vortices, as once explicated by the renowned, though popish, mathematician René Descartes—but, instead, to examine the open casements of suspected courtiers, and of suspected courtier's ladies ("... to have useful knowledge of a gentleman's politic," read *Ye Secret Agent Handbook*, "first have use of a gentleman's carnal knowledge ...."). A "telescope," continued the recruiters, is first for spying on the menses & et cetera, and second for spying on the moon & et cetera. The study of the "telescope" will proceed with generous funding by our Generous Monarch, because our Generous Monarch would have the tools of His Majesty's Secret Service perfected. Even as we speak, the recruiters had concluded, learned men such as Robert Hooke at Gresham, Isaac Newton at Cambridge, and Christian Huygens at Leyton, ponder the possibility that light bends around corners. Imagine the espionage potential if a lens can be ground and mounted in a telescope that could examine, in magnified form, men's secrets around corners!

That had all been at Whitehall the year before he'd matriculated Trinity College in June of 1681, ostensibly to study the quadrivium (Arithmetic, Geometry, Music, Astronomy). However, Francis Colquhoun Craven hadn't required such philosophical justification for his enlistment as a spy. He accepted the Third Assistantship more out of personality than patriotism. Though he could be argued to be a typical seventeenth-century man—superstitious, syphilitic, alcoholic, naive in love, cunning in religion—he was best perceived as a bad apple. His fate was indifference. He made an excellent spy because he had a rotten soul. Without integrity, he might not have sold his own family out, but he would have thought about renting them out. Gawky, pockfaced, with his left foot bearing a sixth toe, Frances Colquhoun Craven was not the stuff of Virtue. He was an introverted scoundrel, and a weakling as well.

With this introduction, it is easier to understand how very much Francis Colquhoun Craven enjoyed reading the private correspondence of the more suspect luminaries of the University, among whom (it should come as no surprise, for His Majesty's Secret Service was always interested in scholars whose work related to their own) was the aforementioned Opticks genius and, sad to say, dissident fellow of Trinity College, now Professor of Mathematics, and rumored Alchemist, Isaac Newton, e.g.:

My Dearest Mother,

The Best & Safest method of ridding yourself of this affliction is to follow my useful instructions with regard an elixir I have developed. I enclose a list of ingredients. The theory is that the apple cider wch you most graciously send me each month provides an excellent medium for this elixir.

I remain in excellent and inexplicable health and am happily engaged in many works with regard a recent heavenly event. A new comet has appeared in the evening sky, wch should be easy for you to espy following sundown in the east. Your faithful and loving son,

Isaac

Woolsthorpe
4 September

My Dearest Son,

Speak not to me of these evening curses. I am often of even temper, but you test me with talk of your ungodly observations. I would rather you increase your allowance to me, or perhaps find it in your soul, which I have cherished more than my own ever since I was abandoned in this dark world by your father's death from drink, to repay me for the Fruits & Drinks that I tirelessly prepare for you each month.

This elixir you have sent word of to me has proved useless. In future, do not write to me of elixirs whose ingredients are suspect as the Devil's work.

The month's cider is both sweet and hard. I trust you find it of Use, though you might have no Use of an aged mother's succor. Your sick, loving

Mother

Trinity College
7 September

My Dearest Mother,

I remain anxious and confused by your affliction. Please accept this new formula, wch I am sure you will find acceptable as not suggesting the Devil's work. The base for this useful elixir is yet the most delicious and greatly appreciated cider wch you send me.

I assure you, good woman, that yon comet in the evening sky is not a product of ungodly observations. It is a useful heavenly event, wch I study for further enlightenment with regard to Our Lord's wonder. I remain Your Most Loving

Isaac

Woolsthorpe
10 September

My Dearest Son,

Any and all experiments from which you have derived this elixir you force upon me can only have been done with assistance of the Black Arts. I speak no more of. Never again send your poor mother, whose days are numbered even as the sickly apple trees on this ill-worked farm are numbered, news of this foul work.

I conclude from your recent correspondence that you have forgotten good and God-fearing ways taught you by my holy and blessed Mother, your grandparent, and that you now traffic in the wickedness of your learned, impious brethren. I am sad, and pray for your soul as I pray for your father's soul, though it is many years since he abandoned me in this dark world. Tearful,

Mother

My Dearest Mother,

I am so persecuted for thinking of you suffering
from these unhappy and aggravating afflictions I
know to be the scourge of pious and loving women
in their later years that I have slept little of late. I
send you now a further distillation of my elixir,
this time enclosed in an empty bottle wch you
earlier sent me containing ye most excellent cider
of our bountiful farm.

I blame my imprudence for rushing a formula of
my elixir to you before I had concluded my work.
A single draught of this present elixir will salve
your internal ills and give strength to your gentle
temperament. Please consider yon comet as you
partake of this elixir, as this might increase its
potency. Your weary but hopeful,

Isaac

At dawn of the first day of fall, walking to work,
Francis mulled again over the risks involved in his Newton
Affaire. He felt that if he mentioned his suspicions to His
Majesty's Secret Agent, he was likely not only to encounter
opposition—for the charge of witchcraft was a delicate thing
in Charles II's Court—but also to lose full credit for his
intrigue. And he had an excellent chance at the moment to
realize his plans without anyone knowing who he was, or
why he was doing it. If all went well, he would have time
enough to apprise his superiors of his strategy. If something
fouled, he could probably hush the matter.

Francis pounded up the back steps of the Bile of Bat
tavern, whistling a catchy tune to himself. His Majesty's
Secret Service branch in Cambridge occupied the third floor
of the tavern, and it was Francis's morning chore to open
shop. He'd never objected to such busy work, because it
gave him an opportunity to examine his colleagues' desks.

This done, and nothing new to be found about the
Beige Buggery Society Affaire or the *La Vice Anglaise* Clubbe
Affaire, Francis threw open the casements, fed the parrots,

lit the candles leading up the back staircase to the observation platform, and, the branch's "telescope" in hand, popped up onto the desk in the gray dawn mist. His first observation was of the River Cam, placid as usual, Francis recording there were no enemy fleets to be seen (this not a joke but the Secret Agent's strict instruction, he having been undone by the Dutch Fleet at Medway fifteen years earlier). His second observation was of the London Post Road, noting in his notebook that the post rider was to be seen clearing the horizon on schedule, with a quarter hour to his stopover at the Bile of Bat. And the third observation was of Dean John Quale's room's adjoining St. John's College, the Dean being a primary suspect in the Beige Buggery Society Affaire, and the Dean's niece being a primary suspect in the *La Vice Anglaise* Clubbe Affaire. There was the Dean, poking open his casements, yawning obesely, casually giving a limp wave to the Bile of Bat. No one had determined if the Dean was aware he was under scrutiny by the Secret Service. And, uh-huh, there was the Dean's niece, through the second-story casements, the beautiful and cruel Evelyn Quale, who was said to have beaten two undergraduates and a fellow of Pembroke College to deafness, at their own request of course, but mayhem most ungodly, nonetheless. It was certain that she knew she was under scrutiny, for every so often she paraded unclothed and lascivious before her windows, making Francis quiver so much he feared for the branch's "telescope" in his sweaty hands. But this morning, the beautiful and cruel Evelyn Quale remained semiclothed and ladylike. Just as well, for Francis could not tarry. The post rider approached. Finishing his notes, returning the "telescope" to its case, snapping up the day's packet of examined correspondence, Francis estimated he had time to breakfast lightly in the tavern before the post rider arrived.

Yet he found, once downstairs, he couldn't eat. He pushed his plate away, finished his wine, and drew out the neatly folded letter he'd received several days before, which had precipitated his Isaac Newton Affaire. He read it again, for the comfort its conspiratorial tone gave him:

Woolsthorpe Rectory
17 September

My Dear Master Craven,

I am pleased to be of some humble assistance to His Majesty's Agents in these matters.

Your name is, of course, well known to me. Your gracious Parent, in his generosity, has, severally, extended many good and generous works upon my flock as well as upon adjoining parishes.

I have never personally enjoyed the privilege of attending Craven Castle for one of its fetes, so that your identification of me could not be based upon our actual meeting, but I would hope this might show otherwise in future.

As to your inquiry of the Health & Welfare of the Widow Newton, I have disturbing and unhappy news . . .

The London post rider pounded to a halt before the Bile of Bat, the banging, bell-ringing, and general clatter interrupting Francis's reading. No matter, for he'd memorized the rest.

The Widow Newton had once confided in her Rector that her son, the famous Professor of Mathematics at Cambridge University, was trying to poison his own Mother with concoctions he could only have prepared in league with "Dark Powers." Moreover, she had once mentioned to her Rector that her son was always attempting to enlist the assistance of "Heavenly Visitors" as well, though the Rector had never thought these could safely be identified as fallen angels. In sum, the Widow Newton had, over a period of many years, communicated to her Rector enough damaging information about her son to shake Newton from his eminent position at the Royal Society. Once, she had even provided her Rector with lengthy letters, which he had wisely kept, in which Newton spoke of many elixirs (all based upon apple cider) that Newton claimed could cure Dropsy, Vapours, Gout, Tumours, Cancer, and the Common Cold—

these cures so suspect, of course, as to send the Court Physicians into paroxysms of denial. (Indeed, Newton had never been politically sound with any clique in the Realm, and especially not at Cambridge, where Newton had refused to take Holy Orders, as was traditionally required of those in his position.)

One of these letters in the Rector's keep was a de facto admission that Newton practiced Alchemy of the most insidious kind. The Rector had promised to send it on to Francis as soon as required (on official stationery) to do so. In it, Newton admitted to his mother that he was developing a potion that could prolong life, which he called "Cider of Eden."

But the most compelling aspect of the Rector's information made even Francis, with his years of experience confronting the irrational, shiver when he thought about what it truly meant. The Rector assured Francis that all his conversations with the Widow Newton had taken place three or more years before, when he'd been called repeatedly to her bedside. It so happened that the Widow Newton had passed on to her Maker in 1679.

Isaac Newton was carrying on a correspondence with a ghost!

Incredible as this all seemed to Francis, he understood that it was merely a strong start for a case against Newton. Charges of Witchcraft had stringent, if extraordinary, rules of evidence. There must be an interrogation by Experts. There must also be evidence of correspondence with Dark Powers written in Newton's own hand.

Sure enough, the post rider exchanged for Francis's packet a thick packet of letters containing the one post Francis had anticipated. The Muse of Espionage seemed at his tit this day! It was on unusually heavy vellum, wax-sealed with an enormous crest that seemed as enigmatic as ominous, reading (in Latin), "Beware Thy Sanity! The Dark Prince's Vanity!"

Francis retired to his desk, slit open the letter, and read quickly. It was brief and warm, signed by the Recording

Secretary for His Majesty's Secret Service's Bureau of Irreligion. But still it made less than sound sense:

> Whitehall
> 21 September

My Dear Agent Craven,

The Theory you have propounded seems evinced by you, not by inferring 'tis thus because not otherwise, that is, by deducing it only from a confutation of contrary suppositions, but by deriving it from some Power in you concluding it positively.

Tho 'tis heartening to read of young gentlemen of so capable spirit in time of General Wavering from True Paths, 'tis not prescribed what shd be made of thy Zeal.

More of these issues are certain to be discussed in circles not open to our pens. In haste.

> Lord Z.

Francis mulled the remainder of the morning and the whole of the afternoon. Had he been rejected by Lord Z., his sanity and vanity in question? Or, contrarily, was he being told, in sentences composed to conceal their true meaning from all but informed eyes, that he was to press on independently?

That must be it, thought Francis at supper, two bottles of claret in him. Lord Z. wanted Francis to obtain tangible proof *before* he took Francis's charges to "circles not open to our pens." Times were impious. There was a "General Wavering from True Paths." Protestants and Catholics were said to cohabit like-minded cabals against divine-righted authority. Politics were everywhere shedding religious principle. (Revolution was in the air!) Men spoke of Property and Progeny as if Salvation and Damnation were irksome, overused concepts. Englishmen deferred to Scots! Scots turned from Ale! With such irregularity at Court, little wonder that Whitehall required precision from its agents.

Tonight was it, then, thought Francis, fortifying himself—cloak, dagger, tapers, floor plan, flask of rum. He sneaked out of the Bile of Bat. He sneaked toward Trinity College. He should have done this before he corresponded with the Bureau of Irreligion. He'd incorrectly thought they'd want to interrogate Newton before impounding his laboratory & et cetera. They actually wanted evidence from Newton's laboratory & et cetera before they interrogated him. The Inquisition on the Continent proceeded otherwise, of course, but then, Englishmen were peculiar about Jurisprudence. Fortunately, the Bureau of Irreligion could call on champions of stealth like Francis, who, despite his resolve, nearly fainted when he chanced upon three undergraduates along the riverbank. They ignored Francis.

"Just there, Nigel, perhaps twenty degrees above the horizon," said one.

"No, no, where?" said a second.

"He is dense from birth, not for stargazing," said a third.

"There! See the very bright star? With the tail?" said the first.

"There are clouds," protested the second. "A storm."

"And you are nearsighted and dense," said the third.

"It's easy, Nigel. Squint. It will get large again," said the first.

"Oh, yes, I see. That's the comet?" said the second.

"One day past perihelion. It will grow its tail again as it returns from the sun," said the first.

"What does it mean?" said the second.

"Infidelity," said the third.

"Fidelity," said the first.

"Shall we sound the alarm?" said the second.

Francis humbugged as he passed them. To think that such men would one day rule England. They were Protestant fodder! Ah, one campaign at a time, thought Francis, crossing the main quadrangle of Trinity College, slipping into a dark entryway at the base of the sooty Gothic tower containing Newton's rooms. Newton should be all night at the observatory at the other end of the university, according to a steward Francis had bribed.

He forced the lock. It gave way with ease, as if it had been jimmied many times. Perhaps the great Professor was accustomed to forgetting his keys. Francis stepped into a black foyer, lighting one of his tapers once the door shut. He studied the floor plan he'd prepared: study to the right; bedroom to the left; closets to the far left; laboratory to the far center; office to the far right; and a small room between the office and the study which had no apparent use. First, thought Francis, the laboratory.

The overall smell was unmistakable. Unripe apples mixed with ripe apples mixed with rotten apples filled the laboratory with a not unpleasant, though strange, odor. Francis recalled all Newton's passages about apple-based elixirs. Buggo! The great Professor stood revealed as yet another dotty yeoman to Francis, whose own family, at Craven Castle, lorded over many apple farms near Grantham, not a score of miles from Newton's Woolsthorpe.

Newton's fruit fetish calmed Francis, who, like many bounders through the ages, mistook personal eccentricity for moral turpitude. To work, then. Feeling morally superior, Francis pawed through the papers on the lab table. Newton was a messy scholar. The rats were his housekeepers. Half-hour gone, then two hours, and little of interest to Lord Z., thought Francis, shoving apart a stack of leather-bound books beneath several large prisms. This was useless— French mathematics, Spanish geometry, Dutch optics. Francis gathered up several sealed vials from the lab rack, just in case they were found to contain, upon examination by experts, ungodly liquids. He abandoned the laboratory for the study. For his efforts in the shadows there, however, he received bumps on the head when he collided with a large model of the universe suspended from the ceiling. A lead ball symbolizing Saturn crashed into him above his ear, followed by lead balls symbolizing Jupiter, Mars, Earth, Venus, Mercury, and the Sun. Stunned, Francis collapsed in Newton's desk chair. Above the chair was another large model. Here was the Earth, Francis surmised, and here was the Moon. Why should a famous mathematician play with toys like these? Francis slapped at the Earth-Moon toy, discovering that it was fashioned so that, when shaken slightly, the ball symbolizing the Moon revolved about the ball symbolizing the Earth. Was this geometry? Was this cosmology? Was this that new concept "mechanics"? In frustration—since he was certain that it wasn't the Black Arts—Francis ripped the Moon ball from its mounting, discovering that it wasn't lead like the others, but was, instead, an apple, with a large bite gone.

"Useless old witch!" cried Francis, considering leaving in defeat, but no, he hadn't examined Newton's office yet. Not much there, either, except, what's this? On a sideboard, some ancient-looking volumes with odd Latin titles:

THE SUM OF THE CORES, OR
THE PERFECT APPLE
by Aristotle & Alexander

THE BOOK OF BAKING FURNACES
by Aristotle

THE INVENTION OF THE TREE OF LIFE
by Pythagoras

SEEDS OF VERITY, OR
DISTILLATION OF APPLE
by Aristotle

Aha! This was Alchemy! thought Francis. No mistake! Francis, ever superstitious, was reluctant to open the books, but he must. A sheaf of writing paper fell from *Seeds of Verity* and fluttered to the floor. Francis reached for it, but it escaped him in the shadows. He lit another taper, went to his knees, picking up a splinter as he reached. Damn! Here it was. Holding it before his candle, he read, in Latin:

CIDER OF EDEN
We can reason, from the Philosopher's supposition regarding Heavenly Events, such as the visit of a Comet, that any distillation of the Apple, in pursuit of the Atoms of Eternal Life, can only be enhanced by performing these Experiments when the Astrologers portend.

The Best & Surest method of this Philosophy seems to be, first to inquire into the Properties of the Seeds, and of establishing these Properties by Experiment, and then to proceed more slowly with Properties discovered not known to have equivalents in Seeds of lesser fruits, and then to hypothesize of the explanations of the Unknown Properties of Apple Seeds . . .

"If this isn't witchcraft, I'm an apple," said Francis as his taper burned out, so lighting another. Success at last! Now he had his proof for Lord Z. Now he could make his case in the open. They might not burn Newton for this, but they would surely hound him from the University, break him from the Royal Society, and open investigations into his scientific discoveries. And all because of my perseverance, thought Francis, who, for the first and last time in his brief life (dead of the pox, or was it a potion, in '89, the very same season William and Mary stepped from their Ship of State into the hot-blooded Sea of Revolution) felt flushed with victory.

Francis stuffed "Cider of Eden" into his blouse. It was time to away. Francis took note that it had begun to rain heavily outside. The great Professor might be moved to cut short his work at the observatory and return early. Francis reached for the door latch absentmindedly, dreaming of rewards and promotions. Instead of the door to the hall, however, Francis had grabbed hold of the door to the room joining Newton's office to his study—the room that seemed to have no purpose on the floor plan. The latch clicked. The door gave way with a rush. Francis, squatting on the floor, heard an irregular sound. He looked up. He didn't have time to scream. He was buried—thump, thump—under a mountain of apples.

"I have often thought that the moon is much like an apple," said a voice from nearby, in Latin. "Where's that apple gone?"

"This is a very interesting analogy," said another voice.

What was this? Francis sat up, pushing apples from his shoulders. His body ached. Apples were heavy and hard. They made little pounding sounds as they rolled across the floor. Francis paused. It was still raining. How long have I been here? What were those voice? They continued, in educated Latin:

"For many years, I have believed that to know the apple is to know the building block of Creation. Surely this is what the Holy Scriptures would have us understand. How else can one read the Holy Book of Genesis?" said the first voice again—high, airy, and knowing. Francis recognized it. That was Isaac Newton.

"Your researches have led you to this conclusion?" said the other voice. No, that was a new one. Francis moved slightly, more apples pouring down about him, muffling the words from nearby. He pushed as hard as he could and righted himself, listening again.

"But you have not come to visit to speak of my study of the Lord's fruit," said Newton. "You say that you have interest in my work on mechanics. Is this so?"

Francis brushed himself free of apple leaves, apple fluff, apple dust, and, this time, popped the correct door. He must escape undetected, for illegal entry would taint his evidence. Where were those voices coming from?

"We have come on a matter of significance to many," said that other voice, slowly, regally. "But here now, would you share this with us first?" Francis supposed they were in Newton's study. This was the worst possible. He must pass that open door to reach the front door. Quietly, now, Francis, going on all fours, snaking along the edge of the wall.

"Of course, generous of you, of course. A fine claret. Now, speak to me of these matters," said Newton. "I can only hope to be of assistance. You have already given me information of great promise. I would be happy if I could return the favor."

"Could you tell us, please, the true nature of monarchy?" said the first, unidentified voice.

"Monarchy?" said Newton. "Why, monarchy is

Kingship. Monarchy is His Majesty ruling with the grace of the Lord God. Usually, I should add."

Francis peeked around the doorway. There was Newton in his desk chair, gesturing with his thin arms. Across from him were three strangers in the dress of Puritan zealots. One was huge. The middle one, with the regal voice, was average-sized, yet held himself in a compellingly noble manner. The third stranger was a dwarf. Who could they be?

"And the true nature of oligarchy, if you please, Professor?" said the dwarf Puritan.

"Oligarchy is said to be a corruption of aristocracy," said Newton. "It is not to be defined by disputations. You know this condition when you confront this condition."

"Does it have a particular demeanor?" said the dwarf.

"Bloody and noisy and vice-ridden," said Newton. "Consider an oligarchy as a pack of fat but still hungry wolves."

Francis suddenly experienced a revelation. These three were from the Bureau of Irreligion. Lord Z. had understood him, dispatching experts to examine Newton's religious convictions. These three were trying to trap the great Professor with his own words. Very clever, thought Francis, who decided it better not to expose himself. Best to leave Lord Z.'s inquisitors to their work. He crept forward silently, reaching the front door, opening it, hunching himself up and easing out into the stairwell as a viper might slide from its roost. He turned sideways to reach back to shut the door. The last he heard was the voice of the dwarf saying:

"And what, then, is the true nature of revolution?"

"Revolution like the comet, you mean?" said Isaac Newton, without whom, it must be said, men of Reason & Virtue in Creation might not to this modern day be permitted to declare, out loud, without threat of detention, house-search, torture, and infamy, that the direction Down does indeed, faithfully, follow the direction Up.

Book III

*Wherein the Principals Gather
at Means Manor for the
"Rites of Spring"*

Means Manor

THE LONG Island, viewed from far above as if it were a constellation, can be argued to resemble a concupiscent female, on her back, head turned coyly to one side, arms crossed demurely on her chest, left knee up, legs slightly askew, sex aroused.

To translate: King's County's electric blaze becomes a first-magnitude star centering her lovely face; Oyster Bay's electric blaze and Babylon's electric blaze become second-magnitude stars centering her voluptuous breasts; Port Jefferson to Patchogue become the trim line of her waist; Orient Point's faint glimmer and Montauk Point's fainter glimmer become her delicate toes; and, of course, her heart-shaped sex, slightly askew, is formed by the patch of stars spreading from the Hamptons to Flanders, that section of the Long Island where it's said the howls of the rutting socialites shape a permanent pleasure dome of sound waves over a moneyed swamp of blood, some spilled, some swilled.

The Long Island as constellation as concupiscent female was not a popular opinion. Its chief proponents, in fact, were the very private Means children, Torrance VIII, Justine, and Christine, who chose to tell people in town (the Manhattan Island, another sort of philosophical property) that their family estate, Means Manor, was at the "sex" of the Long Island. What is more, they also said that the stately Means Manor had been built at the erotic center of the Long Island's "sex." Said the Means children, "Foundation on the button."

All is prologue, of course, the chatter of the fabulously rich, for the Long Island can also be understood as a geological configuration carved by an indifferent ice flow, and Means Manor can be understood as yet another impossibly large home amid impossibly large grounds somewhere in the nest of the Impossibly Large along Peconic Bay.

For fifty-one weekends a year, Means Manor was unapproachable to all but suicidal *paparazzi;* patrolled by an army of guard persons, guard dogs, guard robots, and unguarded grandiosity. On the fifty-second weekend, however, the mistress of the Manor, Mrs. Happy Means, ordered the gates opened for the employees of the Means Corporation invited to an extravagant birthday party for her husband, Torrance Means VII, which she called the "Rites of Spring," but which was more accurately understood by everyone as an opportunity to pay homage to their patron and protector—a corporation fete. And so the guests gathered for wine, women, and humbling, made the more tolerable by Happy Means's sense of the ridiculous. How Happy loved a happy time. The wine was the finest. The women were the rarest. And the humbling was the meanest, for the setting served to convince the guests painfully on their knees that tongue-first was *the* modern lifestyle. The suites of the Manor were redecorated with plush vanities. The servants of the Manor were redoubled with obliging masseurs. And the pleasures of the Manor were reawakened—kitchens, ballrooms, fountains, gardens, stables, and fireplaces.

Especially the last, for Means Manor was architecturally novel in its uncountable ornate fireplaces, each with a separate chimney stack, so that, from above, the sprawling Manor ("a neo-Gothic blockwork strange," said the *New York Crimes* critic) resembled more a playland of barbecue pits than a feyland of vassals of PIT. Some said that the wealth of private fireplaces at the Manor was to compensate for the unusual chill sweeping down upon it from Peconic Bay to the east. Others said that the wealth of fireplaces at the Manor was to conceal the truth of the legend that one of those fireplaces displayed orange'n'blue flames roaring up from the fires of Hell.

Nevertheless, in the bounty of the spring, when the azaleas blossomed, the giant forsythias exploded, and the giant oaks filled again with buds promising leafy madness come May, Means Manor seemed a palace of pure delight, fit to welcome the corporate rulers of so generous an Earth. The color scheme here was the green of Capitalism Itself. Amid such gay renaissance did Happy Means heave her celebration, always the weekend of or before the first of May:

Mrs. Torrance Means VII
cordially invites you to
THE RITES OF SPRING
in honor of the sixty-ninth birthday
of her husband
Torrance Means VII

Means Manor
The Long Island
25–27 April
Nineteen Hundred and Eighty-six

R.S.V.P./Cable MEANS

The younger guests arrived Friday morning, the upper lots filling with sedan chairs bearing colorful hood flags of six continents (but especially the black of the malevolent), the lower lots filling with sedan chairs so overpacked that their springs screamed as attendants emptied them of trunks, suitcases, cosmetic bags, and, of course, handmaidens and handboys. By noon, the Manor was a bustle of

144

glamorous women and dapper men. The wine spigot remained open. The talk flowed. Ad hoc luncheons competed with ad hoc cocktail parties throughout the first level of the guest wings. A casual, curious celebrant (Abbott Broadsword?), if unattached to a clubby clique, might wander through this self-congratulatory maze gathering wineglasses as he gathered smart impressions of the complex social structure asserting itself, as it will, whenever men, women, power and pulchritude share space and time. Here, in one lavish drawing room, Futurism covering the walls, he finds preppie diplomats, State and Energy departments mostly, exchanging anecdotes about their year, on (semisecret) retainer with the Means Corporation, hawking fools and tools for Uncle Sam. Here, in another lavish drawing room, Cubism covering the walls, he finds preppie bankers and (Ways and Means) lobbyists, on (semisecret) retainer with the Means Corporation, flattering foreigners of all colors and politics, each of them understanding that, as distasteful as this seemed, the business of Big Business is not only profit, but also enduring conversation and negotiation with impossibly alien temperaments. And here, in still another lavish drawing room, Abstract Expressionism covering the walls, the casual celebrant finds the plutroleum preppies, on (semisecret) retainer with the Means Corporation, mixing successfully with administrators of Antediluvian Power, that is, Panhandle cowboys, argonautic engineers, Antarctic colonists, and Sheiks of Araby—here the *de rigueur* Western party dress of black and white ties competing with the exotic swish of rawhide vests, Hawaiian shirts, arctic skins, and Islamic robes.

In late afternoon, the few partygoers yet to succumb to hallucinogenic and/or erotic temptations strolled the Manor's garden paths still dripping with Thursday's rain—the deep verdure of midspring, the aphrodisiacal smells of roses budding, magnolias wafting, and the just-planted annuals rioting their colors in the low rays of the Bright One. Birds sang. Music soothed. The beasts grabbed for each other with a lust not even they could have anticipated a bottle of wine before. The sex before dinner (at eight) was energetic enough to make the whole Manor hum. Many of the older guests—arriving in the twilight because it really was the best light for those unspeakable age lines—remarked as they followed servants to their suites that there seemed a "charming" electricity in the Manor. They chose not to comment on the smell. But oh, how the sweet spring sex made a fragrant cloud that hung over the Manor through dinner and into the evening's festivities—more parties, rendezvous, and masochisms. Past midnight, when most of the celebrants thought to retire so they'd have some desire left for the morrow's action, there was a dandy fellow who remarked that, if that cloud bank held, it was likely to sleet orgasms all night, mixed with an appropriate amount of remorse before morning clearing. His forecast was taken more seriously than he'd intended. The Manor was already filled with howls. Howsoever, across the night's games, in those plush suites warmed against late April's surprisingly chill air (from Peconic Bay, they say) by ornate glowing fireplaces, it seems wisest to draw a veil.

There were few casualties, if one, through the night. In any event, all the ambulatory guests breakfasted hurriedly alongside the day-trippers, just arrived in more sedan chairs. Outside, April had served up a dazzling day. The vaulting blue sky made transgressors want to apologize. Nature deafened with chirping, buzzing, and chlorophylling. And, with a bicarb, it was possible to face that sensuous spring breeze, urging one, as if by design, to stroll down to the Great Meadow, where, amid silk-draped lists, pennant-bearing pavilions, silver-plate-heaped banquet tables, and the rainbow colors of giant rhododendrons, Saturday's featured event was about to begin: the Jousting Contest. Hurry now! Take your arm?

"Bother, Bee! We must hurry or we'll lose our seats," said Grace Thyme, apparently recovered from her athletic wounds of the year before, save that inoperable wound in her heart. She looked to be off the booze as well, for the moment.

"We will lose the *Padrone,*" said the Contessa Bianca Stupefacenta Capricciosa, as darkly beautiful as ever in a white flower print dress, carrying both her own parasol and Gracie's. Gracie, in a white flower print dress of only slightly different design, said the parasol made her feel "dumb."

"Probably looking for Abbott again. He's miffed," said Gracie.

"He should not be. These people are Abbott's, uh?"

"Idiom? Still, Abbott should have waited for us today."

"There they are," said Bianca. "By those horses."

"Grace! Grace! Over here!" called Cedric. "Here we are!"

"Did you find him? Oh, hi, Abbott," said Gracie.

"Uh," said Abbott.

"How handsome you look today, *Padrone,*" said Bianca.

"Yes? Well, ahem, we must get on with this," said Cedric. "Have you found our bleacher yet?"

"Lists, Uncle Cedric. You must try," said Gracie.

"You certainly do," said Abbott.

"I'll have none of that today," said Cedric.

"Right. Not on top of things, Father," said Abbott.

"Let me straighten your tie," said Bianca. "Okay?"

"My head is elsewhere, Contessa, but thanks," said Abbott.

"Here. Is this what this ticket means?" said Cedric.

"Yes, I think," said Gracie. "Oh, look, there're people in our seats. We've a good view. Let's sit below. No problem."

"Wait, Grace," said Cedric. "Excuse me, sir. My name is Cedric Broadsword. My ward, here, my son, and my guest. It seems there's some confusion. These are our seats."

"*Che?*" said the man nearest Cedric, a serious, sinewy, middle-aged Italian who was, along with his three comrades, and another, Europa Stupefacenta, at Means Manor not to

147

party but to negotiate certain sensitive art deals with the Means Corporation. They were selling the Florentine Renaissance to the highest bidder, because Italy's cash flow wasn't.

"We have a mix-up, sir," said Cedric. "English?"

"No English, comrade," said the Italian.

"Contessa! Contessa! Come up here," said Gracie.

"What is the problem?" said Bianca. "Bonaventuro!"

"Signora Capricciosa!" said the Italian, Bonaventuro Pellegrino by name, Stalinist by politics, so he shunned Bianca's title. "We'd heard you'd surrendered," he continued in Italian, "to American vanity. To their men as well?"

"Is Mama with you?" said Bianca.

"Not as your mother. As a patriot," said Bonaventuro.

"She's wanted by them! What has happened? Why wasn't I told? Why no letter?" said Bianca.

"That? Politics, Signora. Now they want something from us they cannot afford without diplomacy. Ask her yourself, she's about," said Bonaventuro, waving at the crowd.

"What does he say, Contessa?" said Cedric.

"One moment, *Padrone,*" said Bianca. "You have our seats."

"No. Tell him he is wrong, your lover," said Bonaventuro.

"Is he going to move?" said Cedric. "Just like a Yale game!"

"Padrone," said Bianca. "This is the Minister of Culture of the People's Republic of Florence, Signor Bonaventuro Pellegrino. He suggests an amicable settlement."

"Bounced by a Commie? Liberals! What do you suggest?"

"Father, we're making a scene," said Abbott.

"There are plenty of seats, Uncle Cedric," said Gracie.

"Aye, aye," said Cedric, resigned. "But you tell the comrade for me, Contessa, that I am Cedric Broadsword of Broadsword Hall, Colonel, United States Army Reserve,

Retired, and he should show more respect for someone who liberated his country from his Nazi allies long before he could read."

"Uncle Cedric! Sit here, please?" said Gracie.

"What does your lover say, Signora?" said Bonaventuro.

"Go to the Devil!" snapped Bianca as she sat by Gracie.

"What's this?" said Cedric. "Has he insulted you? Say, you Commie creep, we don't treat our women like that in America. Get down from there and I'll make you apologize!"

"Uncle Cedric!" said Gracie.

"Padrone!" said Bianca.

"Father!" said Abbott.

Just then, on horseback, the host and birthday boy, Torrance Means VII, Chairman of the Board of the Means Corporation, member of the Board of Governors of the Proto Industrial Trust (PIT), and, not incidentally, father to the Twin Sisters Means, cantered to a halt between the lists, to the near left of Cedric Broadsword waving his huge fist at Bonaventuro Pellegrino above him. Torrance VII, as befitted his station, was costumed immaculately in white satin, lace, and leather, a fashion designer's overdone vision of dukish propriety. A peregrine on his left arm would not have been too much, but there was no falcon to be had. He'd tried falconry years before, only to have to give it up, along with a large civil penalty, when one of his prize falcons tore off the face of a Hollywood starlet. Happy Means was not implicated. The falcons departed discreetly. This anecdote to the point that though there was no peregrine on Torrance VII's arm, his own beak (a savage proboscis that terrified his vassals whenever he turned it on them) and his claws (long, queerly misshaped fingers with four-inch-long nails after the fashion of centuries of despots) were as sharply vindictive as ever. Torrance VII was not ugly. He was horrible. Decades of corporate sinning had ravaged his once matinee idol face in the exact manner avarice, murder, usury, and impiety is supposed to ravage mortal tyrants. Flatterers might call him striking, but any truly religious man would call him demonic. There were no horn tips beneath his silvery mane. There were no hooves beneath his polished riding boots. There was no tail beneath his snug trousers. That is all that should be said of the matter. He spoke with elaborate, imperial precision. He made no sense.

"This is not happy," said Torrance VII.

"Oh. Mr. Means, sir. Abbott Broadsword, sir," said Abbott.

"On our birthday? Fists? Not happy," said Torrance VII.

"This Commie has insulted my guest," said Cedric.

"Your orders, Mr. Means?" said a burly bodyguard who'd been following closely behind the horse, and who was joined immediately by three of his companions.

"Seat them there," said Torrance VII, indicating the front row with his riding crop.

"No, sir!" said Cedric. "I tried to cooperate. But this Commie has insulted the Contessa. Now I want my right seats!"

"Come along, old fellow," said a bodyguard, stepping up to take Cedric roughly by the shoulder.

"Damn you, man! I'll not be handled," said Cedric, pushing back hard on the bodyguard, who wouldn't have gone down quite so easily as he did if Gracie hadn't deftly stuck her foot out as he tried to skip away from Cedric's ire. The bodyguard crashed off the front row of the list to thud heavily to the grass. The three other bodyguards jumped to his defense. Cedric drew himself up to his full height and breadth, making ready to defend his honor and family. Gracie stepped beside him, ready to join the fray. Bianca saw Gracie's face flash with the intrepid beauty ever managed only by romantic, slightly naive heroines—those ladies who love their vainglorious men till undoing and beyond. For an instant, everyone involved in this masque came to a still pose. An observer might have thought this a larger-than-life tapestry of a medieval conflict. The clothes weren't quite correct, true, but the hearts were exactly like those that had once enjoined in the illusion of chivalry. Then it was gone, as a stranger, dressed as a forester, shouted from the side:

"Well done, stout sir, fine lady!" They all turned to him, a day-tripper by appearance, in dark green, with a leather waistcoat, a quiver of cloth-yard shafts strapped to his back. He leaned casually on an unstrung longbow, which meant that he was probably here today to practice for the Archery Contest scheduled for the grand ball on Sunday evening. He didn't move when more burly bodyguards encircled him from the rear.

"Why interfere? Are you an employee?" said Torrance VII.

"I am engaged," said the forester.

"Your name?" said Torrance VII.

"My name is my concern," said the forester.

"Good for you!" said Cedric, stepping to the forester to offer his hand. "Cedric Broadsword's the name. Glad to make your acquaintance. This is my ward, Grace Thyme."

"An honor, sir, milady," said the forester in a clipped, polite voice. He was bearded and comely, yet with a sad gaze.

"Is this settled, then?" said Torrance VII, waving off the bodyguards with his riding crop, preparing to ride on.

"It is settled, *Padrone,*" said Bianca from the list. "Signor Pellegrino has apologized and will take other seats. Mr. Broadsword and his party will take their correct places."

"Who are you?" said Torrance VII.

"I am the Contessa Bianca Stupefacenta Capricciosa, houseguest to Cedric Broadsword, present today at his invitation," said Bianca. This man revolted her, did not intimidate her.

"Not happy," said Torrance VII, riding on.

"Pazzo!" said Bianca, ebullient as she rejoined Gracie.

"What's she say?" said Cedric, taking his seat.

"She says old Means is crazy," said Gracie.

"Pazzo!" said Bianca, she and Gracie giggling together.

"Exheredared" (sic)

TORRANCE VII rode on to the silk-draped stage situated at the exact center of the gentle ridge forming one entire side of the grassy expanse of the Great Meadow. Here, already seated, were his family in their fanciest gaming dress, looking unearthly. They shimmered in white satin. Justine and Christine sat to the left of the throne chair, bantering with their ever-present pack of admirers, gathered appropriately at their feet at the edge of the stage. Behind the Twin Sisters Means, looking aloof, confident, stood Aaron Verbunko, dressed for a garden party, gray slacks, navy blazer, bow tie. Between the Twin Sisters Means, on a tiny throne chair, sat now eight-year-old Torrance Means IX, son of Christine Means and heir apparent to the Means Family Empire, toying with a scale-model reproduction of the one-eyed pyramid (pictured on the other side of George Washington on the dollar bill) which he'd been given for his birthday the week before.

To the right of the throne chair sat the illustrious Mrs. Torrance Means VII, that is, Happy, to her high-born crowd. From a distance, she seemed an older, more distinguished version of her fabulous daughters, the Twin Sisters Means. This was an impression, however, not a case. Happy Means was only ten years senior to the Twins. She was, as the Twins said when they said anything about a woman they openly detested, a "stepmother." The first Mrs. Torrance Means VII, mother of the Twins and of Torrance VIII, was long since lost into marital history. She was said to be beyond tragedy into apocryphal fragment, beyond apocryphal fragment into gothic (Walpolean) legend. Some even joked that perhaps the Means children had leaped full grown from Torrance VII's imperial passion. Happy Means did not favor such witticisms. In her opinion, as Mistress of Means Manor, wife to the Chairman of the Board, and tempestuous adversary to the Twin Sisters Means, whom she reviled as they reviled her, Happy Means was Torrance VII's sole passion. He was a middle-aged man mad beyond his years, and, inside, wasted. She was a middle-aged woman clever beyond her years and, inside, twisted.

Happy Means looked her part as Mistress as well. Gem-sharp featured, she was empresslike, whereas the Twins were queenly. Thin-lipped, she was imperious, whereas the Twins were aristocratic. Long-limbed, she was supremely powerful—let there be no mistake of this—whereas the Twins were energetic.

Happy's physiognomy was also shaped by a supposedly deep secret that set her apart from her stepdaughters. Happy was consumingly in love with her stepson, Torrance VIII, with a lust best hidden behind the sort of camouflage fabulous wealth can acquire by auction or by august theft. Her lust for Torrance VIII was not unrequited. Their rendezvous, always continents away from the Manor, were filled with animal pleasure. And who could say what Justine and Christine really thought of their stepmother's supposedly secret obsession with their baby brother? More, who could say what Torrance VII really thought of Happy's supposedly secret obsession with his successor and only son? Did they all know? Did they care? There was no sure way to answer these questions; or Aaron Verbunko, for one, a student of the Means Family Empire, would have long ago done so. Not even Verbunko knew how self-aware the Means were, or wanted to be. They remained private enigmas as they remained public celebrities. Verbunko assumed, in his practical, patient manner, that if they did know of each other's hungers, they had chosen, to date, not to act on their intelligence. If, in future, Verbunko reasoned, they did move on each other's intrigues, they would do so for a monumentally novel reason embedded in their blood, the nature of which Verbunko could not hope to determine even with all the resources at his command, even with the godlike help of the Proto Industrial Trust's (PIT's) supercomputer, ORACLE, available through terminals to the Means Corporation. It was *that* much of a mystery.

For the present, Verbunko understood, the Means remained a viable though volatile tableau. They depended upon each other in the tradition of all fabulously wealthy families who are at the same time lines. Their table was bountiful, their feasting athletic. They loved each other and loved for each other. They feared each other and feared for each other. They ruled together, supreme atop a mountain of corpses of those who would have forced a place in the lurid Court that is the Means.

Happy leaned forward to greet her husband, just then dismounting onto the stage, with a blunt question.

"What was that with Broadsword?"

"We're not sure," said Torrance VII.

"Bad form, Tory," said Happy. "Why haven't you ever done anything about Broadsword? A liability. That."

"Who isn't?" said Torrance VII. "And let's not have contingency readouts again. How can you still doubt our success? Plus *n* from launch. Minus *n* from contact. It's beyond compromise. This is a victory celebration. Worry with Verbunko, not us. This is our birthday."

"I'm concerned with your next birthday as well. Say hello to your brood," said Happy, dismissively, leaning back —her long, well-turned legs separating momentarily to reveal, beneath her gown, muscular thighs—to indicate her advice on the subject was done, for now. Happy held herself not only co-conspirator with the President of the Means Corporation, Torrance VIII, but also chief counselor to the Chairman of the Board of the Means Corporation, Torrance VII. It was her happiest conceit. Verbunko, who indulged her advice with courtly finesse, had never challenged her on the matter. He was first councillor, of course, and this meant, among other things, that he did not ever openly counsel against the opinion of a member of the family.

"Daddy! Daddy!" called Justine, springing up and onto her father's right knee. "Have you forgotten again? You have!"

"What is this?" said Torrance VII, hugging his daughter.

"Oh, Daddy, you did forget!" said Christine, springing up and onto her father's left knee. "Pity that Stepmother didn't think to remind you."

"There, Verbunko, what is this?" said Torrance VII.

"They might be referring to Virtue, sir," said Verbunko.

"By Jupiter!" cried Torrance VII.

"By Mars," whispered Justine to Christine.

"What did you say?" shot Verbunko.

"We've forgotten to name a Virtue!" said Torrance VII.

"It's not too late, Daddy," said Justine. "The jousting's yet to begin. Christy and I have a solution."

"Do you want it again?" said Torrance VII.

"Sweet, but no. Nor Christy, but sweet," said Justine, leaning forward to kiss him on the cheek.

"Wait, now," said Torrance VII. "She'll do nicely."

"Who, Daddy?" said Justine, surprised, frowning at Christine.

"There, with the Broadswords. The Italian. Her name is Bianca. A Contessa," said Torrance VII with undisguised admiration.

"Really, Tory," said Happy, picking up the sound of a potential rivalry. "A Jewess? You're not serious."

"That's a marvelous choice," said Justine, smiling now at Christine. "Isn't it, Christy?"

"Yes, someone new and exotic. Even virtuous," said Christine.

"Leave me out of this," said Happy, disgusted, detecting this was more than it seemed, perhaps even a plot by the Twins.

"She's beautiful, certainly. Do you know her?" said Torrance VII.

"We met her last year at the Broadswords'," said Justine. "Aaron was quite taken with her, weren't you?"

"Excuse me?" said Verbunko.

"Her mother is Europa Stupefacenta," said Christine.

"The commissar's daughter? Mmh. Verbunko?" said Torrance VII.

"It might not be appropriate at this stage of the talks, sir," said Verbunko, who was overseeing the Means Corporation's negotiations with the People's Republic of Florence, the Means seeking to acquire a goodly percentage of the Florentine Quattrocento.

"But Daddy!" said Justine, who'd anticipated as much, "it was a winning idea. Why not the Contessa's friend, then, the famous horsewoman, Grace Thyme? She's right there."

"Broadsword's ward? I don't know," said Torrance VII.

"A compromise, then!" said Justine. "Why don't we allow Tory, er, the winner of the Jousting Contest, to choose Virtue?"

"Nicely turned," said Verbunko, who understood Justine's machinations perfectly.

"Girl, take this to the young master, quick," said Happy to a handmaiden, quietly, of course, so that her family couldn't hear that she was sending a note to Torrance VIII, telling him to choose the "Jewess" for his Virtue once he'd won the jousting, as he did every year, and under no account to choose Broadsword's ward. Happy had determined enough of Justine's game to understand it was Grace Thyme she wanted as Virtue. What Justine wanted, Happy didn't.

"We've settled this," said Torrance VII, escorting his daughters to their chairs, then seating himself on his throne chair, waving with lordly indifference to his vassals. "Carry on, Verbunko."

Aaron Verbunko moved to the fore of the stage, microphone in hand, calling for silence once, twice, thrice. The crowd—luxurious and splendid in the lists, displaying fashions so pricey that only those who have trucked with Mammon for more years, and with more sincerity, than can be forgiven can afford to sweat in them—quieted from its cacophonous expectation. The spring breeze flapped the motley pennants and caressed the high grass. Sssh!

Verbunko announced the "Rites of Spring." Today, the Jousting Contest. Tomorrow the Cross-Country Race, and later, at the ball, the Archery Contest.

As to the Jousting Contest, then, Verbunko continued —pausing dramatically while the crowd giggled and blushed as they did every year (the Means' Jousting Contest was an international scandal)—it was open to any man who came forth. The Means would supply him with a mount and proper harness. The only thing a contestant was required to provide for himself was his lance, which had to be shaped according to scale-model standards. Each man's jousting lance had to represent, in precise, scaled-up proportions, his own private lance.

The jousting would commence, continued Verbunko, with the nine top seeds of the previous year taking the field of combat. Challengers were to present themselves next, approaching to indicate, with a dip of their lance, which of the top seeds each of them would ride against. The two groups would then clash. The survivors of each clash would meet equal groups of challengers, as before, until, when all challengers were satisfied, the Means would name the day's champion. The champion would then receive, from the Means, a kiss and a bag of gems. And this year, as an added reward, the champion was to choose Virtue, whose charge it was to certify that the champion's jousting lance accurately represented his private lance.

A cheer and a squeal went up as Verbunko drew back from the edge of the stage and, with a wave of his hand, signaled that the riders were to take the field.

From the left of the Great Meadow, where the contestants' pennant-bearing pavilions billowed before the towering oaks, nine riders amount Arabians cleared the ridge onto the field proper. First rode Joe Brown, Potomac by name, hefting a knobby lance with a swollen head turned up to the left, a lady's ribbon dangling from its end. He cantered by the stage with a proud bearing. Second rode Joe Columbia, Beverly Hills by name, hefting a thin lance with a bumpy ridge underneath, a lady's ribbon dangling from its blunt, turned-down head. He cantered by the stage with a covetous bearing. Third rode Joe Cornell, Main Line by name, hefting a twisted, rootlike lance, broad at the base, tapering up to a bulbous head, dangling a lady's ribbon from its blunt tip. He cantered by the stage with an angry bearing. Fourth rode Joe Dartmouth, Vail by name, hefting a uniformly thick but strangely bent-up lance, a lady's ribbon dangling from its blunt head. He rode by the stage with a gluttonous bearing. Fifth rode Joe Harvard, Palm Beach by name, hefting a delicate, shapely lance, with neat ridges and a well-shaped head, dangling a lady's, or perhaps a man's, ribbon from its blunt tip. He cantered by the stage with a complex bearing seemingly a sum of all the vices in his nature. Sixth rode Joe Pennsylvania, Houston by name, hefting a firm-looking lance, straight and smooth, a lady's ribbon dangling from its blunt tip. He cantered by the stage with an envious bearing. Seventh rode Joe Princeton, North Shore by name, hefting a bent-up lance with an uncircumcised head, a lady's ribbon dangling from its uneven tip. He cantered by the stage with a slothful bearing, too high on something organic to keep his seat, as he crashed unconscious to the ground just as the eighth rider, Joe Yale, Rye by name, hefting a thin lance with an odd, lightbulb-shaped head dangling a lady's ribbon, cantered by the stage with a lusty "Boola!"

And finally, the crowd hysterical, some of the lewder in the lists heaving garlands of roses over the lances, the final —yet the top—seed rode onto the field, Torrance VIII himself, hefting an enormous lance, thick and evenly ridged, that was at least an arm's length longer than any of the eight lesser seeds' lances. This was not accidental. The length of the lances of all the other seeds were generally about the same—within acceptable, believable limits. Only the President of the Means Corporation ever unsheathed a lance strikingly longer than seemed credible. It was said that this was because all contestants wanted to appear properly armed, and endowed, but that none wanted to appear extraordinarily so. Thus, they very likely exaggerated, but not so much as to arouse suspicion. They misrepresented themselves uniformly—similar, one can suppose, to varying the color of a uniform, but not the cut. (Perhaps this explains why their women all looked the same, smelled the same, became their own mothers with similar predictability.) In the end, the seeds, and all the challengers, depended upon the certainty that Torrance VIII won the jousting every year, saving any one of them the unendurable chagrin of being shown a fraud. It was assumed that Torrance VIII did have a jousting lance in proper proportion to his private lance, as he'd passed inspection by Virtue every year since he'd taken his father's place on the field.

It was understood as advantage in the Corporation merely to participate in the Means' Jousting Contest. This accounted for why the younger executives endured the risk here. Favor was to be had. It was manly pursuit. Moreover, it was possible in the jousting to unseat, literally, a rival in the Corporation. It was also possible, of course, to unseat, accidentally, a superior in the Corporation. The watchword here was care—to best your equal and to lose to your more equal. Yet all this is not to forget that, as earnest as the contestants seemed, as aware of the tensions, rewards, and punishments as they might be, they also knew they were supposed to act as if this were fun. The jousting was mortally serious, but it was not to look so. To be caught sober, or appearing sober, was almost as much an error as unseating your own boss. Suck, snort, and be wary was the advice older, former contestants passed on to their protégés.

The top seeds, less the toppled Princetonian, formed a martial line along the right of the field. From the left, again, to the flourish of trumpets and strumpets, to the cries of mates and dates, rode the unseeded pack, hefting knobby, thick, thin, twisted, bent-up, bent-down, bulbous, and tapered lances, much like the seeds—and invariably the same length. There would be no bravura this year. The best horsemen of the pack made their way quickly across the field to indicate, by lance-pointing, their choice for the first pass. The remainder gathered at the far end of the field to wait, and to seek some solace from flasks, funny cigarettes, and the real thing.

The eight challengers then trotted to their side of the field, about fifty yards distant from the top seeds. In turn, both groups buttoned down their helmets, with leather flaps, hard bills, and patterned face cages. As they'd been instructed, they hooked shut their heavily padded breastplates, checked their cups and thigh pads, pulled snug their padded gloves. Attendants ran to their sides to hand up the dollar-sign-shaped shields to be held by the whole of the forearm.

From a distance, as the riders readied themselves, they appeared a not unattractive mockery of what might have been the way it was done in feudal lands, distant time and space to the east, when rivalry meant chivalry, and the only credit a true believer needed was the shy glance, once, when he was very young, of a lady faire. Fancifully, these might have been knights—second-raters, perhaps, as might have been left behind after the great hearts had galloped into legendary doom in the Levant—but knights nonetheless. This seemed especially the case if one directed one's attention to Torrance VIII, proud and stalwart atop one of his prize chargers, he dressed immaculately in dark green with gold trim, bearing a customed shield showing the Means Family crest—a five-towered, pentagonal castle atop a sinister plateau, encircled with the Latin motto *Omnino Omnino Omnino* (By All Means By All Means By All Means)—embossed and gold-embedded on its leather face. Torrance VIII had also thought to tie his stepmother's kerchief to his helmet's crest, his sisters' kerchiefs around each elbow, so that as he paraded across the Great Meadow, his charger tossing its head high and fierce—halter, saddle, and spurs gold-inlaid and flashing in the sunlight—his three ladies' sentiments waved about him with more romance than seemed discreet. He seemed overdone, particularly when one considered that he wore, presumably for effect, a genuine broadsword on his hip.

Aaron Verbunko measured the scene. He nodded to the heralds to raise their horns to the ready. He watched for the two lines of eight to come to relative rest. He nodded again. The horns blasted. The horsemen lurched in their seats, their mounts rat-a-tat across the field, closing unevenly. They met pell-mell at the middle of the field, all individuals momentarily lost in the swarm of flesh, metal, and leather. There were some cracks, a few animal screams, and many thuds, as this fourteen-hundred-pound mass met that fourteen-hundred-pound mass obliquely, legs and lances tangling, perhaps from bad horsemanship, perhaps from the general press, and perhaps from some genuine bloodlust briefly awakened in the slumbering breasts of these once self-aware men now resigned to the self-humiliation of corporate in-fighting.

"Can I look, Bee?" said Gracie, eyes shut tight.

"It is over," said Bianca, who thought this bizarre but also bizarrely engaging.

"Oh, Bee, those poor, poor dears," said Gracie, looking.

"You weep?" said Bianca.

"Those poor babies," said Gracie, meaning the horses, naturally, for once the swarm had split asunder two mounts were left sprawling amid several dismounted riders. One Arabian had broken its leg, and it screamed as it struggled to right itself for escape. But there would be no justice, as attendants ran to the wounded animal and, with a shot, ended its beautiful life—dead for sport. The other Arabian —a gray-star—righted itself easily, with nothing broken or sprained, and jerked away riderless, snorting and pawing, with vengeance in its heart. Gracie moved before she thought where she was. She leaped over two rows of spectators, jerking at her midcalf hem, and charged onto the field. Cedric called to her to stop, but she either didn't hear or didn't care. She jogged easily onto the flat expanse of the Great Meadow, holding her hem up, for she was in fine physical shape after a winter spent exercising, dieting, and philosophizing with Bianca and her great-grandfather, Wavy Rufus (who had told them a zany tale of Halley's Comet).

Gracie halted a few yards from the panicked Arabian, waving and whispering until the Arabian, as if by magic, fell under her spell. It lowered its head, tossing its mane from side to side. Gracie walked up to it, loosed its bit, loosed its cinch, removed both halter and saddle. There was blood where the rider had spurred the stallion. Nonchalantly, Gracie pulled off her half-slip to wipe the wound, press it shut, then check the other flank. She then reached down to pull her dress up, tucking it at her waist, to allow her to spring—up!—bareback on the Arabian. She whispered more to her new mount, turning it gently to trot back to the edge of the Great Meadow. As she neared the lists again, Torrance VIII passed by her, making a show of inspecting her long legs, shouting:

"Want a lance?"

Meanwhile, the wreckage of the first pass had been cleared. Of the sixteen, twelve had stayed amount, three without lances, two without shields, one without the will to continue. Ten more challengers organized to charge the ten survivors of the first pass. It was the same again: the trumpets, ta-da; the pounding, rat-a-tat; the clash, cracks and screams and cries. Only a few of the men were good enough horsemen to stay amount for long, regardless of the combat. Several toppled without being touched. A third pass was organized—fourteen on fourteen; and a fourth, this time only eight riders bearing down on six. After an hour and a half of dust and pain, it was sure the end best be soon. With the pack of challengers reduced, the ten most sentient—that is, most sober—riders arranged themselves five on five, charging. From this pass, six emerged who would be next year's top seeds. Now came an intemperate calm. The six riders roamed across the field to gather the well-wishes of their cliques. Attendants ministered to the dazed and injured on the sidelines. Aaron Verbunko looked to Torrance VII. Torrance VII looked to his wife and daughters. They each gave thumbs-up, meaning they wanted one more pass. Verbunko commanded as much, and with a trumpet blare, the six riders closed once more, three on three. This time there was serious injury as one rider flew from his horse at the end of Torrance VIII's long lance. The crowd gasped as he tried to stand to wave gallantly that he was well enough to walk off. He wasn't, collapsing heavily, blood from his mouth.

Then there were five. Four drew together around Torrance VIII, throwing down their shields to point, with their empty hands, that Torrance VIII was champion. The crowd's cheer seemed to confirm as much, as Torrance VIII, who didn't seem to have been tired by his repeated victories, led the four once around the Great Meadow, collecting garlands of roses and hearty obscenities. They returned again to the stage.

"This is our champion!" said Aaron Verbunko.

"Hooray!" said Justine.

"Hooray!" said Christine.

"Mine," whispered Happy.

And Aaron Verbunko would then have handed down the pearl necklace with which the champion was to choose Virtue—who was then to inspect him and crown him—if not for a ripple of laughter from the list nearest the contestants' pavilions. Verbunko looked up to discover a lone rider galloping onto the field atop a sorrel quarter horse. His horsemanship seemed excellent, if mechanical, as though long out of use. His harness, however, was shabby. He wore a ragged lacrosse helmet, no breastplate, and a tattered foul-weather coat covering him completely to his scruffy boots. That he was no employee was obvious; but what caused even more comment were the two shocking details of the lone rider. First, he hefted a lance every inch equal, mayhap more equal, to the lance hefted by Torrance VIII. Second, and so mysterious as to make the faint at heart swoon, he bore a leather shield with the Latin chalked in white across its face.

"What is this?" said Cedric, suddenly interested.

"I think, *Padrone,*" said Bianca, "that it is supposed to mean 'dishomed,' but it is not correct."

"Not right at all," said Abbott.

"Aren't you suspicious?" said Justine.

"He never was very smart," said Christine.

"Dishomed," said Happy to Torrance VII, "but what right has he got to come on after Tory's tired?"

"Verbunko?" said Torrance VII.

"I have no idea," said Verbunko, not truthfully.

The lone rider proceeded directly across the field to slow thirty yards short of Torrance VIII. He lowered his lance to indicate combat. Torrance VIII kicked his mount into a jump forward. He was for it.

"Tory! No!" cried Happy.

"A new horse!" cried Christine.

"Go get him, Tory," said Justine.

"Happy, happy," said Torrance VII.

The lone rider backed his mount to await his opponent. Torrance VIII, apparently thinking better of his pique, rode to one of his attendants to give an order for a new charger. Presently, another of Torrance VIII's prize Arabians was walked forth. Torrance VIII changed seats. Torrance VIII took up his shield and lance again and walked to the ready. The two adversaries awaited Verbunko wordlessly. Verbunko nodded to the heralds, ta-da! The two lurched forward, rat-a-tat! They closed swiftly, precisely and grimly.

"Gracie! Gracie! Come here!" called Bianca from the top of the list to Gracie, walking her rescued beast behind the lists in order to calm him.

Crash! went the two, the contestants lost in each other's energy. Then, this scene: two riders still amount spinning in opposite directions. They had grazed each other's shields. Torrance VIII found, however, when he'd slowed to a walk, that his lance was cracked at the base. He tossed it down, signaled for another.

"Gracie! *Andiamo! Basta!*" called Bianca. "The pig's prick has broken!"

"Contessa!" said Cedric.

The lone rider and Torrance VIII faced each other again. Verbunko looked to Torrance VII to see if he should stop this. These two were in deadly earnest. These two showed the murderer's nature. A death here would likely, at least, flag the party's spirit. Yet Torrance VII sat a cipher. Happy shook her head—no. Torrance VII sat on a cipher. Verbunko shrugged, which the heralds took as a command, ta-da! The two riders closed again, rat-a-tat, with profound antagonism. They charged without mercy. Verbunko didn't like it, and, in fact, looked to Justine before they crashed again, just in time to see her lunge out of her chair, calling:

"Tory!"

When Verbunko looked again, what he saw he knew could only mean bad trouble ahead. Torrance VIII was on his back, his shattered lance at his side, his shield ten yards distant, his Arabian spinning away in a daze. The lone rider continued on, carrying an also shattered lance, missing his shield. The crowd came to its feet, murmuring, not daring to cheer or call out, lest it be misinterpreted. Torrance VIII did set them to oohing when he sat up, shook his head, then slowly muscled himself to his feet. With a loud, unintelligible cry, he turned toward the lone rider and, in the same motion, drew forth his genuine broadsword.

"Not happy," said Torrance VII.

"Stop this now, Aaron," said Happy. "Before it's too late."

"It is already," said Verbunko to himself, for the lone rider had tossed down his lance, spun his mount about, and with a motion only slightly less grand than Torrance VIII's also drawn forth a genuine broadsword from beneath his foul-weather coat. The crowd gasped. A duel to the death? The Means gave terrific parties.

"Aaron, please, do something," said Justine.

"Yes," answered Verbunko, saying into the microphone, "Gentlemen! Please! We salute you! There is no need! You have both acquitted yourselves magnificently!" Verbunko began an applause that quickly spread from the stage to the lists. Torrance VIII, however, ignored Verbunko and the applause, advancing on foot toward the lone rider, brandishing his genuine broadsword. The lone rider heeded Verbunko, though, urging his mount forward, past Torrance VIII to the stage. There, he pulled up, backed his mount sideways so that he could watch both Verbunko and Torrance VIII, and called:

"My prize!"

"Certainly, sir," said Verbunko, who was not about to await the Means' unanimous approval with Torrance VIII circling hostilely. "But first you must choose Virtue," continued Verbunko, reaching in his pocket for the string of pearls, "with this. Give it to your choice. She must crown you."

The lone rider waved his sword that Verbunko should toss the pearls, which he did, arching them high but amiss, short by yards. The lone rider urged his mount forward again, swooping down to scoop up the pearls with his blade, then continuing on, past Happy, who glared, past Torrance VII, who blinked, past Torrance IX, who waved, past Christine, who frowned, and past Justine, standing, hands on hips, who said:

"That was a mistake, Effert Broadsword."

The lone rider jerked his horse to the side, trotting off to the lists. The crowd anticipated a circuit, beginning a timid cheer, unsure how the Means would understand this unprecedented defeat.

"Is not that the boy from last year?" said Bianca, stepping down from the list to join Gracie, who'd finally returned to the jousting, leading her new friend, the graystar Arabian. The two women came together between lists, at the edge of the Great Meadow.

"What?" said Gracie, looking as to what the cheering was for.

"Madonna mia!" said Bianca, the lone rider halting above her.

"Bee?" said Gracie, also startled, holding her Arabian still, seeing the lone rider.

"This is the boy, Gracie," said Bianca.

The lone rider flipped the string of pearls at Gracie, who let them fall at her bare feet.

"He's chosen you," said Bianca, not sure of this.

"Pick it up!" called Abbott from the list.

"Do no such thing!" called Cedric, crashing down to Gracie.

"Bee? Who is he? What should I do? Does this make me Virtue?" said Gracie, Arabian tethered in one hand, so using her free hand to grab up the pearls. She stooped to conquer once again, and this time for all time, the great heart of the lone rider, Effert Broadsword. How could he resist this plucky person, here in her ripped dress and her shredded hose, covered in sweat and horse blood, asking if these silly pearls made her anything than what she would always be to Effert, no matter how far he wandered, his beloved Gracie.

"Inspect him!" called Abbott from the list.

"Do no such thing!" called Cedric, hurtling over to Gracie.

"What do they want from me?" said Gracie.

"I will do it," said Bianca, advancing on Effert, a sly twist on her lovely face. Effert rocked back in his seat, bringing his knee up defensively. He thought, is she really going to do this? So I cheated a little, so what? What is this woman "Bee"? Yet before he could think to answer his own questions, Bianca had reached his side. She grabbed on to his saddle, rose up on her tiptoes, and, with a final leap, slipped her delicate hand over his thigh, inside the folds of his foul-weather coat, and patted him there, once, twice, thrice, light as a feather, and oh, the whether or not of Bianca's true intentions here must be set aside, for her ignorance of the rider's identity, her ignorance of her own identity, and the fact that she was too much the Tuscany sylph, too little the

American sybarite, make any such inquiry premature and, perhaps, in the English language, impossible.

"Bee!" said Gracie. "What are you doing?"

"You Americans!" said Bianca, spinning about from the rider to march back toward Gracie. She clapped once with delight, which served to animate Effert Broadsword, fugitive, pilgrim, knight-errant, seeker, and slightly delinquent servant of a certain comet. He sheathed his genuine broadsword and left the field, rat-a-tat, fast.

ORACLE

THAT EVENING, after dinner, the guests spread through the Manor and the grounds, in pursuit of each other and of a never-ending gambit in the surly game of night moves. There were so many players this evening, in fact, that no one of authority noticed conspirators —two male, two female—drifting toward the only closed-off and guarded wing of the Manor, where Torrance VII was said to house his private offices.

"This is crazy!" said Yella Kissl, sitting abruptly on a loveseat.

"Herr Schleppend, do something," said Swinyard.

"I'm begging you, Yel, don't do this. We promised Effert. We must," said Schleppend.

"They'll garrote us. These people are bigger than everybody, including Uncle Sammie. The Ways of the Means! Garrote," said Yella Kissl.

"Lyra, help," said Swinyard, creeping over to keep lookout.

"Free the people! Down with the pigs! Off the permanent government! We want our rights, and we want them now!" said Lyra, flopping down next to Yella, mightily stoned.

"This is our partner in crime?" said Yella Kissl.

"Be your seductive self, and we're cool," said Schleppend.

"Chicks up front!" said Lyra.

"Sshh, Lyra, please," said Schleppend. "Yel, think of the future generations. Do this one for them. For me?"

"I don't have any children," said Yella.

"Deal?" said Schleppend.

"You'd go that far?" said Lyra.

"Well, sure, when the time comes," said Schleppend.

"I want this in writing," said Yella Kissl.

"Power to the people! Come the revolution!" said Lyra.

"Of the comet," whispered Swinyard reflexively, thinking better of it, turning to see Schleppend scribbling a note and passing it to Yella Kissl, who stuffed it in her cleavage.

"Psst!" said Schleppend, indicating they were to continue. The four regained the dim hallway, stopped to check a map, then proceeded hallway to passageway to alcove.

"What was that?" said Swinyard.

"She blackmailed me. Not notarized, though," said Schleppend, halting their procession. "Okay, girls, strut your stuff."

"We need half an hour. Mark!" said Swinyard, tapping his watch as Lyra, giggling, took Yella Kissl by the arm to sweep out of the alcove and dead-center down a brightly lit hallway—Lyra the fair, slender tart (twice an Obie nominee), and Yella Kissl the dark, voluptuous tease (twice divorced). They began to sing:

I tip my hat to the new constitution,
Take a bow for the new revolution . . .

"Hold it right there!" boomed a brutish voice from a burly bodyguard posted at the end of the hall, standing up from his desk, drawing a machine pistol from a drawer.

"A gun!" said Lyra. "A big gun! Oh, oh, wow."

"Can we touch it?" said Yella Kissl, and et cetera, as these two clever conspirators clouded the burly bodyguard's senses long enough so that Swinyard & Schleppend, packing flashlights, cameras, skeleton keys, and other tools of the espionage trade, passed unnoticed onto the spiral staircase that took them down to Torrance VII's private offices.

Once there, they discovered they didn't need their skeleton keys, because none of the doors were locked. The Means were that sure of themselves. They also discovered they didn't need their flashlights because the inner chamber, Torrance VII's monstrous desk set before a semicircle of French doors opening onto a lily pond, was lit eerily by the glow from crackling flames in a fireplace to the left, with a mantelpiece bearing a large translucent ball. Further, and most surprising of all, they discovered they weren't alone. There was someone rummaging in a walk-in closet at the far side of the chamber.

"Run," whispered Swinyard.

"No," whispered Schleppend, grabbing Swinyard's coat, dragging him across the room to duck behind Torrance VII's monstrous desk. There, they collected themselves as best they could. They'd spent their whole lives waiting to mess up this profoundly. It was a moment to be weighed. Schleppend did so loosening his bow tie, reaching out to support himself on the desk side. He felt cool metal, and something extraordinary. He ran his fingers down the side, under a ridge, and felt a pod. A pod? What was this? He leaned back as far as he could to find "NASA" printed in federal script on a plate. NASA, he thought, as in the National Aeronautics and Space Administration? Sure, he thought, the Means Corporation, through its subsidiary, Grimmen Aircraft, used to do a lot of work for NASA, but nothing about building desks. He flattened out and peeked under the desk. There were three pods altogether. He tapped the metal lightly. It was hollow. This was the shell of something, with a glass desk top mounted after the fact. He dared to snake around to the front of the desk, where he spied a gold plaque, the sort museums attach to sacred artifacts. Ignoring the risk, he snaked across the front of the desk and raised his head to read the plaque:

THE VIKING PROJECT
VIKING LANDER #3
—*From the Collection
of Torrance Means VII*

"*Viking Three?*" said Schleppend.

"Get back here!" said Swinyard.

"Do you know what this is? It's *Viking Three.* He's made a desk of *Viking Three.* Damn," said Schleppend, impressed, consternated.

"What? There was no *Viking Three.* You're nuts," said Swinyard, deciding to take command, because Schleppend had let his panic flood his self-preservation synapses. He pushed himself up to survey the threat. Once over the edge of the glass top, he found he had to shift to his right for a clear field of vision, because of the toys stacked atop Torrance VII's desk—models of the Great Monolith Southeast, of a rocket, of an ocean-based drilling platform, of an Antarctic nuclear power tower, and what was that, some sort of satellite? Ah, the rich, thought Swinyard, they were all weird.

"*Che?*" came a female voice from behind a blinding torch beam right in Swinyard's eyes.

"God, no!" said Swinyard, throwing up his hands.

"Don't!" said Schleppend, standing up, deciding to bluff with some lawyerly blarney. "This is unusual. Not to worry. We'll overlook your intrusion. Many responsibilities. This and that. Eh, fellow security guard? Huzzah."

"Huzzah?" said Swinyard, also standing, prepared to meet his end, while cataloging, in his mind, the papers in his safety deposit box that would forever defame him before his mother.

171

"Buffoni!" said the female voice.

"What's she say? Deal?" said Swinyard.

"She called us buffoons. Strange," said Schleppend, deciding to try his Ivy League Italian. "No, we are guards."

"Buffoni!" said the female voice again.

Impasse, thought Schleppend. Is she armed? He moved his left foot forward. A small, muffled explosion ripped the carpet at his feet. The smell of gunpowder told him she'd fired something, and a pistol was not a bad guess. Right, thought Schleppend, cataloging the papers in his safety deposit box that would forever defame him before his mother.

"Mama, Mama, non!" came another female voice from behind them.

"Bianca!" said the older female voice, with the pistol and torch, flashing it to catch the face of the fourth intruder. Schleppend looked quickly to the side to realize he'd seen that beautiful mouth before. It was the dark angel from the Broadsword ball, the Contessa, dressed in most fashionable spy style, black pajamas and bandana, ruby sash—a designer's dream. Sigh, he thought, falling a little in love with her forever, and not just because she'd just saved his ass, as she walked directly to her mother, pushed the pistol down, and told her not to do this. Europa asked Bianca what right she had to interfere? This was Party business. To the Devil with the Party, said Bianca, what was Europa doing in her host's office? Europa asked Bianca why she was down here, shouldn't she be with her degenerate companions, frolicking?

"Scusi, signori?" said Schleppend.

"What do you want?" said Bianca.

"Not much. Can we leave? Duty calls." said Schleppend.

"Who are you?" said Bianca, still annoyed.

"Introduction, yes," said Schleppend. "I am Schleppend, humble barrister. This is Swinyard, the same."

"Humbler," said Swinyard. "And blind."

"Deaf and dumb," said Schleppend. "We wandered in here by mistake. Looking for gaming machines. Pinball?"

"I am Bianca Capricciosa. This is my mother, Europa Stupefacenta. Let us not speak jargon. Do you serve the *Padrone?*"

"No, we're independent . . ." began Swinyard.

"Uh!" interrupted Schleppend. "We're not security guards. Little joke, ha ha. As I say, looking for the gaming rooms. Can you direct us? Never mind, we'll find our way out. 'Bye."

Europa grunted them to a halt. Europa told Bianca they couldn't be allowed to leave. It would jeopardize Party business. Bianca sighed, causing Swinyard & Schleppend to sigh. The old lady had the pistol. Her opinion prevailed. The four stood immobile (resigned to the ramifications of the dictum that power comes out of the barrel of a gun, enslaving, as it does, both the gunner and the gunned). Then, with a hum, a rattle, a few bells, and some spring-boinging similar to what one might hear had one slipped a one-eyed coin into a pinball machine, chance intervened.

"There!" said Swinyard, pointing to the theretofore silent translucent ball centering the mantel above the fireplace containing a glowing fire. The ball now glowed also, on, off, on, brighter than the fire below. Boing! Ring! Boing!

"What is it?" said Bianca.

"The Devil's work," said Europa in Italian.

"Looks like a crystal ball that—uh-oh," said Schleppend.

"You think what I think you think?" said Swinyard.

"None other. Oh, God," said Schleppend.

"What?" said Bianca, holding her mother.

"ORACLE," said Swinyard respectfully, as he'd been taught to speak the acronym (Old Reason And Current Loose Energy) of the godlike supercomputer of the Proto Industrial Trust (PIT). Actually, Swinyard & Schleppend had been taught to say the acronym ORACLE respectfully if they were ever obliged to use it in front of their superiors in the Means Corporation. Otherwise, they were not to use the acronym. ORACLE was secret corporation business, and executive employees of the Means Corporation, which was itself controlled by the Proto Industrial Trust (PIT), were expected to be discreet. This was serious—a word as unspeakable as the YHWH of the Old Testament. The employees understood the jeopardy and complied wholeheartedly. Who were they, miserable slaves to feudal capitalism, to do otherwise? It was rumored that ORACLE controlled all high-level decision making in the corporations controlled by the Proto Industrial Trust (PIT); that the bothersomely complex projects, programs, trends, five-year plans, conspiracies, and product discontinuations that rattled through the halls of the Means Corporation's Great Monolith Southeast like marbles were loosed from on high through terminals in the possession of Torrance VII and Torrance VIII. The jargon in the corporation for this process was "the ball." "The ball" ordered this. "The ball" terminated that. Yet that had been so much gossip for Swinyard & Schleppend, who'd never seen one of those terminals. If they existed, fine with them, they'd said, hush hush, cash the biweekly check in peace, stay on the ball, ha ha. But now, by chance, and only because they were where they knew they shouldn't be, they had found one of those terminals—at least, that's what it said it was, Swinyard edging forward to peer through the heat of the fire to the gold plate along the base of the ball, reading aloud, "It says 'ORACLE' all right. Shit."

"No reason to offend it," said Schleppend, scared.

"What's an Oracle?" said Bianca.

"Trouble, ooh, ooh, trouble," said Schleppend.

"A supercomputer, actually. This is just a terminal," said Swinyard. "The computer itself is somewhere secret."

"They say a troubling cybernetic," said Bianca to Europa.

"Buffoni!" said Europa.

"No time for politics," said Schleppend. "Time to flee."

"Look!" said Swinyard, pointing to the face of the ball, which had begun to print out, or televise, or crystallize, or whatever, a message: numbers and symbols followed by

PROJECT: ♂

SUBJECT: HAROLD STARR

"The Macho Project!" squealed Swinyard.

" 'Harold Starr'!" squealed Schleppend.

"What about 'Harold Starr'?" said Europa in Italian.

"That's it," said Swinyard. "I can hardly believe it."

"What does she know about 'Harold Starr'?" said Schleppend.

"Mama, what of 'Harold Starr'?" said Bianca.

"Party business," said Europa.

"She says it is a Florentine secret—foolishness," said Bianca, throwing up her hands.

"Wait'll Effert hears about this," said Swinyard.

"Effert Broadsword?" said Bianca. "You know him?"

"Uh, who? That is, uh, why? Do you?" said Schleppend.

"What about Effert Broadsword?" said Europa in Italian.

"Do you know Effert Broadsword too?" said Bianca.

"She knows Effert?" said Schleppend.

"We all seem to know a lot about a lot," said Swinyard.

"Effert Broadsword is Party business too," said Europa.

"Effert Broadsword is the *Padrone*'s son, Mama," said Bianca.

"What's she say? 'Harold Starr'? Effert Broadsword?" said Schleppend, who would have liked to take notes.

"There's more! Look!" said Swinyard, pointing to ORACLE again, printing, or televising, or crystallizing more.

PROJECT: ♂

SUBJECT: HAROLD STARR
1986   4   27   .0
J.D.   2446548.5

"What's that?" said Schleppend.

"The date, Herr Schleppend. Gregorian and Julian calendars. It's midnight," said Swinyard, who shushed them as he slipped out his billfold/notebook and copied down the figures that then flashed on the ball's face, including the (1) right ascension and declination referred to the mean equator and equinox of 1950; (2) right ascension referred to the mean equator and equinox of today's date; (3) geocentric distance of object; (4) heliocentric distance of object; (5) total magnitude of object; (6) nuclear magnitude of object; (7) the sun-Earth-object angle in degrees; (8) the sun-object-Earth angle in degrees; and (9) heliocentric ecliptic and longitude in degrees, referred to the equinox of 1950.

"Have you got it?" said Schleppend, catching on. They were in trouble, true, but this was hot.

"Yes, now. Wait!" said Swinyard, for the ball wasn't done. It now flashed another series of figures, similar to the above save for reading "no data" for items 5 and 6. "Got it now," said Swinyard, as the message started to repeat. "Let's get out of here!"

"Right. Is it okay, Signora?" said Schleppend to Europa. "We have mutual friends. Effert Broadsword? And 'Harold Starr'?"

"Yes, Mama," said Bianca. "Let us leave. We talk later. Hey, where are you going?"

"This way," said Swinyard, opening the door to the outer office.

"No, much easier, here, follow me," said Bianca, leading all four out of Torrance VII's private office the same way she'd come in, through the bathroom window.

"Harold Starr"

Lost is what! Your fault!" said Schleppend to Swinyard as he hacked back a pine branch with a stick, waving the stick over the moonlit scene before them: a mucky creek bank between birches, maples, oaks, and the melancholy pine.

"Help me!" said Lyra, stuck in mud.

"Oy," said Yella Kissl, lifting Lyra free, stuck now herself.

"You idiot, Herr Swinyard!" said Schleppend, lifting Yella Kissl free. "A simple map. A simple half-hour walk. Lost!"

"No, this way, I'm sure," said Swinyard. Suddenly, from out of the pines, half a dozen perpetrators pounced upon the four conspirators. Before they could think to scream, they were corraled into a clearing amid pine groves. Schleppend demanded:

"Who are you people?"

"I'll ask the questions," came a commanding voice from the shadows. "We have a situation."

"A situation?" said Schleppend.

"Are you Means?" said the commanding voice.

"Off the pig!" cried Lyra, then giggling (funny cigarettes).

"Us, Means? No way, sir," said Schleppend.

"You're from the Manor," said the commanding

"You're from the Manor," said the commanding voice.

"Vain fun-seekers, not Means," said Schleppend. "Tumble in the bushes. Carnal spring joys. I blush to continue."

"We don't believe you," said the commanding voice.

"Make a deal," said Yella Kissl to Schleppend. "I'll do it. Hey, you guys. You want money? We have that. You want sex? We have that. No rough stuff, okay? Don't act like losers. Rob the rich. Feed your despair. Fine, a legitimate solution to societal inequities. Go ahead. Why discuss it? Be felons! We're attorneys. We'll read your childhoods into the court record. No jury would listen to the prosecutor. No court would convict you. I personally know the Court of Appeals is for sale, and cheap. Even The Court, though that's expensive. Get your name attached to a landmark decision? We can do it. The police violate your rights by arresting you. Assert gangsterhood. Seize crime boldly as a civil right. Rip off, lest you be ripped off. Okay? Retain us, and we can't even testify. I'll take a kiss for retainer."

"Why, Yel," said Schleppend, impressed.

"The New Kissl," said she.

"Chicks up front," said Lyra, applauding.

Meanwhile, the gang of perpetrators had retreated behind their commander, cringing before such lawless abandon. They urged flight. The commander turned to Schleppend again, asking, "You aren't Means? From the fete? Spies?"

"We're the good guys," said Schleppend, kissing Yella.

"Visionaries," said Yella Kissl, kissing back.

"Come the Revolution!" cried Lyra, fist in the air.

"Of the comet," said Swinyard quietly, but not so quietly that it didn't get a disciplined response from the commander and his gang of perpetrators. They lunged forward to form a martial line; then each went to one knee, hanging their shaggy heads in seeming adoration of something so supernally compelling that they dared not raise their gaze to confront these four conspirators, now nominally identified as agents of the comet. "What'd I say?" asked Swinyard.

"Cool it," said Schleppend, studying these men, who no longer seemed, as he had supposed, grim outlaws moonlighting from their grim jobs at nearby Grimmen Aircraft (the Long Island's largest employer), but rather seemed something fabulous. These were not felons. Material wealth wouldn't slightly interest them. They radiated the spiritual wealth only great hearts ever enjoy. Schleppend dared to ask, "You guys know of the comet?"

"We serve the comet," said the commander, rising again, leaning on his longbow. His longbow? thought Schleppend.

"Holy Mother of God," said Swinyard, feeling faint.

"Is it, uh, is something, uh, going down?" said Schleppend.

"We are waiting for the comet to come," said the commander.

"Wow!" said Lyra. "Wow, wow, wow."

"Do you know Effert Broadsword as well?" said Schleppend.

"Who?" said the commander. "Is he one of us?"

"Oh, yeah, he's our brother. We're lost," said Schleppend.

"The horseman and the mathematician? By the sea, in the baker's van?" said the commander. "You're not lost. It's just through here." He led them to a briar patch edging a granite incline, pointing down to firelight flickering in the near distance, crashing surf to be heard in the distance.

"Why, thanks," said Schleppend. "Can you come along?" But the commander and his men were gone, as spookily as that. The four said nothing of consequence to each other as they raced down the granite incline to the firelight, each lost in second thoughts about this affair: of Effert's recruiting them last year; of the break-in at Means Manor; of Europa's pistol and Bianca's questions; of the muddy tramp through this eerie forest; of the encounter with those brigands, if that's what they were.

"Effert!" called Schleppend at last.

"Aye! Here!" called Effert, throwing down his Wells, leaping up from the fireside, loping once, twice, to greet them boisterously, much howling, laughing, hugging, and tripping about, them finally led to fireside to wrap in horse blankets, strip off their soaked shoes. The chatter was repetitious, with occasional bursts.

"Means!"

"Macho Project!"

"Europa Stupefacenta!"

"ORACLE!"

"Bianca Capricciosa!"

" 'Harold Starr'!"

"Brigands!"

"Comet! Comet! Comet!"

"What's this now?" said Wavy Rufus, emerging from the van parked at fireside, this van being Effert's "wheels" from his Counterculture days, mothballed these past years at Broadsword Hall, still sporting its once trendy interior (bear-rug bed, reel-to-reel and et cetera electronics, posters of Yardbirds, Animals, Kinks, Doors, Who), and still bearing the always kitschy exterior—enormous mushrooms surrounding the single advertising word "Wonder." This was Effert's "Wonder" van.

"Have you all met my great-uncle Rufus?" said Effert, moving over to guide Wavy Rufus to his sorcerer's stool.

"Far out," said Lyra when she saw Wavy Rufus's usual guise—peaked hat askew, masquerade mask drawn across his sightless orbs, white beard scraggly down over his billowing black robes, only ten cracked fingernails visible from his cavernous sleeves. "How old?" she whispered.

"Old," said Swinyard. "Nice to see you, sir."

"Are these your friends, Effert?" said Wavy Rufus.

"Yes, and they've lots of news, good and bad," said Effert, nodding to Schleppend to begin the debriefing. The four conspirators took turns telling the evening's events. There were contradictions. There were gaps. There were huge mysteries. After an hour of talk, they paused to watch Effert feed the fire. He poked and pried, then said:

"Heavy stuff," explaining that he'd been the one to tell Europa Stupefacenta about the comet last year, that she'd sent him word of "Harold Starr" from her sources in the Party, that she had no more idea what it was than he did, and that perhaps her "Party business" related to some Byzantine conspiracy of her own.

"Heavier still," said Schleppend, who summarized for Effert and Wavy Rufus what he and Swinyard knew of the "Macho Project"—which was next to nothing save that it had been top priority for years at the Great Monolith Southeast; and who reviewed again for Effert and Wavy Rufus what he and Swinyard knew of "Harold Starr," which was very little, save that Abbott Broadsword had brought down a lot of heat last winter by making inquiries as to why so much cash had to be diverted to "Harold Starr." This evening, said Schleppend, was the first time he'd seen the Macho Project linked with "Harold Starr."

"Heaviest of all were those guys with bows and arrows," said Swinyard.

"No comment," said Schleppend.

"You folks still don't believe it, do you?" said Effert. "After all I've told you and shown you? The Babylonian tablet? The break-in that Europa Stupefacenta's sources have reported at PIT Peak? The fact that the Underground is buzzing with talk of something very big, and that 'Harold Starr' comes up right after the whispering begins? Why can't you take it for what it seems? The Comet Incarnate is coming!"

"It's far-fetched, Effert, really," said Schleppend. "You've got to give us a break. A rush, yeah? Though now that I've seen an ORACLE terminal print out 'Harold Starr' with those numbers—damn!"

"What numbers?" said Wavy Rufus.

"Oh, these," said Swinyard, handing over his billfold/notebook, asking, "It's astrophysics, isn't it? We copied it from ORACLE."

"These are points in outer space," said Effert, taking the notebook. "Apparently, the Means, with this computer, ORACLE, are tracking the comet. Watch." Effert snapped up a stick to draw a diagram on the ground before the fire. He made three concentric circles around a large dot. Then he traced an elliptical curve coming in from the upper right, swinging beneath the dot, then out again to the middle left. He lectured, "This point is the Bright One, that's sun to you. The first circle—really an ellipse—is the orbit of the planet Venus. The second is Earth's orbit. The third, Mars's. Now, this pronounced ellipse, or part of an ellipse, is the two-dimensional rendering of the orbit of the comet. I say two-dimensional because while the planets are generally co-planar, the comet is not. It swings retrograde down from here, reaching its closest point to the Bright One, which is called its perihelion, in late winter 1986, then out again, past Venus orbit, past Earth orbit, past Mars orbit and so forth, on its way to aphelion well past Neptune, sometime in the year, uh, A.D. 2024."

"Neat," said Lyra, making circles in the air.

"Now these are two points in space," said Effert, tapping the notebook. I'm guessing, but, being on top of this, I'd say about here, between Earth and Mars orbit. The first point seems like the comet, post perihelion magnitude of its nucleus, its coma. I just don't know what this second point is, I really don't. Perhaps an error factor of some sort. Eh, Wavy Rufus?"

Wavy Rufus climbed down from his stool with a heavy air. Effert bounded up to help him back into the "Wonder" van, where he helped him get comfortable on another stool, get the volume and bass/midrange/treble settings correct on the electronics just then receiving WHIP-FM, Metromaniacal Radio, New York City, rocking Who.

I tip my hat to the new constitution,
Take a bow for the new revolution,
I ain't free, but there's change all around,
Pick up my guitar and play,
Just like yesterday,
Then I'll get on my knees and pray,
We don't get fooled again . . .

"Poor old baby, he was crying," said Lyra.

"Effert says he's been waiting since 1910," said Schleppend.

"And now it's been and gone, almost," said Swinyard.

"Didn't we find out anything tonight? All that?" said Yella.

"Listen, Yel," said Schleppend, "I know you mean well, but it's my advice we try to cool Effert out about all this. You've heard what we have. 'Harold Starr' is desperation time. It's Effert's last chance. He's been all over the country looking for his Comet Incarnate since the Broadsword party. You were there. Did you get a load of his itinerary? PIT Peak Observatory, every Astrophysics Center in the land, Big Ten to Ivy League. He even flew to the Max Planck Institute in Heidelberg. *Nada!* And if the Germans ain't heard, nobody has. You know Teutonic metaphysics as well as me. Not a whiff."

"That break-in at PIT Peak?" said Yella.

"A coincidence, that's all," said Schleppend. "Loose anomalies that only the most flaky detective could take as evidence. Effert knows it too, though he won't give up as long as the old man hangs on. I'm telling you, tonight, what we did, this was the last chance. I admit we came up with a lot of mystery. But thinking about it, there is nothing hard here. Wavy Rufus has a theory. It remains a theory. Nothing has happened empirically."

"Would we know this Comet Incarnate if we saw it?" said Yella.

"You mean those crazies?" said Swinyard.

"Folly," said Schleppend. "We've got to stop it. Ignore the mysteries. Concentrate on Effert, who's not healthy anymore. Too long on the run. It's a long way down where he's headed. We've got to help him, at least get H. G. Wells away from him. That stunt today was literary."

"Whatcha thinking?" said Swinyard.

"We hang in there until Effert himself admits it's a no-exit," said Schleppend. "We owe him that much. And more."

"You got it. Good man gone too long," said Swinyard.

"But what about the poor old baby?" said Lyra.

"He's old," said Schleppend.

"Wouldn't it be nice if he got his heart's desire?" said Lyra.

"What you are asking is too scary to admit to," said Schleppend. "There was something very, very bad about Means's office tonight. Foul. I don't want to mess."

"But he's so old. He's waited so long," said Lyra.

"Just once around for the comet," said Effert, returned of a sudden, flopping down to stir the fire, then continuing, "It reached aphelion the year me and Swinyard and Schleppend were born. I've always thought that was significant. Perihelion last winter, right. It reached comet-Earth minimum separation this month. Now it's off again, riding high, just a one-degree tail tonight."

"Where?" said Lyra.

"There," said Effert, handing her a spyglass, directing her gaze to a spot low in the western sky just off the constellation Leo. At this latitude, he explained, the comet would be visible for over six hours tonight, with an apparent magnitude in excess of 5.5.

"Wow. That's Halley's Comet? Mazda never showed it to me. Wow," said Lyra.

"Believe it," said Effert. "It had a faint forty-degree tail a month ago. Now we, that is, the Earth, well, you understand, us on the Earth as eyes—we've closed the angle, so it seems more a point, its tail away from the sun still, always. It's point seven A.U. out—about sixty-five million miles—and moving. Grand, isn't it?"

"Mind-blowing," said Lyra. "Why were they hyping

collision? It's tiny. No wonder it didn't change my, uh, well . . .

"Five kilometers across at its nucleus, actually," said Effert. "That collision talk was rubbish. They hauled out what old Halley himself once said about comet collision and made it into media munchies. Though point seven A.U. is close, for space."

"Bye-bye, Halley's Comet," said Lyra, waving.

"It is sad," said Yella Kissl. "Halley's Comet is once in a lifetime, if you're lucky, and then gone. Like true love."

"Twice for Wavy Rufus," said Effert, taking back the spyglass, tracking the comet, superb beyond ordinary vanity up there against the deep, imponderable dome of Heaven.

"He is strung out about it," said Yella, bouncing over to cuddle with Schleppend, patting the paper in her cleavage.

"When you wish upon a star, makes no difference how old you are," said Lyra, bouncing over to cuddle with Swinyard.

"Amen," said Effert, wishing Gracie a good night with a magical kiss in the air, smack.

Comet Comes

SMACK, smack, smack," from Gracie at precisely the same moment, disgracefully in her cups again. "Oh, God, that feels good! Whose room is this? Oh, more."

"Ours now," said Torrance VIII. "More wine?"

"Enough, thanks, I'm flying. C'mere," said Gracie.

"Easy, there. Your bloomers are showing," said Torrance VIII.

"You noticed! Watch, wheee! No more bloomers!" said Gracie.

"I should say. Is that all yours?" said Torrance VIII.

"Strong like a stallion, but you're the stud, c'mere!"

"Ow! Not so rough, please," said Torrance VIII.

"Let Virtue nurse her favorite lancer. You are gorgeous. All of you. Gorgeous neck! Gorgeous chest! Gorgeous tummy!"

"Pause," said Torrance VIII.

"I'll take them off. Whee! Oops, sorry, they ripped. Hey, that lance was no joke," said Gracie.

"You're a strange child," said Torrance VIII.

"Older than you, gorgeous. And lonely," said Gracie. "Hold still, now. Let me take this off. Damn, I ripped it too."

"Just go slower. No hurry, really," said Torrance VIII.

"I guess you can tell it's been a long time," said Gracie.

"Thirteen years?" said Torrance VIII.

"How did you know that?" said Gracie.

"Virtue has no secrets. I have sisters," said Torrance VIII.

"I suppose. She has hormones, though, God!" said Gracie.

"Did you just, uh . . .?" said Torrance VIII.

"Yes. Funny, isn't it? It's been a long time," said Gracie.

"Amazing. I didn't do anything," said Torrance VIII.

"You're gorgeous. That matters. C'mere!" said Gracie.

"Ow! Damnit! Not so rough! You horse!" said Torrance VIII.

"Sorry, motor coordination is off. Sorry," said Gracie.

"Let's get this over with before I get hurt," said Torrance VIII.

"That's not very romantic," said Gracie.

"You want romance, screw your Effert," said Torrance VIII.

"What about Effert? Do you know something?" said Gracie.

"Turn over and shut up," said Torrance VIII.

"Hey, what are you doing? Please, Tory? Don't! Not like this. Tory? Owww!" cried Gracie.

"Don't fight me, girl, this is tough enough," said Torrance VIII.

"Stop! Please, stop! That hurts. Stop!" said Gracie.

"Hey!" said Torrance VIII, crash.

"Oh, no! I didn't mean it! Oh, no! Tory? Tory? Come on Tory, please! Are you dead? Oh! Help! Help! Help!"

Sunday brunch at Means Manor, several hours before the scheduled Cross-Country, was more an outpatient clinic than a luxurious outing on the marble patio, bubbly and bagels, lox and laxity. The talk was small when there was talk at all above the pall and the fall of water, gentle and blue, in the Florentine fountain forming the entire far side of the patio. Many chose to slump at the fountain's rim, admiring the restoration work, e.g., the repainting of the center pieces of this *Fountain of Neptune.* When menials inquired of those slumping if they'd like a platter now, they were glared away. Simply, there were many who couldn't face any more products of the ovaries, fowl or fair; and, symmetrically, there was an equal number who'd had their fill of sausages, pig or blood. Thus, the chief activity for the menials was to distribute chemicals, conciliatory "Good mornings," and warm face cloths. Still, these carnal combatants, statistics from the wars of the miswed, deserved some regard. Only a special few—such as Grace Thyme nursing a cruel hangover, and Torrance VIII nursing a cruel head lump—were missing in action; the bulk of the guests were just hissing in faction.

The roll call is momentarily informative: the preppie diplomats from State and Energy, in white slacks, crocodiles, huddled with vodka and very thin ballroom queens, chatted with BOR reps from Elephanta/Assassin/Bloodmoney Records. There was talk the undersecretaries of the southern temperate zone wanted to cut an LP of some captured tapes —native drums segued into AC/DC current humming through revolutionary groins.

The preppie bankers and lawyers, in pastel slacks, horizontal-striped blouses, huddled with gin and big-breasted sailors, gossiped over the financial section of the *Crimes.* The market had been stable for months. Nobody liked it. When the Big Bettors lay off, they said, then they Know. What, is the question? Either Capitalism had changed its face—unlikely—or Capitalism was poised on the brink of something That Big. What a game!

The plutroleum preppies, in buckskin and bravado, huddled with Arabian espresso, leotard lynxes via Farmingdale, and pearl-handled revolvers. They were playing the latest in oil-field pick-me-ups, that is, Levantine (five bullets for six chambers) Roulette—spin, spin, then, click!

Not every table smelled of overindulgence, however. One in particular caused some raised eyebrows, but no remarks. Who knew what they were arguing about. Italian, isn't it?

"My daughter does not speak for the Party," said Europa Stupefacenta, hammering her point on the white tablecloth, splattering her cappucino on her drab suit.

"I was interested to draw her opinion, not to alarm you," said Aaron Verbunko, dapper in a blue suit today, bow tie.

"It is settled, comrade," said Bonaventuro Pellegrino, next to Europa, also in a drab suit, his eyebrows hairy and wavy.

"How can it be? This is criminal," said Bianca, wrapped in cool passion and a bright flowery print, bonnet and bravura.

"In what court?" said Verbunko.

"The court of Reason. Mama cannot sell these treasures. You cannot buy them. These are facts," said Bianca.

"A charming logic," said Bonaventuro.

"One does not reason with the aristocracy," said Europa.

"I am a citizen of Florence," said Bianca.

"Your patriotism rivals your infidelity," said Europa.

"The totalitarian tack," said Bianca. "Disavow by defamation of character. I had hoped for more, Mama."

"Your hope will not nurse the sick, feed the hungry, or even repair the plumbing," said Europa. "We need these things, and now. Exchanging your aesthetics for bread seems a fair bargain."

"My aesthetics? Do we live in the same city? I submit civilization's aesthetic!" said Bianca. "We are not discussing a rose garden. We are discussing the Florentine Renaissance. Who are you to sell it? And who are you, Mr. Verbunko, to buy it? Is there no end to your pride? What wouldn't you sell, Mama? What wouldn't you buy, Mr. Verbunko?"

"These romantic abstractions," said Bonaventuro.

"I follow you," said Verbunko. "But your argument seems overblown in this instance. A simple deficit lessened by foreign trade. Much more palatable than the spoils of war or the squalor of bankruptcy, when the strong rule by cruelty, the meek flee to the churches, when there is no release, not even in death."

"It is off the point for me to speak to your failed faith, Mr. Verbunko," said Bianca. "I ask you to recall a time when humanism was not obtuse to you. I am speaking to this instance. To facts. How does it go? For the Palazzo Vecchio, one hundred millions and a social service center? For the Palazzo Medici, one hundred millions, wheat credits, and a car park? For the Palazzo Rucellai, one hundred millions, three petrol ships, and a high-rise complex? Genius, that, replace the old skyline with a new one. And how many Michelangelos was it? Five? A fine list."

"My daughter does not speak for the Party," said Europa.

"History, then, Mama," said Bianca, "since your Party holds itself a historical inevitability. How dare you cooperate with the Capitalists, allow them to rape our city. What justice is there in feeding a man who has lost his heart, a woman who has lost her soul, a child who has lost truth?"

"You would prefer they starve knowing these abstractions?" said Bonaventuro. "Art must serve the people, or it is worthless. These are stones, cloth, wood, not food, clean water!"

"To wash the blood," said Bianca.

"An emotional remark?" said Verbunko.

"No. Those who lose respect for man's art also lose respect for man. A lesson of their history, all history. Totalitarianism will not permit first-rate art. My mother and her comrades have adapted this fact with their Florentine genius for innovation. They not only prevent modern art, they also destroy received art," said Bianca.

"We aren't discussing a bonfire, Contessa," said Verbunko. "I represent men and women who can afford to preserve these works of art in a manner impossible for the People's Republic. We have the highest respect for the Florentine Renaissance."

"What you do, Mr. Verbunko," said Bianca, coldly, "is more odious to me than anything Mama or her lackeys will ever do. You corrupt. And you do it because you do not, cannot, believe in goodness. You are a fouler of the present, a curser of the future. You would permit a Hell on Earth. You would undo the Creation."

"I believe she must be a saint," said Europa.

"I am speaking to a man," said Bianca. "He knows who he is. I am not saving him, or the world. I am no saint, Mama. I am a Jewess who has loved, erred, hoped. I continue in the face of gross indifference and popular malignancy."

"The choir sings! The fools kneel!" said Bonaventuro. "The sermon transforms us! The Cardinals pray! And to what? A Savior? The Promised Land? Do you know where it is, Contessa? Show us, tell us! Where? And who is our Savior? I? Her? Him? You? The Americans? I answer you. All of us, we are all our own salvation, if we struggle, without petty shame."

"Once again," said Bianca, "it is off the point to speak to a man's failed faith."

"Speak of faith, then, Contessa," said Verbunko.

190

"She knows nothing of faith," said Europa. "She believes in copulation like dogs."

"Sex is human, Mama," said Bianca. "And you have sold love today more cynically than the commonest street woman. You have sold the Florentine Renaissance without even suspecting the tragedy that you don't know what it is to be reborn."

"I . . ." began Europa, trailing off, slipping back into a gray funk beneath her shapeless Party sack. It was Europa's most consuming secret that once upon a time, when she was very young, and hungry, and many of her comrades had lain bleeding without penicillin, or hope—Nazi bullets, Fascist bullets, American shell fragments, and British bomb fragments filling their wasted bodies—Europa Stupefacenta (never wed, because a passionate believer in human freedom without the chains of Italian matrimony) had sold her body for money. And the issue of that shame sat before her now, charismatic in her beauty, denying the very politics that had obliged her creation. An irony beyond Europa, so she pouted, sighed, did not weep.

"Your redemptionism interests me more than you can suppose," said Verbunko. "Is there a Savior? I ask this sincerely."

"And I reply sincerely," said Bianca. "I believe there is. Whether He has come. Whether He is coming. These are creeds. I believe in a Creator. He is the Savior in every creed, howsoever He represents Himself."

"A delicate matter delicately turned," said Verbunko, charmed as he had never been before, "but a Savior for us, for now, for this 'Hell on Earth,' as you say. Is there hope?"

"There are forces, powers. How else can we explain revolution? There are special men and women. There are revelations and visions," said Bianca, trailing off also, unsure what she was trying to say. Why did she think of Gracie's ancient great-grandfather, of something he'd said while telling them those zany stories of a "Comet Incarnate"? She couldn't think it through just now, not with the pressure of debating Marxism-Leninism, Stalinism, and Capitalism all at once. It was something significant though, about personal destiny.

"Contessa? Contessa?" said Verbunko, trying to get her attention. He was standing now, holding a woman by the arm.

"Yes? A thought. I apologize," said Bianca.

"I introduce our hostess, Mrs. Torrance Means VII," said Verbunko. Bonaventuro Pellegrino bounded up to take Happy's bejeweled hand, kissing it courtly, mumbling how lovely Mrs. Means was in her golden gown. Europa nodded to Happy. Bianca said,

"It is generous of you to have us out here this morning, Mrs. Means. I enjoy seeing the *Fountain of Neptune* again."

"Why, yes, wonderful," said Happy, pausing, her Italian not sure enough immediately to discern sarcasm from idioms. Happy grinned the wider as she translated in her mind what Bianca actually meant, replying, "It is refreshing to find someone with refined sensibilities. Europe has been so dreary since the war. And your opinion, Contessa, I would treasure it. I was urged to move it farther from the Manor."

"I especially liked it when it was in the Piazza della Signoria," said Bianca.

"A Florentine with prejudices, how charming," said Happy, sitting abruptly in Verbunko's chair. "And these are our revolutionaries, Aaron?"

"Yes, Mrs. Means," said Verbunko.

"We were speaking of the Revolution," said Bonaventuro.

"Oh? Who won?" said Happy. "Silly me. These are trying days. You've all been enjoying yourselves? We have an exciting race this afternoon. I understand your friend, Grace Thyme, won't be racing after all, Contessa."

"You have been misinformed," said Bianca. "She is dressing now. Athletes need their rest."

"Do they?" said Happy. "Apparently they need other things also. But what do I know? My stepdaughters are the sweaty ones in this family. You have met them?

To meet one is to meet both. Yes? My humor is not Florentine?"

"This is very amusing, Mrs. Means," said Bonaventuro.

"You think not, Commissar?" said Happy.

"I do not joke about children," said Europa.

"How exciting for you! An ideology!" said Happy, waving her hand over the guests. "These children lack many intangibles, but they particularly lack an ideology. You should chat with them, or whatever you call it—proselytize? —while you can. They come and go with no order."

"I shall do that, Mrs. Means, thank you," said Europa.

"My mother doesn't understand that you make light of her," said Bianca. "But I do. Please stop immediately."

"How sweet!" said Happy, rising to go as abruptly as she had sat, grabbing Verbunko firmly by the arm and pulling him to her to whisper, in English, out of the corner of her toothy mouth, "Have you asked them about the bullet hole?"

Verbunko attempted to camouflage Happy's error (she not realizing Bianca spoke English) by clearing his throat noisily, then sweeping her away in a dancing motion. Happy threw a parting wave to the Florentines, then said to Verbunko again, "We must talk, Aaron, at length."

Bianca watched them depart. Happy Means was as dangerous as her stepdaughters, thought Bianca, but there was also something desperate about her. She played the Mistress of the Manor too hard, as if she were afraid of someone taking it from her or accusing her of inadequacy. But she was quick, and of a violent temperament. Bianca knew she had heard "bullet hole." Then the Means were already on to last night's escapade. Bianca hoped they were still as ignorant as she; for Swinyard & Schleppend had fled without explanation, and Europa had refused to discuss "Party business"—another bizarre plot, no doubt, with what Europa would claim were "worldwide implications." Mama, Mama, thought Bianca, when will you learn that persecution is not viable proof that one is righteous? And when will you admit you are too old to combat brutes such as the Means? And now, Mama, your "bullet hole" has jeopardized all of us, including, perhaps—for in the New World anything seemed possible to Bianca—the long-missing Effert Broadsword. Bianca excused herself from the table. She dodged Aaron Verbunko's outstretched arms as she slipped into the crowd and into the Manor house, hearing Verbunko calling entreaties and apologies to her as she passed out of earshot. No more time for flirtatious debate. It was time to get Gracie up, bathed, sobered, and dressed. It was also time to confess what she knew of Effert Broadsword. Maybe then Gracie would confess what she'd been up to late last night, ripping another dress like that.

The Cross-Country course was in the shape of a broken heart, the start and finish at its bottom tip. Marked by white flags bearing the Means crest, the course ran east from the Great Meadow to the sea, along the beach to an escarpment over Peconic Bay, hooked up and down again over meadowland to the midpoint at a stream, where the ford was dodgy, then up again, in and out of country homes recently built at the edge of the Means' estate, turning through rolling hills to the finishing stretch—a perilous run through heavy woods. Justine called the course hearty. Christine said little, for she rode formally, not to win. Torrance VIII, who had lost the male prize only once since first he'd raced, and that time to Torrance VII, called the course bloody. This apt, because if the escarpment didn't get the novices, the stream got the mediocre, the rolling hills the exhausted, and, if one was lucky to survive all that, there was the finish through the dark wood—ominous and branch-infested.

The betting was outrageous. The tally board in the Great Meadow, surrounded with tables of goodies upon which fed the Ungood, had Torrance VIII going off at 1 to 5. Justine would run this year at a mere 1 to 1, because of the entry of the horsewoman Grace Thyme at 3 to 1, which was down to even money by race time. This annoyed Torrance VII enough so that he threw a ridiculous sum in the pot to render all odds meaningless. The major betting, regardless, was on who would finish, and who would last how long. This race thrashed. The one question among the bettors was whether or not "Exheredared" (sic) would ride. Perhaps out of respect for his mysteriousness, the tally board showed him at 20 to 1 before betting on an enigma stopped the flow. Two lawyers said to work for Cedric Broadsword & Sons, Ltd., were seen betting heavily on the lone rider, however, and the word got around that there might be some hustling here.

There were six dozen riders numbered and presented by the time, past 1 P.M., Aaron Verbunko again took the microphone on the stage to commence the festivities, to clear the crowd of well-wishers from the field, and to announce the rules. The rules, he said, did not exist. Go and come back. There were no shortcuts worth taking. If you cheated in some creative way, so be it. There were attendants along the whole of the course to aid the injured, shoot the horses, and monitor the sluggish past dark, calling back numbers so the audience could follow the race at the Manor. Good luck, he added, and may the Best win, whatever the cost in flesh or friendship. Verbunko then held up his hand, looking to Torrance VII on the stage behind him for approval. The riders, splashy in reds, greens, motley, and all variety of costume (ape suits, chicken heads, a duck's ass, and a Godiva, of course), readied themselves. This was a dismounted start. Verbunko dropped his hand. The heralds tooted. They were off, under a threatening, blackening sky.

In the lists: "Are you sure of her?" said Cedric.

"Yes, *Padrone,* she is strong," said Bianca.

"Did you find out what happened last night?" said Cedric.

"She felt dizzy and went to sleep early," lied Bianca.

"Hello," said Abbott, with a spyglass, "what's this?"

"That looks to be the fellow from yesterday," said Cedric.

"Where?" said Bianca, taking the spyglass from Abbott.

"By the far trees, do you see him?" said Abbott.

On the stage: "Who is he, Verbunko?" said Torrance
VII.

"I have yet to determine accurately," lied Verbunko.

"It won't bother my Justy," said Torrance VII.

"No, nor our Tory," said Happy.

"What does that mean?" said Torrance VII.

"I agree with you, don't I, Aaron?" said Happy.

"Yes, Mrs. Means," said Verbunko.

"Don't tell me any more. You two are up to something, and I don't want to know," said Torrance VII.

"A done thing," said Happy.

Gracie didn't spy Effert, of course, since her equestrian philosophy, adapted from a Counterculture epigram, was "Don't Look Back": Gracie easing into her English saddle with the grace of a woman born to the breed of horse available in heroic time, she chiding her gray-star (the rescued beast) with consoling commands as she guided him at a trot to the edge of the swirling pack, aiming to stay clear of the amateurs, provocateurs, and torturers, but keeping within quick sight of the leaders, who were, from the first, Torrance VIII and Justine atop splendid white Arabians, leading the bunching from the Great Meadow through a woodcopse, turning left on the leafy lane down to the sea, Gracie choosing to ride the shoulder of the unpaved path, holding her gray-star back, for he was a randy, impetuous mount, eager to pass the lesser grays, overtake the whites, Gracie leaving the shoulder to detour up onto the tree-lined bank for some slaloming, in and out, accustoming herself to the feel of her mount (whom, though Gracie would blush to admit it, she had renamed

Come Home Effert (All Is Forgiven)

—or "Come" for short), Come responding becomingly to the slalom and two quick jumps, neither reaching too far nor too high with tight, controlled motions, conserving his strength as he seemed to find Gracie's rhythm—her heartbeat—

which did pace the horse's heart, let this piece of horsewom-
anship be clear, thump-thump from Gracie so rat-a-tat from
Come, under a willow, over pine logs, down into the shoulder again, easing through the pack which jostled dangerously as the lane narrowed to a bend, one sorrel going down
before a "Curve" sign, two grays (one with Lady Godiva)
piling up, bodies askew, some screams, nothing terrible, as
the race's inertia was yet too low for butchery, Gracie
tempted to pause to check the fallen horses but thinking
better of it as she glimpsed the lead whites, and another
(Christine), bend to the left again to begin the final twisting
descent to the seashore, Come jerking for some fun so Gracie
deciding to give him a thrill, up, up, up, and over a ridge to
leave the lane and cut off the worst of the winding, hearing
cries of

Tally-ho-Thyme!

from the pack as she left it permanently behind, into the
shrubbery, paralleling the lane now, moving away from the
rumbling, alone with her equinity (all that in femininity);
yes, there, through the pines, the gray-blue sea, Gracie slowing Come to a walk as she searched for an opening down,
aha, fixing a mental image of the course map she'd memorized in her bath this morning (Bianca over her scolding and
teasing her with news of Effert)—here's the red-dotted line
showing Gracie's path—in order to intersect the course's
flags there, let's see, thought Gracie, turning through here:

DANGER

"Horseshit!" from Gracie, for the giant sign warned her that
her overgrown path ended at the edge of a forty-foot gorge,
a split made in the highest dunes overlooking the sea, so no
wonder the lane had wound so oddly, Gracie pulling Come
because she had to double back, losing ten minutes on the
leaders, but Come resisting, anxious, earnest, Gracie smiling
at the risk of it—an easy six meters across to an uneven
landing—but Come for it, so Gracie yelling, "Come on!" and
off, rat-a-tat, whoosh! up, up, Gracie flying atop her gray-

star, concentrating on the landing, keeping his head up and her own weight forward and even, her knees up for guidance, but what's this??? did she feel this???

"Wings?"

said Gracie, as they landed, ooff, too busy to think now, right, left, hard work down the decline, over loose rock, soft sand, clumps of sea-grass, faster, faster, as she kept her weight back, reining Come through a break in an aged dune and out, onto the course again, and now in the front dozen behind the two white leaders, Gracie shaking off the wonder that her horse had sprouted wings back there in that mighty jump—but knowing, as she got her breath, that once upon a space and time Athena had tamed a certain Pegasus—none of that, thought Gracie, Pegasus is still up there in the sky (must check tonight), Gracie leaning into her ride as Come took to the beach curving in a crescent along a swirling surf beneath storm clouds approaching fast from the south, perhaps a dozen riders dropping out as they tired on the sand, or reconsidered, seeing that escarpment ahead, menacing indeed, twenty-five degrees at its worst, as the two leaders took it easily, back and forth up a snaking path, Gracie spying Torrance VIII above her as she passed the last of the stacks and headed over a slate slide, easing Come back so as not to bunch with the vanguard as they waited their turn on the narrow path: Now! as Gracie urged Come onto the incline, clop-clop, up and up, sighing excitedly as the sea breeze whipped her pigtails: ten minutes to the top: easy, and when she cleared the top there was a hidden depression of soft sod lipping quickly up onto the plateau that fooled a stallion before her, rider and ridden crashing badly with Means attendants running to their aid, Gracie veering left dangerously along the edge to avoid trampling the damaged stallion, then up onto the meadowland—rye grass and briar patches as far as she could see—Come ready to pass the six ahead, then to match the two leaders, but Gracie cautious about blazing a trail she'd never ridden, so content to glide close behind across the fields, her professional manner relaxing enough to give her time to daydream of recent conversations:

> "What about a bullet hole, Bee? Effert's not been shot? No, then what? Tory said Effert too. Every time we see the Means, Effert's name comes up. Really? You think that was Effert? But where is he now? Why won't he come home to me? Why? Why?"

> "Tory, uh, I want to apologize about last night. Tory? I'm sorry I acted so childishly. Can you forgive me? Tory?"

—but then out of the meadow and into a white-water stream, so concentrating again, for this ford was said to be tricky because wide at the bank, narrow in midstream, and hooking sharply to the left at the far bank (to shape the exact midpoint of the race, the heart's dip in a V): but no problem for Gracie, splashing quickly past tired riders being swept away at midstream, Gracie hurtling white water left, as she'd observed the leaders do, her weight back on her left stirrup, Come like a seahorse now, shoving off his legs to float-flop onto the bank, then onto to the steep incline leading to a paved highway, an opulent sedan chair filled with celebrants from the Manor racing by, honking, Gracie ignoring them as she kept Come to the shoulder round a towering cliff face sporting graffiti:

GNOSSOS PAPPADOPOULIS, ONE DAY SHORT

and through a musky crossroad, across a narrow bridge, and into a shadowy glen, the course now to follow the graveled private roads of three mansions bordering the Means estate, first, Bufotenine Keep, its architecture from overhead noteworthy:

and second, Sernyl Towers, and third, Ditran Inn, their ar-
chitectures from overhead also noteworthy, but Gracie not
amused by the ruling class's sense of humor (for hallucinogenics had done her wrong again last night), though she
wondered momentarily where Mescaline Manse and LSD
Meeting House might be; then, near catastrophe, for Come
was spooked by the stares of the guests at Ditran Inn so
veering into a chicken coop, Gracie having to jump him over
the henhouse, alley-oop, hen blood in his tracks, egg yolk
on his hooves as they regained the course, over rolling hills
for several miles, Gracie unable to pick up ground on the
leaders as they cleared the final ridge before the forest: there!
dark, deep, and dreadful, a horse race through such thick
being thick, but so be it, Gracie seeing the leaders would
have to wend right to take an open bridge before scooting
into the pine cave, so here was her chance to take charge
before all strategy was drowned in the imminent rain (thunderclaps to the southeast, lightning streaks across the pine
tops): Gracie yanking Come off the course, down through a
pasture, over one fence, another, a third, running along the
stream now, Torrance VIII approaching the bridge from the
opposite direction, spying Gracie and giving her a wave with
his riding crop (apparently thinking she couldn't possibly
reach the bridge before him, which she couldn't), but Gracie
with plans, nearing the narrowest, deepest section of the
stream—still, fully seven meters across—but this was IT, so
away and Up!

"They are wings!"

from Gracie, giddy with good nature as she landed Down!
on soft Nature, Come immediately leaping onto the roadway to take the lead finally, him giving a burst as Gracie
swept under the first pines a hundred yards ahead of Torrance VIII as the rain began with big drops, pop-pop-pop,
on the needle carpet, then, with foreboding gusts, transformed into a torrent of cold water, the light in the forest
nearly extinguished by the huge black clouds tumbling atop
each other overhead, the forest screening out the worst of

the lightning, but not the thunder as—flash—Gracie counted, one million, two million, three—

KerPOW!

a boom like a hammer followed by three more flashes and three more: "Kerpow, KerPow! POWPOWPOW!" fell on Gracie and her trusty steed, Come Home Effert (All Is Forgiven): see them there as they twist deeper into the forest, straining to follow the flags through the withering shower, visibility largely by lightning light, Gracie losing the turn once, then twice, only to chance upon the flags through saplings bent back by the wind, Come shaking his head, nervous, so Gracie leaning forward to sing him a lullaby:

> . . . I ain't free, but there's change all around,
> Pick up my guitar and play,
> Just like yesterday,
> Then I'll get on my horse and pray,
> We don't get fooled again . . .

but needing someone to comfort her too after a while, as the storm transformed the forest into groaning cataclysm with branches cracking and crashing, and worse: yet Gracie pressing onward, Come strong as ever trotting into a clearing, lit up by flashes from above, the marshy ground green and glorious with mud spattering onto Come's shoulders, onto Gracie's legs, but she was such a mess she loved it, homo and equus versus Mother Nature and Father Time, a fair match, thought Gracie, reining Come through a quartet of pines at the far end of the clearing, giving him a pat and then,

"God!"

a snap, a squeal, a tumble: girl and stallion askew on their backs, pause, the rain in a sheet, pause, and still girl and stallion askew on their backs, stunned.

"Get the wire first!"
     "What'll I do with the horse?"

201

"Shoot it. Quick! Not here! Over there!"

"Is she bad, you know, hurt bad?"

"Just dazed, I think, help me. She's big, isn't she?"

Bam! Bam! Bam!

"I missed it! Help! It's crazy!"

"Look out! It's crazy. Chase it. Here, use this."

"She's big, isn't she? Look at those hips and shoulders."

"Society bitch, that's all. Get her under the tarp."

"The horse got away, okay? Crazy."

"Yeah, well, we'll see if Murtrux buys that explanation."

"We gotta stay out here in the rain?"

"Till dark. Those are my orders. You wanna cross her?"

"Naw, it's just that . . . what about her?"

"What about her? Tie her down. I'll dope her."

"Could I have a go? You know? Okay?"

"You're insane. If Westergaard ever finds out, forget it."

"You don't see nothing."

"She's kinda big, isn't she?"

"Have a drink and shut up."

"What's he doing back there?"

"You don't see nothing."

"Rider coming in!"

"Where? Are you sure? Get off her. A rider!"

"Rider coming in. It's Means!"

"Does he see us? Oh, shit, he's seen us. Shit!"

"Come out here!"

"Yes, sir, Mr. Means. It's me and the boys."

"What are you doing there? This isn't a way station."

"We're waiting for riders that wander off the trail."

"I don't believe you. Come out here, all of you. Him too."

"That's a rider, sir. She fell. We were helping her."

"Who? Who is it? It's Grace Thyme. Is she hurt?"

"Not too badly, sir. Can't tell. Her horse threw her."

"Tory! What's wrong."

"These servants have found Grace Thyme. She's been thrown."

"Where is she?"

"In there. Take my reins. Now, where is she?"

"Right here, sir. I was just about to give her something."

"What's going on here, man? Who did this? Grace?"

"We just loosed her belt. She took a bad fall."

"Tory?! Come back here. How is she? Tory!"

"You go on, Justy. She seems all right."

"Leave her, Tory. We've got a race to finish. Tory!"

"Hiya, Tory. What happened? Wow, my back."

"Grace. You fell. How do you feel? Can you stand?"

"No problem. Whoa. My head too. This is grim."

"Can you walk with me? Lean on me, now. That's it."

"She fell, Tory. She'll be fine. Let's go!"

"Something's wrong about this, Justy."

"That's it, Mr. Means. She was thrown. Over there."

"Shut up."

"Listen to them, Tory. Leave her. Do as I say."

"Where am I, Tory? What's happened to Come?"

"These men will take care of you, Grace. You fell."

"I did?"

"We've got to finish the race. We'll see you later."

"See, Tory. I don't know why you're so suspicious."

"Justy, you know who's responsible for this as well as I do."

"Maybe."

"All right, let's get out of here."

"Hold it right there, Means."

"Effert!"

"Gracie!"

"Oh, Effert, Effert, it's really you!"

"Sure, Gracie, easy. Are you going to get down, Means?"

"Stay where you are, Tory."

"I'll handle this. You ride on."

203

"What shall I do, Mr. Means?"

"Stay back and shut up. You've done enough damage."

"Listen to me, Gracie. Take my horse. Get out of here."

"No, no, I won't leave you now. No, Effert, no!"

"Can you ride? You're not gonna let Justine Means beat you? Win it for me and Father. A kiss for luck. Up you go! Please, Gracie? For me, because I love you. I do."

"Oh, Effert, oh, Effert, oh, Effert, there are five of them. Oh, Effert."

"Go fast and sure, Gracie. See you at home."

"Justy, you go on as well."

"Yeah, me and your baby brother got something to discuss."

"I'll do no such thing."

"We'll take care of things, Miss Means. Don't worry."

"You can worry if you want, Justine."

"Go, Justy!"

"This one's for Gracie, Means."

"Hey!"

"What'll we do? He's out bad."

"Get him. Get him! Get him!!!"

Gracie was off again, dazed and sore, soaked and shuddering, bonnetless and beltless, yet running with the wind and rain at her back, Effert's horse not as strong as Come, but energetic and relaxed, possibly even better equipped for the sloppy track (a quarter horse), Gracie turning back at the first bend in the course—violating her own dictum, "Don't Look Back!"—but she must: Justine Means hard on behind her, also glancing over her shoulder; six men amid the quartet of pines, one down, four closing on one standing, Effert; a bolt of lightning, a clap of thunder, a flutter of the pines, and three new figures on the scene, one tiny, one graceful, one gigantic; the four surrounding Effert to kick him down, smash him with clubs as he lashed out; the three new figures closing on the four; and then . . . Gracie around the bend so losing sight of the action, back into the cave of pine limbs so leaning into her ride, rat-a-tat, must get help, thought she, must must must, as she spied the last of the forest ahead, huge pines swaying in the torrent, Gracie using her reins and knees, faster, faster, out of the woods! into the fields! across a lane! over a fence! and another fence! hard on to the Great Meadow in the distance, Grace Thyme, horse-woman-in-love with a passionate mission past the deserted pavilions, past the abandoned finery, past the empty lists, woman and horse a whirl of mud and rainwater as Gracie went up on her seat and gave her mount the whip for the first time ever: through the "Finish Line" with only half a dozen attendants still about, yet Gracie spotting indefatig-able Uncle Cedric alone on the stage, he opening his huge arms like a great bear, Gracie twisting her mount to the stage, shouting, "Effert!" as she collapsed off her seat into the embrace of Effert Broadsword's puzzled father.

A Great American Family

WHILE the weekend had been especially for the em-ployees of the Means Corporation and assorted VIPs linked by bribe or by tribe to Means interests, the ball capping the "Rites of Spring" was intended for the full spectrum (color and confessional) of the Manhattan Island's and the Long Island's society. The opulent sedan chairs formed a continuous black line in the rainstorm, snaking into Means Manor to discharge their viperine passengers. Everyone who might have been, wanted to be, or was some-one was there, including, of course, the *Crimes* society re-porter, who reported:

It was another night to remember at the Means family's Long Island estate, as the rich and famous gathered to celebrate the "Rites of Spring."

"No one gives parties like this anymore, dear," commented Princess (Esther) Aga Gah, who has homes in Cold Water Canyon, Houston, Palm Beach, Monte Carlo, and Riyadh and travels a good deal with her husband, an energy executive.

In excess of fifteen hundred guests filled the three cavernous ballrooms that comprise one entire wing of Means Manor, a sprawling mansion near Peconic Bay that architecture critics have called "neo-Gothic blockwork strange."

The theme for this year's ball was, once again, "May Day." This year's surprise was that a dozen members of the Soviet General Staff, handsome in their severe gray uniforms festooned with magenta ribbons, were on hand to waltz with the ladies. A long line of beauties formed for this treat. The orchestra in the main ballroom played the "Blue Danube" six consecutive times before the Soviet officers pleaded for a rest.

Mrs. Torrance (Happy) Means VII presided over her ball. Coiffured like Marie Antoinette, with a striking diamond hairpin, and dressed in a revealing gold lamé and silk chiffon gown, topped with platinum-trimmed silk and a bald-eagle-feathered cape held at the neck with petrified eagle claws, Happy Means moved from room to room dispensing cheer and novelties.

Also in spectacular attendance, to the delight of the younger gentlemen particularly, were the dazzling twin sisters, Justine and Christine Means. With their fine golden hair dangling in corkscrew curls and dressed in identical, simple white silk sheaths slashed high up the side, the sisters danced every dance.

"How do you tell them apart?" asked one newcomer. She was informed that, though the sisters wore identical diamond chokers valued in excess of a quarter of a million dollars each, Christine Means wore the nosering encrusted with an additional tens of thousands of dollars' worth of gems. . . .

. . . and the evening was capped, at midnight, with an archery contest held under arclights by a Florentine fountain. Because of inclement weather, the Means had raised an enormous canvas over the shooting range. Many guests wagered on the contestants, and a favorite was Dr. Trinity Ystorm, a cousin of the Means, who is also President and Chief Executive of Grimmen Aircraft, a wholly owned subsidiary of the Means Corporation, and the Long Island's largest employer.

Dr. Ystorm, a former Olympic archery medalist, excelled, striking the target dead center many times. However, an unidentified man said to be a technician at Grimmen's Transportation Division bested Dr. Ystorm by splitting his arrow. Intriguingly, the unidentified winner left without collecting his cash prize of gems valued at ten thousand dollars.

And was a good time had by all?

"Does a chicken need lips?" replied Dotty Ystorm, comforting her husband, Trini, with a kiss. "One leaves the Manor feeling rejuvenated, like the spring. No one believes in parties like this anymore, dear."

A matter of faith, then.

Kong Weekly's "Rock Ghoul" had it decidedly different, as one would expect:

Over two hundred rock'n'roll celebrities (whose names we are sworn never to print until after life) were at their bourgeois best for a depraved gathering given by ex–Straw People **Justine** and **Christine Means**' Midas-rich Daddy in the family's heliport-and-telekinema-equipped Long Island mansion.

"Just a few old friends from the Revolution," said Justy Means. It was closer to two thousand partiers, bored to death by the rattling of the exclusive society band **Keith Moon Rising.**

. . . **Justy Means** denies for the eighteenth consecutive year her engagement to the late **Jim Morrison** and/or **Jimi Hendrix**. . . . **Christy Means** joins her identical sister in this denial . . . and did you know a bearded reincarnation of the late **Errol Flynn** is a longbow champion?

Yet the most telling reportage of the evening was written by the editor of the *Grimmen Bulletin,* a company weekly distributed gratis to the executives, scientists, and engineers of the Grimmen Aircraft Corporation:

> Former Olympic medalist Dr. Trinity Ystorm demonstrated his considerable prowess once again at an unusual archery contest held under lights and an enormous canvas pavilion as part of a ball given by the Chairman of the Means Corporation, Torrance Means VII.
>
> Dr. Ystorm easily proceeded to the finals in the contest with high scores at 30m, 50m, 70m, and 90m. At the 90-meter range, Dr. Ystorm scored the exceptional 7-7-10.
>
> However, another contestant, who refused to give his name but was recognized as a technician in the Grimmen Transportation Division, tied Dr. Ystorm at all ranges, scoring 8-8-8 at 90 meters. An unorthodox, sudden-death match was then organized by the presiding official, Torrance Means VII.
>
> At the astounding distance of 100 meters, Dr. Ystorm struck the target firmly on the dividing line h and i, scoring 9 points. The challenger quickly stepped to the line and loosed an arrow that split Dr. Ystorm's arrow, carrying through to the target to affix itself at such an angle that its tip was adjudged closer to center. The challenger offered to shoot again, but Dr. Ystorm magnanimously conceded the contest, adding that he had been bested by a "chivalrous champion."

Enough of the strident voices of the media. The "Rites of Spring" was a success. The "May Day" ball was a success. The weekend celebrants ebbed as they had flowed, making their bubbly ways back to their always comfortable despair in the early morning hours of 28 April 1986. By dawn, only broken glass and fixed stares remained in the great home. The quiet was refreshing. From room to lavish room, clocks ticked, fireplaces crackled, servants silently cleaned. Not a discouraging word was to be heard in the whole of the Manor—except in the office wing. Here, in the firelit study adjoining Happy Means's private office, where she monitored the credits and debits of her husband's empire, several discouraged vocabularies sounded. Five, to be exact: Happy, Justine, Christine, Torrance VIII, and Aaron Verbunko, all exhausted by the weekend, by the ball, and by the threat recently posed to a great American family by a series of inexplicable events seemingly originated by a fugitive from justice (goat's blood on a Senator's suit), Effert Broadsword, and by those who would abet this fugitive now inopportunely returned from the "Holy Wars" to his homeland.

"Have you told them it's corporate security?" said Happy.

"Yes, Mrs. Means. They are not hostile," said Verbunko.

"Then what business is it of theirs?" said Happy, placing her hands firmly, palms down, on her knees. She sat at a writing table on one side of the room, with Torrance VIII, nursing a swollen jaw, sprawled casually in an armchair behind her. The Twin Sisters Means sat together on a divan on the other side of the room. Verbunko stood. He was the go-between.

"Saying that it's corporate security is not enough for them just now. They want specifics. Justine feels that these are her guests and that she has a right to know," said Verbunko.

"Did you hear that, Tory?" said Happy.

"Yes, yes, yes," said Torrance VIII.

"Make a decision, now," said Happy.

"I'd prefer this settled unanimously," said Torrance VIII.

"You didn't think of unanimity when you went after that Thyme girl. Don't deny it. I know," said Happy.

"It was a game, that's all, a game," said Torrance VIII.

"Your 'game' has contributed to a serious breach in our security. A breach, I add, that could well bring authorities of mixed allegiances down upon us. Tory, you have . . . tell him Aaron," said Happy.

"I know Mr. Means understands the gravity here," said Verbunko. "Thankfully, it is not out of hand, as of yet. If we contain now, we have reason to be optimistic about this indiscretion. And in the near future."

"Indiscretion. Blunder. What matter?" said Torrance VIII. "I agree. Let us contain now. Regardless. Perhaps Father . . ."

"Your father is not to know of this," said Happy. "He has already said as much to us. He wants to be left out."

"Is this true, Verbunko?" said Torrance VIII.

"Yes, Mr. Means, it is so," said Verbunko.

"All right, then, how many names?" said Torrance VIII.

"Eleven, sir," said Verbunko.

"Eleven! God! Why not a dozen?" said Torrance VIII.

"The Broadswords are three," said Verbunko.

"Damn Effert!" said Torrance VIII. "How could he have gotten me back here in his condition? How? A concussion. How?"

"And what happened to our servants?" said Happy.

"An indiscretion on your part," said Torrance VIII.

"I acted in your interest," said Happy.

"Of course," said Torrance VIII. "Go on, Verbunko."

"Grace Thyme and her friend the Contessa," said Verbunko. "And the Contessa's mother, and her associate, who may or may not have burglarized your father's office."

"We'll have to buy more silence in Italy," said Torrance VIII.

"And finally the two lawyers, Swinyard and Schleppend, and their lady friends," said Verbunko. "Eleven in all. As far as we can determine without direct interrogation,

Swinyard and Schleppend effected the break-in last night. At Effert Broadsword's direction, apparently."

"Another mess, another mystery," said Torrance VIII.

"No mystery what they were after," said Happy, opening a drawer in her writing table, producing Swinyard's billfold/notebook, which she'd had removed from Effert's coat after he'd finally fainted from his wounds. "They clearly have knowledge of 'Harold Starr.' If that were to get to . . ."

"Yes, yes, yes, we know," said Torrance VIII.

"We are agreed then? Containment?" said Verbunko.

"We're agreed," said Happy. "But not my daughters."

"We could mislead them," said Torrance VIII.

"I think not, sir," said Verbunko.

"Yes. How much do we have to tell them?" said Torrance VIII.

"What would they accept is more apt," said Verbunko.

"You handle it, Aaron," said Happy, reaching out to touch Verbunko's dinner jacket sleeve. "We'll abide by your achievement. If you think they have to know about 'Harold Starr,' so be it. You know best, Aaron."

"Thank you, Mrs. Means," said Verbunko, moving over to sit on a French antique chair opposite Justine and Christine. He reached inside his jacket to produce his silver cigarette case—a gift from Justine on a happier occasion— from which he removed a European cigarette, tapping it, placing it on his lips in European fashion, and lighting it with an ancient Ronson lighter, another gift from another female admirer—his mother, upon the occasion of his leaving the Dominican monastery. He leaned back in the chair, then crossed his legs. He glanced once at the fire, then up at Justine and Christine.

"Do you have to lie to us, Aaron?" said Justine, tilting her head to rest it on Christine's shoulder, both sisters wrapped in a single mink coverlet, their four golden slippers peeking out from underneath—a portrait of innocence.

"No," said Verbunko.

"How much are you permitted to tell us?" said Justine.

"The Broadswords have made threats," said Verbunko.

"To Tory? To Daddy? To whom?" said Justine.

"To the family. Threats which must be confronted," said Verbunko. "And cannot, I say, cannot be overlooked."

"Why did Effert beat up Tory today?" said Justine.

"I have no explanation," said Verbunko.

"Who beat up Effert? Those were her thugs, weren't they?" said Justine.

"I have no explanation," said Verbunko.

"Don't do this to me, Aaron. And who were those three other men who attacked Stepmother's men?" said Justine.

"This is the first I've heard of it," said Verbunko. "Did you see these men, Christine?"

"No, I was too late," said Christine. "All I saw was Effert Broadsword carrying Tory near the Meadow. That's when I came for you. The storm. I didn't see any others."

"Our search parties?" said Justine.

"Found nothing but Broadsword and Tory," said Verbunko. "Perhaps now you understand why we have to protect the family."

"Perhaps. But from the Broadswords? Fire them," said Justine. "Unless . . ."

"It is past the point where termination is adequate," said Verbunko. "This involves the Corporation too."

"Unless something big has Stepmother scared," said Justine.

"I do not understand you," said Verbunko.

"Yes, you do," said Justine.

"Do you mean violence, Aaron?" said Christine.

"I should say not," said Verbunko. "This is business."

"He means nothing radical, merely certain," said Justine.

"We will reduce our risk," said Verbunko.

"Where are they now? The wine cellar?" said Justine

"Hardly, Justine. This is serious," said Verbunko.

"I saw them leave," said Christine. "Before midnight."

"Yes, you did see them leave. We had them driven away in three family vehicles," said Verbunko.

"But they aren't going back to Broadsword Hall, are they?" said Justine, sitting up, nodding her head, guessing.

"Not just yet," said Verbunko. "Eventually. Not now."

"Where, then?" said Christine, but then she, too, sat up, nodded her head, and guessed, out loud. "Not Craven Castle?"

"Craven Castle?" said Justine.

"Craven Castle," said Verbunko. "Yes."

Doing

"Tradition eats its mothers."
—Cain

Book IV

*Wherein His Majesty Is Found
but Principals Go Missing Deep within
Everpine Forest*

Back at the "Wonder" Van

WAVY RUFUS adjusted the bass on his earphones, but he couldn't debug them, that interference consistent set after set on the radio:

> . . . *Just like yesterday (snap-crackle-pop)*
> *Then I'll get on my knees and pray (snap-crackle-pop),*
> *We don't get fooled again (snap-crackle-pop)* . . .

This maddening, Wavy Rufus flipped dials, floated levers, and, when all else failed, pounded the preamp. Still the bug. He reasoned it couldn't be WHIP-FM, Metromaniacal Radio, New York City, since the quality control there was fanatical. Engineers who lost transmission were shot. DJs who sabotaged were packed off to AM news. Once, in apocryphal time, the legendary WHIP-FM DJ Winnie-the-Fool (for Love) scraped out his own gold filling with a pop-top in order to jerry-rig a circuit, thus protecting a fifty-nine-minute set from Yardbirds to Jailbait exploring the break-up of the Party in Northern Europe. No, the bug wasn't in the transmitter, which meant that it must be either (a) in the

"Wonder" van equipment or (b) an extra-rock disturbance, like jamming or a local radio source.

Wavy Rufus fiddled another half-hour, but the bug survived. He abandoned it in frustration, since it had already disturbed his concentration on his translating. He cleared his tape recorder, slipped in a fresh cassette, and was about to begin again with his oral notes when a fresh wave of melancholy swept over him. He sat back on his sorcerer's stool, removed his earphones, and listened to the heavy rain on the roof. If Effert were here, he thought, he could fix the radio. But no, Effert had ridden off like a vainglorious clown. Wavy Rufus had not tried too hard to stop him. He loved crazy Effert despite, and perhaps because of, the seventy-year difference in their existentialism. *Fin de siècle* symbolism and Counterculture romanticism were extraordinarily similar stimulants, or, as Effert said, "downers." Besides, thought Wavy Rufus, if it hadn't been for Effert's extraordinary faith in Wavy Rufus's theory of cosmological phenomenon, well, he would be even more depressed than he was —rain on the roof, bug in the set, the comet flying off to deep space again without a sign of action (well, perhaps a sign here or there, like the PIT Peak Observatory break-in). Still, he thought, if Effert were only a little less seminiferous, a little more even-tempered, something more might've been done to locate His Majesty and His Majesty's entourage. What, Wavy Rufus couldn't say, as consternated by what could have been as he was by what Effert's efforts had discovered of significant note—"Harold Starr."

Wavy Rufus flipped and floated the reel-to-reel to replace the FM radio. He didn't like it as much, since he knew his tapes so well that they often put him to sleep, like counting sheep, track after familiar track; but there was no choice. Without music, there was no work. Worse, without music, there was the fear of being a blind old man all alone where he knew not. Wavy Rufus rolled a deck to the closest thing to star-drive yet produced, forty-four minutes odd of music to carry a willing pilgrim to galaxy escape velocity minus one [courtesy of those space captains all, Townshend,

Daltrey, Entwistle, and (dead but not down) Moon], that is, *Who's Next.* He slipped his earphones back on and, punch, float, climbed into the music. Now back to translating, he thought, running his fingers over the speckling to find his place. He was working on the Babylonian tablet, converting Assyrian (derivative Babylonian) astrology to American astronomy, hoping to find some error in his calculations about the position of the comet when an audience with the Comet Incarnate was most likely. This Comet Incarnate, "His Majesty," seemed to come, Wavy Rufus theorized, when the comet itself was visible to mankind. His Majesty seemed to go when the comet itself was no longer visible in the night sky. But things were far more complicated, and far less clear, than even these two ambiguities. Was it necessary for the comet to be visible to the naked eye before His Majesty walked among men? Probably not. Did man's ability "to retrieve" the comet in ground glass affect the quality or quantity of His Majesty's walk among men? Probably not. Was there any way to predict, to systematize, to guarantee the apparition of a comet? Probably not. The matter paralyzed mere positivism. Rufus faced the apparent (ha ha) irony: not for nothing did the Comet Incarnate later called Halley's Comet—the most famous, most spectacular, most transporting comet in the history of man—refer to himself as "Voluntas," or "Freewill": any part of mysterious Creation as profoundly mysterious as a Comet Incarnate seemed to be able to do any God-blessed thing it willed to do, and do it without concern for history, tradition, or magic. His Majesty seemed truly free, Wavy Rufus sighed (of everything but gravity and Virtue). There was one minor oddity, though, which might be a pattern. The tablet indicated something about weather, about rain.

Wavy Rufus worked past midnight, obsessed with his task, existing in that place that has no name other than Thought. The life of the mind is a terrible thing, making up songs one might never sing. So for Wavy Rufus, refining his translation, isolating the Pole Star at 623 B.C., determining the mean equinox of the seventh century B.C. And then there was this queer reference to "floods." Wavy Rufus knew that medieval lore generally associated comets with catastrophes —disasters actually, that is, literally, "bad stars"—and that one recurring disaster linked with the apparition of a comet was flooding. Perhaps that spoke to the other reference on the tablet—to rain. Who could say? Wavy Rufus relaxed on his stool. What did it matter anyway? None of this would bring the Comet to him. The reel-to-reel finished, so Wavy Rufus flipped and floated back to the FM, back to the speakers. The bug was still there, stronger, "snap-crackle-pop," oscillating as if it were moving. Wavy Rufus pounded the preamp. This was too much! No WHIP-FM! No Effert! No Comet Incarnate! And he couldn't even see the comet in the night sky, not only because it was raining, but also because of the achingly irreversible fact that he was blind! He had to remember the comet, see it with his mind's eye, those hundred of sketches and paintings he'd produced of the comet splashed magnificently above that wonder-filled spring of 1910, seventy-six Earth revolutions before, when he, Rufus Broadsword, had truly seen the comet. Never more! Never again! It wasn't fair. This was theft of imagination. He'd always expected to die curious. But he was damned—damned!—if he'd accept in silence dying like this: Oh, please, dear God, this I pray, before the Angel of Death gets here, let me know that this hairy star, whom I love, that he truly walks among men. Failing that, God, prayed Wavy Rufus craftily, perhaps I might watch my health enough to get to A.D. 2062? How credible was a 183-year-old man? But then, how credible was a Comet Incarnate? There came a rapping at the "Wonder" van's door.

Comet Talk

WHAT'S THAT?" said Wavy Rufus.

"Worthy Father," came a deeply resonant voice in antique English, "here are poor wanderers bewildered in these woods, who give thee the opportunity of exercising thy charity and hospitality."

"Who's next?" said Wavy Rufus. He readied himself for the worst, reracked the Who on the reel-to-reel. Any mother's son who came in here looking to trouble an old man was going to get 400 watts per channel blasting full volume of the world's most deafening rock'n'roll band. Crush their eardrums. Confusion to the enemy, as Effert would say. Wavy Rufus put one hand on the volume dial, then flipped the switch that opened the "Wonder" van's rear door, click, Wavy Rufus adding, "I am one of God's humblest creatures. You are welcome to my shelter, if you come in peace."

"Certainly, worthy Father," said another voice, softer and differently accented (Polish?) than the first. "May we enter?"

"Yes, but I'm expecting my servant, Effert, and his huge companions at any moment," said Wavy Rufus.

"Yes," said the softer voice again. Wavy Rufus listened as three bodies climbed into the van. The first made sounds associated with a normal man struggling into a confined space. The second made sounds associated with a child doing same. The third made sounds—indeed, tipped the truck back—associated with an oak tree doing same. The three sat opposite Wavy Rufus, on Effert's bear-rug bed.

"Nasty night," said Wavy Rufus. "Are you Means men?"

"Means?" said the softer voice, whispering something

222

unintelligible to normal ears. Wavy Rufus's were not normal, however; he heard Ciceronian Latin.

"Means, Majesty. We are close. Shall I inquire more?"

Wavy Rufus sat straight up on his sorcerer's stool, grabbing his chest with both hands. Heart, he thought, don't fail me now, thump-thump. He breathed deeply, trying to slow his pulse. Joy can kill. Ever the would-be positivist, he asked himself for his true feelings at that precise moment. He felt free. He was in the presence of a belief. He believed in the Comet Incarnate as once upon a time other men had believed in such seemingly wild ideas as Newtonian mechanics, or Maxwell's electromagnetism, or Einstein's general and special relativity, or quantum mechanics. He believed from the bottom of his heart, thump-thump, lowering his hands from his breast. He'd rehearsed what he would do at this moment for decades—his speech in Latin, of course, as he'd set himself to learning Ciceronian Latin after his blinding vision. He turned toward the sensation nearby, full of wonder and grace, and said reverentially to that sensation:

"My name is Rufus Broadsword, cosmologist, cometologist. I was privileged to have an audience with you, Majesty, in May of the year A.D. 1910, as a member of the Rockefeller Expedition, at the Persian Gulf port of Abadan. Your servant."

"So?" said the softer voice.

"I would prefer to speak in the English tongue, worthy Father," said the deeply resonant voice, who has no need for a name, of course, being an idea embodied, but has been called through the ages: by the Chinese, "Broom Star"; by the Greeks, "Comet" (meaning long hair); by the Romans, "Sword Star"; by the Mayans, *"Agent Provocateur"*; by the Iroquois, "Chief-Who-Walks-in-Rain"; by the Europeans, "Hairy Star"; and by the proto-positivists, "Halley's Comet." The Comet had taken for himself the name *"Voluntas Hallei"* (Freewill of Halley) two apparitions before, ever willing to accommodate mankind's talent for naming, for the act of naming, for the idea of naming. And though his

223

subjects chose freely to address him with cosmic deference, "Majesty," he liked it best when thought of as "Freewill."

Freewill continued, "I have been studying the language of the English. The Latin tongue seems gone forever. Is this true?"

"It seems sad when you say it like that," said Wavy Rufus.

"No," said Freewill, "I did not mean it pathetically. I did not like the Romans, even at the first. They were— thieves."

"Not thieves, Majesty," said the softer voice, "gangsters."

"Yes, gangsters, thank you, Laddy," said Freewill. "Ah, English! A confusing language. They say 'love' when they mean 'hate.' They say 'war' when they mean 'peace.' Very emotional and ambivalent for a supposedly scientific language, do not you think, worthy Father? You must help us. It is new for us. We have been trying to understand the subtler levels. It is more difficult than I had anticipated. The language seems to change daily. And our experience thus far is largely secondary. Laddy says we have reached the limits of your cinema."

"Excuse me? Cinema?" said Wavy Rufus.

"I have misspoken?" said Freewill.

"What do you mean, Majesty?" said Wavy Rufus.

"We have been much at your motion pictures. Rollo grows fat on the popped corn with butter," said the softer voice with obvious delight. "Especially at His Majesty's favorites, the Errol Flynn retrospectives on the Manhattan Island."

"*Captain Blood, The Adventures of Robin Hood, The Sea Hawk, Elizabeth and Essex, The Prince and the Pauper, Virginia City, They Died with Their Boots On, The Santa Fe Trail, The Master of Ballantrae,*" said Freewill wispily. "And more. Sublime philosophical achievements. Certainly an amalgam of centuries of learning. I enjoy them more each time. A dozen times now for *Captain Blood.* Why, just yesterday . . ."

"I am an old blind man, Majesty," interrupted Wavy

Rufus, deeply puzzled. "Errol Flynn? Who is Errol Flynn?"

"Oh? Laddy?" said Freewill.

"Let us begin anew, Rufus Broadsword," said the softer voice. "I am Count Wladyslaw Wrathnitski, Lord of Dominoes, Ringer of the Bell, and First Councillor to His Majesty, *Voluntas Hallei,* who is known in your indexes as Halley's Comet."

"You're the dwarf. You're Polish," said Wavy Rufus.

"Once," said the Count, known to all subjects of His Majesty as "Laddy," and henceforth so, "but that was long ago."

"And the silent giant?" said Wavy Rufus.

"Rollo?" said Laddy.

"The Viking chieftain Rollo?" said Wavy Rufus.

"You have much knowledge of us," said Freewill.

"Yes, I . . . Majesty, please forgive me, I forget myself," said Wavy Rufus, picking a candle out of a drawer and lighting it hurriedly. "I did not mean to be so impolite. Or do you need light? No matter. I am at your complete service."

"How is it that you know of us, Rufus Broadsword?" said Laddy. "Our meeting in 1910 was brief, inconsequential. As I recall, we confused you with a famous capitalist."

"I have what is called a 'prepared statement.' If I may?" said Wavy Rufus.

"As you will," said Freewill.

Wavy Rufus fought for control of his pulse, won. He recited: "Seventy-six years ago, my accidental meeting with you aboard the *John D. Rockefeller* changed my life in two ways. First, I renounced fashion. Second, I devoted myself to astronomy. At the time, I didn't know why. Now I understand. I wanted to see you again. However, I didn't understand that seeing you again was a qualitative endeavor, not a quantitative one. It was easy enough to be misled. In the years following your last apparition, the quantitative sciences exploded. Einstein and his colleagues addended Newtonian physics with what has come to be called general and special relativity. Heisenberg and Schrodinger and their

225

colleagues developed what we call quantum mechanics, in order to speak nuclear mysteries. What is more to the point, astronomy, my special field, moved away from the poetic into the analytical, not only with Hubble's work at Mount Wilson, but also with the clever application of chemistry and physics to our observations. Visible light, which had been the sole basis of astronomical statements, now became only a tiny fraction of our work. Today, astronomy is entirely a quantitative science, without a heart, and without a direction. But even back before I lost my sight, when we still worked primarily in the visible light band, there was no room for a man like me. I wanted to see you again. Politely, they called me a 'cometologist'—something akin to a hobbyist for them. It didn't bother me. I filled my nights with stargazing of all sort, and especially comet-watching, when it was available. And my days—I researched. I'd met you in 1910. I chanced upon sketchy evidence of your 1835 apparition—some drawings by a fellow named Thyme, whom you met, I believe. From there, with the help of my family's records—and it was here my pursuit began to feel like destiny—I gathered evidence of your 1759 apparition. Do you recall Elijah Broadsword? This led me to your 1682 visit, a bad fellow named Craven, I believe. And so forth. Though, before the seventeenth century, the records are almost worthless. I guessed. I hoped. Some shred always seemed to lead me from one visit to the previous visit. Back and back I went, till the fourth century B.C. And there the path disappeared altogether, with only random clues for the whole of time back. My chief solace these years of utter confusion was stargazing. It was here, I thought incorrectly at the time, that I might discover an objective correlative to my theory—which intimidated even me for decades. I tracked comets incessantly. I forced my facts, as quantitative scientists are wont to do when confronted with the ineffable. From this work, I extracted three likely explanations for my theory of a Comet Incarnate.

"First, I reasoned that our solar system was filled with all manner of unexplained phenomena. So far from there being nine planets, there were likely dozens, just a few of which were popularly called planets. We know that Mercury displays properties associated with, say, our Luna. We know that Venus developed along similar lines as the Earth, but that solar radiation has produced considerably different results in its atmosphere. We know that Mars has a Terra-like evolution, as well as mysteries which I shall speak to. And that Jupiter seems a failed star, a peculiar aberration that we cannot yet explain in terms of star life. Saturn, Uranus, and Neptune don't especially concern us here. Pluto again has properties similar to our Luna. And this is not to slight the asteroids, which fill near space in all their eccentric shapes and properties. We have even come to call some of these asteroids minor planets, especially the ones that frighten us, passing within point five A.U. of the Earth.

"Now the comets. These, the strangest members of our solar system. I tracked dozens in my years alone—computed their orbits, and considered this: what could be the cause of more than a few having orbits with hypothetical intersections at a common point between Mars and Jupiter? My answer seemed a breakthrough at the time. I theorized the calamitous explosion of a large planet past Mars, one large enough to explain the odd orbit of Mars, the asteroid belt, and other variables. I reasoned that this explosion had sent pieces of this planet into orbits around the Bright One, even more pieces on trajectories which took them out into interstellar space. I named my hypothetical planet *Voluntas,* in your honor, Majesty, as I believe you named yourself after 1759, or perhaps before? No matter. Further, I reasoned that perhaps some strange development beyond my imagination had caused the comets from this planet to have properties that explained what happened to me in 1910.

"My second explanation was an attempt to remain consistent and current with general cometology, with which I have had infrequent contact these past two decades, due to the extended holiday of my reader, Effert. It had been proposed that comets originated from an outer comet cloud located between fifty and one hundred fifty thousand A.U.

from the Bright One. In this cloud, there were said to be over a hundred million comets. When perturbed by collision with each other, or perhaps by the vagaries of interstellar space —such as the rotation of the galaxy, the passing of another star—individual comets fell toward the Bright One, making a single pass, in a hyberbolic or parabolic orbit. General cometology also argued for an inner comet belt, consisting of comets escaped from the outer comet cloud. The inner comet belt was said to sit about forty A.U. out and contain comets which by and large go unobserved from Earth. A few, however, fell toward the Bright One either to pass once, or to lock into an elliptical orbit, or to crash into the furnace. In any event, I reasoned that the outer comet cloud could perhaps contain properties similar to my hypothetical planet, *Voluntas,* and that in some bizarre fashion . . . well, you understand. General cometology did argue that the unusual number of comets observed during what we call the Middle Ages and the Renaissance were the result of some gravitational disturbance in the outer comet cloud, or the inner comet belt.

"From this argument I developed my third quantitative explanation. I reasoned that perhaps the outer comet cloud was insufficiently rigorous. That what the concept of the outer comet cloud actually attempted to explain was the noninterstellar origin of comets, that is, that comets originate within the gravitational reach of the Bright One, and not from interstellar space. I theorized an outer gravitational disturbance of enormous proportions, sending comets from the outer comet cloud plunging toward the Bright One in eccentric patterns, capable even of shattering *Voluntas,* ripping the atmosphere from Mars, inhibiting Uranus and Neptune, tearing Pluto from its orbit around one of the major planets. A monstrous disturbance! I reasoned that the only gravitational source significant enough to do such a thing would have to be either (a) a very large planet on the order of Jupiter (the failed sun); or (b) another star. Yet this seemed silly. Anything that large would easily have been observable. There would be extensive records, from

Mesopotamia and Egypt onward. There are not. Mind, I developed this explanation before the concept of binary systems was popular. And long before the discovery, not twenty years ago, of what we have come to call the neutron star, that is, a collapsed solar furnace so dense no light escapes its gravitational field—and not only superdense but also superfluid. No matter here. Quite simply, Majesty, I supposed that the Bright One—Earth's sun—was in orbit with an unseen star. I called it the Dark One. It was a shock to me that later quantitative science provided shaky justification for my thinking. Regardless, I thought that in some way the Dark One was responsible for comets—that perhaps comets entered orbits around the Bright One for a secret purpose to do with the relationship of a bright brother, Abel, and a dark brother, Cain. We have these stories—ah, yes. And it was not beyond me to believe that you, comets, carried in you the makings of life on the planets. That the struggle between two brother stars should account for sublime gifts. This, too, has come to be a consideration of the quantitative sciences, in pursuit of what they call the 'polysaccharides.' There have been instances of the discovery of substances closely associated with 'polysaccharides,' that is, life soup, in meteorites called 'carbonaceous chondrites.' And we both know that meteor showers are closely linked with the apparitions of comets. What is more, comet spectra are said to contain the C_3 radical, and HCN and CH_3CN are held to exist both in the interstellar medium and in comets. All these molecules are closely associated with life soup, of course. Well, you can see how I reasoned. The Dark One flinging comets from the edge of the interstellar medium. Comets colliding with planets, with Earth! And if meteorites have been demonstrated to contain lifelike substances, why not the comets that seem to trigger the most intensive meteor showers?

"Yet, no, no, no, all this, no! My three explanations. No! I tell them to you so that you understand the full weight of my declaration that I abandoned them all unequivocally. They have intriguing elements. But none of them can explain the event that led me to you, truly—an event that just so happens to have taken my eyes.

"It was mid-century. One night, a new comet. With comet-watching, that's the way it happens. Out of nowhere. There is usually a scramble to have the new comet named for the observer. A vulgar game that I've always wanted to stop. But my position in the scientific community is nonexistent. I've neither corresponded nor published. This comet, then. It was the most promising I'd seen in years. I estimated its nucleus about three kilometers across. The coma seemed tear-shaped, melancholy somehow, but resigned. The tail, at the last, was fifty million miles long, wide and wavy. Its inclination was similar to yours, Majesty, at sixteen degrees. And it had imperium. As Effert would say, it had class. Plumed and fierce and proud—like an old warrior held upright by vainglory alone. Unfortunately, the time of year, its speed, it was virtually unobservable at night from Earth. Only the last hours to sunup by naked eye. There was no mention in the papers, or on the radio. I watched, though, with my four-incher, and my eight-incher, especially because once it had reached a total magnitude of five point zero, I computed that it was falling into the furnace. I was witness to the death of a noble comet. I became a prisoner of my telescopes. I felt that the comet should not perish alone, that someone who knew its glory should be with it at the end, however abstractly. The last day, before its consumption by the heat, I wept. I was weeping over my eight-incher's viewfinder when the Bright One came up and took my eyes. I was delirious for months. The light ripped through my head and did peculiar things to my biology. But nothing as peculiar as what I'd seen, but not understood, the last instant before my blinding. I couldn't make sense of it for years afterward. It was nearly inexpressible. It was a blinding vision. I saw you.

"I must elaborate. I mended slowly. My only comforts were my great-grandnephew, Effert, and my great-granddaughter, Grace, who came to my sickroom as children to read to me and chat about what was going on outside my tower, which I knew I would never leave again. I shunned my cometology in self-pity. I wanted to see you again. How could I see anything?

"All was melancholy until one night, listening to this special music on the radio—which my Effert had taught me to call 'the Rock music'—I was transported into a trance. I had a dream. Or perhaps I had a vision. Does it matter which? I dreamed of what I'd seen just as the comet plunged to its death, victim of the gravity which imprisons us all so lovingly, so absolutely, and so profoundly. The laws of nature are not complex, are they—for all is subordinate to the eternal law of gravity, yes? And in this dream I saw a tablet being buried near a fantastic city. I recognized nothing of the architecture. I saw human natures alien to me. I understood little. There was great strife. There was fratricide, infanticide, matricide, and the most terrible and grand, regicide. A name for the fantastic city came through: 'Babylon.' And a glimpse of a clay tablet came through, with the single fragment of a line: 'Mar'zi'pan declares . . .' Nothing more. When I awoke from my dream, it all seemed so simple. Why had it taken me so long to suppose? If there was one comet with these, uh, properties, then why not others?

"What I'd seen, or known, at the last, before blinding, was the death cry of another Comet Incarnate.

"And in the cry was the vision of a request, or a concern. The Comet Incarnate called Mar'zi'pan cried out for something that had happened long before in the ancient city, 'Babylon.'

"But what? I thought and I meditated. I reviewed my dream or my vision. There was something in it that was very important. And then, after much travail, and much of the radio's wonderful music, I realized that standing amid those strange figures burying that clay tablet near the gates of Babylon was a figure I had seen before. It was you, Majesty, burying that tablet. You alone, without your entourage. Perhaps you . . ."

Wavy Rufus halted his lesson abruptly. He sensed great sorrow. He listened. There was weeping.

"Majesty, is there anything I can do?" said Laddy.

"He was a great friend," said Freewill.

"Yes, Majesty. It is the very same document, is it not?" said Laddy.

"Yes. Our information seems accurate," said Freewill.

"I am sorry if I have offended," said Wavy Rufus.

"You have not," said Freewill. "I knew that he was gone. To hear it in detail, though. . . . Can you understand how completely he is gone?"

"No, Majesty, I cannot," said Wavy Rufus.

"It is difficult for me as well, Rufus Broadsword," said Laddy.

"Thank you for that, Count," said Wavy Rufus.

"Laddy, please," said Laddy.

"Yes, Laddy," said Wavy Rufus. "Should I continue?"

"There is no need," said Freewill. "An unusual tale."

"Is there any merit to what I say?" said Wavy Rufus.

"Yes, but not the way you mean it," said Freewill. "If you had hoped that I could tell you which, and not which, I cannot. There is no language in which I could explain to you what you call 'Comet Incarnate.' "

"Yes, Majesty," said Wavy Rufus, lost, but respectful. What, after all, had he anticipated—diagrams? "I am content. I have spoken my confession. I am content."

"Not ever content. That is contrary to our common history," said Freewill.

"Yes, Majesty," said Wavy Rufus, smiling. "If not 'how,' then, why do you come? Can you tell me this? Why?"

"This is the most difficult of all," said Freewill. "The philosophy of history. The history of thinking of history. Your Errol Flynn says it best when he says, 'Over the side, lads.' But you deserve a more complete response. Laddy?"

"What His Majesty means," began Laddy, "is that we might commence an answer to your profound inquiry by asking you what you think it means to act in history."

"To act in history? To make history? To change history?" said Wavy Rufus, puzzled.

"Try to be precise. The language is fragile. To act in history. Only that," said Laddy.

"Can you give me an example?" said Wavy Rufus.

"There are many stories. You are superstitious?" said Laddy.

"Very," said Wavy Rufus.

"My favorite," said Laddy, "concerns the Demon Rum. More seriously, consider what it means when it is said that something extraordinary acts in history. For example, the Devil is said to walk the Earth, put evil in the hearts of men, bring ruin to civilization, eat the cunt of the woman and the prick of the man, set chaos loose upon the land. Horrible deeds. All of them speaking to the phenomenon of Evil acting in history. Conversely, there is talk of God the Father acting in history. Of His angels bringing goodness and light to mankind. In one instance, there is the story of the angels bringing the Savior, Jesus of Nazareth. This is a long, deceptively splendid story, and I am sure you know one or more versions. You have considered, have you not, what it means when it is said that the Christ acted in history? As it happens, Jesus of Nazareth is said to have acted once, epiphenomenally—similar, I suppose, to the passing of a comet once, perhaps?

"All the tales, then, demons and angels, the Evil One and the Holy One, speak to actions in history, do they not? As His Majesty says, we must concern ourselves here with the history of making history, with the philosophy of historical causation. A popular anecdote might have one warrior saying, 'The Devil rides with the enemy,' as his companion says, 'And the angels ride with us.' "

"I anticipate, Laddy," said Wavy Rufus.

"As you will," said Freewill.

"First, I must say that I now understand you when you say it is best to speak to all this by acting, not philosophizing. Hence the phrase 'Over the side, lads.' " said Wavy Rufus, pausing, sighing, deep breathing. "Otherwise, for my own heart, when men have said, in history, that the comet in the sky—bright, ominous, inexplicable—has brought war or famine or pestilence, simply put: disaster; and, contrarily, when men have said that the comet has brought victory, bounty, and the birth of kings, this is all a manner of speaking of the comet acting in history. It is not superstition. It is not inarticulate barbarism. It is an approximation of a truth so deep and rich that an approximation must suffice for mortal beings. Fear the apparition. Praise the apparition. Know the apparition. The nature of the comet in the sky—bright, ominous, inexplicable—derives from mankind's perception of the comet in the sky. It is a matter of vision. A comet acts in history each time it enters history's purview—fact or fancy, it matters not—from the black dome into the black dome. But then, of course it is a matter of inner vision as well, for the comet is always up there, always available to the seers among us. And a man who believes that a comet brings flood, fire, failure, is no less legitimate an observer than a man who believes that a comet is a catalyst for war, rebellion, murder. Even a man who insists that the comet is only dust and frozen gases, and has no rational correlation whatsoever to events upon Earth, he too expresses a legitimate observation; for ignoring or belittling or quantifying, even indexing, an apparition is as significant in history and as meaningful for history as worshiping the comet or damning the comet. It has always been and will always be a matter of vision. Sing of the sun, the moon, the stars, and hairy stars! Dance with the comet!"

"Enough, worthy Father, enough," said Freewill.

"Have I touched, just touched, the matter?" said Wavy Rufus.

"It is enough," said Freewill.

"It is very hard to hold it in front of my mind," said Wavy Rufus, placing his right index finger to his lips, for these were primeval secrets: Sssh!

"There is no need to strain, worthy Father," said Freewill.

"An old habit," said Wavy Rufus.

"Yet you believed before without benefit of explanation," said Freewill.

"An old habit as well. Faith," said Wavy Rufus.

"Happy man," said Freewill.

"I am honored," said Wavy Rufus.

"This is what attracted me to Errol Flynn," said Freewill. "A man of great faith. Yet of greater action. A magnificent combination. Do you know where we might find him?"

"No, Majesty, but Effert might," said Wavy Rufus.

"Your servant?" said Freewill.

"My great-grandnephew, Effert Broadsword. Unfortunately, the last I heard from him he was riding off to do battle with the Means. He, too, believes in you. He's younger, though, and restless. Rash."

"A man of action and faith?" said Freewill.

"I suppose that would summarize him," said Wavy Rufus.

"These Means you speak of, Rufus Broadsword," said Laddy. "They are the Means of the Means Corporation? They are the Means of the Means Manor, near here, yes?"

"Those are the Means," said Wavy Rufus. "A bad lot."

"The tablet you have mentioned, worthy Father," said Freewill. "Did you go to Babylon to find it?"

"No, but Effert did. Half of it anyway. Here," said Wavy Rufus, turning to pull back the oilcloth to expose it.

"So? Half? So?" said Laddy. "Majesty, half!"

"Yes, Laddy," said Freewill. "May we have this when you are done with it?"

"Please accept it now. A present." said Wavy Rufus, feeling a giant hand reach by him and snap up the tablet like paper.

"This is most generous," said Freewill. "We have been searching for it for some time. I made a grave mistake. I never should have buried it. It should have been destroyed. We were looking for it when we visited with you in 1910. It eluded us. Very generous. Thank you. He was a great friend."

"You wouldn't know about the other half?" said Laddy.

"No, nothing. This is all Effert brought me. He's been looking for you, you know. Helping me. Oh, I can hardly wait till he meets you, that is, if you can stay. I expect him back at least by morning. He has many things to tell you. Apparently, many people have been waiting for you. The Means. And others. Effert knows. There's something about 'Harold Starr' too."

"So?" said Laddy.

"Do you know about 'Harold Starr'?" said Wavy Rufus.

"There are many worrisome questions," said Laddy heavily. "You say Effert Broadsword knows of the Means and their overlords?"

"I think so. He's informed when he wants to be," said Wavy Rufus.

"This Effert Broadsword is quite a fellow," said Freewill.

"Majesty?" said Laddy.

"We shall wait for Effert Broadsword," said Freewill.

"Have I said something wrong?" said Wavy Rufus. The "Wonder" van hummed with extraordinary anxiety.

"There are many worrisome questions," repeated Laddy.

"But surely you have powers," said Wavy Rufus.

"We have no powers," said Laddy.

"We are revolutionaries," said Freewill.

"Not supermen," said Laddy.

"Oh," said Wavy Rufus.

"You sound disappointed," said Laddy.

"I'm sorry. I don't mean disrespect," said Wavy Rufus. "It's only that you make it sound, well, as if revolutionaries were more, uh, sort of . . ."

"Troublemakers?" said Laddy.

"Oh, no!" said Wavy Rufus. "I didn't mean that! 'Trouble' is not the right word at all, is it? Effert, he's a real troublemaker."

"Effert Broadsword is our man," said Freewill.

"Effert Broadsword, the man for us," said Laddy.

"Yes, Effert, yes," said Wavy Rufus, confused, but relaxed before their strange desires. He turned around briefly to rack up some rock'n'roll on his reel-to-reel, readjusting the volume, checking the mix through his earphones. He'd give them some Who, some Kinks, some Jailbait, a lot of bop-she-bop, perhaps even a taste of "Rock Around the Clock" by Bill Haley and the Comets if they got far enough into the music so that this didn't seem impudent. Wavy Rufus suspected very little about pop culture would annoy His Majesty. He seemed trendy, in his odd way. Wavy Rufus said, "While we wait for Effert, Majesty, I think you might enjoy what is called the Rock music. It's said to be revolutionary."

"Most considerate," said Freewill. "And we can talk," said Laddy. There was the pop of a wine cork. "I am hoping, Rufus Broadsword," continued Laddy, "that you can tell us the true nature of rock'n'roll."

Kidnapped!

NEAR MIDNIGHT, in the downpour, Gracie busied herself overseeing the attendants as they carried Effert's body, sedated against the pain, from a side door of the Manor toward the three waiting sedan chairs. She didn't dare turn her back, lest Effert disappear again for thirteen years. He was back now, and nominally hers, even if damaged. But Gracie wasn't about to quibble with fate. Holding umbrellas over the body, the attendants lifted the stretcher into the rear of the first of three sedan chairs the Means had put at the disposal of the Broadsword party, Cedric's single vehicle being much too small for Effert's stretcher (not to mention all his friends). Gracie climbed in after Effert. Europa followed. The surgeon the Means had provided then attempted to follow. Europa snarled him back out. Bianca stood patiently outside the door beneath two enormous umbrellas—one held by a servant, the other held by Verbunko—explaining to the surgeon that her mother was a licensed nurse and could easily care for the patient until they reached Broadsword Hall. Without a word to Verbunko, but with one curious look, Bianca then climbed into the sedan chair. Verbunko backed off with the surgeon. The three women shook off the water, sighed individually, then sighed as one. They hugged each other. Gracie rolled down the window on her side, stuck her head out into the rain, and yelled, "Uncle Cedric! Let's go! Now!"

Cedric cringed, letting his umbrella slip for a moment, getting a face full of water. He pulled his dinner jacket tighter about him, nodded to Gracie. Never had she been so angry with him; never had she said such awful things; far worse than Effert himself had ever dared. But what did she expect from him? That he welcome Effert back as if nothing had happened? Bah! thought Cedric, the injustice of it, being made the heavy here. Cedric slipped his silver flask from his coat, uncorked it, swigged, swigged again, corked it, and slipped it back, before turning to Abbott and the Florentine Stalinist, Bonaventuro Pellegrino (who insisted upon accompanying the Contessa's mother), saying that it was time to get in.

Abbott protested anew. He didn't want to leave, as the ball was good business, the Archery Contest was about to begin, and the dancing would last half the night. Cedric very calmly told Abbott he wanted his whole family with him, so please get in the sedan chair. Abbott exploded:

"Why should I do anything for that child? He deserted all of us, not just you. I have worked hard for five years to learn how to run the firm. It's all that's mattered to me since mother died. But you didn't know that. All you care about is the Hall and that silly drunken woman. You think she cares about Effert? She has a desperate need for romance, that's all. She's never going to be happy. Look at her so-called friend, the Contessa, a society witch of the sickest variety. Those two are willful and unscrupulous. They're using you, Father, and you don't see it. I do. I love you, and I'm trying to protect you from their manipulations. They don't care how hard we work for what we have. Why should they? Neither of them has ever worked in her life. I work hard. You work hard. We fight to keep the Hall, the firm, to keep from drowning in that morass that comes in over the phones, the wire, and the ball. Could those two girls do it for one hour? Could Effert? Of course not. Does Effert even give a fig for you, or me, or the Hall, or the firm? Of course not. Him on his dreary charger, that's all he ever wanted. A hippie dreamer, an impractical fool, a selfish, petty, insincere brat. I'm not impressed by his independence, his so-called 'time in the wilderness.' Or his quest. Why should I be? Quest for what? He doesn't know. He has no purpose. He lacks a point. He's getting older, and more self-destructive, that's what his behavior this afternoon means. I belong, Father. He doesn't. Make your choice." With that, Abbott turned away and hunched over in dejection.

Cedric stepped to his adopted son, reached out to place his arm on his shoulder, and said, "I have two sons now." With that intimacy, Cedric and Abbott climbed into the sedan chair. Bonaventuro Pellegrino followed. Cedric rolled down his window to wave back to Swinyard & Schleppend, who had asked to accompany their bosom buddy, Effert, back to the Manhattan Island.

"What do you think of Abbott?" said Swinyard, waving to Lyra, who dashed from the Manor to the third sedan chair, where Swinyard helped her in.

"I never would have believed it," said Schleppend, who waved to Yella Kissl, who also dashed from the Manor to the sedan chair, where Swinyard helped her in. Swinyard & Schleppend then climbed in. The caravan of three opulent sedan chairs—driven by Means pros—moved slowly away from the Manor into the private roadway system. "I don't

agree with *nada* he said. Like the all-American way he said
it, though. Maybe these California dudes got something
under the paste. You think he's got a point?"

"Nah. Just the Establishment breathing hard," said
Swinyard. "Notice they do not raise voices or fists. Talent."

"Meanwhile, Herr Swinyard, we could use some of
it," said Schleppend, "if happens what I think is about to
happen."

"You mean if Verbunko's got our number?" said
Swinyard.

"He's got that. You see what they did to Effert, and
that boy was in shape," said Schleppend. "Only question
now is how long we got before the goon squad telephones
us."

"How far can we run?" said Swinyard.

"How fast is what I want to know," said Schleppend.

"How much time we playing with?" said Swinyard.

"Oh, Mama, could this really be the end?" said
Schleppend.

"To be stuck inside the Means machine," said Swinyard.

"With the Righteous Blues again," said Schleppend.

"Hey," said Yella, "you telling what's the double-
talk?"

"Ssh!" said Lyra, finding the radio panel, fiddling until
she came upon WHIP-FM, hearing an unusually anguished
tone in the otherwise very mellow voice of the legendary DJ
Winnie-the-Fool (for Love), riding the overnight airwaves,
now into a rap:

> . . . and I'm tellin' you this thing's got me strung
> out. We can't find it in our system. Please stop
> calling the station. We are on it. Man here just got
> off the line with the head dude at the FCC. He
> says every radio station in the tri-state area, maybe
> more, is having the same hassle. We didn't do it.
> But I'm worried. Sure there's a mean storm out
> there, but that shouldn't matter. I mean, I read
> books. And this is precisely the way it's supposed

to go down when those dudes Vonnegut met from the planet Trafalmadore, or what have you, come down. Radio interference is the number one UFO. Wow, now I've said it. We don't need this grief. If it wasn't for the bug in the system, I'd play something right now, and cool out this nonsense. What! What! Oh, yeah? Dig this. Man here just told me he was on the line to his buddy at a radio astronomy lab in West Virginia. The word is that this interference is being investigated by scientists. Intense! Excessive! And it's nonsolar, which means, I think, it's not sunspots. Okay, maybe I'd better play some music. Play with your bass. Cut down the . . . (snap-crackle-pop) . . .

"Far out, huh?" said Lyra.

"How high are you, Herr Swinyard?" said Schleppend.

"Not nearly high enough to think this," said Swinyard.

"Maybe there's help for us yet," said Schleppend.

"Do we need that kind of help? said Swinyard.

"What are you talking about?" said Yella Kissl.

"That radio interference," said Swinyard.

"The comet," said Schleppend.

"Those guys in the woods last night?" said Yella Kissl.

"Comet Incarnate?" said Swinyard.

"Maybe even 'Harold Starr'?" said Schleppend.

"You're crazy!" said Yella Kissl.

"I think it's neat, don't I?" said Lyra.

The four fell into a tense silence. Swinyard & Schleppend leaned their worried heads against the cool glass on opposite sides of the sedan chair to watch the rain and the wide stripe along the road zip by. Lyra rolled her lovely head of wet kinks back to watch, through the rear window, the hypnotic mass of power lines zip by. Yella Kissl rolled her lovely head of wet curls back, and would have watched the power lines if she hadn't noticed something unusual. She noticed they were not returning to the Manhattan Island by the popular route—trunk road to the Long Island Freeway straight into the city—but instead roared through the rain on a private road that wound up and down, right and left, through a menacingly thick pine forest bending before the torrent to reveal, now and again, through the breaks in the groves, swirling surf to the left. Yella Kissl concluded they must be driving along the North Fork shore of the Long Island. But if they were headed back to the city, shouldn't the surf be on the right? She started to say something, but was interrupted by Schleppend yelling, "We forgot Wavy Rufus! He's still back there waiting for Effert!"

"Poor old baby," said Lyra.

"We've gotta go back," said Swinyard.

"No, not wise," said Schleppend.

"Oh, yeah," said Swinyard. "Not wise."

"He's out there alone. We must," said Lyra, sitting forward to pound on the glass separating the driven and the driver. The driver ignored her. She reached for the intercom.

"Is there something you're not telling me?" said Yella.

"Well, Yel, it's like this," said Schleppend.

"This guy won't answer me!" said Lyra, pounding, beeping.

"What?" said Swinyard, turning to discover the Means chauffeur was indeed ignoring Lyra. In fact, far from stopping, the sedan chair accelerated, taking a sharp curve to the left, toward the sea, that sent them all sprawling and squawking.

"About your question how much time we got," said Schleppend.

"Yeah, I hear you. No time," said Swinyard.

"Enough! Enough! I want facts!" said Yella Kissl, buttonholing Schleppend in her best White House versus Capitol Hill manner. Look out! They tumbled over each other again as the sedan chair powered over a rise, then left, then right, slowing as it mounted a wooden wharf—the bumpity-bump of boards beneath as the caravan of three opulent sedan chairs moved past pylons and bait shacks. The sea air, the pounding surf, the merciless rain, all such sensations joined in Schleppend's mind to lead him to conclude:

"We're not going back to the city."

"Don't stall with the trivial. Facts!" said Yella Kissl.

"Here's the dope, then, straight and fast," said Swinyard. "We fought the Means, and the Means won. We thought maybe we could get back to the city before the sky fell in."

"And the sky fell tonight?" said Lyra.

"Not just yet, but bad, very bad," said Schleppend.

"Can we deal?" said Yella Kissl.

"Not this time, but," said Schleppend, assuming his noblest posture, "maybe they won't mess with you and Lyra. They want to damage me and Herr Swinyard, for sure, for last night—we saw ORACLE. That means they probably want Effert as well—maybe more. Right! That must be it! Herr Swinyard, first chance, we're out of here. Don't worry, Yel, we'll come back for you. When we can. Here." He paused, removing the wad of winnings from the Cross-Country Race (Effert paid off at 20 to 1, since he'd carried Tory across the finish). "You take half. Do what they tell you. Do some fast talking. Feign everything. Listen for bugles."

"Lyra?" said Yella Kissl. "Get this line."

"Stand by your man!" said Lyra.

"Sister, we speak the same language. Listen for bugles, ha!" said Yella Kissl.

"Now, Yel, don't get political now," said Schleppend.

"Here we go," said Swinyard, meaning their jeopardy was upon them. The caravan purred to a halt before a heap of lights and shadows, which, when examined closely, could be seen to be a ferry rocking at its moorings, its mouth yawning open, prepared to gobble up the three sedan chairs. Swinyard tried the door, surprised to find it unlocked. That's right, the Means didn't lock doors. They were that sure of themselves again. Swinyard paused momentarily, shaken by the futility of this. Oh, well, he thought, give it that funky Yale try. Come the Revolution (of the comet)! He cracked the door open, signaled to Schleppend it was flight time. Yella reached forward to draw the curtains, lest the chauffeur spy their escape. Schleppend gave her a kiss on the cheek as he dove through the door. Yella shook her head. He wasn't about to escape her as easily as he escaped the Means. She broke off the heels of her shoes. She dove through the door right after Schleppend, too quickly for Swinyard to stop her. Lyra, also breaking off her heels, followed immediately. Swinyard, alone in a sedan chair moving slowly up a ramp, thought to grab the lap blankets and a flask of gin, then plunged out the door as well. Crash! He'd waited so long he was half on the ramp, half dangling over the surf twenty feet below.

"Who goes there!" boomed a voice from the ferry deck above. A search beam cut through the rain to play along the ramp, sweeping over Swinyard's dark form. Thank you, Mommy, he prayed as he hung there, for forgetting to pick up my white dinner jacket from the cleaners. He pulled himself up, then rolled on his side, over and over, down the ramp. He hit the wharf with a thud. He lay there waiting for a 7.62-millimeter bullet to cut a swathe through his ambitions to leave law for his own rock'n'roll label. It didn't happen. In shock, Swinyard stood on wobbly knees and fought his way through his own fear down the wharf, one step two, looking for peace of mind. He found Lyra on all fours looking for one of her contact lenses. Swinyard picked her up, threw her over one shoulder, and churned on.

"Psst!" from the side.

"We give up!" said Swinyard.

"This way!" said Schleppend, grabbing his partner, leading him by the hand down a staircase from the wharf. They nearly tumbled when Yella Kissl jumped them from below—so excited she'd run the wrong way. Lyra screamed to be set down. The four charged onto the sand, without even considering the sea monsters, bottomless pits of quicksand, and other large-jawed horrors attendant upon beach walking past midnight. They fled pell-mell, finally turning inland, out of the water into the dunes, thrashing through the undergrowth, on and on, holding each other's hands now and again when the rain blinded them to all but the rocks before them. They ran until they couldn't run anymore, so they walked, then waddled. Lyra yelled for a halt. Swinyard insisted they reach the cover of the forest ahead. But Schleppend knew the women were exhausted, and that if they tried to spend a night without shelter in this storm there'd be no tomorrow. He scanned about for an answer. There! A shack. He pulled them toward it. They crashed against its locked door. Swinyard kicked through a window. They pulled themselves inside. It leaked. It smelled. It was heaped with nets, traps, and other abandoned-looking fishing materials. It did, however, contain enough kindling for Swinyard to build them a small fire on the sand and gravel floor. Schleppend pulled out oily tarps to cover them as best he could. The girls tucked each other into the lap blankets. The boys tucked each other into the gin flask. Around and around went the flask as the fire filled the shack with a semblance of warmth and hope. Not until the crackle of damp wood matched the whine of the wind outside did they dare conversation.

"I smell like a dead fish already," said Yella Kissl.

"Are we going to die?" said Lyra.

"Kidnapped!" said Schleppend, "They kidnapped the Broadswords!"

"Let's pray this hut's above the water line," said Swinyard.

"You mean we might drown!" said Yella Kissl.

"I can't swim in cold water!" said Lyra.

"Nice going, Herr Swinyard. More?" said Schleppend.

"Calm down, everybody. We're gonna be fine," said Swinyard.

"Sing us a song, Lyra," said Schleppend.

"I can't stop shaking," said Lyra.

"Let her flip out in peace," said Yella Kissl.

"Come here with me, Lyra," said Swinyard. "Better?"

"Do you love me lots?" said Lyra.

"Lots and lots," said Swinyard.

"How about you?" said Yella.

"Give us a kiss," said Schleppend. "Anybody got any ideas?"

"We could sleep," said Swinyard.

"I'm too scared," said Lyra.

"And stinky," said Yella Kissl.

"Tell us a parable," said Lyra.

"Me?" said Schleppend.

"Yeah, Mr. Listen-for-Bugles. A parable," said Yella Kissl.

"What kind of parable?" said Schleppend.

"A gin-swilling parable," said Swinyard.

"That kind of parable?" said Schleppend.

"Please, please, please?" said Lyra.

"All right, but not gin," said Schleppend, producing from his vest a little plastic box containing six fat, funny cigarettes. "I'll tell you a doper's parable."

PARABLE PAUSE

THE BIRTH, THE CRIME, THE PEACE, AND THE TRIUMPH OF THE STRAW PEOPLE (1968–1978)

PART THE FIRST

THE BIRTH

BY LEVIATHAN STRAUSS AS TOLD BY SCHLEPPEND

BY Bastille Day 1968, it was clear to exempt observers in the West that the Revolution wasn't coming well in America, the land to which the *ancien régime* had once upon an irony advanced a cash sum against royalties. Of course, things were not all that grand in Paris either, what with DeGaulle cutting bait, throwing Pompidou to the red wolves, launching battalions of *flics* against philosophy majors who concerned themselves a little too much with how their barricades would look in the film Jean-Luc Godard would certainly dedicate to their martyred comrades. But then, in the Old World, fashion predicates fascism just as bulls predicate bullshit. Not so in the New World, where fashion rests exclusively in the manicured hands of the sexually inert. And the Revolution in America was nothing if not a sexually charged affair. Everybody was packing erections, some of flesh and some of iron. It was strictly shoot first and call a press conference later—call it Caliber Crit. January '68 had not only shot off *Surveyor VII* (eyes and ears for Apollos to come) to drop onto Luna near Tycho Brahe's crater, but also had reopened Washington's Ford's Theater, where the first salvo in the war on Yankee imperialism was fired in the spring of 1865. February '68 had shot off General Giap's Tet Offensive in Vietnam, of course, with the Marines up in I Corps (off the 17th parallel) mucking an impossible assignment, that is, retaking Hué's tactically meaningless Citadel pint by pint: see the childlike Marines die, see the olive-drab body bags heap. March '68 had shot off a mixed bag, such as Robert McNamara out of the Pentagon (the first long-range score for Tet); then, testing a secret spy plane, Yuri (Captain Russia) Gagarin out of the sky, splat; and finally, Lyndon Baines Johnson (imposed by gunfire so deposed by gunfire) out of his mind, the month ending with some heavy foreshadowing as LBJ, too late, copped a plea: "I shall not and will not

accept the nomination of my party as your Chief Target."
April '68 first shot off Martin Luther King, whose death
triggered some weird firefights in Washington, the question still open as to who called in the napalm off Pennsylvania Avenue; and then shot off a megaton bomb half a
mile below the Las Vagas Bombing and Gunnery Range,
it not being clear if they got the message in Hanoi that
what goes down a mineshaft can just as easily go down
a bombsight. May '68 had shot off the Vietnam War
Peace Talks in Paris, Averell Harriman hyping reactionary
reason, Xuan Thuy and Madame Binh (code name: "Victoria Charlotte") hyping reasonable reaction, while outside the Majestic Hotel, across the river, the red flags
flew, the barricades grew, and the Latin Quarter made of
nothing new much ado. June '68 shot off Bobby Kennedy,
three times, bam-bam-bam, watch him die on the pantry
floor, the word out that it was open season on open
mouths. So to July '68, everybody still packing their erections, some of flesh and some of iron, but cool now, no
sense calling down those ballistics. The smoke cleared
momentarily. Body counts were, as always, misleading. In
Vietnam they called casualty reports "SWAG"—stupid
wild-ass guess. In New York City, they called casualty
reports "heinous." Very different things, if you are concerned with semantics, which nobody seemed to be.
Rhetoric was in ascendance. Reason was in eclipse. The
erections, remember, everybody was aching with erections, looking for something to f——. Candidates
abounded. F—— the White House; f—— the Pentagon;
f—— the Commies; f—— the VC; f—— the Peaceniks;
f—— the hippies (especially the hippies); f—— the Constitution; f—— the blacks; f—— the Jews; f—— the Enlightenment; f—— Jane Fonda (a.k.a. Barbarella); f—— Paul
McCartney's double; even f—— Donald Duck. There were
no rules to this game. Still, alas, alas, if all you need is ass,

the Revolution in America was in trouble. None of the above solutions seemed adequate. What was needed was something so bizarre, so beyond-Disney, that not only would they be unable to write novels about it for decades, but also they would never truly realize why it felt so good but hurt so bad once the major players had long since retired to Texan ranches and Manhattan co-ops to write their memoirs and to greet the Reaper. What was needed was genuine self-disgust. To best the Devil, you must become (sort of) the Devil—an old dictum, resurrected one more time from the romantic ruins of feudalism. It was the season of the nasty f——. There could be only one nasty f—— that would waste everybody packing erections, and waste them regardless of annoying considerations of right or less right, or wrong or less wrong.

"America," said the Revolution, "go f—— yourself."

By Bastille Day 1968, the Revolution in New York City, though innately convinced of the strategy of urging America to f—— itself, was in a state of confusion. Ever trigger-happy, some revolutionaries had drifted into triteness out of sheer exuberance. The balmy weather could be blamed, but the deeper fault was disorganization. True, the dope supply was excellent, with blockade runners dashing onto the island from as far away as California's Air Force bases, where they'd picked up certain olive-drab body bags (from Danang, AFB, Vietnam) full of Thai dynamite—take yer head off. And, true, the airwaves were partially liberated, with WHIP-FM, Metromaniacal Radio, in its first year, playing those cosmic sounds, especially the Dead, the Fish, the Doors, the Animals, the Who, the Kinks, and even (then) the Stones. But the troops in the front lines were shell-shocked by the mail (particularly the hate letters in the *Crimes*), in need of a little direction.

There were very bad people in the land. Some had names: Johnson, Humphrey, McNamara, Rusk, Westmoreland, Abrams, the entire staff, down to the mail room, of the SS (Selective Service). And though some of these very bad people were huffing in their infamy, there were new very bad people on the march. Some had names: Nelson Rockefeller, Richard Nixon, George Wallace, Ronald Reagan, and Mister XYZ (whose name, so secret, was never revealed). The Revolution needed a plan to go up against such foul legions. In particular, the Revolution in New York City on Morningside Heights—defined as the thirty blocks north of the Thalia Theater, west of parks and east of the Heartland—was a mess of motives. The Strike at Columbia University in April/May had radicalized folk haphazardly. Elitists are inconstant revolutionaries by nature; their recruitment must be done guilefully, respectful of the thought in their heads that if this civil war doesn't go down right, one can always split to Dad's beach house in the Hamptons, et cetera. What was needed on Morningside Heights—if the Revolution was to address itself to the Long March ahead—was not Spring Fever transformed by newspaper headlines and final exam panic into knee-jerk trespassing, but serious, dispassionate, and brutal agitation. America was so ripe for f——ing itself that all that was required was the suggestion of stimulation, not assault and battery. The major lesson of guerrilla warfare is that one should never use a bomb when a bomb threat will suffice. In occupying those few buildings at Columbia University, the SDS (Students for a Democratic Society: and therein lies more irony than might be possible to plumb), though unquestionably committed to troublemaking, had committed tactical self-fragging. The occupation itself became so huge an issue that it smothered the profound issues, such as imperialism, capitalism, slavery, and murder. Worse, Columbia University

251

open for action was a hotbed of hotheads, many of whom could be cajoled into worthwhile revolutionary acts; but Columbia University shut down was no use at all. Might as well be Neanderthalic Princeton or Cro-Magnon Yale. School out, the kiddies trundled home, lost to summertime indolence. Nothing could be done to garner media hype of (looks like) outraged radical cadres until the fall. Moreover, while Columbia was open, it was possible to terrorize the likes of President Grayson Kirk by urinating on his desk, defecating in his drawers—exactly the sort of theater that makes history interesting; or it was possible to terrorize the likes of the *Crimes* editorial staff by suggesting that if you can spell "iconoclasm," you don't know what it is. But with Columbia shut down, the "pigs" had the summer to regroup. The Revolution had to go looking for new battlefields. And it still needed a Plan.

Which was, in effect, the only item on the agenda of a very unusual, very secretive conference scheduled for the late afternoon of Bastille Day 1968, in an expensive (for the Upper West Side) townhouse just off the Great White Way. The townhouse was mottled brown. The townhouse had a view of other townhouses and, obliquely, the Hudson River. The townhouse had five floors, four bedrooms, three telephone lines, two permanent residents, and one entrance. It was furnished unevenly, some rooms lavish with antiques and Pop Art, others shoddy with butcher block and motorcycle parts. The townhouse had a lease signed by "Torrance Means VII." Consequentially, the logo on the air conditioners, kitchen appliances, television sets, stereo equipment, and the two English racing bicycles parked in the front hall was that of the "Means Corporation." The names on the engraved plates attached to

252

the seats of the racing bikes were, respectively, "Christine Means" and "Justine Means," both Barnard College students, class of 1968, and, not incidentally, identical golden twin daughters to Torrance Means VII.

The guests for the very secret conference (the dramatic details of which one can now only surmise, fictionalize) started arriving past 4 P.M. It was withering outside— 98.6 degrees all afternoon—so the downstairs maid, Ruby Monday (whose recollections more than ten years later provided the only firsthand evidence of this scene), had turned the air conditioning to polar levels. Each time a new guest was escorted from her limousine into the swelter of the city and then up into the Means townhouse, she turned as blue on the outside as she seemed on the inside. Ruby Monday had her small rebellion against the ruling class. By 5 P.M., there was an icy and elegant crowd, bluebloods all, in the library. They sprawled uneasily around a long oaken conference table cluttered with a year's worth of periodicals—including several copies of a garish new tabloid, *Kong Weekly*, vol. 1, no. 1—and two years' worth of antiwar propaganda. The only sound to be heard other than the swish of chiffon was the Mozart on the sound system, for the guests, though they might have recognized some of their number, certainly could not have known each other to chat. Sad to concede, there is no guest list to be found, and the identities of the gathered, aside from a few good guesses, will remain forever apocryphal.

At 5 P.M. precisely, the grandmother clock chiming the moment, Christine and Justine Means are said to have swept into the room from the secret panel door. They wore wooden sandals, comfortable blue jeans, faded blue workshirts, light makeup, and several tasteful items of jewelry, such as turquoise and silver bracelets, rings, necklaces. Their white-golden hair was extremely long and silky over their shoulders. As ever, more beautiful than mortal, they are said to have appeared strangely older than their twenty-two years. Behind them trooped four ladies-in-waiting hefting stacks of looseleaf notebook reports. The conference began quietly and earnestly. Howsoever, its major substance seems irrecoverable, the tapes either destroyed or left too much in the open ever to be found. Needless to say, though one must, none of the participants has ever reported of the particulars of the discussion. It is only possible now to deduce the conclusion of the affair.

There is some certainty, though, with regard to the themes at the birth of the Straw People. The question at hand was, Why are we still in Vietnam? The immediate goal sought was, What is to be done? The immediate priority was, Who is to do it?

After several hours of what must have been informed though languid debate, in which everyone in the room must have had an opportunity to sniff in approval or disapproval at everything said and everyone who said it, with regard to a wholly novel plan for the Revolution in America, Christine Means once again took the floor, saying:

"What my sister and I propose has considerably more risk than the solutions you have shared with us today. Tom Hayden's rebellion might succeed. Jim Morrison's solipsistic indifference doesn't need to succeed. David Eisenhower's Republic already exists. Daniel Berrigan's awakening, is, by definition, imminent. Thomas Pynchon's enigmas provide the innate comfort of paradox. And Julie Christie's insouciance charms all. What we propose combines all these recommendations, but not in a stable formula. It will place all of us in great personal as well as mythical danger. We call ourselves the 'Straw People.'"

"As in straw?" said Julie Nixon (she was certainly in attendance).

"Yes, yes," said Christine. "Straw People as in straw men. A weak, fictitious force constructed ostentatiously so that it might easily be confronted, criticized, castigated, and even vilified by all observers. The Straw People. We here, and many, many others—hundreds of thousands of us, and millions more who would pretend to be what we are. All of us daughters of the zealous American Revolution. Well born, well educated, well funded, well loved, and well pleased. The Straw People."

"What will you do once you've organized?" said Julie Nixon:

"We are everywhere. You are us," said Justine.

"We perceive the American civilization as well as most," continued Christine. "Our fathers, our brothers, our husbands, our sons—all of them our issue—they own the American civilization. We would therefore guarantee the American civilization sincerely. There are two means to our end. We choose the Revolution. We choose to foster the Revolution flagrantly. Our solution, then, is to avoid ultimate solutions. Our dogma is to avoid dogmatics. Our tactic is to proceed tactlessly. We, the Straw People, will do nothing."

"But how can nothing be a plan for Revolution?" said Julie Nixon.

"Opulently, fabulously nothing," said Justine.

"Nothing," confirmed Christine.

(to be continued)

The Comet Clubbe

SWINYARD, first awake, surveyed the scene, estimated their chances as abysmal as the weather outside the leaky shack. It still poured, though the gray light indicated the sun shone somewhere high above the storm clouds. Swinyard checked his push-button watch. It was near noon. They'd escaped the Means for ten hours, though at any moment he would not be surprised to see Means troopers crash through the door brandishing pistols and doom. Swinyard listened for helicopter blades, dune buggy engines, the baying of hunting dogs. He heard Lyra moan.

"Ooo," from Lyra, in Swinyard's arms.

"It's true, all of it, I swear," said Schleppend sleepily.

"Herr Schleppend! Wake up!" said Swinyard.

"Have they got us yet?" said Schleppend, snapping to attention from a dopey dreaming. This wasn't Studio Beefcake. He listened for helicopter blades, dune buggy engines, the baying of hunting dogs, and, in addition (being Jewish, more of a historical pessimist than American Lutheran

256

Swinyard), pistol cracks. "It could be a lot worse," concluded Schleppend.

"I'm hungry," said Yella Kissl in Schleppend's arms.

"This place have a toilet?" said Lyra, awake now.

"Exercise! Exercise!" said Swinyard, leaping up.

"Here," said Schleppend, producing two chocolate sweetmeats—one Mars bar, one Halley's Comet bar (a reconditioned Milky Way)—breaking them in half and distributing.

"You told me you were off them," said Yella Kissl, grabbing.

"Gimme," said Lyra, bouncing up to join Swinyard stretching, soon joined by Yella and Schleppend, each of them in turn moving behind the heaped nets and traps to evacuate what they could of their despair. And so preoccupied were they with their fretting that none of them heard the door open slowly until the forester—lean and intense, his longbow and quiver of cloth-yard shafts over his shoulder, holding a bundle of foul-weather gear in yellows and reds—was upon them, saying:

"Good morning! Good morning! Good morning!"

"We give up!" said Swinyard, grabbing Lyra close.

"We know nothing!" said Schleppend, buckling his pants.

"He's no Meanie," said Lyra, pointing to the obvious.

"Isn't that . . . ?" said Yella Kissl, pointing to the obvious.

"Haven't we met before?" said Schleppend. "You jumped us?"

"This time, I introduce myself as Grandtour, Captain of the Comet Clubbe," said Himself, Grandtour, once upon a time, under another name, a precocious engineering student who'd taken the dream for what it had seemed, thrown in his lot with astrophysics and aerospace sciences, first to obtain prestigious degrees, second to obtain prestigious appointments with the National Aeronautics and Space Administration, and third, in brief, to be rewarded for fifteen years of obsessive dedication to America's space program—

at the sacrifice of his family, his career in private industry, his mental health—with a pink slip, services no longer meaningful, good luck living the rest of your life with a broken heart.

"You serve the comet, correct?" said Swinyard timidly.

"Affirmative," said Grandtour.

"So, uh, what can we do for you?" said Schleppend.

"For me?" said Grandtour, laughing, throwing the bundle of foul-weather gear at their feet. "It's me for you."

"He's kinda cute," said Lyra, covering her lensless eye.

"Trust him," said Yella Kissl to Schleppend.

"You haven't seen an army of goons?" said Swinyard.

"They passed over you riding dragons just past dawn," said Grandtour. "Very professional. This storm protected you. Why are they searching for you? The comet again?"

"Dragons?" said Yella Kissl to Schleppend.

"There he goes with that comet," said Swinyard.

"All right, hear me out," said Schleppend, who, hesitantly, told Grandtour what they knew of their kidnapping, starting with Effert, then to Gracie, Cedric, Europa, Bianca, Verbunko, and finally to "Harold Starr."

"What about 'Harold Starr'?" said Grandtour excitedly.

"That's all we know," said Schleppend.

"Isn't there anyone else? So close! There must be," said Grandtour.

"There's Wavy Rufus," said Lyra to Swinyard.

"The mathematician! He's not taken?" said Grandtour.

"I, uh, I don't think so," said Schleppend.

"Can you help him? He's all alone, poor baby," said Lyra.

"Get dressed, quickly. Follow me!" said Grandtour, spinning to the door and charging out. The four conspirators looked at each other. Yella Kissl made the first move. She snapped up a foul-weather coat and hat, pulled on the sea boots, saying:

"*Mishugenah* or not, I'm with him."

"Ask yourself," said Schleppend, also pulling on foul-weather gear, "what's the alternative?" Soon they were all dressed, peering out into the storm. There was Grandtour, halfway up the slope to the forest above the dunes, beckoning them to come along, which they did, silently, in the gusting rain, thunder and lightning above as they trudged in the mud and weeds below. Grandtour set a ferocious pace, which did not slow as they entered the dark forest, pine trees swaying rhythmically. It might have been romantic, if it hadn't been so scary. Swinyard & Schleppend tried to comfort Lyra and Yella after each thunderous rip—"kerPow!"—but words were drowned with all else as the rain pounded them in sheets. Suddenly, Grandtour called a halt, pulling a rusty motorbike from beneath a bush, ripping open its saddlebags to produce a loaf of hard bread and lumps of cold cheese for the conspirators. They ate while Grandtour reburied the motorbike, upon which he had followed them the night before as the Means kidnappers had driven them northeast of the Manor to the sea. Now they had to walk back, for the side roads were sure to be closely watched by the Means pros pursuing the escaped four. Wordlessly, they were off again, deeper into the forest along a thin but clearly defined animal track. The conspirators struggled heroically, but after several hours of sloshing and stumbling, with the little light above fading as evening approached, they had managed only half the distance to the Manor. Grandtour called another halt, ordering them to collapse below a towering, thickly skirted white pine. He used his knife to fashion a cozy waterproof shelter over them. He flung down his pack, producing more bread and cheese, and then, saying, "Friends, I shall be back before total dark," was gone.

"You don't suppose he won't?" said Yella, tearing the bread.

"This was your idea," said Schleppend, tearing the cheese.

"Grandtour, he says! Captain of the Comet Clubbe, he says! Whatever that is," said Swinyard.

"I still think he's cute," said Lyra.

"He's cra-a-a-zy," said Schleppend. "Like us, for following him. The Means wouldn't have tortured us." He groaned as he removed his sea boot to find his blisters. The others found even uglier blisters, torn and bleeding. They washed them as best they could in Swinyard's gin. Schleppend passed a funny cigarette to numb them to the damp and wind. They cuddled, two by two, and soon found some peace in uneasy sleep. See them there, four souls dreaming as one of deliverance, as the day passed into evening, as the evening darkened to another stormy night.

"Hello!" called Grandtour of a sudden.

"Baby, he's here," said Lyra, nudging Swinyard in her arms. Lyra sat up to rub her eyes, then covered her lensless eye to study the figures gathered before the lean-to. She counted eleven, five on one side of the pine, six on the other, all dressed in foresters' tunics and breeches, all hefting quivers of cloth-yard shafts and longbows, all smiling politely.

"Stretchers, Grandtour?" said a large, broad man. Grandtour nodded. The big man waved to the others.

"What's this? Grandtour?" said Swinyard, sitting up.

"We will make hammocks for you," said Grandtour, squatting before them on a toadstool. "We must push on to the mathematician. I have him under surveillance now. The Means have not taken him. But they will find him before morning."

"Who, uh, Herr Schleppend?" said Swinyard.

"My men?" said Grandtour. "The Comet Clubbe. I am Captain."

"I'm never gonna know what I died for," said Schleppend, sleepy.

"We've told you the truth," said Swinyard.

"Affirmative. I copy," said Grandtour, bowing his head, then looking up sadly to begin his tale by dangling the Freedom Medal he wore around his neck, awarded him by Richard M. Nixon in 1971 as a member of the ground crew at Houston Control who'd brought the crippled *Apollo 13* spacecraft home against all probabilities. Grandtour let Lyra touch it, then said that he was seventeen years old when the National Aeronautics and Space Administration and Council (NASA) was established in 1958, headquartered in and completely beholden to Washington, D.C. He had a childhood, a mother, a father, and a future. All things had seemed possible. He'd dreamed of starships a thousand miles long, of hyperdrive, and of glistening galactic empires spilling exploration teams into the cosmos. Truly, he'd told his comrades, as he'd swept through seven years of higher education, two years with North American Rockwell's aerospace division in the old L.A. bomber plant, before shifting to NASA at the Jet Propulsion Lab as a member of COMPLEX (Committee on Planetary and Lunar Exploration), Descartes had been thinking of space adventure when he'd said, "There is nothing so far removed from us to be beyond our reach, or so hidden that we cannot discover it."

"Fortunately for the generations that followed Descartes," continued Grandtour, "the old Jesuit never heard of congressional committees bullied by party henchmen, of Pentagon lobbying, of the American political phenomenon called 'priority funding.' Otherwise, there might not've been Cartesian philosophy. The Democrats wouldn't have funded the telescope, copy? They preferred territorial wars, public relations about civil rights, and submarines. Useless tin tubes full of bombs. What sense is a bomb? When I think what we could have done with an R&D budget worth half the maintenance on their stockpile of bombs. But no, we were expendable, whereas the Vietnamese plutocrats, they were 'priority.' My starships became interplanetary spaceships by one-niner-six-seven, when Grissom, White, and Chaffee cooked on the pad as a direct result of desperate economizing—sacrificing quality for results. By one-niner-six-niner, all we had were space shuttles. Glider planes! We told Agnew in one-niner-six-niner, at the moon launch, that we could have orbital space stations around the Earth and the moon, and a lunar base, and a Mars base, and all by one-niner-eight-six. This year! He grinned. The next thing we knew the White House canceled our budget. The dream was gone by one-niner-seven-two. I don't dream at all. I have nightmares. I hope you understand when I tell you that archery helps me sleep. These arrows are the only projectiles I have left me. What could have been! We could have done anything! Do you know what they keep me to do at Grimmen? I design lounge cars for rocket trains. Choo-choo! Trains!"

"You poor baby," said Lyra.

"And your men? The same?" said Swinyard.

"We are poor, ma'am," said Grandtour. "But not because we have no money. What is money? All the money of the Means could not buy back the wasted years when we could've been building a space fleet. We are poor, oh, yes. Outlaws, because what is the law to men without meaningful work, without families, without purpose? We have nothing. We do nothing. Except, of course, wait for the comet."

"The comet, yes, the comet," said Schleppend, fascinated.

"The Comet Clubbe," said Grandtour, gesturing. "Once engineers of our fate, now passed over by all fates save the fantastic. Each of us twelve, without earthly identities, waits for the comet in his own way. There . . ." he continued, pointing to his men, sketching their bios. "Ranger, who tinkered for General Dynamics until joining NASA for Project Ranger, the early moon crashers.

"And Orbiter, a tailor's son, a Zen-microelectronics genius who quit North American Rockwell's Mach-Three bombers for Project Lunar Orbiter, first circling the moon in '66.

"And Mercury and Gemini, one a flight mechanic off the Korean War's U.S.S. *Essex,* the other a fighter pilot off the same, both joining NASA as ground personnel at Cape Canaveral for the early manned rides.

"And there, Apollo, our sun-kissed ingenue, who was crew chief for a B-52, before joining NASA to be there, twenty-one January 1967, to burn off his fingertips trying to get Grissom, White, and Chaffee out of that billion-dollar oven . . ."

Grandtour broke off for a moment, his deep anger choking him. He recovered to run through the rest—Surveyor, Skylab, Mariner, Voyager, Pioneer, each named for a canceled NASA project, each inconsolable in his grief at what could have been. Of note, all had brushed with the splendor of the Apollo program before being transferred to the Mars project (which was never named) and then terminated, heartbroken.

"Then there's me," said Grandtour. "I co-designed the never-built Project Grand Tour. Imagine our thrift—one vehicle to tour Saturn, Uranus, Neptune, and Pluto, perfectly aligned as they would not be again until A.D. 2150. And they robbed us! They tried to buy me off with Houston Control, but I was a troublemaker. I told the truth! They dumped me on the Mars project when they knew it was a ticket to termination. The crime!"

"The Comet Clubbe," said Schleppend, shaking his head.

"Who could've guessed?" said Yella Kissl, amazed.

"A lot of people," said Grandtour, "most of whom are long retired to their Junior Chamber of Commerce power bases playing bad golf."

"Ready now, Grandtour," said Mercury, meaning the hammocks for the conspirators were finished. Lyra and Yella were slung. Swinyard & Schleppend elected to walk awhile with Grandtour, asking questions. The party moved out in the storm, with only their sense of the forest to guide them. The pace was again ferocious, and soon Swinyard & Schleppend had to retire to the hammocks. They stole over roadways, grassy tracks, manicured golf courses, and marshy lakesides, staying as much inside the forest as they could, reaching the woods around Means Manor just past midnight, and the granite incline above the "Wonder" van an hour later, where awaited the twelfth and final member of the Comet Clubbe, that is, Viking: taciturn Greek stock, son of an exiled Communist guerrilla, graduate of Amherst and MIT—the aerospace genius here—joining NASA as a member of Werner von Braun's brain-trust team, always in the VIP crowd watching launches from the Cape, then back to his charts, personally shoving Project Viking until Congress bought it as a publicity stunt for the Bicentennial, *Vikings 1* and *2* on the surface of another planet perfectly, keeping alive in men's hearts, if not in their billfolds, the ill-fated Mars project—never named—which he alone had to terminate with a memo to his staff, he being asked to stay on at HQ, but drinking, fuguing, until his termination, heartbreak.

"We have contact," said Mariner to Grandtour, meaning that Viking was at the head of the column.

"Down, then," said Grandtour, "we're coming up on T plus one minute, Stay–No Stay." The party collected beneath several pines. Viking crashed through the bushes to ask:

"What's our status?"

"We're going in for the mathematician," said Grandtour.

"Nothing in or out since fifteen hundred," said Viking.

"Copy," said Grandtour, turning to Schleppend behind him. "Will you go down with me? He knows you."

"We'll all go with you," said Swinyard, getting Lyra and Yella Kissl from their hammocks, joining Schleppend next to Grandtour.

"We must hurry, my friends," said Grandtour. "We have a ninety percent probability that the Means will have a security sweep through here when the rain abates."

"Say no more," said Schleppend, waving to Yella, Lyra, and Swinyard to follow. Schleppend had had time to ponder the Comet Clubbe now. He believed he understood them. They were middle-aged hobbyists, like mountaineers or motorcyclists. This was merely a club, like veterans of foreign wars or domestic elitists, except that these twelve grouped not to encourage business contacts but to keep each other from depression. Nostalgia for NASA was more their enemy than their theme. Like Schleppend's daddy, Mort, and especially like Swinyard's daddy, Ingmar—both of whom had reached young adulthood just as the world burst into Fascist flames, obliging them to commit their imaginations forever to the mythology of *"c'est la guerre,"* regardless of how profoundly different the world became after the Third Reich fell to a Hollywood hype—these twelve men, the Comet Clubbe, had reached young adulthood just as Jack Kennedy (himself shaped by wartime fairy tales) had committed NASA to space adventure with the words "This is a new ocean, and I believe the United States must sail on it"; and having pledged themselves to sailing the ocean black, these twelve couldn't readjust to political sea changes that made their talents seem quaint, their imaginations seem childish. The Comet Clubbe was their treehouse. And so what if they carried bows and arrows and frolicked with eagle feathers stuck in their caps? He thought of Laurel and Hardy at the Sons of the Pharaoh conventions, or Ralph and Norton at the Raccoon meetings. They were certainly no funnier to look at than the New York Athletic Club. Schleppend assumed they all worked at Grimmen Aircraft. That would explain their antipathy toward the Means Corporation, corporate overseers of the Long Island's largest employer. The Comet Clubbe's gamboling in the woods was weekend recreation (though it was Monday night, so why weren't they home?). It was true that Grandtour's talk of the comet was suspiciously flaky. But then Schleppend had learned years before, when first he'd taken money for lawyering from a business community anxious to put sixties dissent and seventies regicide behind, that corporate America abuses serious minds into defensive games better played than analyzed. Since when, for example, had professional sports encouraged rationalism when a championship loomed? Modern times had no reasonable games, just fetishes and fevers. The Comet Clubbe seemed, to Schleppend, acceptable zaniness. Schleppend reasoned it wise to play along with Grandtour until he could fashion a more discreet plan. Not to forget, Herr Schleppend, he thought, that Aaron Verbunko himself, evil sorcerer of a technocratic realm, is on to you.

"Huzzah!" cried Schleppend in his confusion.

"This is a Go situation," said Grandtour beside him.

Schleppend sighed more deeply at that. Grandtour was truly spacey. He talked funny too. The five of them reached the "Wonder" van. Schleppend hugged Yella. Swinyard hugged Lyra. The remaining Clubbe members gathered in the near distance. Schleppend looked at Swinyard, who nodded exhaustedly. Schleppend said, "Wavy Rufus? Are you there? It's me, Effert's chum."

"Who's there?" said Wavy Rufus from inside the van.

"Schleppend," said Schleppend, "and the, er, Comet Clubbe."

"Is that you, Effert?" said Wavy Rufus.

"No, not Effert," said Schleppend.

"Don't say that!" cried Swinyard, but too late, for the "Wonder" van's rear door clicked open and swung out on its hinges. Then the sky fell (almost), Swinyard & Schleppend and Lyra and Yella Kissl screaming as one as four enormous speakers, 400 watts per channel, flattened them with 120 decibels of the Who—Daltrey screaming:

Yeaaaaaaaah . . .
Meet the new boss!
Same as the old boss!!!

The Rescuers

LYRA ROLLED over, still holding her ears. The ringing was shallower now. She would live. She sat up in the mud. There was a giant foot beside her, attached to a giant leg attached to a giant man, standing over her, in dark robes, bearded, unfriendly. He had his arms crossed as if on sentry duty outside the open door of the "Wonder" van. Lyra tapped Yella Kissl next to her. Yella, holding her nose up to stop the bleeding, looked once to see the giant. Why not? She looked past the giant to the open door of the van to spy a dwarf standing in the light of a single candle inside. The dwarf was talking. Yella couldn't hear him, her first clue that she was momentarily deaf. She fainted in Swinyard's lap. Swinyard felt Yella slump on him. Automatically, he reached to cradle her, seeing the giant nearby as he did so. He giggled. He was high on sound, a sensation he hadn't had this badly since the last of the heavy metal concerts at the Garden. He cocked his head. There was a dwarf in the van. Swinyard giggled again. The giant reached down toward him. Help, thought Swinyard. But no, the giant reached past him to lift Schleppend toward the van.

Schleppend had regained his senses by the time the giant deposited him in the van. Still, he was numb. He staggered to a seat atop a speaker. He assessed the scene. Here was Wavy Rufus apologizing tenderly for his error. Here was Grandtour detailing the events of the past twenty-four hours in pithy declarative sentences. Grandtour gave the most thorough debriefing Schleppend had ever witnessed. Whatever else, Grandtour had a flair for facts. And here was a dwarf dressed in dark robes, bearded, carrying a walking stick. A dwarf? thought Schleppend. Perhaps I'm not recovered just yet. He leaned back on the Who poster, realizing there was yet another figure in the van, opposite Wavy Rufus. The giant was bizarre. The dwarf was absurd. But this third—fabulous. He was the most casually extraordinary man Schleppend had ever seen. He had a majestic air of election. Lyra would have said, "heavenly." He was dressed in dark robes, like the other two, his hood pulled forward, so obscuring all but his long nose and the spread of his beard and hairline. Indeed, his most distinguishing characteristic was his hair, which seemed, even in the dim van, the color of stellar flares. Schleppend stared harder. Just then, Grandtour shifted in the van, momentarily cutting off the light of the single candle falling onto the third stranger.

Schleppend gasped. The man glowed in the dark—not obtrusively, but distinctly. Should I be frightened? thought Schleppend. I don't feel scared. Schleppend spied an empty bottle of claret at Wavy Rufus's elbow, dated 1910—a French claret. Before Schleppend could groan with shock, Wavy Rufus asked him a question.

Outside the van, Swinyard had recovered enough to see to Lyra and Yella Kissl, with the assistance of Surveyor and Apollo. He thought to ask how much longer they'd be out here in the rain. What he and the women needed was drying out. He ambled to the back of the van, pulling himself in just as Schleppend—sounding very shaky—began a description of their kidnapping, Swinyard looked about the now crowded van. The dwarf was to his left, also listening intently to Schleppend. Swinyard studied him, because he'd had a prep school roommate who'd suffered the same birth defect—achondroplastic dwarfism, where the head and trunk grow generally correctly, but the limbs remain childlike. Swinyard had an abiding affection for folk so malformed. Swinyard didn't want to remember his roommate's tiny coffin. He smiled down at the dwarf, who smiled back. Swinyard looked past the dwarf. There was another man back there Swinyard didn't recognize. He seemed to glow. Uh-huh, thought Swinyard, where are you when we really need you, Effert?

"And one other thing," continued Schleppend, who was tiring of repeating himself so trying new material. "I forgot to tell you, Wavy Rufus, in the woods Saturday night, about the *Viking Three* dummy that Means has for a desk. I didn't think it mattered, but . . ."

"Viking! Report!" called Grandtour.

"Hey, take it slow, Grandtour," said Schleppend, surprised.

"Ready for copy," said Viking, hopping into the van.

"He says Means has the *Viking Three* mock-up," said Grandtour.

"You were right, then," said Viking. "That confirms."

"Confirms what? Hey, Grandtour, explain," said Schleppend.

"We've often wondered what happened to NASA's hardware and software after obsolescence. The Means bought it," said Grandtour, "or at least there is a fifty percent probability that the Means Corporation acquired enough of it."

"Enough of it for what?" said Schleppend.

"At this time, we have insufficient data," said Grandtour, "for me to answer that completely. We were hoping the mathematician could provide us with additional data. He says he cannot. He says that Effert Broadsword has the information we need. A notebook."

"That's my notebook," said Swinyard. "What's important?"

"We are the Comet Clubbe," said Grandtour gently.

"Please, Mr. Grandtour," said Wavy Rufus, "you are among friends. Can't you explain with more clarity?"

"We serve the comet, or, at least, we'd like to. We're spacemen," he said.

"So?" said Laddy of a sudden. "How is it you know of the comet?"

Swinyard's & Schleppend's mouths gaped open. That voice carried several lifetimes' worth of wisdom and patience.

"As I've told you," began Grandtour, "we are veterans of the best team of spacemen ever assembled. But now we work for the Means Corporation, at Grimmen Aircraft. In general, none of us had touched a space vehicle for years until an odd project we were assigned to three years back. That's how we met. They put us in the same auxiliary shop. The project was supersecret, of course, and they didn't give us very high clearance. But there was a rush. They'd fallen behind schedule. So they recruited us for backup and gofer jobs. Even still, they took our work from us each night, just like wartime security. Many of us complained. A few of the more troublesome disappeared. We stopped complaining to the foreman and stuck together. We knew enough to realize

that we were working on on-board systems for a space vehicle, perhaps many space vehicles. We were relatively happy,
until the schedule went brutal early last year. They imprisoned us until completion. It was because of the hurry-up
that security got sloppy. I was the one who chanced upon
the photograph of the tablet, and a translation."

"What kind of tablet?" said Wavy Rufus.

"A Mesopotamian tablet," said Grandtour. "Babylonian actually. Just half of it. It concerned a rebel named . . ."

"Mar'zi'pan," said Wavy Rufus, holding his chest.

"You know about this?" said Grandtour.

"Continue, continue," said Wavy Rufus.

"Copy," said Grandtour. "Mar'zi'pan's tablet explains
that 'hairy stars,' or what we call comets, are, in fact, revolutionaries. They visit the Earth as men. Mar'zi'pan was such
a Comet Incarnate. And he identifies one of his companions,
who he hopes will come and revenge a failed rebellion which
he has led against Assurbanipal of Assyria. Interpolating the
Babylonian astrology, the companion he refers to is the
comet we call Halley's Comet. Who is called Majesty, by the
way, since each Comet Incarnate is said to be sovereign in
his realm."

"This photograph," said Wavy Rufus, "the Means
have it?"

"Affirmative," said Grandtour. "It was part of an appendix of a Grimmen Aircraft study for the Means Corporation."

"So the Means know of the comet too?" said Laddy.

"In a manner of speaking," said Grandtour. "I would
doubt if they believe the tablet, though. It was an appendix.
That's how projects proceed. All the available data, without
bias, are fed into the computer. The computer then weighs
the data to produce responses to inquiries as to what can and
cannot be done. It's how we did it at NASA, and we were
the best. The Means probably assembled all data pertinent
to comets for their project, which they called 'Harold
Starr.' "

"So!" said Laddy.

"But what is 'Harold Starr'?" said Wavy Rufus.

"We have insufficient data," said Grandtour.

"But you must know. You say you're the Comet Clubbe," said Wavy Rufus, frustrated.

"We are," said Grandtour. "Waiting for our . . . Majesty! We serve him. You might not understand this, but we are spacemen. This planet doesn't mean anything to us anymore. It doesn't want us. We are spacemen. The Comet Clubbe!"

"I didn't mean to offend," said Wavy Rufus. "Please accept my profound apologies, Mr. Grandtour. It's just that, well, I too serve the comet. And what you have told me upsets me very much. There is something ominous and dreadful about what you say is part of 'Harold Starr.' Please, if you can, try to tell us more. Any little thing you recall."

"Copy," said Grandtour, nonplussed. "Along with the translation of the tablet there was mention of an expedition in 1910 by the Rockefellers."

"Ah! I should have guessed," said Wavy Rufus to Laddy apologetically. "There are no secrets from such evil men."

"Brother Grandtour," said Laddy evenly, "you have mentioned your work on a space vehicle. What was its intention?"

"An ion drive space vehicle," said Grandtour, "approximately ten thousand kilograms in total mass. We know we worked on at least one such spacecraft. The weight is mostly fuel, of course. A thousand-kilogram spacecraft mass. A two- to three-hundred-kilogram payload. Smart and clean, with an on-board computer, and an on-board computer terminal link to Earth. Spacecraft power is solar electric."

"Ion drive, I'm sorry?" said Wavy Rufus. "Does this mean, for instance, that it could rendezvous with the comet?"

"Viking?" said Grandtour, turning to the Greek.

"We can say with fifty percent probability that this spacecraft, or these spacecraft, has, or have, a capability of rendezvousing with the comet and landing on the comet," said Viking.

"Landing on the comet?" said Wavy Rufus. "Why?"

"The probability dips to thirty percent of a return flight from the surface, however," said Viking.

"But what purpose?" said Laddy.

"Yes, why? What is 'Harold Starr'? Why?" said Wavy Rufus.

"We have insufficient data," insisted Grandtour.

"There is a ninety percent probability that this spacecraft, or these spacecraft, is, or are, part of 'Harold Starr,'" said Viking patiently.

"But you agree with me," said Wavy Rufus. "You do believe that 'Harold Starr' is hostile to the comet? To His Majesty? That's why you seek the comet, yes?"

"We are the Comet Clubbe! We despise the Means! The Means own Grimmen. 'Harold Starr' is bad science! We must find His Majesty and warn him! Come the Revolution!" cried Grandtour.

"Of the comet," mumbled Swinyard, sighing deeply.

"We need more data, sir, in all respects," said Viking.

"We will be in a better position to answer your inquiries once we speak with Effert Broadsword," said Grandtour, recovering his calm. "That the Means have taken him is surely a warning light."

The "Wonder" van grew eerily quiet. Swinyard stood holding his head, lest it overflow with the incredible. Schleppend sat against the wall, also holding his head, and his fantasies as well. He didn't want to do any guessing yet. He wanted to watch the stranger in the corner, who'd not been introduced, who'd sat motionless throughout the exchange between Wavy Rufus, Grandtour, Viking, and the dwarf. Schleppend wanted to hear him speak, thinking that hearing his voice might confirm a suspicion he had that was unimaginable under any other circumstances save those coming together tonight in the rain in the woods surrounding Means Manor, late April 1986. He thought, too, that he might still be tripping on the rock blast. Please, dear God, thought Schleppend, let it be in the music. Or did he really want it to be true?

"Effert Broadsword, then," said Laddy. "It seems to come down to him. Where might he have been taken?"

"Do you know, son?" said Wavy Rufus to Schleppend.

"What? Oh, no, no," said Schleppend. "Herr Swinyard?"

"Me? No, no," said Swinyard.

"There is one location with a ninety percent probability," said Grandtour. "Two others with fifty percent. Below that, an assortment."

"Yes, yes, the ninety percent?" said Wavy Rufus.

"The Means Corporation maintains a fortress retreat deep within Everpine Forest," said Grandtour. "A European structure they had transported overseas in the early part of this century and rebuilt, stone by stone. It has family significance. It is guarded by dragons and the masterless fire."

"Do you mean Craven Castle?" said Schleppend, befuddled by Grandtour's eccentric terminology, swinging between feudal syntax and NASA jargon.

"Meansylvania!" said Swinyard.

"Yes, Craven Castle," said Grandtour.

There were more declarations, interrogations, and exclamations, but the course was determined. It was agreed that Effert Broadsword and company had been taken to Craven Castle, deep within Everpine Forest. It was agreed that by rescuing Effert Broadsword and company from Craven Castle, more information ("data") might be obtained with regard to the true nature of "Harold Starr." And it was agreed that all present, plus the Comet Clubbe, plus Lyra and Yella Kissl, would join the quest to Craven Castle, deep within Everpine Forest. Notably, all these matters were determined with a minimal amount of anguish and ambivalence, which would have been impossible had all those present been normal, mortal, and understandable adventurers. They were not, however. One of their number was a Comet Incarnate. And this Comet Incarnate settled their qualms at once, when, sitting forward just before daybreak in the storm outside, he urged them to prepare for the trail with the simple (yet philosophically complex) sentence:

"Over the side, lads." Then he let down his hair, and they knew him.

Book V

*Wherein the Proto Industrial
Trust Conceals Its Plan
for Conquest*

Craven Castle

THERE WAS a time, before the plague of American turpitude, that a great pine wood covered the western Atlantic seaboard, from the tip of Newfoundland stretching across the Gulf of St. Lawrence through the Appalachian mountains onto the Atlantic coastal plain to the very edge of the Florida Keys. It was, according to the diaries of the pilgrims fleeing Europe's degenerate monarchists, an utterly sublime forest. Verdure was its color, and it knew not time, as evergreen as it was evermore, its aroma so powerful that folk strolling quarterdecks fifty leagues at sea could scent the pinegreen. And these were not ordinary of the pine nation, as can be had for cheap in the landscaped twentieth century. No, these were trees touched by the munificence of the forest primeval, so that their needles were as sharp as quartz, their cones as ballooned as guillotined heads, and their bark as tough as the Pathfinder. North American Indians, who were yet unapologetic savages, squat and fratricidal, without bronze, called the pine nation absolute and left it alone—in deference to its magical suzerainty—to

conquer field and mountainside. The pines themselves—
genus *Pinus* in Foul Rome's tongue—followed tribal rites.
There were the prolific softwood white pines, who, along
with the occasional refugee from the West (the giant sugar
pines, the long-lived foxtail and bristlecone, the edible
piñon), lived gentle, virginal lives. There were the diffident
firs (balsam, silver, red, and white) who were said to reserve
the best of the fallow settings for their naked cousins, the
larches. There were the cedars, proud relatives of the trees
that served the monomaniacal fleets and monotheistic tem-
ples of the Levant. There were the learned spruces, ever shy
and high-minded, with their even-grained wood ready-
made, by God the Father's hand, for the commodity with
which all noisy iconoclasts fight the despots—paper, of
course, God gave them paper to tell the Truth! And there
were the warlike hardwood pines as well: the gigantic red
pine; the jack pine for paper; the pitch pine, seemingly ill
fashioned, but ruling the rudest soils; and the yellow pines
of the Southland (longleaf, shortleaf, loblolly, slash), good
for bridges, railroad ties, and burning crosses—though this
underside not the yellow pine's fault.

The pine nation, then, once absolute ruler of the
coastline which came to be, through politics and revolution, the thirteen colonies of Mother Britain, soon, through
more politics and revolution, the thirteen states of mother-
f——ing America: this pine nation to fall victim to the advance of agrarian civilization. Sadder still—though there
were chroniclers to mourn passing of the red man's nation
—there were never any novels to bid fare-thee-well to the
passing of the pine nation. The unsentimental *colons* just
hacked. White pines went for the colonial manse. Firs
went for the colonial barn. Larches went for the colonial
fireplace. Spruces went for Ben Franklin's *Weltanschauung.*
And the hardwood pines went for plows, muskets, and
statecraft. The single most important resource of young
America was its forest, not its soil. The pine nation built
the Philadelphia hall, fashioned the furniture for that hall,
protected the birds whose feathers made the pens used in

that hall, and warmed the chambers of that hall, where men who called themselves revolutionaries made a nation, 1776–1789. It is more true than it is fanciful, though it is fanciful, that the idea of the Republic of the United States of America grew first in the glens of the great pine nation, and second in the hearts of Tom Jefferson and company.

Perhaps, then, the fall of so much wood can be justified in terms of liberty, fraternity, and equality. Judgment seems superfluous here. The question remains: what good is a state that must make a plain (not a desert) before it makes a peace? Peace was had, but at the terrible cost of the pine nation. The copses fell to cities first, Savannah to Boston, then to communities along river valleys, Connecticut River to Savannah River, and finally to the push of road systems, settlers chopping up the wood even as the soldiers charted it. The nineteenth century was one long slaughter. By 1900, there was only a remnant of the Northeast's virgin white pine, only a remnant of the whole pine nation, north and south. Instead of verdant glens, there were sylvan metropolises. Instead of verdant hollows, there were sylvan farms. And instead of verdant mountains, there were sylvan logging camps. In despair, the pine nation called a full retreat from the double-bladed axes of men who, claiming to be politically conservative, approved the defoliation of a continent. Eventually, an equilibrium was established, though it was actually a devastation. Coal and oil replaced wood in the furnaces. Brick, stone, and iron replaced wood in the architecture. The early twentieth century brought a truce. The remnant of the pine nation gathered north of the Allegheny Mountains, assessing what was left it. A decision was reached. Let the sickly, inconstant broadleafs entertain man in his sickly, inconstant abodes. The pine nation would regroup in valleys too cold and rugged for fragile *Homo sapiens.* There, the pine nation would plan for its return, fathering ever-sturdier strains, mothering ever-heartier cones. But, most important, there the pine nation would mourn its felled children. A tree with every reason to rejoice its design

—green, proud, stalwart before wind and storm—turned to sad matters. The pine wood became a melancholy forest. In its last redoubt, this living forest wept. Without the need to be vengeful, it chose to remember and to regret. Thus, and ever thus, Everpine Forest.

North of the Allegheny Mountains, then, north of the Catskill Mountains, the Taconic Mountains, the Green Mountains, the White Mountains, north even of the splendid Longfellow Mountains, the Everpine Forest reigns over diminished but not diminutive lands. And it is here that this adventure now moves, deep within Everpine Forest, east of the Atlantic, north of the Longfellows, west and south of the St. Lawrence River. This is as exact as one can be, for it is impossible to keep one's bearings once within the grip of Everpine Forest. The greens are too deep, the pine carpet too thick, the pine-draped ponds too clear, the passions too overcome by the vanity of the last redoubt of the pine nation. Soft woods and hard, cedars and firs, spruces and larches, and even the unjustly maligned hemlock populate the valleys and plateaus, the glens and lakeside lanes. Everpine Forest is a place where there is no true space. Everpine Forest is an idea. To get there, one must believe in Romance.

One particular path through Everpine Forest is of interest, winding down from a mountain, through a series of sharp cliffs, falling onto a flat, broad meadow, proceeding snake-like through a pass opening onto a lakefront, around this lake into the cover of the trees again and then, suddenly, out of the trees onto a trestled pine bridge over a waterfall and up, up, at a sharp angle, cutting through a cliff edge to the flat top of the most peculiar high rock in the area, atop which sprawls the Means Family crest come to life—a five-towered, pentagonal castle atop this sinister plateau. Below: a dark and deep lake spilling over the waterfall to disappear into the tributary system of the St. Lawrence. All about: the forest thick and thoughtful as far as the eye can see, farther than the mind's eye can imagine. And above: Craven Castle.

In its original setting in Lincolnshire, Craven Castle dated from the second generation of Norman warlords scuffling for power in Saxon Britain. Its walls had comforted —and maddened—dukes and lechers, bishops and assassins, and the occasional happy man. The unending combat in Lincolnshire wore it down, however, so that, by the Renaissance, only two of its original five towers remained. The civil wars reduced the castle more, until taxes and fashion abandoned it to slow disintegration, scattering its stones about the moors. So it remained, a forgotten ruin, until those American cousins of the defunct Craven family, the Means, reached out with their wealth and hubris to gather the stones, blueprint the plans, and remove the concept of Craven Castle to North America, deep within Everpine Forest.

There was nothing extraordinary about its design— high, thick walls with toothed battlements, guardposts, bartizans, and palisades; drainage pipes ending in grotesque gargoyles; five towers, each shaped differently, reflecting the original haphazard construction of the castle. The two most forward to the gatehouse were roundish with overhanging, windowed turrets. The next two were squarish, unfinished-looking, with exposed stones. The rear tower was taller than the others, with a richly carved exterior staircase winding around its sides from the top turret down to disappear in the walls. Even the bailey, or courtyard, was ordinary, serving now as a parking lot.

What gave Craven Castle its unmistakably ominous presence was something other than its parts. During daylight, the forest animals kept clear of its walls and the walls of the high rock. At dusk, Craven Castle didn't seem to reflect sunlight. This seemed to worry the pine nation, so that its trees seemed to lean away from the castle, groves growing permanently bent back as if from the epicenter of a blast crater. At night, Craven Castle was blacker than the night, and yet seemed to radiate an evil heat.

One other aspect should be noted. Craven Castle was

not haunted. It was not filled with inhuman wails past midnight. It was not even uncomfortable, fitted, as it was, as a retreat and hunting lodge for the Means Corporation and VIP guests. Craven Castle was, however, garrisoned by a company of professional soldiers—mercenaries on permanent call to any part of the far-flung Means Family Empire. Their heliport filled the bulk of the plateau atop the high rock. When not on duty, in harness, armed as a light infantry strike force, these professional soldiers served the Means as custodians and bodyguards. Craven Castle was their headquarters. Craven Castle was said to be impregnable. Craven Castle was where the Means had Effert Broadsword and his company taken—kidnapped, imprisoned, and helpless in a fortress retreat deep within Everpine Forest.

Captives

A T THE beginning of the fifth week of captivity, at luncheon, Cedric lost his temper over the temperature of the soup, and thrashed a guard into the corner. Abbott and Bonaventuro—cellmates with Cedric in the squarish tower to the left center of Craven Castle—tried to pull him off before either damaged the other. Presently, half a dozen more guards arrived, muscling the three captives into separate parts of the largish, whitewashed, room. The captain of the guard, Westergaard, swept in. He was short, broad, gray, and correct, speaking three languages passingly and one language, violence, loquaciously. Truth to tell, Cedric liked the man. Abbott was indifferent. Bonaventuro

Pellegrino thought him typical of capitalism's "Fascist" military.

"Another escape attempt, sir?" said Westergaard.

"If it was, I wouldn't be here now," said Cedric.

"What can I do to make you relax?" said Westergaard.

"If you were in my position, what?" said Cedric.

"Point well made, sir," said Westergaard.

"The soup was cold," said Cedric, flinging off a guard.

"It shall not happen again," said Westergaard, nodding to all three, waving his guards out. "For your information, sir, I have made inquiries to my superiors. It still isn't possible for you to visit Miss Thyme. Was there anything else you'd like me to investigate?"

"A good place of refuge," said Cedric.

"Threats again?" said Westergaard.

"I will have my satisfaction," said Cedric.

"Yes, sir, good day," said Westergaard. The door whomped shut behind him. Cedric, Abbott, and Bonaventuro returned to their meal.

Abbott, obviously annoyed, asked, "Why must you antagonize them, Father? For soup?"

"Very clever man," said Bonaventuro in the broken English he'd picked up from his cellmates. In five weeks, they'd become reasonably chummy companions.

"Aye," said Cedric. "Harass the enemy. Officer's duty."

"Your famous adventure in Europe was forty years ago," said Abbott. "Though I wonder if you ever really took off the ribbons."

"It would've done you no harm," said Cedric.

"It's gone," said Abbott. "And it derived from political circumstances impossible in the modern world. No informed person believes in your so-called nationalism anymore."

"You're beginning to sound like the peacenik," said Cedric.

"Father," said Abbott, cleaning his glasses.

"You're damn content for a man in chains," said. Cedric.

"We are not in chains. A misunderstanding," said Abbott.

"Misunderstanding!" said Cedric, dashing his utensils. "This? The Means will pay for this! Maybe I am old. But I know an enemy. I know how to fight. Your sophisticated politics, Abbott, perhaps that's just a way of making excuses. Life is not politics. I have done things I'm not proud of. But I've never murdered, and I've never broken my word. I give it now. I shall kill Means if one of my children is harmed. Regardless, I shall have satisfaction. We have been kidnapped by the private army the Means claim they keep to rescue kidnapped executives in foreign countries. An outrage! We have rights. They cannot do this with impunity. I shall see them in court. If that fails, I shall act."

"Bravo, bravo!" said Bonaventuro Pellegrino, raising his glass high in respect. Though he understood only a little, he sensed the defiance. Bonaventuro Pellegrino had been imprisoned three times before in his life, once by the *fascisti* for brigandage, once by the *Wehrmacht* for suspected partisanship, and once by the Christian Democratic party for inciting riot. He knew jail was hard for proud men like Cedric. He knew Cedric must rage to remain sane. It was the only way. This wasn't his fight, he knew. It was Cedric's. But he could cheer him on. Cedric Broadsword was an investment banker—a rascal and a pigheaded landowner—but he was also a father. He guarded his territory. "Bravo! Bravo!"

"Don't encourage him," said Abbott, walking away from them.

"I'm sorry, Abbott," said Cedric. "It's not you."

"I understand," said Abbott, who, truly, didn't understand. They'd had this same argument repeatedly over the last month. It always ended with Cedric indulging melodramatics, ignoring Abbott's explanations. This was a misunderstanding, Abbott was sure. Multibillion-dollar corporations didn't imprison loyal employees for no reason. They had done nothing wrong. Their "detention" was a mistake. It would surely eventually be corrected. Already the Means showed signs of relinquishing. Hadn't Abbott been permitted wires to New York? Furthermore, there was the possibility that the Means might not be responsible. The orders might be coming from elsewhere. Where? Cedric always demanded. From that Abbott repeatedly blanched, just as he blanched now. He retreated to the secretary in his room. He composed himself, took out the log he'd begun. The first few days had been puzzling but pleasant. Then Cedric had tried to bust out of the bailey, so their exercises had been discontinued. The restlessness of life permanently indoors showed in Abbott's handwriting, and in his supposing. The acronym "PIT" predominated in his log, perhaps because the unknown was a tempting scapegoat. It was unhappily true that Abbott Broadsword, though a highly paid executive in the Means Corporation, knew nothing substantive of the umbrella organization, the Proto Industrial Trust (PIT). He'd always assumed it was just a function of modern business techniques. Now, Abbott pondered other ideas. It seemed to him not even Aaron Verbunko would have dared the operatic arrogance of kidnapping American citizens unless he'd been forced by something more malevolent than stands idle puzzling. Something very big and very secret was on, confirming suspicions Abbott had had for over a year. There were only one hundred corporations in the world larger than Means. And what with interlocking boards, agreements, and interests—with the unwritten collusion between the Western bloc's business interests and the Communist bloc's business interests—there were only two dozen hypothetically independent organizations in the world. One of them was PIT. But PIT was a shadow, wasn't it? What was PIT? thought Abbott. Had the Means Corporation been backed into this indiscretion by a Byzantine affair beyond itself? Perhaps even beyond PIT? What was beyond PIT?

And so forth, Abbott pondered, freethinking as he

hadn't done since seminary. There was knowledge of God and knowledge of man, Abbott knew. His knowledge of God was as sketchy as the next man's. His knowledge of man was keener. He had always assumed himself well within his freeborn rights to engage in laissez-faire capitalism. Now he paused to reconsider. Does one lie down with wolves and expect to get up? Can there be justice for men who shirk philosophizing for obedience to Andrew Carnegie's "Gospel of Wealth"? Abbott Broadsword was experiencing a crisis of faith. Which might explain why he wrote in his log again the acronym "PIT," adding for no especial reason, almost by intuition, or by romance, the name he had casually mentioned to Aaron Verbunko at Gracie's ball that had precipitated an unsettling alarm in Verbunko's demeanor: "Harold Starr."

"Oh, no," said Abbott, dropping his pen, realizing what it means to be ignorantly innocent yet at the same time guilty of everything, by one's own words, no less.

Europa Stupefacenta had refused—tenaciously—to be separated from her charge, the badly mauled Effert Broadsword, and so Westergaard had been obliged to permit her to be quartered in the same tower—the squarish one opposite Cedric's—with the young Broadsword. The first fortnight was a struggle for Europa, since she felt the food improper for an invalid, and since Westergaard refused her request for a hospital bed. Europa, in retaliation, refused the castle's surgeon, accepting only his medicines. Europa knew enough of what was going on to despise the thought of a Means hireling touching her compatriot. She had a fierce sense of camaraderie, of course, a legacy of her anti-Fascist partisanship. What is more, she believed in returning profound favors tenfold. Effert had saved her at Broadsword Hall the night of the ball, when the Means thugs had pursued her relentlessly. Europa intended to nurse him back to health and then assist him to escape his jailers. And she would do it alone, if she had to. By the second fortnight, Effert was sitting up, mumbling through his wired jaw, trying to converse with a nurse who had only a few odd English words. The two improvised a code of sorts. By the end of the fourth week —Effert strong enough to exercise in the bailey—Europa and Effert had puzzled together, in code, the revelation that they loved each other in the way young, motherless men can love older, sonless women, and the way older, husbandless women can love young, wifeless men.

There was an additional, mysterious consideration for Europa. Once she'd set herself to clipping Effert's greasy locks, to shaving off his greasy beard and moustache, to dieting him to shed his excess poundage, to shaping him up in the manner a mother might tend an infant long neglected by nature and maternity, a new personality emerged— though it was really the old personality arrested these many years of adolescent indulgence—that Europa responded to shyly. Effert came to look younger than his thirty-eight years. He came to look like someone in Europa's murky past, someone she might have met at the close of the war—an American soldier? It was possible. Yet Europa's fancies came fleetingly, only when Effert's head was turned and relaxed. Once, she thought she saw something of Bianca's bone structure in his face, but she shook that off as the fantasy of a mother concerned for the safety of her only child. Europa didn't trust this part of her mind anyway—her fey-ness. It had gotten her into more trouble than pleasure in her youth, attaching herself to eager firebrands making rousing speeches to the workers on the banks of the Arno. Those silly boys, spouting Babeuf, Tolstoy, and Apollinaire, they had taken advantage of her affection for maverick temerity. Europa had put that behind her once Mussolini showed himself the tyrant. She had concentrated, instead, on her logical pursuit of peace, order, and justice in the world. She had joined the Party, broken her mirrors, and pulled on gray wool. No more speechifying, just hard work organizing, pamphleting, and marching, waving the red banner high. Indeed, she had been, still was, a romantic Marxist-Leninist. This could not be denied. She'd wept for Kirov. She'd wept for Kamenev, Rykov, Kinoviev, and Bukharin, when they were dispatched, in their turn, by a failure of nerve in Russia. She'd even wept for Trotsky, though secretly. If challenged about her romantic socialism, however, Europa would say, politely, that her sense of romance was only for dinner conversation with the capitalist warmongers she was obliged to charm in her role as mother hen of the People's Republic of Florence's pecking politics. She preferred to think of herself as cunning and antisentimental. Such a fiction served her well in sentimental Italy. Here, in the New World, with the wilderness draping everything so compellingly that the great monster himself, Stalin, would have been hard-pressed not to smile in the spring, Europa's self-estimation showed itself as contrived. She was only sentiment, had never been anything else, Jew or not, woman or not, Communist or not, correct or not. When Europa looked at Effert doing his sit-ups before the fire, late at night, just before bed, her nostrils flared, her heart thumped, and she recalled something warm and happy, long ago. What, or whom, she would never know.

For his part, Effert Broadsword thought Europa wonderful. She cared for him as he'd never been succored before. She mothered him, a novel experience for Effert, whose own mother, Elizabeth, or "Bess"—the much lamented Bess—had acted indifferently toward him the eight years he'd had her. An only child, he'd taken his mother's neglect casually. Effert hadn't realized how much his mother might have been for him until her Super-constellation collided with a Delta-constellation over the Grand Canyon and she was gone, a star-crossed casualty, falling one mile to the earth and another mile inside it. Effert could not now remember actual times when Bess had extended half the affection toward him that Europa gave just feeding him through his wired jaw. In four weeks in close quarters, Effert hadn't once thought of leaving her. For Effert Broadsword, this was amazing. His biographical theme, after all, was dropping out. He'd abandoned every endeavor he'd ever enjoined. He dropped out of childhood to situate himself four feet from television,

287

worshiping the Mickey Mouse Club, which many opine is the secret to the Counterculture. He dropped out of television when he discovered Cedric didn't mind his going to the movies, usually alone, though occasionally having to take along a plump, cousinish Gracie. He dropped out of schooling early, that is, he attended but did not participate, sitting in the classroom physically, somewhere in the nether reaches of romance philosophically. He kept his fascination with science fiction and swashbuckling to himself, lest he ruin his perfect do-nothing, think-nothing, know-nothing record. He dropped out of sports after the first practice of each sport, each season. He dropped out of teenage courting after an embarrassing indiscretion by a cheat implicated him in a lingerie theft. This interruption of his otherwise fetishistic but healthy sexuality was happily corrected once his appetite for hormones, his and hers, had turned on Gracie, from whom he would later drop out, of course. Yet he dropped out of Yale first, an impish act given that Cedric had purchased his son's matriculation in the Class of 1970 (a class so red that they were to be remembered in beer gardens with the phrase "Free the Yale 70!"). Once out of Yale, and out of the reach of Swinyard & Schleppend's SDS rhetoric, Effert dropped out of the Revolution, though Cedric never understood how slopping goat's blood on that especially timid Senator was a counterrevolutionary endeavor. It was, however, and this is an important, revealing distinction. Effert was only rebellious. He was never revolutionary. He countered, like a juvenile delinquent. He did not ignite, exploit, manipulate, or transcend. He had no politics other than selfishness, which is no politics. He was reflexive iconoclasm, not ideology. He was a premeditated dropout. His final leap, with Gracie abed mending from the miscarriage, with Cedric stalking the corridors of Mass. General swearing revenge, with the FBI distributing a poster to the effect that he was wanted for questioning regarding the violation of the civil rights of a United States Senator, with America on the brink of vouchsafing the most depraved war crime since the second war (the Christmas bombing of

Hanoi/Haiphong, December 1972), Effert needed only one look to understand that his life of irresponsibility seemed merely calisthenics for what was ahead. Effert dropped out of the twentieth century. He fashioned himself a crusader en route to the Holy Wars on the other side of the planet—their being on the other side of the planet their chief attraction.

One fey night, at the beginning of the fifth week of captivity, Effert pulled out an atlas from the bookshelves, offering to show Europa where he'd dropped out to those thirteen missing years. Pencil pointer in hand, Effert was childishly animated while showing off. Europa was more sober. She listened attentively, but like a concerned mother, not like an admirer. For an hour, he revisited six of the seven continents, but as he finished, Europa did not smile. She despaired. She had the measure of the man now. He had spent his young life a self-critical vagabond. Effert Broadsword was an unadulterated romantic, and, being so, punished himself for not measuring up to the romantic idea of himself. Europa had met this type before. Sadly, they were irresistible to sentimental women with spirit and brains. They were also unbearably inconstant. They substituted wanderlust for purpose. Rather than endure life's little compromises, they drifted from one fabulous circumstance to another. Eventually, too long the mysterious outsider by choice, they forgot what it was to relax and be accepted as citizens of Western civilization. Effert, for example, could no longer acknowledge anything less than the shimmery splendid. He'd reject anything of human proportions. Europa suspected he saw things larger-than-life or not at all. The "comet talk," then, she realized how foolish she'd been to believe his "comet talk" was rational. It was no euphemism for an uprising by the legendary Underground. It was no clue to a plot by the Means and their kind. That there was talk of something titanic and sinister was only a coincidence. Effert's fears spoke only to his own personality, not to anyone else anywhere. He had invented the "comet talk" to reinforce his eccentric sense of reality.

"Bedtime," said Europa in Italian to Effert. Effert

understood and nodded, shuffling off with his atlas in hand. Europa moved to the overstuffed chair before the fire. "Harold Starr," she said in English, and then laughed at her gullibility. But then, she thought, doubt stabbing at her heart, why am I here?

Gracie escaped three times in the first fortnight. She wanted her Effert, and no tower (the right roundish one above the front gate) intimidated her. They caught her on the spiral stairs. They caught her in the bailey. They caught her in the laundry off the postern room. Westergaard admired her pluck. He made a point of visiting her daily the second fortnight in order to discuss escape methods she'd not tried. Gracie cursed him, threw things at him, all of which amused him. She set to demolishing the furnishings. She smashed lamps, chairs, porcelain, beds, and bookshelves—emptying her four rooms of civilization. Westergaard had everything replaced as soon as she was done, no matter how many times she did it. Westergaard hoped to siphon off Gracie's energy for escape. Gracie knew she was being indulged like this, but continued. What is more, her hysteria lulled her keepers. She established a routine of a wild fit in the morning, two in the afternoon, and one at midnight—clockwork. In between, she sat at the windows overlooking the vast green of the forest below sketching escape capers on a pad Westergaard had given her.

Gracie reasoned she was in that chestnut of feminine predicaments: The Princess in the Tower. Rapunzel had let down her hair. Gracie's hair was too short and thin. Gracie's champion also was imprisoned across the yard. Worse, Gracie's momentary thought of climbing down on bedsheets, rug runners, or bunched drapery cords was abandoned when she estimated the drop at about two hundred feet straight down to the rock-strewn shore of the lake. Climbing up was equally impossible, for Gracie knew herself to be much too big to attempt catlike maneuvers on the parapets. "What would a princess do?" asked Gracie of herself, conceiving

several versions of a less than ladylike plan. She could seduce the guard, club him senseless at a critical moment, and
then away in his uniform. But even thinking of what she
should say to entice the guards (who, after all, did at least
leer at her when they brought in her food, carried out the
shattered furniture) made her tongue dry. It seemed, Gracie
realized, she had some innate sense of modesty—even virtue
—that ruled out erotic plots. Even her body balked, for the
very morning after she'd first thought of seduction as a
ticket to escape, she menstruated a week early. Abandoning
stealth and/or sex, Gracie, at the beginning of the fifth week
of captivity, decided to try trickery. She borrowed a routine
from Fielding, or perhaps Pynchon. She smashed two chairs
and a large leather couch to scrap, then made loud demands
to the night sentry to have this junk out in the morning. At
breakfast, Gracie repeated her demands, then slammed her
bedroom door, as if pouting. Actually, she hopped into the
gutted belly of the couch, pulling the chair hulks over her.
Soon, the change of the guard brought attendants who
removed the couch with her in it. They seemed not to notice
her extra weight. They wheeled her out on a dolly, down the
corridor, into an elevator, down, then to a halt. Gracie
waited a few minutes, then, hearing nothing, popped out,
only to discover they'd deposited the couch in the midst of
the horseshoe-shaped table that filled the Great Hall. Westergaard, his first lieutenant Murtrux, and several other
officers of the guard were at breakfast. They applauded her
as she straightened herself. Losing her temper, Gracie leaped
atop the table and savaged their food with her boots. They
laughed and laughed. In tears, she ran back to the portal to
the spiral stairs up to her tower, Westergaard and his subor-
dinates following her, apologizing for their bad manners.
Gracie slammed her tower door shut, ran to her bed to bury
her face in the pillows, weeping heroically. She suffered the
whole of the day. The attendants tried to interest her in
lunch, then supper, but Gracie wailed, all vanity gone. Her
life seemed to her one interminable frustration. She had
been frustrated in childhood by her orphaning and then

wardship to a portfolio estate (administered by Cedric) toward which she had marked indifference. She had been frustrated in girlhood by her athletic talent for horses. She had been frustrated in young womanhood by lost love and lost child. And now she was frustrated in mature womanhood from recovering what little opportunity she had left for true love, motherhood, and domestic bliss, by a series of gothic events that could not bear review. Her history seemed one of perverse reversal.

And what would you recommend, Mary Shelley? Should Gracie apply to Cedric for a pension, retire to Broadsword Hall to breed horses along South Street and fashion journals of Effert's wandering? And what would you recommend, Jane Austen? Should Gracie accept an arranged marriage with Abbott or someone of his ilk, and apply her energies to accepting her lot, uncurious of what might have been? And what would you recommend, Emily Brontë? Should Gracie resign herself to life without Effert, standing idly by while he consumed himself with more vainglory?

"Not yet, by God!" said Gracie, pounding her fists into the pillow. She looked up to discover it was twilight. She went into the living room, sneering at the food and wine (she had sobered herself up again). She flopped down in the window seat to watch the day end in the forest. The peace and beauty down there made her feel calm, if no less miserable. But then, without warning, she felt a new wave of tears coming on. A creak from the corner behind her caught her attention. She turned, the wall opened.

"Okay," said Gracie, trying to remain nonplussed in the face of a paneled wall swinging open to reveal a secret passage into the castle walls. Gracie walked over to stare. It was a secret passageway all right, two feet across and four feet high, in the wall by the main fireplace. Gracie even felt a gust of stale air sweeping up and over her. To enter or not to enter was the question.

If Gracie had been philosophical, she might then have returned to the window seat to ponder how much like geopolitical adventurism is a secret passage into an unknown tunnel. Would there be light at the end? Would it simply wind on itself to deliver the seeker, exhausted, back into the same maddening predicament as before? Would there be a bottomless pit at the end? What was an unknown tunnel? Was it life, a sophist might opine, all unknown tunnels analogous to the mysterious vagina into which and out of which life flows? Or was it a fool's game, since any passage worth exploring does not open up of a sudden, but introduces itself politely? Passageways! Tunnels! Vaginas! Black holes! And more! Thank the God who made her that all this wind was well above Grace Thyme.

"Here I come!" said Gracie, grabbing an oil lamp and stepping in cautiously, to the left, feeling her way along a stone wall. She was moving between the castle walls, the architect having built rooms within towers within walls. The wall ended abruptly at wooden steps, narrow and deep, plunging down to the right. She wiggled her toes in her riding boots as she descended all fifteen steps carefully to an earthen floor. She found herself in a low, wide, sloping tunnel. Down there was a dim light. She made for it, trying not to think of spiders and rats. It was an air vent. She heard voices she recognized.

"Word is we're due visitors," said Murtrux, the lieutenant.

"A job?" said Squelk, a sergeant of the guard.

"Word didn't say," said Murtrux.

"Them there?" said Squelk.

"If I was a gamblin' man," said Murtrux.

"You are," said Squelk.

"Since when?" said Murtrux.

"Tay Ninh? Santiago? Zanzibar?" said Squelk.

"Watch yerself. Just watch it," said Murtrux.

Gracie waited until they were gone. She had no idea what they were talking about, but she intuited imminent jeopardy. It was time to act effectively. She crept onward, thus fortified, ducking lower as the tunnel seemed to shrink. She heard a whining sound up ahead, so she went to her knees to crawl toward it, reaching a panel some twenty yards on. She pressed her ear against it and accidentally popped it in. It crashed with a bang. She stuck her head through to discover she'd chanced on part of the ventilation system. She worked her hips through and dropped down five feet. The shaft wound in a large curve, back toward the rear of the castle. It was lit every dozen yards by a naked lightbulb. She charged on, hoping it might take her all the way around the circumference of the castle to Effert's tower. Soon, however, the air shaft ended at a hatchway. Gracie unlatched it and looked through. Here was another passageway. She supposed now that the original builders of the castle had constructed a network of secret passageways, and that the rebuilders, updating the castle's power, heating, and ventilation systems, had used the network here and there for modern conduits. Otherwise, they'd left it alone. Gracie dropped back into the original network, moving to the left, hoping to continue around the walls. There was another air vent ahead, and more voices to be heard.

"Man sez dust off for Quebec in five," said a trooper.

"I'm not off duty for ten," said another trooper.

"Man sez be there," said the first.

They moved away. Gracie reasoned she must be near the barracks in the rear of the castle, off the postern gate, overlooking the heliport where they'd flown them in on May 1. That had been the last Gracie had seen of her companions, and of Effert. "May Day, indeed," Cedric had said in parting. Gracie sighed as she felt her way onward, bumping another protuberance. This was the fourth or fifth one she'd hit. This one she grabbed firmly and pushed, pulled, then lifted. The wall swung open. So this was how it worked. That meant someone had opened her wall from inside. But who? Gracie put that aside with all the other enigmas and looked through the open wall.

It was a men's clubroom. There was a darkwood bar. There were billiards tables, snooker tables, lounge furniture, bookshelves, and a walk-in fireplace. Above the fireplace was a plaque bearing the Means Family crest. The room seemed empty. Gracie edged forward, thinking there might be some way for her to stow away aboard that helicopter ("dust off?") leaving for Quebec. If this was what it seemed, an officers' lounge, then she certainly was near the barracks. Her chances for success were poor, but better than not trying at all. She took a bold step into the clubroom. Suddenly, she felt herself being watched. There were eyes on her. She shivered, spun around to confront her fate, then nearly choked swallowing her scream. "God!" she husked, almost collapsing. Above her was an enormous wall, twenty feet by forty feet, covered with trophies. Some of them were stuffed bear heads. Some of them were stuffed lion heads. Some of them were stuffed buffalo heads. Most of them, however, were stuffed human heads, grouped by race, yellow to the upper right, white to the upper left, black to the lower right, a mixed bag of Arabs, Jews, and Indians to the lower left. The taxidermist had done a neat job of patching the bullet holes and fixing the eyes, glassy and accepting. The mouths, though, were often half-open, in surprise. Gracie stood frozen. Here was American corporate policy, 1945 to present, but Gracie wasn't the sort to joke, "Live by your luck, die by the buck." How could anything be so vile? she thought. Westergaard and his men were more than hired guns, Gracie realized. She'd been a fool to regard them so lightly. They were high-priced villains. This was their idea of the regimental chronicle. (And yet, Gracie, it must be asked, who is to judge? If challenged, Westergaard and his men would say they followed orders. The men who gave those orders will say they followed orders. If pursued logically, this bureaucratic dodge will eventually offer the "people" as their own victim, for the will of the "people" gave the orders also. And aren't the heads just a dramatic representation of diplomacy? What would any war, civil or international, look like if reduced to a wall of stuffed heads? What is war? What is execution? What is murder? These and other ethical questions are meant to give pause to the self-righteous who would unblinkingly condemn the politics of falsehood. They might actually stop some folk. But not Gracie.)

"Devils!" she cried, jumping back into the passage-

way, pulling the wall shut behind her. She was panicked by
the hideousness of that room. She ran, missing two steps
down and sprawling forward in the dust, the oil lamp
smashing against a wall. Rather than explode and burn, it
snuffed itself out, leaving Gracie sweaty, dirty, tired, and in
the dark. She pulled herself up. She rejected turning back to
the clubroom, deciding to pull the next lever available and
accept whatever fate it exposed. She knew she was well
under the castle now, in the depths of the high rock. She
stumbled on, feeling the wall. There were steps down, two
flights, then a sloping tunnel. The air was stale and dry. She
couldn't find another lever. Then, here, she grabbed, pulled,
pushed, then lifted up. The wall opened. Gracie walked
through.

"Peace in our time," said a child.

"What?" said Gracie, hands balled up, stepping sideways.

"Atoms for peace," said the child, who was male, very
fair, very thin, bearded, seated in the lotus position in the
middle of a long, narrow room. He was pale enough not to
have seen the sun for a decade. He seemed translucent,
wraithlike—a goblin, thought Gracie. He wore a white laboratory coat, a hospital green frock underneath. His room was
filled with Eastern culture: prayer rugs, brass hookahs, lit
candelabra, jade buddhas, a sleeping mat rolled neatly in the
far corner. The room reeked of incense and, underneath,
hashish.

"Far out," said Gracie, spotting what looked to be a
flying carpet suspended magically behind the child. Wires?

"You must be one of the prisoners," said the child.
"My name is Monarch Means. As in the butterfly, not the
regent. Welcome, little sister. My home is your home. Will
you take tea with me? Nice, biting jasmine tea?"

"Who are you?" said Gracie. He spoke older than he
looked. Gracie upped her estimate, anywhere between
fifteen and thirty-five (he was actually twenty-six) and
weird.

"Monarch Means, little sister. Physicist, naturalist,

bastard," said Monarch Means, bowing his head. He seemed the gentlest of creatures. Gracie wondered if he was prisoner here also—a doper's version of the Man in the Iron Mask.

"Did you let me out? The wall?" said Gracie.

"I am not of your world," said Monarch Means.

"Can you help me escape, then?" said Gracie.

"There is no escape," said Monarch Means.

"Oh, yeah?" said Gracie, always a sucker for mystic jargon. "A coal chute? A cellar door? I'll take it from there."

"Where would you like to sit?" said Monarch Means, standing to fetch a teapot, tea servings, a bowl of moon-flower seeds.

"Do they keep you here? Westergaard?" said Gracie, watching him walk. Actually, he seemed to float. "Are you the family shame? You can trust me. My name is Grace Thyme. I don't want to hurt you or your family. Just help me and my friends."

"The true path is inward," said Monarch Means, set-ting the tray down before her. Gracie squatted down, tasting the jasmine tea. It was bitter. Gracie waited a moment, then asked:

"What's your act, kid? Are you putting me on?"

"Physicist, naturalist, bastard," said Monarch Means, offering moonflower seeds. "I smash atoms, culture bacteria, and listen to my mother. Would you like to see my labora-tory?"

"No, thanks. Unless, of course," said Gracie, glancing over to the door he'd pointed to, "I can get out that way."

"Out is in. In is out," said Monarch Means.

"I read all about it," said Gracie, walking over to make sure. She popped the door and peeked. It was a laboratory, all right, out of Dr. Frankenstein's dream life. Dim green light emanated from panel displays. The vast carpeted floor glowed with neon tube lights strung like runners. It seemed a subterranean barn, filled with crates, coils of wiring, lab tables covered with twisted glass tubing. To one side, filling nearly a third of the room, was a horseshoe-shaped struc-ture, with heavy black cables shooting from all sides. It

reminded Gracie of the time she'd visited Effert at Yale and
they'd gone down to the physics lab to get stoned and watch
white-coated gnomes swarm over machinery Effert called
"Seymour Cyclotron." Monarch Means's lab smelled of asbestos, alcohol, ozone, new plastic, and old air. On the far
side of the barn was a two-story-high metal sphere, with
ladders and catwalks attached, with the words

DANGER

POSITIVISM

printed in blue-black on its side. It hummed forebodingly.
The whole scene seemed unhappy. Gracie shut the door,
turning back to Monarch, saying, "You ought to get to the
beach more."

"I have simple needs," said Monarch Means.

"Sure. If you'll excuse me now," said Gracie.

"Do come back. Bring your friends," said Monarch
Means.

"I'll take that rain check," said Gracie. "You do remember rain. Wet and stormy?"

"There are many storms," said Monarch Means.

"'Bye," said Gracie, grabbing up one of his lit candelabra and stepping back out into the passageway. She
slammed the wall behind her. She wondered what he meant
by "storms."

The Contessa Bianca Stupefacenta Capricciosa occupied her
time in captivity with novel-reading, cantata-playing on the
baby grand Westergaard provided her, and, above all, meditating upon why she and her companions had been
"detained" (according to Westergaard) at Craven Castle.
Otherwise, she seemed the perfect guest. She kept her two
dresses neat and clean. She retired early, rose early, drank
lightly, ate healthily, and deferred to everyone. Her captors
thought her a musky jewel. In contrast to their mocking of

Gracie, they treated Bianca with a deference befitting royalty. Each evening, when the attendants brought her supper, they found her seated demurely in the window seat, her head held high and proud, her hands crossed daintily before her—a portrait of civility. She always had a kind word for her jailers. They were charmed. Was this an Italian Jewess or a fairy princess?

Bianca knew full well she had them bewitched. Her conduct was as calculated as it was uniform. She intended to neutralize her opposition with feminine grace just as Gracie neutralized her opposition with feminine sassiness. As an alien here—woman, Jewess, European, aristocrat—Bianca felt that any display of defiance would invite only the cruelty associated with American xenophobia. Her jailers were stupid, but strong, numerous, and merciless. She was clever, but weak, alone, and ambivalent. And her ambivalence was a telling characteristic. Bianca could not come to a holistic understanding of the New World. Its very heterogeneity thrilled her as much as it worried her. The citizens of the New World seemed as unpredictable as their passions. They loved as deeply as mankind can love. They hated as viciously as mankind can hate. They were generous with their surplus as well as with their own portions. They were greedy for material, regardless of its country of origin or its rightful ownership. They practiced enlightened education, championing an internationalism informed by their Constitution's sublime addendum, "The Bill of Rights." They made war with a deranged temper on helpless peasant populations. The Americans, North and South, fought like saints when attacked by tyrants. The Americans, North and South, slaughtered like demons when engaged in colonial expansion. It was as if the New World had two faces, front and back; neither was completely the truth. Bianca suspected that the citizens of the New World themselves didn't know beforehand, sometimes even after the fact, which face they would turn, or had turned, on their friends and enemies. They were precocious children at best, toying with pistols and plows, with plastics and plutonium. If the New World was a melting pot, then it surely was a cauldron too, capable of tempering, but just as likely to erupt.

No, thought Bianca, that was too fanciful. She'd been reading too many novels. She must keep to the facts at hand, with discipline, meditating upon the mysteries that had brought so much passion to Craven Castle. She made a list:

1. What were the Means afraid of? "Harold Starr"?
2. Was the Swiss, Aaron Verbunko, afraid of her?
3. Why did she feel strong affection for Effert?
4. Why did the forest below seem as enchanted as it seemed fearful?
5. Who was "V.Y.M."—initials engraved on many of the leather-bound novels Westergaard had provided her?

There were other questions, of course, especially with regard to Europa and her burglarizing at Means Manor, but five seemed enough just now not to be able to answer. Not that mysteries intimidated Bianca. The opposite was more true. After all, she was the only child of a Marxist-Leninist —enough mystery there to require another century of class warfare before the totems could be sorted. She was also a bastard, the mystery of her father's identity never resolved by Europa, who'd always feigned heart-sickness when questioned by Bianca, mumbling some fiction about Communist "free love." What is more, she was a Jewess—the mystery of the survival of her people beyond contemplation. Out of mystery Bianca had come, then, and accordingly dispensing mystery wherever she journeyed: whether to Britain to wed a ghoulish, proletarian rock'n'roll star, with whom she had engaged in the compelling mystery of the birth of a child before he succumbed, under mysterious circumstances, to his own hallucinogenic phantasms; whether to Naples to wed an impossibly gallant Count with a weakness for dueling, Nazzareno, who would subsequently be undone by his misunderstanding of how vital further mystery (in the form

300

of confidantes, rendezvous, trysts in first-class coaches whipping through the Alps) was to his beloved Contessa; or whether to America (a land named for an extremely curious Florentine adventurer, Amerigo Vespucci, so irresistible to the extremely curious and adventurous children of Florence) to repair the life and love of an all-American girl, Gracie.

Not too surprisingly, then, the darkest human mystery of all, death, interested Bianca increasingly as her weeks in captivity passed, one, two, three, four, and now into her fifth week, alone in the left, roundish tower above the front gate. Death, death, death, thought Bianca, trite as it was, there was death in Craven Castle. There was death in the forest below. Bianca had premonitions of her own death. Bianca imagined her last moments. Would they be as grotesque as this gothic scene? Would she know peace before the end? It suddenly seemed very important to her to know, as if the vulgarity of the Means had to be countered by thinking of ideals such as peace, justice, and truth. Was Europa's self-realizationism finally gripping her? Was she becoming her own mother after all?

Bianca, in the window seat, watching the fading twilight, reached out to tap the window pane. She was perfectly composed. As it darkened outside, however, her own reflection in the glass brightened with the eerie glow of the fire behind her. Her anxiety increased as she studied her own image. She thought she could see something beyond her own image. There seemed a hidden identity there, another face—the face of her unknown father? of her dead husband? of her imprisoned husband? of her neglected child? of her murderer? Bianca broke the spell by smoothing her hair. Vanity returned her to the present. Something else did as well. She heard footfalls, nearby, behind her. She felt a cold presence. She turned.

"Don't look!" said the hag.

"Perchè?" said Bianca.

"None of your gibberish, child," said the hag.

"Are you to slay me?" said Bianca.

"Look away, or I might," said the hag.

"Yes," said Bianca, looking away, toward the window again, but the image was there too, in the reflection—frightening, ghostly, and unforgettably sad. The old woman seemed terribly wrong. She was dressed in a sweeping, translucent white gown, satin and chiffon, with gold-brocaded sleeves puffed out at the elbows and shoulders ruffled with chiffon, like swan wings, with a low neckline trimmed with more gold stitching. More, the gown was covered with garlands of blossoms, around the waist, like a girdle, around the shoulders, like a stole, and especially around her neckline—rosettes, daisies, and ferns wound together like Edenic necklaces. The old woman's gown glimmered. It smelled sweet, like a garden, though it was tinged with the overripe smell of a dying flower bed. Of course, thought Bianca! That was why it seemed familiar. Here was Spring, that is, the dress of Spring—an overdone imitation of Sandro Botticelli's *La Primavera,* the ersatz woman, in her many faces, for whom half the West's elite has made a pilgrimage to Florence's Uffizi Gallery, the other half intending to when they got the fare together.

Yet, God in His Heaven, thought Bianca, the old woman beneath the dress was horrible. She seemed a demimondaine's self-persecuting hallucination. Her face and her visible flesh were cracked, as severe drought cracks the bed of a dry pool. Her hair was lifeless—dry, thin, like gray snakes out of a misshapen skull. Her features were twisted: thin mouth crooked and scaly; nose repeatedly battered to resemble a tiny igneous rock, bubbled, cratered, and frozen in the midst of a drip; and her eyes were indescribable pits. Bianca could not think of those eyes descriptively save to use the word *corrotto,* that is, corrupt.

"If you are to slay me, may I make a letter?" said Bianca.

"Are you afraid of me?" said the hag.

"I am afraid of you," said Bianca, wondering if she had fallen asleep, if they had drugged her, if this was as morbid an interview as it seemed.

"You are lovely, child. What is your name?" said the hag.

"I am the Contessa Capricciosa," said Bianca.

"Are you with the Broadswords?" said the hag.

"Yes, yes," said Bianca. "I am in their party."

"Why did they put you here?" said the hag.

"I do not know," said Bianca.

"Because you're a Jewess?" said the hag.

"I think not. Ask the Means," said Bianca.

"Which ones?" said the hag.

"All of them. Mrs. Means especially, I think," said Bianca.

"Happy Means put you here?" said the hag.

"If that is her name," said Bianca. "The Swiss also."

"The girls? The boy? Tory too?" said the hag.

"Yes, yes, all of them, especially Mrs. Means," said Bianca.

"Why, why?" said the hag. "Tell me. You know. Why?"

"Because they are . . . *odiosi!*" said Bianca, making a gesture with her hands. She meant hateful. Her message was unmistakable.

"You hate the Means?" said the hag.

"No, I do not hate them. They are full of hate. I have no feeling for them. To them? I do not hate them," said Bianca.

"Hate is better than fear. Hate them. They will kill you. I won't kill you. Hate them," said the hag.

"Who are you?" said Bianca, turning to look at the old woman again. She stood horrible as before, and yet helpless too, a human being who had abandoned hope.

"If you cannot guess, you are not worth telling," said the hag. "Now look away! You've had your fun. Don't look!"

"It is not fun," said Bianca, looking away.

"Do not pity me! Forget me! They have!" said the hag.

"Did the Means imprison you here too?" said Bianca,

watching the old woman in the glass. At the question, the old woman dropped her head in thought. She reminded Bianca of more than Spring. The more she studied her, that absurd dress, the decrepit features without form, the more Bianca thought she could see a young girl's face and form —the maiden in the corpse. Bianca experienced a monstrous revelation.

"No," said the hag finally, breathing asthmatically, sucking for breath, gobbling memories with air, "I am my own keeper. I condemn myself. I let them."

"Who are you?" said Bianca.

"I am not she. She is dead," said the hag.

"You are not who? Who is dead?" said Bianca.

"How old do you think I am?" said the hag, pirouetting once with an energy that surprised Bianca. The woman looked ancient, but her twirl was an act of middle age.

"I do not know," said Bianca. "Ninety years old?"

"I am sixty-five," said the hag.

"Accidenti!" said Bianca.

"I was prettier than you," said the hag.

"I am forty," said Bianca.

"It will come. We rust. The tears. The hate," said the hag.

"For the Means?" said Bianca.

"I hate myself. I hate the Means. The same," said the hag.

"They did put you here," said Bianca.

"Stop saying that!" said the hag.

"I do not want to hurt you," said Bianca.

"Liar! Don't look! You think I'm ugly," said the hag.

"No, I do not think this," said Bianca.

"Liar! Liar!" said the hag, then dropping into her raspy voice to say, "Yes, it is true. They threw me away. Because I wasn't beauty anymore. They condemned me. I lied. He is my child. There was no love for me. I love him. Their hate made me hate. I became ugly. She did it. He did it. Hate!"

"Please," said Bianca, but the old woman had leaped

304

away, going into a wild spinning dance about the room, laughing:

"Kee-kee-kee! Kee-kee-kee!"

Bianca reached out to comfort the woman with a touch as she spun by her. The old woman leaped away, screaming:

"No! Do not touch me! I am wicked! I am ugly! Only wicked women become this ugly! Don't I disgust you?! They said I was disgusting! Adultery is wicked! I did it! My husband! My babies! I am a wicked and ugly mother!"

"Are you a Means?" said Bianca.

"I am dead! Dead!" cried the hag, twirling faster.

"What is your name?" said Bianca.

"It wasn't adultery! Monarch is his seed! That's a dead woman's secret!" cried the hag, faster still.

"What is your name?" said Bianca, pounding the windowsill.

"Vernal!" cried the hag, spinning so fast now that flowers flew off as the gown wrapped tighter and tighter about her bent, bloated, tortured body. "Vernal Ystorm Means!" she screamed. "Mrs. Vernal Ystorm Means! They are my babies! I am their mother! Mine!"

"Pray God forgive them," said Bianca.

PARABLE PAUSE

THE BIRTH, THE CRIME, THE PEACE, AND THE TRIUMPH OF THE STRAW PEOPLE (1968–1978)

PART THE SECOND

THE CRIME

BY LEVIATHAN STRAUSS AS TOLD BY SCHLEPPEND

THE Boeing Chinook tore the gray sky apart as it tore east one thousand feet above the highland jungle mat, with a May Day dawn to its rear. It crossed the unmarked international border, passing from the airspace of the Republic of South Vietnam into the airspace of the Khmer Republic, a.k.a. Cambodia. The whop-ch-whop of the Chinook's two giant blades, one fore and one aft, shook the machine's three dozen passengers, Americans all, weighted with weaponry, information, and mendacity. The high-speed gears penetrated to their hearts. Riding a forty-foot chopper was sexy. Riding a forty-foot chopper into a war zone in the bloody spring of 1970, with nineteen-year-old flower children seated beside you better armed then the most grizzly of the 2nd SS Panzer Division, *Das Reich*, twenty-five years before, was pornographic.

The Chinook did not incur Cambodia alone. Loaded with VIPs, it rated a showy escort. To eleven o'clock high, another Chinook churned along, loaded with three rifle squads of airborne troopers from the Air Cav (known as the 101st Airborne when it went up against *Das Reich* twenty-five years before), under the command of a southern gentleman named Caw and a lifer noncom named Westergaard. To two o'clock high, two Bell Huey Cobras floated in precision, their pilots holding them back as cavalrymen might have held back a spirited mount, for those Cobras could do 220 mph flat out, packing three barreled 20-mm cannons in their chin turrets, and rockets, machine guns, and more cannon in their stubby wings—killer birds, those, which Victor Charles (VC, a.k.a. the Viet Cong) knew not to dare down unless without alternative. And to seven o'clock low, a Bell Huey Iroquois bobbed, loaded with a chicken colonel and his brigade staff, riding below and before the chopper formation, brassy pointmen daring Victor Charles's fire.

The VIP Chinook was filled with a neat blend of Yankee classes. The fourth estate was represented by three overweight correspondents from the *Crimes* of L.A., N.Y.C., and Dallas; by a haunted-looking waif said to be a stringer for a consortium of underground newspapers, headed by the weekly *Kong* out of New York, by a correspondent, a cameraman, a soundman, and a gofer girl from the Public Broadcasting System (with an attached Psyops noncom from the Mission); and by a chubby, eager, alternative radio news reporter—later known as the legendary Winnie-the-Fool (for Love)—from an FM broadcasting chain called Metromaniacal.

The third estate was represented by two geologists, wiry and secretive, said to have credentials good enough to get them into any palace compound in the Middle East, said to receive their paychecks from a cartel of British, Dutch, and American oil companies seeking uranium deposits in the Third World.

The second estate was represented by a Mormon preacher named Otis Smith, who doubled as a liaison for the projected Saigon Commodities Exchange.

The first estate was well represented. There was a French refugee, now a California State Representative, beholden to Ronald Reagan politically and financially, on a junket with his mistress to revisit his birthplace in Cambodia, once part of France's Indochina Empire. There was the legislative aide of a flamboyant, sexagenarian United States Senator who liked to order his staff about the world like Rosencrantzes. There were three United States Congressmen, each accompanied by an embassy guide (who reported to the CIA), and a legislative aide, since all three Congressmen sat on a subcommittee of the House Committee on Space and Aeronautics called Nuclear Rockets and Aircraft. And, finally, there was the former United States Special Ambassador to SEATO (South East Asian

Treaty Organization), Pierce Polychron Ystorm, called "Polly," now on special assignment for the Secretary of State, K., reporting directly to Ambassador Ellsworth Bunker in Saigon. Polly was accompanied by a major from MACV (Military Assistance Command Vietnam) named DiBetta; by a bodyguard on detached service from the 3rd Marines; by a nonuniformed CIA translator from the mission named Elvis Presley; and by two female aides, who were also, not coincidentally, his nieces, their names fashioned with tiny diamonds in brooches attached on their uniform blouses where ordinary GIs wore their name tags. This was not the only unusual aspect of the two, who seemed goddesses dressed in combat garb—*Vogue* fashion for war groupies. They sat side by side, smiling at everyone, holding themselves as if untouched by the whop-ch-whop of the blades, the smell of the grease in the Colt M-16 across the Marine bodyguard's lap, the fact that one thousand feet below was a hot war. They seemed angels of frivolity, not angels of death. They seemed magical, these two, according to their diamond brooches, "Christine Means" and "Justine Means."

("The Twin Sisters Means in Southeast Asia," read the entry in the *Annals of the Straw People*, "action taken Friday, May 1, 1970, to Tuesday, May 5, 1970, at Iz Christine, Cambodia, and the Intercontinental Hotel, Saigon [later Ho Chi Minh City], Vietnam. Operatives: Christine and Justine Means.")

"Begging your pardon, sir!" said DiBetta, climbing over some television equipment to the Ambassador's side in the relatively quiet center of the Chinook. "Pilot says ETA five minutes! We hold until our escort is on the ground to secure! It's a hot Iz, sir!"

"Fine, Major!" said Polly, wagging his long fingers, as was his habit when thinking, of which thirty-five years of service in the State Department had required its share,

from Moscow to Mozambique, from Montreal to Monte-
video, from Manila to Melbourne—Pierce Polychron
Ystorm, Princeton, Class of 1929, youngest son of an oil
magnate who'd once said yes to John D. Rockefeller, Sr.,
and never had another worry. "Who's commanding the
Iz?" asked Polly.

"Colonel Schweppenburg, sir!" said DiBetta. "I've
no personal knowledge of him, sir! Newly assigned to First
Cav!"

"Name like that, could be Jerry! Full name?" said
Polly.

"It's Beyr den Schweppenburg, sir!" said Elvis Presley, across from Polly, a wan, fair man who looked childish, wasn't.

"I remember a name like that!" said Polly. "SS general!"

"Couldn't be the same!" said DiBetta, smiling.

"Oh? They were good soldiers!" said Polly.

"Just joking, sir!" said DiBetta.

"Yes, sir! They were good soldiers!" said Presley.

"We were better, of course!" said Polly.

"Yes, sir, much better!" said Presley.

"We weren't much better, young man!" said Polly,
who remembered a similar conversation long before—
London? St. Lo? Paris? "Just better!"

"I shall remember that, sir!" said Presley.

"Firepower! That was the difference, then! Not sol-
diering!" said Polly. "Man for man, I'd say Jerry had us!
Tough, disciplined, and they could take casualties! Better
than us! They took forty, fifty percent casualties, and still
fielded a brigade! How do you explain that?! If we took
twenty percent at division level, we were inoperative!"

"We value life!" said DiBetta, trying to understand
the Ambassador. His chief had told him Ystorm was rich
and peculiar, related to a powerful Pentagon contractor

corporation, Grimmen, and to an even more powerful international corporation, Means. But then they were all peculiar at State. They were either grubby intellectuals chattering statistics, or tall, stern, silver-haired foxes roaming Indochina as if it were a province of the empire. DiBetta himself—squat, dark, chain-smoking professional since '59—regarded both types as hostile to the Army, and therefore deserving of distortions, misstatements, lies. That was his job—a liar in uniform. He was expert at it. But now he had to figure the Ambassador, before he could lie to him effectively.

"No!" said Polly finally, wagging his fingers.

"We don't value life?!" said DiBetta, thinking, Christ, another f——ing ironist.

"Lucidity!" said Polly. "That's what we value! Give us a clear goal, and we'll get there! Without it, bust!"

"Then you should appreciate this operation, sir!" said DiBetta, seeing his chance. "Crossing the border in five places! Parrot's Peak, Fish Hook, Se Sanh, Tay Ninh, and here, Pleiku! Corps strength! Find and destroy Charlie's command center! Neat! Direct! Very clear!"

"That's what I'm told!" said Polly.

"Should be over in a month!" said DiBetta.

"Ever hear of Operation Sea Lion, Major?!" said Polly.

"Sir?!" said DiBetta, confused again.

"Code name for the Nazi invasion of Britain, 1940!" said Polly.

"I'm not following, sir!" said DiBetta.

"How about you, young man?!" said Polly.

"Not really, sir!" said Presley.

"Christine?!" said Polly to his niece at his side.

"Yes, Uncle Polly!" said Christine, who'd listened attentively to their conversation. "When one state

311

invades another, even thinks about it, no turning back! Go! Or don't go!"

"That's exactly right!" said Polly, beaming.

"An incursion, sir!" said DiBetta, concerned as to what sort of power the two girls held over their uncle. DiBetta was charmed by them, of course, but had thought them, to this moment, American debutantes soaking up the romance of war in order to make cocktail conversation high above the Manhattan Island. DiBetta didn't believe in beautiful women in combat. They were difficult to manipulate. They exaggerated emotions around them. They tempted men to act larger than life, which, in war, often means death.

"Yes, Major! An incursion!" answered Polly finally, but not as if he cared. He was more concerned with smiling first into Christine's azure eyes, then into Justine's. He adored them, never having had time, inclination, or luck to have children of his own. He'd married a Corsican Dragon Lady in '39, and they'd separated amicably after Yalta, without issue. Over the years, he'd poured his paternal affections upon Christy, Justy, and the young Tory. How very much their white-golden beauty reminded him of their mother, his beloved, deceased baby sister, Vernal, God rest her soul.

The VIP Chinook veered off into a holding pattern. The Cobras circled overhead. The other Chinook, Caw and Westergaard commanding, swooped down to the chopper pad on one flat side of a small, double-peaked mountain (Hill 444), now obvious above the foliage because it had been stripped of jungle by the drop of a specially designed bomb, called a "peacemaker." Replacing elephant grass were thousands of sandbags heaped to shape admin buildings, artillery bunkers, ops shacks, an air traffic control tower, brigade med, a command latrine, even a post office/officers' club bunker. Replacing elephant trees were prominent iron tubes atop other iron tubes— Howitzers, both 105s and 155s. And replacing elephants and estimated enemy strength was a brigade firepost, Colonel Beyr den Schweppenburg commanding.

The Huey carrying the chicken colonel, Fyfe, was first down, barely touching the chopper pad to unload before it whipped off again, back to Pleiku. Fyfe and his team hunched beneath the blades, saluting Schweppenburg and his staff as best they could as they duck-walked toward the TOC (tactical operation command) bunker. Schweppenburg, a scarecrow-thin man in dark glasses, returned their salute and turned toward the Chinook settling down. Caw and Westergaard dismounted, counting their men as they deployed them in a tight line as honor guard for the VIPs following. Their Chinook lifted off slowly. The scene was set for the VIP Chinook: forty paratroopers in parade dress, a cluster of combat officers to one side surrounding a fierce colonel with a profile fit for a postage stamp. The absurdity of dress formality on a hot lz didn't seem to bother the participants. There were those who noticed, however. Along the ridges of the double-peaked mountain, teams of artillery men stood worn and sloppy by their dirty fieldpieces, men and guns exhausted after a night and a day and a night establishing yet another fire support base ten thousand miles from homemade irony. And beyond the gawking artillery men, just now sashaying up the hillside, a four-man fire team of Baddies, back from another dull night of (not) finding Victor Charles, pulled up to watch the artillery men watching the theatrical bullshit of the brass. These Baddies were typical of the child-mutilators, mother-rapers, and dog-torturers the United States Army hired to scourge Vietnam's free-fire zones. Their name, Baddies, derived from

313

the understanding they were Bad Company. Victor Charles feared them above all else (even the B-52s). Victor Charles knew that if the Army ever fielded more than one Bad Company, say, a battalion, then Hanoi might actually have to deal. Victor Charles also knew that the Army had no faith in the Baddies—for reasons to do with the American ambivalence toward the paladin. Baddies, and their counterparts in other roles—like the Lurps, or Green Beret Bushmasters, or isolatos, or outriders—were as disliked by their theoretical commanders as by their theoretical enemies. Baddies scared everybody living in Southeast Asia. They were an all-American assassin team armed with M-16s, M-79s, frags, C-4, bowie knives, and two thousand years of Western delight in slaughtering Infidels. Maverick carnivores in a counterinsurrectionary war, nobody would, on paper, admit to responsibility for their actions. They were too dangerous. They were nonchalant war criminals. They didn't have real names, calling themselves "Grf" and "Clat" and so forth. Most distressing of all for the Army, they got the job done, as long as the job was body count. They counted bodies with a faultless logic: if it's dead, it's an Indian. No arguing and no conversing with such minds, who, years later, would find a (misrepresented) place in popular legend as the subjects of a rock'n'roll tune.

Certainly the artillery men on the ridges of Hill 444 didn't want to antagonize the four-man fire team of Baddies, back from another dull night of (not) finding Victor Charles, just now pulled up to watch the artillery men watching the theatrical bullshit of the brass. The artillery men backed away quickly, overhearing their jargonish conversation nonetheless.

"Chone comin' in," said Bldg.

"Slope chone most likely," said Gyk.

"Uncle Sugar chone. Can smell it," said Bldg.

314

"I'm in Charlie land. No Uncle Sugar chone," said Nrff.

"Honkey chone. More'n one, for sure," said Bldg.

The four gathered together to watch the three Congressmen step from the rear door of the VIP Chinook, followed by their guides and aides. The press came next, the *Crimes* men stopping nearby to take notes, the *Kong* stringer and Metromaniacal reporter drifting immediately to the latrine to score some Thai dope. The PBS television team pulled off its equipment, setting up behind the honor guard. The French refugee and his mistress were met by a Cambodian government official. The geologists and the Mormon preacher were met by an ARVN major, who marched them off to an FMC M113 armored personnel carrier (amtrack) parked in the distance. The Senator's legislative aide was met by a Vietnamese civilian with one eye. By now, the PBS television team had set up, and directed the Congressmen back on to the Chinook, so they could dismount again, this time for a film library. DiBetta then hopped off, pointing his swagger stick at the PBS, meaning fold-up, which they did, moving to the ridge where the California gofer girl had spotted a commercial television team shooting location footage. DiBetta waited until they'd gone—he distrusted the camera—then signaled to the Marine bodyguard, who hopped down to extend an arm to the Ambassador. Polly struggled out, his fatigues whipped by the chopper wind. He turned to help down Christine and Justine. Elvis Presley was last out, his eyes ever moving over the lz. The CIA was a crazy man's refuge. Elvis Presley talked sane, wasn't.

Because of the general confusion—the wind, the dust, the saluting brass—the three hundred men on Hill 444 didn't immediately espy Christine and Justine. From a distance, after all, small blond beauties in combat dress can be seen as ARVN officers. Their misidentification was

315

corrected by the time Christine and Justine had passed the honor guard to be introduced to Schweppenburg. Half the fire base turned to the other half of the fire base to say, "Ffff——!"

So much for the regular Army perceiving ethereal presence. The Baddies had the Twin Sisters Means spotted the moment their tiny combat boots touched the tarmac.

"Skin one of those, man might not skin again," said Mmn.

"There's half a chone apiece there," said Bldg.

"Odds say no. Boo-coo friendlies," said Mmn.

"Might be a score, if we're cool," said Bldg.

"I'm thinking yer outta yer skull," said Mmn.

"Might be worth it. Hairy tho'," said Nrff.

"We been there," said Mmn.

"Bad bush tonight," said Gyk.

"Screw bush. Lookit that chone! Number One!" said Nrff.

"Number One, twice. Gotta plan?" said Mmn.

"We expectin' rain?" said Bldg.

"No way," said Mmn.

"I gotta plan. No rain. Make rain," said Bldg.

"When?" said Mmn.

"What down. Must up," said Bldg.

"As it happened, Victor Charles did rain a little metal on Landing Zone Christine (renamed by Schweppenburg over breakfast with his guests) that May Day. About noon, as Polly and DiBetta prepared to mount an amtrack to tour the main road west to Lumpaphat, Victor Charles lobbed an 82-mm round one-half a click short of the chopper pad. Amid bellowing cries of "innn-coming!" the VIPs were swept into a bunker, the artillery men battened down their hatches, the choppers waiting to land hot lunches were waved off, and the TOC called for

316

Cobras and Phantoms. As Victor Charles was known to say, you can beat the Man, but you can't beat the airwaves. By the fifth round, walking up the chopper pad, two Cobras were buzzing the opposite mountainside, loosing a terrible but malappropriate vengeance. The mountainside was shredded. The monkey population was reduced. Presently, three McDonnell Douglas F-4 Phantoms dipped below the cloud layer to the north. Their pilots, bored flying cover for an enormous operation that had yet to make serious contact with Victor Charles, performed their ritual with gymnastic precision. From two clicks out, at three thousand feet, the Phantoms rolled on their backs so that the pilots could keep sight of the target on the long run in. Belly up, the eight mean objects on the Phantoms' undercarriages showed heavy and frightening. The pilots throttled for a hi-lo-hi strike, rolling over at the last possible moment to release two loads of Dow Chemical's napalm, then veering off, climbing so fast the Phantoms disappeared into the cloud cover just as the napalm struck the mountain. Each Phantom made one pass. That was enough. These pilots were deft pros. The NVA would enjoy torturing them. They burned the earth. The mountain was an orange fire, an evil black smoke pouring off Mother Nature. In return for five poorly aimed mortar rounds, the United States Army had launched enough devastation to exterminate a battalion of Victor Charles or his NVA allies. And an 82-mm mortar, with ammo, can be fired and transported by five very short people—men, women, or children.

The all-clear whined within five minutes. Folk popped out of their holes in Hill 444 to resume their lives counting the days backwards till they could get out of this game.

Rain means rain, as they said in Nam, however, so no sooner had the evil black smoke blown free than the sky served a thunderstorm, rain down in sheets. Hill 444 battened down again. The hours dripped by. The rain slackened, then strengthened, then slackened again— weather in the Annamese Cordillera being a combination of all the shit they got in the south with all the shit they got in the north. Finally, Polly made a decision. Rain or no, he and DiBetta would proceed to Lumpaphat in the am-track. They'd return at sundown, dine, and then spend the night at Iz Christine. Schweppenburg's aide-de-camp, a West Pointer named Catfiss, grimaced at the idea of a VIP pajama party. Night in the bush tended toward the un-speakable. Men didn't just die, they vanished. But there it was, Catfiss knew, and the best he could manage after a half-hour of charm was that the Congressmen would leave tonight for a dinner in Saigon. Otherwise, Iz Chris-tine was honored with the presence, for the night, of a sharp-eyed Ambassador, two duplicitous operators from the Mission, and last, but certainly first in the fantasy lives of the five hundred American men spending the night within Hill 444's wire, two unimaginably beautiful Ameri-can females.

"Could be worse," said DiBetta to Catfiss. "Maids."

"They got maids?" said Catfiss.

"Four ladies-in-waiting in Saigon," said DiBetta.

"F——ing aristocracy," said Catfiss.

"Excuse me?" said DiBetta.

"Sorry, sir," said Catfiss.

"That's frigging aristocracy," said DiBetta.

Christine and Justine had asked to be excused from the trip to Lumpaphat. Polly, of course, obliged, leaving them napping in Schweppenburg's quarters, which had been made over hastily (hot showers, bar, stereo/radio) into a VIP apartment. The Congressmen were scheduled to dust off at 5 P.M. Caw and Westergaard divided their com-mand between the Congressmen and the Ambassador.

318

Alpha squad would remain the night at Iz Christine. Beta and Charlie squads lifted off at 0500 hours.

Curiously, Caw chose to stay with Alpha squad. Westergaard, amused, stayed with his lieutenant. But then, perhaps it wasn't so curious, since Caw had fallen in love with Christine Means, or was it Justine? No, it was Christine, the bolder, more outspoken of the two, who asked questions of field commanders like a touring Vice-President. After a week of watching her from a respectful distance, Caw loved Christine with the kind of intensity that scars sentiment forever after. He worshiped her. He envied anyone who could touch her. He pined at every separation from her presence. He died for her.

Caw was a familiar story in Nam. Westergaard had met dozens of them with the same terminal sense of romance. A taciturn, red-haired man out of U. Va., '69, he'd volunteered his southern preppie ass into the airborne immediately, intending to score some glory before scoring a law school. He'd been in-country six months now, and, dazzled by his own second lieutenant's figure, had already mentioned to Westergaard that he was thinking of extending his tour. He toyed with career. His father had missed the Second World War—too young—had volunteered into the Marine Corps for Korea, had been chewed up so badly that long winter of '52 that he didn't talk about himself the same afterward. He'd urged his sons toward medicine, had come up with a second son in the Air Cav. It was better than the Corps, he'd told his friends in Virginia, it was much better than the Corps. The Corps was f——ed, bad boys badly led, tripping over their invincible image every time Victor Charles probed. Lifer noncoms, like Westergaard, in the Air Cav (transferred in from the 1st Cav in mid '68), said that if it weren't for the Army, there'd be no Corps; and if it weren't for the Corps, there'd be no need for the Army. Westergaard had told

Caw grisly stories about the Ia Drang Valley in '65, Dak
To in '67, that mean time called Tet in '68, and *beaucoup*
Corps messes ever since. Oh, yes, J. S. Caw was glad to
be airborne, was proud of his rank, of the way the leather
of his .45-caliber holster shone when he walked. He liked
his snug jungle boots too. The only feet he'd seen in Nam
more precious to him than his own belonged to Christine
Means, which might explain why, on May Day afternoon,
supposedly strolling over to the TOC to monitor the Ambassador's movements with Presley, Caw diverted by the
colonel's quarters.

"Hello, Lieutenant," said Justine, emerging from
the bunker with an elegant, stretching yawn, her tanned
arms over her head.

"Yes, ma'am, yessiree," said Caw, unsure which
one she was.

"I'm Justine, remember me?" said Justine.

"Pleasure, ma'am," said Caw.

"Were you looking for me?" said Justine.

"Well, ma'am, I was on my way to the TOC," said
Caw.

"Tell the truth," said Justine.

"Wouldn't lie to ladies, no, sir," said Caw.

"You're looking to sit with Miss Christine, isn't that
so?" said Justine in a delicate, magnolia drawl.

"You from the South, ma'am?" said Caw, surprised.

"My mother was born in Tennessee," said Justine.

"That makes you southern, certainly does," said
Caw.

"I've never thought of myself as a belle. And you'd
come calling every Saturday night?" said Justine.

"Me and the whole valley," said Caw.

"For me, or for my sister?" said Justine.

"If a man had to choose, I think he'd take up serious

320

drinking beforehand. For me, the pleasure of talking with you is all I could ever wish," said Caw.

"Are you flirting with me, Lieutenant?" said Justine.

"Ma'am?" said Caw.

"Will you walk with me? Christy's asleep," said Justine.

"An honor, ma'am," said Caw, offering his arm. The two followed a slit trench across the double peak of the mountain toward the television crews still shooting late afternoon location footage. They looked, for the *Kong* stringer and the Metromaniacal reporter to see from atop a bunker wall, like a debutante and her beau out of the heat of the ball to stroll the garden's edge.

"How about out there?" asked Justine, pointing down the mountain, over the wire to a grove of trees and orchids.

"That's Cambodia all right," said Caw.

"I'd like to walk there," said Justine.

"Across the wire? Out of bounds. There's hostiles out there. Charlie and his Khmer Rouge buddies," said Caw.

"Where?" said Justine. "I don't see anything. Jungle."

"Yes, ma'am, but no, I'd never get over it if anything happened to you," said Caw.

"How dear. Do the Communists take prisoners? Do they make us become socialists?" said Justine.

"I've seen some rough things done to women," said Caw.

"You won't tell me, will you?" said Justine.

"No, that wouldn't be right. I hope not to offend," said Caw.

"I think you gallant beyond your day," said Justine.

"Well," said Caw, turning slightly away from her. He

felt half the men on the mountain watching his every move, the other half watching Justine's trousers. Was Victor Charles watching?

"Would you get me an orchid, then?" said Justine.

"Yo!" said Caw, knowing he was a fool to agree. He broke into a loping run, past a trench, left to hop a communications wire to the outer redoubts. Here comes Caw, he thought, and wouldn't J. E. B. Stuart Himself (that's Jeb Stuart Caw) have been well pleased with so healthy a specimen of southern chivalry risking reprimand and RPG round in the chest to pick a flower for his lady? Now he was outside the wire. What did the artillery men on the ridges think of a wild-assed Air Cav trooper wind-sprinting to a jungle grove? What did Justine think? Caw felt her azure eyes burn his flank as he ran, over a clump, fifty yards to go, then there, winded, though running a quarter-mile in a flak jacket was grim work. Caw snapped a yellow blossom, rejected it, chose two white flowers, which he stuck in the netting on his helmet. Going uphill, he didn't run. He walked quickly, in a crouch. There hadn't been sniper contact all day, he told himself. He went over the wire at a checkpoint. He regained the redoubts. There was applause from the mountain as he reached Justine. There were also jeers. The betting had been spontaneous —even-up he got greased. Money exchanged hands as Caw handed Justine one of the two orchids, then the other, saying,

"For Miss Christine."

"She'll kiss you herself. This one's from me," said Justine, placing her hands on his flak jacket, raising up to kiss him hard on the mouth, but not erotically—just hard.

Caw staggered back from Justine's kiss. He knew this was the apogee of his life. The gallery knew it too. Nobody made a remark for a long minute. Justine turned back to her bunker. Caw skipped after her. The gallery

322

cursed low and sad. Many went to their bunkers to take out a snapshot of a woman, think about how clever God was to make girls like that.

"Why did she do that?" asked the *Kong* stringer, stoned.

"Why did he do it?" said the Metromaniacal reporter.

"That's what I said."

"Ain't it classic, though? Spider weaves web. Eats fly."

"I don't like her. I don't care what they say."

"Yer stoned outta yer mind. That's a woman!"

"Give me a nice, plump Jewish girl."

"Who's givin' you anything?"

"Yeah, well, let's get out of here, before. Before."

"Before what? Yer wrecked. Before what?"

"Where is justice? Where is it? Where did it go?"

The *Kong* stringer and the Metromaniacal reporter toked deeper and deeper on the Number One grass. It passed the rest of the day. They got a chopper out at sundown, missing the rest of the tale, but picking it up later from a corpsman, who swore it was all true, no kidding.

Dinner in the officers' mess was at eight P.M., or 2000 hours. It was hot, plentiful, and as attractive as the resourceful Catfiss could make it—white tablecloth, crystal, china, silver settings, candelabra. Catfiss had called a lover in the Quartermaster in Danang, who'd sent out two Filipino waiters and table settings from the officers' club immediately in a chopper. Nam was nonsensible like that. Spookily, San Francisco could materialize in a rice paddy. There was a story about a château outside Saigon doing flagellation orgies for a fee.

323

There was a story of a crucifixion club on the China Beach, but it was never confirmed. Americans were funky crazy to begin with, in a cinematic way. In Vietnam, they dropped *auteur* control along with the other ordnance. They opted for the decadently grandiose. Mention the most macabre Emperor Nero story, someone could top it in Nam. Southeast Asia, 1965–1975, was disgust. If it's true that revolution eats its children, and that tradition eats its mothers, then it's also true that counterinsurgency warfare (revolution versus tradition) eats its own shit. Vietnam succored American men's most savage impulses. You were only as bad as your imagination. Some of those imaginations were very, very bad. The Dark Ages lived again.

Two of the fairest princesses in the West were guests of honor that evening in the officers' mess. Christine wore a flower print dress, adding black sandals. Justine wore her combat garb, with a white shawl. They both wore their hair down, with orchids pinned at the part. With perfume and makeup, the effect was less than Fifty-ninth and Fifth, but for a hot Iz, it was stunning. The brigade staff officers stood speechless before Christine's legs. Catfiss, who was happily homosexual, hopped to the Twin Sisters Means. They made his harried preparations worthwhile. Catfiss took Christine's arm. Polly took Justine's. They circled the table, admiring the spread. The menu was announced. The wine was red and expensive. Christine and Justine sat on either side of their Uncle Polly. The staff officers arranged themselves along the long sides. Toasts were proposed.

"To Christine!" said Catfiss. They cheered.

"To Justine!" said Polly. They cheered.

"To womankind!" said Elvis Presley. They cheered.

"To the First Cav!" said Caw. They cheered.

"To the Air Cav!" said Fyfe. They cheered.

"To the President of the United States, God strengthen his arm!" said Schweppenburg. They cheered.

"To the United States Army, the greatest fighting force on the face of the earth!" said Christine. They cheered.

"To sweet second lieutenants!" said Justine.

"Hooray," from the officers, followed by an embarrassed silence. Caw stood dumbfounded, pink-faced, and wide-eyed. Justine exchanged smiles with Christine. Dinner was served, along with the usual gung-ho conversation.

"My opposite number at the ARVN Rangers claims thirty kills," said Schweppenburg to Polly. "And over one hundred and twenty AK-47s in a cave five clicks from Lumpaphat."

"Our recon reports have the Communists falling back," said Catfiss to Polly, "along a five-hundred-mile front."

And later: "Charlie's just running for the hills," said Fyfe.

"What does that mean, Colonel? That you've met no organized resistance?" said Christine. "Where is the enemy, Colonel?"

"Begging the colonel's pardon," said DiBetta, volunteering to handle Christine's inquiry.

"Yes, yes," said Fyfe, looking to Schweppenburg with a shrug.

"Where is he, then, Major?" said Christine forcefully.

"Oh, he's out there," said DiBetta, who was getting used to Christine's manner now, after two weeks of her arrogance. Still, he could see his condescension had struck his fellow officers as ungentlemanly. He was forced to continue, "This operation is turning up tons of equipment. Guns and butter. The Ho Chi Minh Trail is cut in five places. The enemy has lost tactical superiority completely."

"Well said, Major," said Polly. Christine smiled.

And later: "Is it not true, Colonel," said Christine to Schweppenburg, "that the Army's objective in Vietnam is to kill the Communists in great numbers?"

"Yes, ma'am, that is true," said Schweppenburg.

"I have been in-country two weeks. From the Z to the Delta. From the Corps to the Navy operating amphibs at Rach Gia. I have yet to see an enemy soldier," said Christine.

"The action this afternoon . . ." began Schweppenburg.

"That?" said Christine. "A platoon with fifty-mm mortars could hold down two rifle companies if they just sat there and called in air." Schweppenburg looked to DiBetta.

"Excuse me, Miss Means?" said DiBetta, trying to stop her.

"My sister means to say," said Justine demurely, "that we marvel at your ground-to-air logistics. But we feel they are defensive only. They lack aggression."

"You don't win a ground war with air or artillery," said Christine to Schweppenburg, who started to smile, then didn't.

"What is it you are saying?" said Schweppenburg.

"I find our tactics excellent. Our strategy poor," said Christine, putting down her wineglass.

"Uh, if I may . . ." began DiBetta, but too late.

"What would you recommend, Miss Means?" said Schweppenburg.

Christine pushed herself from the table, walked to the wall map display detailing North and South Vietnam, bordering China, Laos, and Cambodia. The company of officers made a half-start to stand. Justine waved them down. An observer might conclude that Christine and Justine were now C in C of a 1st Cav Brigade HQ. Christine, as head of S-3 (operations), took the pointer and placed its tip firmly on Haiphong, North Vietnam, the primary port facility receiving Russian and Chinese supplies for the NVA and VC, saying:

"Here is where I'd drop the 173rd Airborne Division."

"But," said DiBetta.

"Here," said Christine, moving the pointer to Hanoi, capital of North Vietnam, "is where I'd drop the First Cav."

"But," said DiBetta.

"And here," said Christine, moving the pointer to Nam Dinh, to the southwest of Hanoi, forming a triangle with Hanoi and Haiphong, "is where I'd drop the Air Cav."

"They couldn't be resupplied or supported," said Schweppenburg automatically. "They couldn't last a week."

"Four days at the most. Ninety-six hours," said Christine.

"What?" said Schweppenburg, looking at DiBetta.

"Then I would launch an amphibious assault with the Fifth Marines behind the Z, and another with the Third Marines at Haiphong," said Christine. "Simultaneous with the drops."

"Do you know what you are saying?" said Schweppenburg, who still wasn't sure if she was serious.

"Just like that?" said DiBetta, as lightly as he could.

"In four days, I would expect fifty percent KIA. Another twenty percent WIA. But they would have to shake every tree in Southeast Asia to find what would be left of the Communists after the Seventh Air Force and

327

Navy support strikes. How long would it take the Soviet Ambassador to drive to the White House to inform the President that the Soviet Army was on Condition Yellow, and to suggest that perhaps it was time to discuss a settlement for Vietnam? I would call the expenditure of our three best divisions, and the sacrifice of the Marine Corps, an honorable price for total, unconditional victory." Christine was not smiling.

"And the Chinese?" said Schweppenburg. She was casually discussing the death of thirty thousand American soldiers.

"I believe our fleet in the South China Sea is equipped with sufficient ordnance," said Christine.

"Nuclear?" said Fyfe, hooked.

"Yes. But this is moot," said Christine. "There'd be no intervention. The Soviets would settle. End war."

"Uh," said DiBetta, looking about the room to see that every officer's face had a dreamy, lean, and ravenous fix—the Medal of Honor face. Elvis Presley looked transformed. "You're joking, of course?"

"What's that, Major?" said Christine softly, returning the pointer to the stand, folding her hands before her.

"I said that you're putting us on, aren't you?" said DiBetta. God, make her be joking, he thought. He suddenly had a vision of what it would be to have this woman in charge. She terrified him. She moved him. As informed and cynical as he was about America's "Vietnamization Policy"—the withdrawal of American ground forces with the concomitant escalation of American bomber forces—he felt that if this woman ordered him, he'd lead that airborne strike on Hanoi himself. What officer who wore the uniform of the airborne didn't have the fantasy of himself catapulting into Hanoi at the head of a battalion of blazing M-16s? They all read D.C. comics. The scene touched them at their most vulnerable because most juvenile. When they said the moon and the stars for women like this, thought DiBetta, they were right. She ruled their souls at that moment. Fall on their swords for her—Get some! Then the moment passed, as Christine said:

"My little joke," laughing high and lyrically. Justine joined her sister. Their laughter filled the mountain. The officers relaxed. It had been a good jest. Polly loved her for it. And as the dinner finished, and as Caw and Catfiss escorted Christine and Justine to their quarters, and as Polly and Schweppenburg retired to the TOC with a bottle of bourbon to monitor the situation reports coming in from listening posts and ambushes, and as all the officers present at Christine's lecture took their turns at whiskey and watches, not one of them, not even Elvis Presley chatting Mission gossip with DiBetta, dared to say aloud that he didn't think Christine Means had been joking. Vietnam being a place for little lies, it was easy to lie a little to themselves as they lay down to sleep, prayed the Lord their souls to keep, please, God, never allow a woman like that to be appointed Chairperson of the Joint Chiefs, let alone run for President.

Not that anyone slept well that night. Victor Charles lobbed in mortar rounds every half-hour. In the dark, they had to take it. This was nuisance fire, not prep fire. Still, everyone knew, if Victor Charles wanted to score big, one human wave overrun of a brigade HQ would make headlines for days. It didn't happen. By 0500, Hill 444 was alive again with Americans pissing, shaving, sipping, and chewing—another muggy day with leech crawlers and breech loaders in the romantic tropics. Westergaard had his squad saddled up without further ado, nodding to Caw to fetch their party, since the chopper was due at sunup plus ten. On his way across the mountain, Caw spied the Ambassador already awake and dressed, chatting with DiBetta. He detoured to them, only to have DiBetta tell him to check on the Misses Means. Caw ignored the sarcasm in DiBetta's voice, and in the Ambassador's look, and continued to the colonel's quarters. He knocked.

"Come in," said Justine. "We're almost ready."

"It's Lieutenant Caw, ma'am," said Caw. "Chopper's due."

"Can't hear you, Lieutenant. Come in," said Justine.

"I said," said Caw, ducking under the beam into the bunker, "that our chopper is due. Half-hour." He stopped. Before him was heaven on Earth. Justine sat on one cot in her trousers and T-shirt, with her foot on the opposite cot, pulling on her sock. Christine, completely dressed except for tucking in her shirt, sat before a makeup mirror at the colonel's desk, doing her eyes. The room smelled of sawdust, French perfume, and sleeping beauty.

"How are you this morning, Lieutenant?" said Christine, without turning to look at him.

"Fine, ma'am," said Caw.

"Did you hear the news on the radio?" said Christine.

"Pardon, ma'am?" said Caw, staring at Justine's naked foot.

"Back home. The rioting. Sounds as if they're burning the campuses down," said Christine.

"How's that? Burning you say?" said Caw.

"Never mind. You've enough to worry about," said Christine.

"Yes, ma'am," said Caw. "I'll be on my way. The Ambassador asks that you join him for coffee in the mess."

"Would you help me with my boots?" said Justine. "Christy won't, and there're so many lace holes."

"Your boots?" said Caw, confused by her teasing tone.

"That's an order," said Justine, holding up her foot.

330

"Certainly," said Caw, walking over, taking her foot to place it on his thigh, over his M-16 clips, lacing it correctly, tying it tightly. He did the same with the other foot. His heart was thumping hard as he finished with a flourish. He grinned broadly as he put Justine's foot down gently.

"Something amusing?" said Justine.

"It's a fine day," said Caw.

"I think you'd better go on without us," said Christine from behind him.

Caw turned to see her standing cold and exquisite. He blanched. He left the bunker wordlessly. He was hurt and puzzled. Had he said something wrong? Was it because he helped Justine with her boot—sisterly rivalry? It didn't seem that simple. The twist of it was that he favored Christine over Justine. Justine seemed giddy, supercilious, the makings of a genuine Jezebel—come today, go tomorrow. Christine was all-woman and all-powerful. The way she'd manipulated the staff officers had awed Caw. What Christine was made of, it might look like what Justine was made of, but seemed profoundly sterner. Perhaps he should have refused the boots. Wasn't a boot boy a sign of something submissive and sacrificial? He wished he'd read more. There was a literary feel to the Means. And he was trying to solve them with cinema and the myth of the Lost Cause. It'd take him a long time to make sense of them.

And it should have. Caw was naive, and Caw was stupid, but neither is warrant for his arrest at the age of twenty-three. The ugliness here was the crime of the Straw People. There was no other explanation. Crane tried, Conrad tried, Hasék tried, Hemingway tried, Mailer tried, Heller tried, even Pynchon tried, yet none came up with an explanation for why young men have to die in old men's wars.

The Chinook arrived on schedule—whop-ch-whop

331

—hovering to windward, awaiting clearance down. Caw and Westergaard set their squad in a smart line. The Ambassador and his party passed. The Chinook touched down, idling its engines to minimize the dust kicked up by its whirly wind. Still, everyone's eyesight was hindered. This was the most vulnerable moment for an lz, with the machine committed, the men committed, and the noise so loud it was difficult to think.

They came up the hill in a line twenty meters apart —sappers in black pajamas, their AK-47s lowered before them, running, screaming, opening fire. The man on the left tossed a frag. The one on the right did the same. Their target was Caw's squad, standing like tenpins. Their 7.62-mm fire, at the rate of ninety rounds per second automatic, ripped into the troopers. The two frags exploded, wham! wham! The dead and wounded slumped together. The four sappers kept coming, directing a withering fire. They were fifty yards short of the Chinook now, split into two and two. They threw more frags to keep the colonel's staff pinned to the ground at the edge of the tarmac. Then came a smoke grenade, obscuring everything. On the ridges, the artillery men stood stunned, thinking of themselves first, the men down there second. Victor Charles had four men through the wire. There might be more. All went to ground. Meanwhile, Caw and Westergaard, to the side of their men and thus out of the direct line of fire, had slung their weapons down and begun to return fire. Westergaard dropped one sapper, down but not dead. Caw shouted to Westergaard that there were two more on the other side of the chopper. Westergaard went to one knee. He saw Schweppenburg, pistol in hand, and DiBetta, pistol in hand, pushing the girls and the Ambassador into the Chinook's rear door. A door gunner stood straight up to help. Gunfire tore through the chopper to throw the door gunner into a belly flop, dead. Westergaard worked to his men to rally them. Some moved. Westergaard waved to the Chinook pilot, pointing thumbs up, screaming, "Go! Go! Go!" The pilot waved back calmly. He'd dusted off of hot lzs before. He throttled back, lifting his forty-foot bird slowly a few feet at a time, waiting for his crew chief to give an all-clear. As the Chinook came up, Caw spotted the two sappers behind it, crawling forward on their bellies. He assumed they were a suicide squad after the Ambassador. Schweppenburg was dragging Elvis Presley to cover. The Ambassador and one of the girls were already in the chopper as it hovered there. Another girl, Caw thought it was Christine, was half in, half out, trying to pull herself up. She wasn't going to make it. She was an easy target from the waist down. The sappers were not shooting at her, however, directing their fire at the chopper's engine, wap! wap! wap! They were trying to down it. One of the chopper's engines choked, kicked in again. The Chinook dipped, then rose up, still waiting for Christine to get inside. Caw could see his duty. He did it.

He gave his best Rebel yell as he launched himself into motion, a flat sprint across the pad to the Chinook thirty yards distant. He felt stinging in his back, but didn't stop. He kept firing short bursts at the two sappers as he ran. One of them stood up to charge at him. It was a race to the chopper. Caw took a hit on his flak jacket which pushed him sideways. He compensated and kept running. He passed Schweppenburg, covering the CIA man with his own body, firing his pistol like a cool pro. Caw and the sapper reached the Chinook at the same time. Caw clubbed him back with his rifle, reached up with one hand to grab Christine at the waist. The sapper came at him again. He threw his rifle at him. Christine had her

333

hands in the Chinook, was being held from inside by the shoulders. Caw fixed his feet, fixed his hands, and heaved. The last thing he felt on this Earth was Christine's impossibly soft ass.

Three mornings later, on the terrace of their penthouse at the Intercontinental Hotel, Saigon, Christine and Justine Means toyed with their breakfast as they toyed with their television, watching satellite-beamed news from America.

"Today, four students were killed and another . . ." said Walter Cronkite.

"Turn it off, Christy," said Justine.

"And now for a report . . ." said Walter Cronkite.

"May I join you?" said Polly, at the door of a sudden.

"Do, Uncle Polly," said Justine. "Christy's a bore."

"What's going on?" said Polly, sitting with his back to the Sony.

"The rioting, you know. Cheap thrills," said Justine.

"Did you get it?" said Christine, clicking off the Sony.

"Here," said Polly, handing her a packet of papers.

Christy opened it up, took out photocopies, and read: ". . . gunshot wounds through and through, back and buttocks. Also knife wounds through abdomen. Killed in action."

"What does it mean?" said Christine, handing it to Justine.

"He was killed by bullets and bayonet," said Polly.

"But who killed him? It doesn't say," said Christine.

"It says 'Hostile.' There. Checked off," said Polly.

"That's not what we were told," said Christine.

"I think we should limit ourselves to the official Army report, don't you agree?" said Polly.

"Is this it, then? No more?" said Justine, returning

the packet, reaching over to take Christine's hand.

"There will be no commendations," said Polly.

"Why not?" said Christine.

"I'm not sure," said Polly.

"But Major DiBetta said that . . ." began Christine.

"Major DiBetta spoke before the official Army report. I am sure he would now comply with the official report," said Polly.

"That's obscene," said Christine.

"Christy, that will be the end of it?" said Justine.

"Something's gone wrong," said Christine.

"Is there anything I can do?" said Polly.

"Leave us," said Christine.

"Yes, of course," said Polly, bowing out, disturbed.

"Tell me what it is, Christy," said Justine.

"That wasn't supposed to happen. It touched me," said Christine. "I felt it. I can still feel it."

"We agreed we must be patient, and hard," said Justine.

"I embarrass myself," said Christine.

(to be continued)

335

Captors

EXHAUSTION felled Gracie from her time of grace between Craven Castle's walls. She pulled one more
lever, walked out into a corridor off the Great Hall,
and made her way back to her tower. She ignored the
guards' looks of discovery. Perhaps it had been Westergaard's doing after all, knowing she couldn't escape. She
reached her room, slammed the door behind her. She needed
a shower. She needed breakfast. She needed sleep. She noticed through the windows as she stumbled to her bed that
storm clouds hurtled across the top of the mountain range
to the southwest, headed for Craven Castle. There was a big
bird there too. Gracie walked to the window to stare. A big
metal bird, she thought, diving toward Craven Castle. Stripping her filthy clothes, she was asleep as she dove toward
the pillows.

"Hello!" called a voice. Gracie stirred. "Hello!"

"Go away!" called Gracie, covering her head with a
pillow.

"I'd like to come in to talk," said the voice.

"What time is it?" said Gracie. She could hear rain.

"Four P.M. I'm coming in now," said the voice, who did, Torrance VIII stepping into Gracie's bedroom.

"You'd better have my lunch with you," said Gracie.

"I'll ring for it," said Torrance VIII.

"Oh, it's you," said Gracie, peeking from under the pillow to see him there, dressed dapperly in cotton, linen, and conceit. She looked up to her windows. It was raining hard.

"I'm told you've been resourceful," said Torrance VIII, pulling over a chair, sitting. "Where were you last night?"

"In your bloody prison," said Gracie.

"Westergaard says you escaped, then returned," said Torrance VIII, lighting up an English cigarette. He was beautiful.

"I fancy the plumbing. Leave, and I'll use it," said Gracie.

"Modesty before me, Grace?" said Torrance VIII.

"All right," said Gracie, ripping back the covers, marching naked to her w.c., slamming the door. She sat down on the toilet and considered how she could poison him. She finished, washed her face, slipped on her bathrobe, then returned to her bed, flopping down, saying, "Ugly weather."

"I didn't come here to antagonize you," said Torrance VIII.

"Phooey. I've read the books. You are the 'Man,'" said Gracie.

"I am as unhappy about this as you. It was unavoidable. It was corporation security, not personal grudge. Some decisions are made for the greater good. You've been well cared for."

"Westergaard's a peach," said Gracie. "The cage is cleaned regularly. It's not so bad, if you go for isolation. Me, I'm the rangy type, I like to choose my own stalls."

"I hope we are still friends. Aren't we?" he said.

"I was waiting for that," said Gracie. "You might have

the biggest thing I've ever seen, but that doesn't mean we've shared everything. I hate you. For what you've done to me, and to Effert, and to all of us, I hate you. Simple hate."

"There was no choice," he said. "It will be clear to you someday. This was precautionary, for a greater good."

"Save it for the judge," said Gracie. "If Effert doesn't settle things first."

"The fabled knight-errant of the Broadswords," he said, "riding across the field. Romantic. Rubbish, too, I think."

"He dumped you good," said Gracie.

"You persist, Grace," he said. "Effert is a fool. This is the real world. Men like him follow an ideal that went out of fashion five hundred years ago. And it was always an ideal. Chivalry, Grace, is not only dead. It never existed. A hollow code, invented by poets. Not for politics. Not for business."

"You're smarter than I am," said Gracie. "You know that stuff. I just know my Effert. He came back to me. That's what I know. If he's so foolish, how come he got this far? His ideal must live all right somewhere."

"When it doesn't interfere," said Torrance VIII. "There are savages who live in animism, who burn sacrifices to river gods, mountain gods, star gods. That doesn't mean they are valid life-styles. They exist as long as they don't interfere with progress. If they do, they must change or perish."

"You make a jingle out of this?" said Gracie.

"I am trying to explain matters to you," he said.

"Sounds like threats to me. If you were a colt, I'd know how to handle you. Horses don't threaten," said Gracie.

"It will amuse you, I suppose, to have me deny that I am a horse," he said, "I am not. I am president of a major corporation in the affairs of men. I use horsepower, whatever is necessary to attain my goals. I have been obliged, in your case, to use obvious force. I am not proud of this. This is my message to you. Your detention will end soon. You will go free again. There will be compensation for your time. I have here a document that I would like you to sign." He produced several papers, in bright colors, from his coat pocket. "On the line here and here. Initial the copies, please."

"Nervy, you are nervy," said Gracie, taking the papers. It was a contract, more specifically, a waiver, excusing the Means Corporation, and its officers, of wrongdoing in a series of events which were described in completely unintelligible legal language. "Sign this?" said Gracie. "I'd eat it first."

"A signature is sufficient," he said, handing her a pen.

"Souvenir for me?" said Gracie.

"Yours will be the last," said Torrance VIII.

"What's that mean, Mr. President?" said Gracie.

"Your guardian. His son," said Torrance VIII.

"Effert signed this?" said Gracie.

"No, Abbott Broadsword," he lied. "There is an outstanding federal warrant that makes Effert's signature unnecessary."

"And the Contessa? Her mother? Being foreigners, they're less than people?" said Gracie.

"Not that," he said. "But international law is vague about temporary detention. Now, please, Effert's waiting."

"If I sign this, that's the deal?" said Gracie.

"Part of it. There's a large reward too," he said.

"When can we get out of here?" said Gracie.

"Soon, very soon," he said, smiling gorgeously.

"No!" said Grace, throwing pen and paper.

"What is it? What can I offer you?" he said.

"The truth. Why are we here?" said Gracie.

"You wouldn't begin to follow," he said.

"Give me that patronizing act again. That's sure to win my heart. Stupid old Gracie, ripe for the masculine mystique. Well, I don't want to play," said Gracie.

"I see. You're to be difficult. Now it is you who insist upon making a decision for a presumed greater good. For which your friends must suffer," said Torrance VIII.

"Oh, really, torture and death?" said Gracie. "You gonna seal us up in the dungeons. Like the little kid?"

"What? Who?" said Torrance VIII.

"Your little brother?" guessed Gracie.

"I don't know what you mean," he said unconvincingly.

"Monarch," said Gracie. "Little, fluttery Monarch and his test tubes. Blowing dope and sipping tea. A nice bit of tragedy. Is that what happens if I don't sign?"

"I don't know what you mean," he said.

"What if I said that I think the reason you put us here was because you and your major corporation are in something really dirty? What if I said I think one of us, maybe all of us, know something that could burn you guys? What if I said that I'd take a flying leap from that window before I'd ever sign anything you gave me? Now get out. And say hello to little Monarch for me. Tell him to save me a place at the hookah. I'll blow dope till Kingdom come before I'll deal with you, President Means."

"I'm not disturbing you?" said Aaron Verbunko in Italian, hat in hand at the doorway. "I can come back? Not come back?"

"I am your prisoner, Mr. Verbunko," said Bianca, shutting her English novel, H. G. Wells's *In the Days of the Comet,* which she'd found in Effert's coat pocket the night after the Cross-Country race. She gave a last glance at the operatic storm outside, then moved to sit on the loveseat before the fire. The servant served tea while Verbunko paced to her right, before the mantel. He seemed courtly, like a suitor, but anxious, like an inquisitor. It was futile, she knew, to hope he might tell her the truth of why he'd come to Craven Castle after over four weeks of this captivity. But she did wonder—the mystery of him. Bianca respected Verbunko's intellect. He was Swiss, after all, German Swiss from his accent, which slipped now and again from Oxbridge English or Tuscan Italian. That made him doubly fortified. The Germans had not gained their reputation as fierce competitors by accident. The Swiss had not gained their reputation as fierce neutrals by accident. There was a sublime cunning in a people who'd talked every tyranny in Europe, for one thousand years, out of invading them. The Swiss were not pacifists. They were dealers. Aaron Verbunko was even more bloodless and calculating than the Americans. She suspected they disliked him for this but trusted him for it as well. Bianca didn't favor men like Verbunko. She preferred boisterous, poetic, naive men, for they made earnest lovers and amiable, sad-eyed acquaintances. Yet there was a quality in Aaron Verbunko that intrigued her. As bland as he seemed—thin, mechanical, gray—he had an air of imminent danger. He was too dull not to be exciting. The money, experience, and savoir-faire showed through. He seemed a man who knew what should not be widely known. He seemed imperially removed. The seat of his soul seemed his tongue. Bianca decided to test him, asking:

"We are far from home, are we not?"

"Yes, we are, Countess," said Verbunko, crossing before her, taking a seat in the chair opposite, taking up a teacup, adding, "Why do you say that?"

"The Americans," said Bianca, waving her hands.

"I'm a citizen here now. You don't like it?" he said.

"It lacks subtlety," said Bianca.

"The master need not be discreet," said Verbunko.

"And you?" said Bianca.

"The servant, but you know this. I have been thinking of you, Countess. Do you recall our conversation on the terrace? The 'Rites of Spring'?" said Verbunko.

"When I accused you of losing faith?" said Bianca.

"You also said I was a corrupter of the Garden," he said.

"I spoke figuratively, as we Florentines do," said Bianca, taking her teacup. The tea leaves told her nothing. Bianca relied on her feyness. Verbunko was seeking her attention in the oddest way. He wanted her to disagree with him, and to judge him, and all at once. Bianca was charmed, adding, "I wouldn't repeat myself now."

"Oh?" he said. "You should know that I was once, well, I left the Church as a young man."

"I am not surprised," said Bianca.

"I was a brother. A Dominican. The Inquisition's order. I lost my faith. No Viennese calamity. A gradual dissipation. I awoke as my faith disappeared. This is accurate," said Verbunko, sipping, putting his cup down, lighting a cigarette before he continued. "I left the Church to enter University at Geneva, to traffic with the Protestant saints, whom I greatly impressed with my learning. The French are too easily impressed by Teutonic metaphysics. You know this. I retain vestiges of god talk. My theology is not as adept as it once was. My talent is language, but the language of men, not of God. Yet I am interested by your language. How did you mean that I am a corrupter of the Garden? Like the serpent?"

"The famous serpent," said Bianca.

"A turn of phrase?" said Verbunko.

"My Old Testament. There has been much said of the Old Adam and the New Adam," said Bianca. "There has been little said of the Old Eve and the New Eve. Grant me that I am the Old Eve's representative. The famous serpent. An intimate."

"You turn and turn," said Verbunko.

"I do believe you have forgotten your manners," said Bianca. "You hand me the whip. You ask me to use it on your oldest wounds. As my friend Gracie would say, 'I do not know you that well.' I return the instrument of abuse. This is not my idiom. I adjourn to feminine restraint."

"Not you," said Verbunko. "Watching you address your mother and her compatriot, the unreconstructed Stalinist, I would not believe this were you to swear it."

"What is it that you want to know from me?" said Bianca.

"Your redemptionism," said Verbunko. "If it is true that you hold out the possibility of a Redeemer, if such a person—a force, you mentioned—exists, then I am in need of guidance. The counsel must seek counsel."

"Let me answer you plainly," said Bianca. "I hold out the Redeemer. Not the possibility. The Redeemer. The Kingdom will come, Mr. Verbunko. This is my faith."

"I do not mean to challenge your faith," he said. "I wish that you would appreciate my position. When I abandoned the Church, I abandoned God and the Devil. It is not as straightforward as it might seem living in a world where there is no evil, where one does not believe in the bad. I must make decisions on the basis of the task at hand, not on moral absolutes. I choose from a field. Each person, thing, has its own merits and demerits. There are no clear-cut cases. I sometimes think it would be easier if I were religious. Then I could judge men for their crimes with both the lower law —which I read as well as make—and with the higher law, which tradition provides. Instead, I am left with intentions, and with the information provided me by futuristic machines that answer questions in terms of percentages of credibility and noncredibility. Do you see? My ally is the logical machine. Given the amount of superstition that persists even among expensively educated men, the machine is often my only ally. Only the machine—I am thinking of what the Americans call the supercomputer—joins me in regarding ethics as ritual chanting before and after events. Contessa, it is hard being a man of compromise, all compromise, only compromise. I do not elect. I do not condemn. I enhance."

"This machine. It troubles you?" said Bianca.

"It exists. But it is, more importantly, for the Americans, a figure of speech. They have their poetry, though a Florentine might not think it from the heart. It is their poetry. They believe in the machine. They sing of the machine. They reward men who defer to the machine, the percentages, rather than to their own wisdom. As the Americans say, 'It pays off in the long run.' They have no need of speaking of the Millennium. They are intrinsic millenarians. They are here for the 'long run.' Their machines assist them.

343

That's all. Assist. Not rule. You see, a Redeemer in America would be celebrated as a technical hero. The Americans would assume he had access to better machines, wherever he comes from. Is this not amusing?"

"I'm not sure," said Bianca. "What does trouble you?"

"I long for depths and heights. I have been long in the middle," said Verbunko.

"You miss the Whore of Babylon?" said Bianca.

Aaron Verbunko laughed long and low. He was transformed by his mirth. Bianca smiled, seeing the man beneath the "learning." He had her attention now. She had never thought to underestimate him. Now she no longer thought to overestimate him. Laughing, Aaron Verbunko revealed his humanity. It was fraught with contradictions, was stained, was even stale, but it was immediate. She liked him for his laugh, and for his mock anguish. Could she love such a man? Bianca wasn't sure. At some point in his past, Aaron Verbunko had abandoned more than the Church—as he too readily admitted. He'd also abandoned hope. Even if he was now seeking to retrieve it, the gap in his personality showed. He was atonal.

"A colorful remark," said Verbunko, which, being glib, angered Bianca, who wanted conspicuous vulnerability when her men were being confessional. She bridled.

"I think you've come to me because you think me totally alien to you!"

"Wait," said Verbunko, holding up his hand.

"Because I am a Jew," said Bianca. "That's why you are here. I am unclean for your abandoned brethren. And so I seem ready-made for you and your faithless struggle. You do miss the Whore of Babylon. You think me a worthy substitute. If not actually her. You might even believe we are perfectly paired. The defrocked arbiter and the Jewish aristocrat. I, from the country of confession. You, from the country of arbitration. I do not confess my uncleanness. You do not arbitrate your faithfulness. We are not merely far from home. We are homeless. You propose a sanctuary in mutual contempt for their—how did you put

344

it—'superstition'? It is an intriguing idea. I, the Old Eve. You, the serpent. And Adam, he is a fool. Tilling the soil somewhere. We can enjoy ourselves, eat apples, reflect, perhaps make music of a sort."

"You are unfair. Your poetry misguides you," he said.

"Possibly," said Bianca. "But I am not the only one who is misguided. What rules you? Not them. That is your conceit. What guides you?"

"I told you," said Verbunko.

"The machine, yes, charts and dots. An electric god," said Bianca.

"This is the late twentieth century," he said. "There is no need to resort to antique categorization. I am not a defrocked arbiter. You are not a Jewish aristocrat. We have names and histories. Certainly the humanism you profess teaches you that such talk of religion is self-denying. You are an intelligent person. A woman of the world. I am not uninformed. We are both from the Old World. We are both in the New World. I have come here today to offer you the Best World. For us. Not for some higher morality. Not for a formula that only your Dante could appreciate. For us. I understand," he said slowly, pausing, softening, "that you have been restless these past ten years, since the birth of your child."

"What do you know of her?" said Bianca.

"That she deserves a father and a mother," said Verbunko.

"Are you making love to me? I think you the coldest man I have ever met," said Bianca.

"I am speaking of 1986. Of my resources and your desires," said Verbunko.

"And vice versa," said Bianca, pausing, thinking, not unamused, adding, "What of the Means? I had thought you beholden to them in many ways."

"Yes," said Verbunko, standing at that to take a turn about the room, climbing the two steps to the window seat to consider the storm outside. It raged, as he must not if he was to succeed with the Contessa. He had anticipated it

345

would come to this. His relationship with Justine was at the center of his protracted anxiety. The Contessa was aggressive and brilliant. She was also a woman. She would not share him with Justine. Verbunko acknowledged the correctness of this. He was in love with Justine Means. He had been since first meeting her in Paris in the early seventies. And yet, after all these years, he had no tangible proof of her love for him. She played with his talents. She leaned on him whenever it was convenient. He had once thought Justine an important link to the Means Corporation. But he had quickly discarded that once he'd come to America. The Means Corporation thought itself too modern to respond to melodrama. Verbunko's relationship with Justine meant nothing in terms of his relationship with the corporation. More to the point, though, he knew Justine would never wed him. He accepted this. They had a compelling respect for each other's weakness. She knew his insecurity as a contrived antagonist. He knew her insecurity as a genuine antagonist. They belonged to each other without need for contract. He had thought to continue this arrangement indefinitely. The Contessa offered another possibility. She offered partnership. From what his agents had told him of her history, she was primed for an American period—race bigotries aside, epiphenomenal wealth at every turn. America was not only the land of opportunity, it was the land of guiltless, ruthless abandon. The Contessa could confront this temptation and subordinate it to her will to survive. Underneath all this as well, she was extraordinarily beautiful and quick. He wanted her. That, after all, was why he was here. Passion never looked rational upon reexamination. He had come to negotiate his way clear of Justine's charms. He must bear down. The Contessa was as tough a negotiator as he was. It was time to tell her more than she needed to know. Without turning, he said:

"The Means have become obsolete. They have become counterproductive."

"Treachery, then?" said Bianca.

"You yourself said it. They lack subtlety. You are

correct. I misrepresented myself when I said the master must not be discreet. He, above all others, must be. The Means have had their day," said Verbunko.

"And you? You're the New Order?" said Bianca.

"I think you are being only half sarcastic," said Verbunko. "The Means are typical of a number of commercial family empires that have dominated American capitalism since the Industrial Revolution. Their true power is more in their name than in their wealth. They have been useful as icons, to which any number of ambitious young men and women have attached themselves. These families have served as the American aristocracy, entering into the tasks appropriate to an omnipotent elite, such as unapologetic acquisitiveness, blood purification, providing for the common defense by serving in elective and appointed governmental posts. In brief, they have ruled clubbily and selfishly."

"You make them sound like ruses," said Bianca.

"Not always," said Verbunko, turning back to her now. "They have had genuine power. They have served with legitimacy. When critics denounced the Astors, the Vanderbilts, the Rockefellers, the Fords, they were speaking to the effective power center. What was called the 'Permanent Government.' It did exist."

"And now?" said Bianca.

"It still exists. But it is changing," said Verbunko.

"To what? Yourself?" said Bianca.

"It is more general than names," said Verbunko.

"A faceless Big Brother. You are trying to impress me with your insinuations of conspiracy. Conspiracy is seductive," said Bianca. "To this, I will admit."

"I am trying to explain why the Means have had their day," said Verbunko. "And your poetry misleads you again."

"The world is not nearly so simple," said Bianca. "But you know that. You condescend to explain it to me. At any moment, and you know it, chaos might drop again, in the night. Your New Order, or whatever you want to call it, could merely be another way of pretending there is order. You talk of civilization while you mock it. The Means seem preferable to your nebulous amorality."

"The known scoundrel preferable to the unknown scoundrel?" said Verbunko.

"Answer me this," said Bianca. "How do you keep from going down with the Means? It seems to me you are heavily implicated in this present fiasco. It is a fiasco. What you call 'Harold Starr.' A fiasco."

"You know nothing," said Verbunko.

"What is it? A desperate ploy? It's why you've put us here, I can guess that. But why? Because they are in danger of making their final mistake?" said Bianca.

"No corporate mistake is final," said Verbunko. "There are only calculations and miscalculations. The Means Corporation has calculated that keeping you here will protect its immediate interests. The Means Corporation must answer to others. In corporate life, no man, no company of men, acts alone, without checks and charges. And if there is a miscalculation, there must be an adjustment. You do follow?"

"You, then, are the man to adjust?" said Bianca.

"Yes," said Verbunko, bowing slightly.

"So your treachery is that you are loyal to appropriate calculation," said Bianca. "Not to people. Not to ideas. Not to yourself."

"I am corporation counsel," said Verbunko.

"I concede my admiration," said Bianca.

"Thank you, Contessa," said Verbunko.

"I also ask that you withdraw. You shall have my answer to your proposal when this present matter is concluded. When 'Harold Starr' is done, one way, or another."

"A condition?" said Verbunko.

"I have my secrets," said Bianca.

"But you don't even know what it is," said Verbunko.

"True," said Bianca, glancing down at the Wells. "But I am getting to like him, it, whatever, more each day. An old habit."

348

"Poetry again," said Verbunko, noticing the Wells.

"Faith," said Bianca.

The Means' private apartments at Craven Castle filled the upper reaches of the rear tower, with the elaborately carved staircase attached to it externally, winding from the turret down to disappear in the wall. Climbing up that staircase now, pausing twice to catch his breath, to shelter his head from the whip of the storm over the castle, was Westergaard, dressed in his usual martial livery, campaign jacket buttoned tight, campaign cap pulled tight. He could have used the inner stairs, or the elevator, and saved himself a soaking. But that wasn't his style. He paused again at the top of the stairs to study his command. In the bailey were two Landrovers and the baker's delivery truck his men had found in the woods surrounding Means Manor during the search for the missing bodyguards (the "Wonder" van). On the walls, five guards made their precise turns along the battlements. In the distance, on the trestled pine bridge, two more guards made their precise turns. Westergaard, like the excellent captain of the guard that he was, restudied the scene—the gray walls, the five towers, the bailey, the heliport to the rear of the castle, with its hangar, its blunt control tower, its fleet of six machines less the six off on assignment, its well-marked chopper pad. He nodded to himself. Last light, and all seemed well at Craven Castle. The Means should be pleased. But what nagged him? He couldn't name it. It was a twinge, like the countless twinges he'd had on countless battlefields around the globe all his adult life. He might be getting old—his arthritis, or one of his old wounds. There it was again. In his kidneys. The queasiness of impending alarm, or worse, an intuition of disaster. He popped the door, walked up more stairs, tapped on a heavy wooden door.

"Enter," said Happy Means, seated elegantly, in cashmere and cunning, at her Louis XIV antique desk. Indeed, her apartments were all Louis antique, as befitted her temperament—delicate, painted, and propped up by a philosophy that makes the piracy of the nineteenth and twentieth centuries seem as triumphs of egalitarianism.

"Reporting, Mrs. Means," said Westergaard.

"Sit with me, Westergaard," said Happy. "I've been reviewing your log. Excellent."

"Thank you, Mrs. Means," said Westergaard, sitting nearby.

"The Thyme girl's been a bother?" said Happy.

"Nothing out of the ordinary," said Westergaard.

"What's this about last night?" said Happy.

"My lieutenant is still investigating," said Westergaard.

"I'm sure. And the Jewess?" said Happy.

"Pardon?" said Westergaard.

"The Contessa," said Happy.

"A model prisoner. She reads," said Westergaard.

"What books do you give her?" said Happy.

"There are books in her room. I saw her reading something about comets yesterday," said Westergaard.

"Oh? I want a list as soon as possible," said Happy.

"Very well, Mrs. Means," said Westergaard.

"Do you know why these people are here?" said Happy.

"No, I do not," said Westergaard.

"Would you like to know?" said Happy.

"I am a soldier, Mrs. Means," said Westergaard.

Happy didn't respond immediately. Westergaard irked her. He was good at his job, of course. He and his command were there for the "extraordinary" in corporate life—detentions, smuggling, courier duty, escort duty, swift force—the usual necessities of international business in a world of impotent nation-states. For the record, Means did not employ the largest private army among corporations, but the one it did support was a considerable presence. They were not thugs. They were professional soldiers. They were well paid. Still, something in Westergaard's manner annoyed Happy. It might have been that he'd developed more

350

of an attachment to his vocation than to his employer's welfare. It might have been that he was getting too old for his job.

"And a very efficient one," said Happy. The buzzer on her desk sounded. There was a visitor at the front door.

"Shall I retire?" said Westergaard.

"No," said Happy, moving to the door to usher in Torrance VIII, saying to him, "Westergaard's just told me how dull our guests have been."

"Not dull enough, I'm thinking," said Torrance VIII, crossing to pour himself a whiskey from the bar.

"Did they sign?" said Happy.

"Just a minute," said Torrance VIII. "Where was Grace Thyme last night, Westergaard?"

"My lieutenant is investigating," said Westergaard.

"Was she in the playpen?" said Torrance VIII.

"I don't know, sir," said Westergaard.

"Well, get on it," said Torrance VIII. "I want a full report by morning, is that clear? Get it out of her."

"Yes, sir. Good evening, sir. Mrs. Means," said Westergaard, leaving by the outer door. The door shut firmly.

"Grace Thyme knows about Monarch," said Torrance VIII.

"What about the other? What about *her?*" said Happy.

"I think not. The Contessa might. She's dodgy," he said.

"If she's on one of her sprees again," said Happy. "Oh, God, Tory, how did we get into this mess?"

"Verbunko says we underestimate the misinformed," he said.

"What's he doing about it?" said Happy.

"He spent the afternoon with the Contessa. He fancies her, I think," said Torrance VIII sarcastically. "She teases him."

"Oh?" said Happy. "Pity that your sisters aren't here to see it. You say Aaron likes her? I hadn't realized. Don't walk away from me when I'm talking to you."

351

"Happy, please," he said. "I'm exhausted. Cedric Broadsword is as thickheaded as his son. The whole family pains me. Now even Abbott Broadsword won't deal with us. The most obsequious of men. He claims to have discovered some philosophical reason to resist our 'temptation.' I do believe they think they're better men for this. Can you account for it? If I were only a violent man."

"Then none of them signed?" said Happy.

"Reward doesn't interest them. They scream for 'justice.' It follows perversely that minor players want intangibles. And you should hear Grace Thyme. She took to teasing me with Monarch. None of them knows anything, I'm sure. But they bait me. Me. If I were only a violent man."

"That's why we have men like Westergaard," said Happy. "Put it out of your mind. Perhaps we should have handled it entirely through Aaron. Then again, whose idea *was* it we come here?"

"You should have seen Grace!" said Torrance VIII. "She pranced around like an Amazon. Hilarious."

"It was Aaron's idea we come up here, wasn't it?" said Happy, mostly to herself, walking toward Tory. "You should have been more persuasive with her, dear. I understand you have been previously."

"Don't," he said, covering his eyes. "I made a mistake. Justy set me up, all right? Ring for dinner, will you? I'm going to bathe and change."

"What you need is a soak and then a rub," said Happy, wrapping her arms around him from the rear. "Maybe a nap before supper? Wouldn't that be heavenly?"

"Mmh," said Torrance VIII.

"A long, hard rub," said Happy, biting his ear until she tasted sticky sweet, then leaning forward, leaving a bloody smear across his cheek, to chew on his mouth, teeth butting teeth, until it hurt them both. Happy hurt Tory, and Tory hurt Happy. They continued, unclothed, hearts and parts, arms and charms, finger to linger where heat and meat combine. They renewed the joys of exchanged fetishes: bone-cracking, blood-tasting, bruise-raising, then a bath together, apart, scalding and freezing. Their understanding was that when vassals won't roll over and comply, it's time for master and mistress to roll over and apply their frustrations on each other's wants. If it pains, even better. To come perchance to cope was the deeper message, just about as deep as Tory took Happy and Happy took Tory, entranced with each other's chosen identities—he the chosen churl, she the mock mother. They supped on each other's hormones, and then, still hungry, ordered midnight supper on Happy's enclosed terrace overlooking the pentagonal castle, the high rock, the murky lake, the heavy forest, and, this evening, the wild storm. Verbunko arrived with the fourth bottle of wine.

"I've been on the line with New York," said Verbunko.

"Glass of wine, Aaron?" said Happy, giggling—pop!

"Thank you," said Verbunko, "I'm told matters proceed."

"Did you talk to Father on patch?" said Torrance VIII.

"Operational silence," said Verbunko.

"Has Father been in touch?" said Torrance VIII.

"The silence is complete," said Verbunko.

"That's impressive. Word from our friends?" said Torrance VIII. "Or do you mean complete?"

"Yes. Nothing in or out of PIT Peak," said Verbunko.

"What right have they got? Considering our investment?" Happy was drunk, but sharp. "Answer me, Aaron."

"The situation is complex and ambivalent," said Verbunko.

"Happy, we've gone through this," said Torrance VIII.

"Enough so to muzzle several hundred of the most important corporations in the world?" said Happy. "I think it's childish, and excessive."

"There are no surprises. This was agreed upon generally years ago. A final variation," said Verbunko.

"Contingencies, Happy," said Torrance VIII.

"We are near complete success," said Verbunko.

"I don't like it. Who're they to do such a thing?" said Happy.

"Us, Mrs. Means," said Verbunko.

"It's been a long day," said Torrance VIII.

"Don't apologize for me," said Happy.

"We will all rest easier once 'Harold Starr' is resolved," said Verbunko. "New York tells me they have already received an agenda for ensuing operations. The harvest will justify both our expense and concern, Mrs. Means."

"You see, Happy?" said Torrance VIII.

"Don't convince me. Show me," said Happy.

"Your criticism, from the beginning, has been valuable in assisting us to proceed with discretion. You have greatly contributed to our impending success," said Verbunko.

"Have I now? Your charm might work better on the Jewess, Aaron. I've seen your dossier. She hasn't," said Happy.

"Pass on this, Verbunko," said Torrance VIII.

"Don't tell him what to do. It's after hours. Tell us about the Jewess, Aaron. And how you will reap that harvest."

"What is it that you want to know?" said Verbunko.

"Oh, Aaron, without you, none of this would be half as much fun," said Happy, giggling, drinking, giggling.

"When can we expect confirmation?" said Torrance VIII.

"Within twenty-four hours we can anticipate confirmation of contact. This is the most crucial time now. The larger affair will be made public as the larger picture emerges. There are some, like our prisoners, who may have guessed wildly about 'Harold Starr,' but I can assure you that no one knows anything about the big picture. They still call it the 'Macho Project.' After all these years, they still can't see what's in front of them. It's so involved, I doubt if anyone will even blink when they do know."

"Doubt, doubt, doubt?" said Happy.

"None whatsoever," said Verbunko.

"Have some more wine, Happy," said Torrance VIII.

"You do think of me," said Happy.

"Yes," said Torrance VIII. "Just think of it, Verbunko. What we will have contributed to. A whole new market."

"A new factor as well, sir," said Verbunko.

"Feeling your drink, Aaron?" said Happy.

"Yes, I am, Mrs. Means," said Verbunko.

The three relaxed in silence. The night outside was black with violent possibility. They finished the magnum, opened another, drank on. In hazy stupors, tired as they were, the knock on the terrace door went unnoticed. The knock quickened, became a pound, ending with:

"Excuse me for intruding," boomed an extremely agitated Westergaard, which was the last any of them heard before they were brought completely alert by the blaze of lights on the chopper pad below. Simultaneously there came the whirling roar of a helicopter feeling its way down in the storm.

"What is this?!" demanded Torrance VIII.

"Chopper coming in, sir," said Westergaard.

"We can see that!" said Torrance VIII, up and pressing against the glass of the terrace, throwing open a small window, leaning out to watch the machine settle toward the pad.

"Who is it?" said Verbunko calmly.

"I do not know, sir," said Westergaard, who was so deliberately trying to control himself that he seemed in slow motion. "We have lost radar and communications. Something is jamming us. It's all down."

"What! How can that be?" said Torrance VIII.

"Tell us, Westergaard," said Verbunko.

"Permission to go to Action Stations, sir," said Westergaard.

"This isn't one of your wars," said Torrance VIII.

"Yes, sir, but communications are down. In fact, all our electronics are down. Our power remains satisfacory, of course, but I've already gone to auxiliary in order to . . ."

"Nonsense!" interrupted Torrance VIII.

"Tory, look," said Happy at the open window, pointing to the helicopter already on the ground. The rear door opened. Two figures paused at the edge, each carrying oversized portfolio cases, each dressed in yellow rain suits. "What are they doing here? Who is responsible for this? They're supposed to be in the Med."

"Please, Happy, slowly. Did you know about this, Verbunko?" said Torrance VIII.

"No, sir, I am as surprised as you," said Verbunko, peering down to the chopper pad. There was a rush of guards from the hangar. Several attendants cleared away the tarp on a small tow car, intending to chauffeur the new visitors across the expanse of the high rock to the postern gate. Verbunko thought he understood the excitement below. This was the first time, to his knowledge, that the Twin Sisters Means had ever come to Craven Castle.

"What is this, Westergaard?" said Torrance VIII, controlling himself now. "I think you'd better explain."

"I have not come because of the bogey," said Westergaard. "It's this, sir."

Verbunko reached out to take a cloth-yard shaft from Westergaard. It looked to him to be handmade. There was a piece of parchment tied tightly below the shaft's head. Verbunko held it up to show Torrance VIII and Happy. Then he carefully removed the parchment. He unrolled a letter, read it. He read it again, then again, looking up, saying:

"Did you look at this, Captain?"

"Yes, sir," said Westergaard.

"Does it make any sense to you?" said Verbunko.

"No, sir," said Westergaard.

"Where did you find it?" said Verbunko.

"Fixed high on the inner gate, sir," said Westergaard.

"Why are you standing there?!" said Happy. "Get down there. Contain them. Aaron, get down there. We can't have them wandering around the castle unattended. My God, get down there!" She was near hysteria.

356

"Happy, wait," said Torrance VIII. He knew she was right.

"Read this," said Verbunko, handing the parchment letter to Torrance VIII, turning to Westergaard. "You say that you've lost communications, Captain. That means we're cut off?"

"Technically, yes, theoretically no, sir," said Westergaard. "With half my command away on assignment, I'm concerned for the security of my perimeter."

"You're not being alarmist?" said Verbunko.

"No, sir. The lines are down as well," said Westergaard.

"But I was on with New York just before midnight," said Verbunko.

"Down, sir," said Westergaard.

"The storm? It might be?" said Verbunko. For the first time, Verbunko noticed that Westergaard was heavily armed.

"I think not. From the paper, one thing is clear," said Westergaard.

"Go on," said Verbunko, sitting down.

"We are under attack," said Westergaard.

"Yes," said Verbunko.

"You don't actually believe this?" said Torrance VIII, handing the letter back to Verbunko, sitting down also.

"Under the circumstances, sir," said Westergaard, "I would advise it best to conduct ourselves as if we were faced by a superior, hostile force that has successfully isolated us from reinforcement and resupply."

"What do you think, Verbunko?" said Torrance VIII.

"I would prefer you make the decision," said Verbunko.

"Tory!" screamed Happy, seeing the Twin Sisters Means stepping down from the helicopter into the tow car. She threw down her glass and charged off to get dressed to attend to matters herself. Happy didn't care about a silly arrow. She believed she had a potentially more damaging family crisis. Still, given Torrance VIII's arrogant

357

ambivalence, given Verbunko's mysterious passivity, given Westergaard's armed anxiety, Happy should have read the letter:

> We, Swinyard & Schleppend, attnys-at-law, with the assistance of our allies, Rufus Broadsword, mathematician, and the good pilgrims Wladyslaw Wrathnitski, Rollo, and he called Freewill, and the company of freemen called the Comet Clubbe, and Yella Kissl and Lyra, citizens, accuse you men of Craven Castle with having unlawfully kidnapped our friends, Cedric and Abbott Broadsword, bankers, Effert Broadsword, pilgrim, Grace Thyme, athlete, Europa Stupefacenta and Bonaventuro Pellegrino, Florentines, and Bianca Capricciosa, Contessa, and with having imprisoned them against their wills in Craven Castle.
>
> We demand that you release our friends and loved ones, in good health, before dawn.
>
> If you do not, we will regard you as villains and fiends, and we will attack without quarter.
>
> This we swear, in the name of Revolution and Justice, 1 June 1986. S&S.
>
> P.S. One of our vast number will visit you within the hour to ensure the good health of our friends and loved ones. S&S.

Free the People

OUR LETTER said one!"
"How come he's going?"
"He wants to!"
"Where he goes, I go!"
"Crazy!"

Three cloaked figures trudged out of the shelter of the pines, into the heavy rain, up over the trestled pine bridge, past the abandoned guardposts, up the earthen ramp to the gatehouse of Craven Castle. The lead figure, Schleppend, pounded on the portcullis, demanding entry, claiming he was a "Humble Child of God!" The portcullis cranked up just high enough to permit him to duck underneath. A taller, broader figure, Swinyard, had to duck even lower. A squat dwarf followed without blinking. Once between the portcullis and the inner wooden gate, they waited for a command. Instead, at the side, a large stone swung back, revealing a sally port. They walked through it, following a narrow, dim passageway. Grandtour had told them Craven Castle was powered by "a masterless fire," but it seemed to Schleppend that the defenders had gone to torch power. The three emerged from the passageway and halted. Before them was a huge, beamed, pennant-draped chamber, with suits of armor, crossed spears, trebuchets, and maces, mounted along the stone walls. In the middle of the chamber—the Great Hall—was a horseshoe-shaped banquet table with a single fierce soldier leaning casually against its exact center. Schleppend gulped a big breath and stepped once toward the warrior.

"Hold!"

"Sure," said Schleppend.

"State your business!"

"I am a Humble Child of God," said Schleppend. "A large band of blackguards has forced me to come here as their emissary."

"I'm to believe that?"

"That's my story," said Schleppend. It did sound lame.

"Who are these two?"

"My associates?" said Schleppend.

The single fierce soldier laughed, pounding the table in his amusement, finally saying, "Go on, do your duty."

"What's funny?" said Schleppend.

"Go on!" he commanded, pointing to an archway

leading to a staircase. Schleppend tiptoed toward the stairway, passing several armed guards he hadn't initially seen.
He paused at the base of the spiral staircase. The guards
waved him on. Schleppend, with Swinyard and Laddy close
behind, climbed the stairs, round and round, up and up. He
reached the top landing, heaving for breath. He turned.
Swinyard and Laddy were gone—just vanished. Schleppend
listened down the stairs, thinking he heard footfalls far
below. Clowns! If they wanted to get themselves racked,
that was their tough luck. Swinyard wasn't himself anymore. He doted on the little fellow, Laddy. But then none
of them were quite on top of things, after one solid month
of walking in the rain. Their brains were waterlogged. And,
too, long walks in caravan with a long-haired dude who
glowed in the dark and with wacked-out aerospace engineers from beyond a binge would unhinge anyone. This was
what his friends in Oregon would call a "Major Visitation,"
though not even they would be comfortable with the details.
Schleppend caught himself. He had promised himself that
he would not, that is, NOT reflect upon what he'd been
through the last month, chanting, "This is not happening.
This is not happening. This is not happening," as he walked
to the single torch at the end of the hallway. There was a
heavy, wooden door, unbolted. There were no guards to be
seen. Schleppend opened the door to shout:
    "Hello! Hello! Is anyone alive?!"
    "What's this?" said Cedric, emerging with a lamp
from his bedroom. Schleppend jumped into the room,
shouting:
    "Mr. Broadsword! It's me, Schleppend!"
    "About time," said Cedric, moving to pound on Ab-
bott's door, then to pound on Bonaventuro's door. "Get
dressed! We're being rescued! Abbott! Signor!"
    "Not just yet," said Schleppend.
    "Why not?" said Cedric, as Abbott and Bonaventuro
appeared.
    "A long story," said Schleppend. "But for the mo-
ment, it's just you. Take my cloak and escape as me."

"Who's with you? FBI? The Mounties?" said Cedric.

"You wouldn't understand," said Schleppend. "But they're waiting outside the castle for you. They attack at dawn if the Means don't let you go. I'm supposedly here to check that you're okay. Actually, we switch, see, because they need you outside. You know the layout. You must hurry!"

"Preposterous. Not until we all go. Abbott?" said Cedric.

"You're the man for the job, Father," said Abbott.

"Signor?" said Cedric, offering the cloak.

"Non, Fra," said Bonaventuro.

"Please, hurry. They're waiting for you," said Schleppend.

"Who's waiting?" said Cedric, still hesitating.

"Uh, the Comet Clubbe?" said Schleppend.

"Who? Are you joking with me?" said Cedric.

"No. It's a bunch of guys from Grimmen. And elsewhere," said Schleppend.

"A bunch of guys. The Means have a company of mercenaries. You come here with a bunch of guys?" said Cedric.

"Has this anything to do with 'Harold Starr'?" said Abbott.

"You hip, then?" said Schleppend.

"Getting there. Father, I think you should do as he says. There's more here than can easily be explained," said Abbott.

"Got that right," said Schleppend, winking at Abbott. Suddenly, in one of those rushes that leads to wisdom, Schleppend decided he'd misunderstood too much in his brief life, including, for example, Abbott Broadsword. He wasn't a bad man—enough said. Fortified by this fleeting insight, Schleppend said, "Get going, Mr. Broadsword! In the name of Revolution and Justice, get going!"

"Aye, but I protest," said Cedric, pulling the cloak over his head, lacing his shoes, opening the door, pounding down the hallway, hearing Schleppend calling from behind.

"If they hassle ya, tell 'em yer a 'Humble Child of God.' "

Cedric grunted, charged down the stairs. He had one mission in mind before meeting any "bunch of guys." He was going to free Gracie. That was his compulsion. All else would follow or not. He thundered down the staircase, pausing at the bottom to catch his breath and to orient himself in the shadows. His best guess was that Gracie's tower was at the top of that stairway. He rushed across the periphery of the Great Hall and up the spiral stairs. Queer, he thought, there being no guards about. Queerer still, the torchlight. Cedric reached the landing, expecting trouble. But there was no guard here either. He unbolted the door, calling:

"Grace! Grace! I've come for you!"

A bedroom door opened. A woman emerged, pulling on her robe, saying, *"Padrone?"* and rushing to throw herself in Cedric's arms, kissing his breast, weeping for joy, "Oh, *Padrone."*

"Don't Contessa, it's all right now," said Cedric.

"I knew you'd come for me," said Bianca.

"You did?" said Cedric, surprised by her ardor.

"What is happening?" said Bianca. "I will dress."

"I don't know much," said Cedric. "We're being rescued by, uh, friends. Revolution and justice, aye." He walked to the bank of windows over the forest. That was an ugly night out there. He called, "Do you know how to get to Grace?"

"It is the one across," called Bianca from the bedroom.

"Aye," said Cedric, realizing he didn't know Craven Castle as well as he'd thought. He'd been here twice since his firm had been acquired outright by the Means in the fifties, both times on corporate VIP junkets—hunting and drinking weekends. He'd thought he'd mastered the tunnels and towers. He understood now that was his conceit. The Means Corporation, with its protean power, had constructed a protean fortress. It seemed to change shape depending upon its masque, whether fete for the fortunate or fate for the unfortunate. It was profoundly different from Broadsword Hall, which stood as a monument to commercial enterprise. Broadsword Hall could only be acted upon by its inhabitants. Craven Castle seemed to act upon its inhabitants. Cedric shook his head hard. That "bunch of guys," thought Cedric, they'd need a lot more than his help —fantastically more—if they hoped to storm Craven Castle on a night like this.

"I am ready now, *Padrone,*" said Bianca, tying back her hair, ripping off the hem of her dress at mid-calf so that she could run. "Where do we go? What do we do? Gracie? Mama?"

"I have to think, Contessa," said Cedric, pressing his head against the glass, trying to discern direction from the treetops, which were weaving as if beckoning. He felt weak.

"And Effert Broadsword," said Bianca, taking his arm.

"Effert," repeated Cedric. He had a son—a big, violent adventurer. There was direction there. But what would it look like? Cedric said, "You're all safer here until the Means are done. And Westergaard beaten. But how, how?"

"I am how," said the wall, which, opening, revealed Vernal Means, as before, adorned like *La Primavera,* aged like Corruption. Vernal screamed, "Get out, child! Don't look! Get out! No! Look away! Get out!"

"Come on!" said Cedric, grabbing Bianca to run.

"No! Stay, Cedric Broadsword!" said Vernal. "Get out!"

"Come no closer," said Cedric, holding up his fists.

"*Padrone,* I shall go to Gracie, then Mama," said Bianca.

"No, wait!" said Cedric, reaching to stop her, but she was gone too quickly, leaving the door open behind her. He started for it, but the deformed shadow was too fast for him. She slammed the door. She said, "Light a lamp, Cedric."

"Who are you?" said Cedric, repelled by her smell and her mad voice.

"Do as I say, Cedric," said Vernal.

"Not until you tell me who you are," said Cedric.

"You haven't changed, *cheri*," said Vernal.

"What?" said Cedric, lighting the lamp now. He saw a horror. He choked, "Who in God's name are you?"

"Bess!" exploded Vernal. "Your sweet Bess! Bess! Bess!" Vernal swirled into her mad dance, laughing, "Kee-kee-kee!" with flowers flying off as her gown twisted tightly on her body, screaming, "Bess! I'm your sweet Bess!"

"God help me!" said Cedric, revolted, mesmerized.

"This is she! Isn't she hateful and ugly? You see what happens? Bess!" Vernal twirled so hard she knocked the table over. Cedric just managed to catch the oil lamp, crying:

"Have mercy! Stop saying that! Please, God!"

"This is Bess! I am the ghost of Bess! All the Besses! Coming for you, old man! See what you did to me! Hate!"

"No," said Cedric, crashing against the wall, barely able to hold the lamp. He couldn't breathe. He felt his heart thump. He beat his chest with his free hand. Get hold of yourself. You're tougher than this. This is fraud. Bess is dead. In the ground thirty years. He screamed, "Stop! My Bess is dead! I know that! Who are you?"

"I am dead. A ghost of her," said Vernal, stopping flat.

"You are not my Bess," said Cedric angrily, gathering himself now, standing straight, pointing at her. "Now tell me who you are or don't. I'm leaving."

"I am their mother! They are my children!" said Vernal, dropping her voice to a hoarse whisper. "Don't you remember our summers? We had such lovely moments at the Manor. Bess was beautiful, and you were so proud. The summer before she died? She looked best in blue."

"Vernal," gasped Cedric. "How can you be Vernal? She's . . ."

"Dead, dead, dead," said Vernal. "I've enjoyed this chat. Now go and tell your rescuers they must attack. And when they see me on the high tower, they are to run for their lives. For the lives of their children. Tell them as I say. I am how. I am how. I am how." She paused, then screamed, "Go! And damn you to Hell! Damn all men like you! Damn!"

Then she was gone, back into the wall, pulling the panel shut behind her, leaving Cedric open-mouthed. He couldn't begin to make sense of this. Vernal Means? Impossible! She was over twenty-five years dead. A miscarriage at forty. Sudden and tragic. He'd attended her funeral. A huge affair. It'd been a twin catastrophe—mother and child. They'd buried them together. Impossible! Cedric tore open the door, telling himself to forget the crazy hag and to remember Grace and the rest. He returned to the Great Hall. It was so dark he walked into the arms of three guards.

"What have we here?" said one, pushing Cedric hard.

"Humble Child of God," said Cedric.

"Where're yer buddies?"

"Humble Child of God," said Cedric, backing away from them, looking over his shoulder for a door, any door. He saw a dark passageway. The guards stood still, conferring confusedly.

"Should we hold him for Murtrux?"

"He's the one they sent. Can ya believe we've had to scramble for this? Westergaard must be getting soft."

"Beat it, you!"

"Humble Child of God!" said Cedric, shuffling backwards. He had no choice. That or nothing. He dove for it.

"Hold it, you!"

"Nah, let's let him go."

Cedric turned around and ran down the passageway, throwing himself at a stone wall. He was trapped! No, the stone swung back. He was outside, underneath the gatehouse, between the inner gate and the portcullis. He leaped at the portcullis, screaming, "Humble Child of God! Humble Child of God!"

The portcullis came up, hesitated, came up, and stopped three feet off the ramp. It started down again. Cedric threw himself to the ground and rolled underneath, a free man. The rain was blinding. He lurched up, down the ramp. He ran pell-mell. He crossed the bridge in a looping stagger. He crashed into the underbrush. He crashed into a man's arms—a giant man's arms.

Book VI

Wherein the Proto Industrial
Trust Is Temporarily Thwarted in
Its Plan for Conquest

The Devil's Work

WHY HAD the Twin Sisters Means come to Craven Castle? The act of coming is a many-splendored verb. It begins as much as it ends. Still, they had come. Why now, though never before? A tentative answer must mention the mystery of the Broadswords' imprisonment; the fact that Torrance VIII, Happy, and Aaron Verbunko had departed secretly for Craven Castle within a fortnight of seeing the Twin Sisters Means off on a Mediterranean holiday. Yet the full answer is deeper, is more mixed with the metaphysical aspects of the Twin Sisters Means. Justine and Christine had come to their father's castle. They had come on a pilgrimage. They sought revelation. They were drawn as much as they came of their own freewill. They came for a confrontation with fate. Their choice of arena—a medieval fortress—was telling of their immortal souls: vulnerable, guarded, defeatist.

Then there is the significant detail that their Mediterranean holiday was in celebration of their fortieth birthday.

They were no longer young. They were not old. They were no longer young.

Through the postern gate they came, Justine in the lead, Christine close behind, their yellow rain suits over black silk pajamas, both carrying oversized portfolio cases. The cases were heavy, but they refused help. They passed into the guards' quarters, where there were greeted by an agitated Westergaard. He ushered them into the officers' clubroom, where a meal had been prepared for them. They ate lightly, marveling at the wall of heads. Westergaard seemed at peace telling them stories about this or that visage. He soon lost his concentration, however, and excused himself, leaving his first lieutenant, Murtrux, in attendance. Soon, Justine asked that they might be directed to the family apartments. Murtrux offered to escort them as soon as Westergaard returned. Justine insisted they go now, alone. Murtrux protested that the elevator banks were temporarily out of order—a power reduction. Justine ordered Murtrux to obey. Reluctantly he walked them to the base of the tower's internal staircase. Guided only by the light of their oil lamps, they began the winding climb to the top. Their footfalls made tiny echoing clicks on the stone as they reached the first landing, the second, pausing to rest.

"You think that was Happy's game?" said Justine.

"Yes," said Christine.

"Westergaard was shaky," said Justine.

"Yes," said Christine.

"Because of us?" said Justine.

"I couldn't be sure," said Christine.

"What do you think of the place?" said Justine.

"I don't," said Christine.

"It is trite. Damp too," said Justine.

"No damper than the Manor," said Christine.

"No . . . do you think Tory will be upset?" said Justine.

"Furious," said Christine.

"Aaron too?" said Justine.

"Especially Aaron," said Christine.

"Yes, especially," said Justine.

"We do want to do this, Justy? I feel cold about it," said Christine.

"It's the damp," said Justine. "Up we go, then, 'Harold Starr,' whatever you really are, here we come."

"We don't know that," said Christine.

"Soon, soon, soon," said Justine.

They slowed their pace at the third landing, larger than the lower two, with several heavy doors bolted shut around the walls, and with an archway giving onto an open-air balcony passing off to the left to the battlements, now being pummeled by torrents of rain splashing over the walls. The wind whipped spray into the landing. Justine and Christine had to edge a pool of slimy water. They sheltered their heads as they crossed the open archway. Two steps up the staircase, they started at the sound of one of the bolted doors creaking open. Justine held up her lamp to see. A head peeked through. Christine held up her lamp, but it slipped and shattered on the landing, spilling oil into the slimy pool. The oil exploded, whoof! so that a sludgy sea of yellow fire separated the Twin Sisters Means from Gracie and Bianca.

"Caught in the act," said Gracie.

"Hello, Miss Thyme," said Justine.

"We've just arrived," said Christine.

"Horseshit, girls," said Gracie.

"My friend means to ask what you have to do with our imprisonment," said Bianca, stepping to Gracie's side, and slightly before, looking that much more fey in the dance of the firelight across her black hair and blacker-still eyes.

"You don't look fettered to me. Sister?" said Justine.

"Free as birds," said Christine.

"Funny you should mention birds," said Gracie.

"My friend refers to the mythological creature. The half-woman, half-bird," said Bianca.

"Oh, harpies," said Christine.

"We are agreed." said Bianca.

"Can we help you? We're in a teensy hurry," said Justine.

"Stay awhile, Miss Means," said Gracie.

"We are innocent," said Christine.

"Prove it," said Gracie.

"Come on, Christy, they won't listen," said Justine.

"I said to stay awhile," said Gracie, reaching her long arm around the flames to grab Christine by the wrist and to pull.

"No!" said Christine, frightened by the fire. She screamed.

"Let her go!" said Justine, swinging her oversized portfolio case awkwardly, fanning the fire so that it swept to the threads of Bianca's ripped hem. The flames caught hold. They exploded upward and over Bianca. Bianca was wrapped in an aura of fire. She stood motionless, blank-faced; she seemed consumed by fire. Then it passed. Just as quickly as the flames had flashed, they died. The air was heavy with moisture and the odor of singed cloth. .

"Bee? Are you all right?" said Gracie.

"I think so, Gracie," said Bianca, who laughed, ha ha, because she really was. It had been a phenomenal trick. Bianca felt spared and tempered.

"Never," said Justine.

"Ever," said Christine.

"Something in the goods, I guess," said Gracie.

"Why don't you two come with us?" said Justine.

"She needs to sit," said Christine, meaning Bianca.

"We can explain," said Justine.

"Explain what?" said Gracie.

" 'Harold Starr.' We've figured it out," said Justine.

"Maybe," said Christine.

"Then you know?" said Bianca.

"Yes, but Aaron didn't have to tell me," said Justine.

"Mr. Verbunko has told me nothing," said Bianca.

"Do tell," said Justine, turning to charge up the steps.

"Come on, Bee. Lean on me," said Gracie as they pursued Justine's lamplight to the top of the fifth tower, though they had no idea where they were. They had gotten lost within fifty steps of Gracie's door. Coming upon the Means had been fate.

"Do you believe them?" said Gracie.

"They are not happy people," said Bianca.

"Amen, sister," said Gracie, struggling to help Bianca, who, despite her claims, was wobbly and sluggish. They staggered to the top landing and through a heavy door, finding themselves in a luxuriously fitted anteroom bathed in shadows. Justine and Christine busied themselves lighting foul-weather lamps and moving furniture in the next room, which looked to Gracie to be a boudoir. She was right. This was Happy's sitting room. The enclosed terrace was off to the right. The candles still burned on the abandoned supper table.

Justine and Christine transformed the boudoir into a gallery. They unzipped their portfolio cases, removing an assortment of photographs, drawings, and paintings, all encased in stiff plastic. The only thing not in plastic, Gracie noticed, was an oilcloth-wrapped, rectangular tablet, very heavy, which Justine set on a sideboard. Everything else they set up along the walls, the chairs, the couches, and the tables. Gracie and Bianca sat on a loveseat to watch them construct an exhibition. Gracie asked Bianca if she knew what they were doing. Bianca said she didn't know what they were doing, but that she did know "what" they were doing—arranging facsimiles of two thousand years of Western comet art in chronological order.

"For example," said Bianca, pointing to a photograph of a Roman mosaic that Bianca thought resembled the *Persian Battle of Issus*, circa first century A.D., at Naples, her hesitating because of a large ball of fire with a tail in the upper right of the mosaic that Bianca couldn't recall. Then there was a photograph of a Roman mosaic that Bianca thought resembled the *Assassination of Caracalla*, circa third century A.D., at Ravenna, her hesitating because of a large ball of fire in the upper left that Bianca couldn't recall. There was also a photograph of a Byzantine mosaic that Bianca thought resembled *Empress Theodora and Her Attendants,* also at Ravenna, her hesitating because of a large ball of fire with a tail in the upper right that Bianca couldn't recall. And there was also a print of a section of the 230-foot-long Bayeux Tapestry, circa eleventh century A.D., at Bayeux, which Queen Matilda had commissioned to commemorate her Lord William's conquest at Hastings in 1066, this portion of the tapestry showing the star with a tail that was generally agreed to be the comet called Halley's.

"Bee?" said Gracie, intuiting a theme to the exhibition.

"Si, si," said Bianca, continuing her exposition. There was a print of an Italian fresco that Bianca thought to be Giotto's *Adoration of the Magi,* circa early fourteenth century A.D., at Padua, showing a large ball of fire with tail above the Christ Child. There was also a photograph of a detail of another Italian fresco that Bianca thought to be Andrea de Firenze's *Triumph of the Church,* circa fourteenth century A.D., at Florence, except that she couldn't recall that large ball of fire with tail between Heaven and Earth. There was the easily recognizable print of the manuscript page from the *Nuremberg Chronicles,* circa fifteenth century A.D., at Nuremberg, bearing an illustration of an eight-pointed star with a veil trailing behind. There was a photograph of the ceiling of the Sistine Chapel showing Michelangelo's detail, *Creation of Sun, Moon, and Planets,* circa sixteenth century A.D., at Rome, except this picture also indicated a large ball of fire with tail above the hand of YHWH creating the sun and moon. And there was a large canvas of an oil that Bianca thought resembled one of Caravaggio's series of the Apostles, perhaps the *Calling of St. Andrew,* circa seventeenth century A.D., except this one included the now familiar detail of a large ball of fire with tail.

Bianca did not recognize many of the facsimiles and could identify none of the sketches, watercolors, and letters with line drawings, each with the distinguishing large ball of fire with tail.

"Is this funny?" said Gracie.

"I do not know," said Bianca.

"A comet gallery," said Gracie, summing up, deciding to assert herself again. It hadn't worked before. The Twin Sisters Means had fended her off as they might dismiss a mule. But Gracie was hardly discouraged. Falling off, Gracie knew, one got up again immediately. "You girls want to explain?"

"I thought you knew," said Justine. "It's why they imprisoned you."

"Try me," said Gracie.

"It's 'Harold Starr,' " said Justine.

"Who is?" said Gracie.

"Look around you, Miss Thyme," said Christine, moving to join her sister on a loveseat opposite Gracie. "These are."

"The comet, then," said Bianca. "And these?"

"Don't you know them?" said Justine. "We collected many of them from Broadsword Hall. Here's a letter to the Royal Society dated 1683, by a student named Craven. An unattractive ancestor of ours, coincidentally. See the comet sketch? And here's a page from a map book by an officer named Oliphant who was in the Royal Army in America. See the comet, '1759' on the reverse. Here is a sketchbook that might pique Miss Thyme's imagination, by a Dr. Michel Thyme, spelled the same, from the Paris Observatory, 1835. See the comets? Finally, we have Rufus Broadsword's watercolors—well, some of them—as part of the Rockefeller Expedition of 1910. More comets. You understand what I'm saying?"

"Yes, we do," said Bianca.

"We didn't know it was real. We thought Wavy Rufus made it up," said Gracie. "He's sweet, but old and . . . cranky."

"Tsk, tsk," said Justine. "The 1683, 1759, 1835, 1910 material is from his tower at the Hall."

"You stole them!" said Gracie. "Did you hurt him?"

"Please. He wasn't there," said Justine. "We borrowed."

"Damn you Means," said Gracie, pounding the love-seat's arm.

"We are not without resources, my sister and I," continued Justine, ignoring Gracie's outburst. "We have used our resources, over the last month, to assemble this display. In doing so, we have reached the conclusion that the Means Corporation is involved in an elaborate scheme relating in some way to the current apparition of Comet Halley."

"Halley's Comet is 'Harold Starr'?" said Gracie.

"More, hairy star is 'Harold Starr.' It's not really Aaron's sense of humor, but then he's been surprising me recently," said Justine.

"Perhaps," said Christine.

"We haven't got all the pieces," said Justine. "These photos and whatnot are the best we could do for now."

"Please elaborate." said Bianca.

"Yes, do, yes," cawed Happy Means, swooping into the room from nowhere like a genuine harpy, her beak held high, her fingers curled like talons. She looked aroused and violent. Her poncho was Inquisition yellow. She'd been out in the storm. She trailed water as she stomped across the room examining the comet gallery.

"Hello, Stepmother," said Justine finally.

"Congratulations, girls," said Happy. "Really excellent work here. So that's why the Mediterranean. And this. My! Bribery again? Or did you dirty your hands with burglary? You shouldn't play with employees. Bad for business."

"Stepmother?" said Christine.

"Yes, Christy dear," said Happy.

"Don't," said Christine.

"Thank you, Christy," said Justine.

"Don't they work well together, Contessa?" said Happy, walking behind Bianca, reaching down to brush her shoulder. "Sooty, sooty. Did you have to crawl to get out?"

"Uncle Cedric freed us," said Gracie. "Your plot is turning on you, Mrs. Means. There's nothing you can do."

"I wouldn't anticipate Stepmother," said Justine.

"Thank you, Justy," said Happy, backing away from Bianca. "Now, why don't you and your exactly equally droll sister pack up again and troop back to the heliport? I'm sure we can find someone to fly you home. There is nothing for you here. Cold and stormy. You've discovered nothing. The truth is that it's too late regardless of what you know. And you know nothing. You're not needed. You're not wanted. Imagine that."

"Truly," said Justine.

"Verily," said Christine.

"We'll decide after a good sleep," said Justine.

"After we've seen Tory," said Christine.

"And Aaron," said Justine.

"You are leaving now!" said Happy. "Must I call the guard?"

No one moved. Happy jumped toward her desk and her callbox. Gracie stood quickly, however, blocking Happy's path with her large self, fully six inches over Happy, who, seeing she was temporarily thwarted, turned to flop down in an armchair. She crossed her arms. She laughed to herself.

"Let me tell you something, Stepmother," began Justine. "We are guessing that 'Harold Starr' has to do with Comet Halley. We are guessing that the corporation— Daddy and Tory and Aaron—has had Grimmen working on something to do with Comet Halley, because we found a lot of these photographs shoved aside in Cousin Trinity's study."

"Trinity betrayed us?" cried Happy, her hatred looking for victims, the Ystorm family, in the guise of its senior patriarch, Trinity Ystorm, President of (Means subsidiary) Grimmen Aircraft (and actually just a [high-priced] flunkie to the Means Corporation), fitting into Happy's delusions of treachery.

"We found them, Stepmother," corrected Justine. "Trinity had nothing to do with it. Your exaggerated concern reinforces our guessing, however. We are further guessing that Grimmen has built a spacecraft to fly to Comet

Halley. That surely is an element of 'Harold Starr.' We are also guessing that the spacecraft was launched last fall, during Tory and Aaron's trip abroad. We are guessing that the Broadswords found out something about that launch, or about 'Harold Starr' in general. Given your obvious paranoia, it might have been nothing more than one of them saying 'Harold Starr' on the telephone. Regardless, it is why they're here, prisoners. We are guessing that there's a deeper significance to all this, beyond Comet Halley, perhaps even beyond the corporation. How am I doing, Christy?"

" 'Harold Starr,' whether it's a plot, a conspiracy, a subplot to a more grandiose machination, is nearing completion," added Christine. "We are guessing that is why you are here. To release the Broadswords. Probably also to get them to waive prosecution. You did kidnap them, which was very tacky, wasn't it? We admit we haven't put everything together yet. But something's got you very frightened. Something huge."

"Soon we'll have it all," said Justine. "Unless you want to concede the point and tell us. Surrender, Stepmother."

"You know nothing!" screamed Happy in reply, laughing again, this time in a higher pitch, more intensely sad, like "Kee-kee-kee!"

Bianca looked up at that. The sound was different. But then, it was the same. Bianca watched Happy. Is this what the Means did to their women? Happy was deeply troubled. She was near more than surrender—complete breakdown. The Means girls were too much for her. Bianca wanted to help her. Despite all that Happy had done to hurt Bianca, Bianca still pitied her, saying:

"Please, let her alone."

"What do you mean?" said Justine.

"Your stepmother is not well," said Bianca.

"What do you see, Contessa?" said Christine.

"Can you see, Gracie?" said Bianca.

"Bee's right, girls," said Gracie. "She's shaking. She

376

doesn't hear us. And her color is bad. Bee's right." Gracie stepped toward Happy.

"Don't come any closer!" screamed Happy.

"She's not the sickly sort," said Justine.

"Yet you might have something, Contessa," said Christine.

"She's as pale as spacey little Monarch," said Gracie.

"No! No! No!" cried Happy, tearing at her face, squirming in her chair as if she'd been attacked by invisible insect-sized demons.

"Who is spacey little . . . ?" began Justine.

"Dear God, help her," said Bianca, rising to glide to Happy's side, reaching down to soothe this pathetic human being now seeming to descend into her own vision of Hell. Happy was disintegrating. Bianca started to cry. One of the most sated and fortunate (as in rich, not blessed) women on the face of present Creation was perishing inside herself. This was soul waste, thought Bianca, who touched Happy on the shoulder just as Happy had touched Bianca moments before. The result was profoundly different. A hiss and a spark and a puff of foul smoke exploded at the point of Bianca's touch, ripping the yellow poncho like tissue. Importantly, the flame seemed to come not from Bianca, who had been tempered from this wickedness, but rather from Happy, who screamed:

"Ahhh!" and flattened back against the chair.

"What was that!" said Justine, jumping up.

"Justy, Justy!" cried Christine, grabbing hold of her sister.

"Bee, get away from there!" said Gracie, rushing to Bianca's side.

Bianca raised her hand to examine it. There was no mark. It didn't hurt. Her fingers worked. Yet that flame had seemed to leap out of Happy and envelop Bianca's hand. As on the stairwell, the fires of Hell, rising from something determinedly bad in the true nature of the great American family Means, had not harmed Bianca.

However, there was a smoking hole in Happy's poncho that penetrated to her flesh. Happy should have been in agony. Instead, she sat transfixed by something invisible before her. She looked to be possessed. Gracie grabbed Bianca away forcibly, clutching her to her breast. Gracie was prepared to carry Bianca to safety. But Happy, suddenly breaking from her trance, dazed them all, screaming:

"Witch! Witch! Witch! Get her away from me! Witch!"

"Shut up," said Gracie.

"Witch, witch, witch," muttered Happy, recovering her human features as she lowered her voice. She looked the torturer, not the tortured.

"This is sick," said Gracie.

"Christ killer! Witch! Christ killer!" screamed Happy.

"Control your stepmother," said Gracie to Justine.

"What is happening here?" said Justine.

"Your stepmother is a sickie," said Gracie. "I think you Means are all loonies. We're getting out of here before . . ."

"Gracie," interrupted Bianca, in Gracie's arms, nodding toward the other side of the room where the wall was opening. Bianca knew what was about to happen. Perhaps she *was* bewitched, for she knew. She struggled to free herself from Gracie, as if there were something she could do to prevent the imminent tragedy. There wasn't, of course, she should have known, because this series of events had long since been set by the secrets of empty hearts, broken hearts, and heartlessness. Bianca struggled free nonetheless, raising her hands to push back the shadow that emerged from the wall. The shadow came forward anyway, into the light, now revealing a soggy dress of flowers and satin—Vernal Means in from the storm to do her worst to the people she loved most.

"Follow me, my children," said Vernal evenly.

Happy reached for a weapon. The nearest to hand was the oilcloth-wrapped tablet on the sideboard. She took hold of it with two hands and lifted it slowly above her head.

Across the room the Twin Sisters Means, not yet recovered from Happy's burning, staggered anew. They recognized the voice.

"Follow me! Follow me! Follow me!" said Vernal, her voice rising now. She leaned back into the wall again. Happy walked murderously toward her. Bianca reached to stop her. They met, sparks flying, Happy stunned sideways with more holes in her poncho.

"Christ," said Gracie, also stunned; yet not even He, of the light, could have stopped this now. This was the Devil's work; of that, Happy had been right. She'd accused the wrong soul. The demon was within the Means.

"Don't look!" screamed Vernal, erupting from the wall, immediately into her swirling dance, laughing "Kee-kee-kee!" Vernal spun across the room, wet flowers sailing, her bloated body never more energetic.

"You! You! You!" cried Happy, stepping around Bianca, taking two quick steps toward Vernal, raising the heavy rectangle above her head again and smashing it down on Vernal's back. The rectangle splattered in Happy's hands. Pieces of clay clunked to the floor. Happy was left with a slab of hard clay. (Babylonian cuneiform scratched in its surface), shaped like a pike, in her right hand. She raised it to swing again. But Vernal had spun away, seemingly unharmed, although that was not the case. Her dress was ripped down the back. The blood started to gush out. Vernal walked awkwardly to the open wall. She seemed to regain her presence through her pain, saying:

"Follow me, my children. Follow me." Then she screamed at them, "Look away! I hate you! Follow me!"

"Bee, don't," said Gracie, reaching for Bianca, but too late. Bianca moved toward Vernal, whose dress began to drip blood.

"Help her," said Bianca to Justine and Christine. "Don't you know who she is? She's your mother!"

"Don't touch her!" cried Justine at Bianca.

"Get away from her!" cried Christine at Bianca.

"Follow me!" cried Vernal.

379

"You!" cried Happy.

And then they were gone, Vernal back into the wall, Happy close behind waving the clublike clay, Justine and Christine following with wild looks, and finally Bianca, holding her arms straight out with motherly concern. Gracie was left alone, as quickly as that. Gracie took a huge breath, saying: "Effert."

(Agent of) "Harold Starr"
Meets (Agent of) Hairy Star

AARON VERBUNKO squirmed in his seat before the plastic wall of instrument panels in Craven Castle's Communications Center. He watched the operator again punch in the correct sequence. He placed the earphones over his head and listened. He should have heard the Manhattan Island. He heard "snap-crackle-pop." Power remained constant. The signal appeared, on the panels, to be going through. The signal appeared to be returning. Yet, nothing—the machinery might be working perfectly, still, nothing. Something was jamming, "snap-crackle-pop." Verbunko dropped the earphones to the table, thanked the operator and his crew, and left the room. His conclusion was that Craven Castle either was experiencing intense atmospheric disturbances or was confronted with a technical genius who knew how to interrupt the Means Corporation's private communications network. The first was fanciful. Sunspots were a joke. The second was unrealistic. Technical geniuses of that sort were owned by the Means Corporation and its friends. Therefore, Verbunko reasoned, he had no explanation for the breakdown.

Verbunko popped the hatch, crossed the long, neon-lit hallway to a hatch reading, "TOC Restricted," and buzzed. Squelk ushered him in. The chamber was large, low, and metallic. Near the center stood Westergaard, Torrance VIII, and several other senior noncoms of the guard. Above them, before them, and around them were maps and electronic displays. This was Craven Castle's tactical operations command, its bunker. From here, Westergaard dispatched his mercenary company worldwide to enforce the policy of the Means Corporation. Just now, the problem was much closer to him, within a mile.

"Well, Verbunko?" said Torrance VIII.

"Still nothing, sir," said Verbunko, walking over.

"Your permission, then, sir?" said Westergaard.

"Are you sure about those patrols?" said Torrance VIII.

"No, sir," said Westergaard.

"They could have lost their way in the storm. Whatever this interference, it could be jamming them," said Torrance VIII.

"That is possible, sir," said Westergaard.

They all stood by saying nothing, because no one wanted to say the obvious—that this was likely foolishness. The most conservative line was to treat it as a genuine assault.

"Verbunko, have you a thought?" said Torrance VIII.

"No, sir, I do not," said Verbunko.

"Carry on, then, Westergaard," said Torrance VIII.

"Yes, sir!" said Westergaard, who nodded to Squelk. Squelk left hurriedly with orders to the awaiting helicopter to get through to the backup Communications Center on the other side of the mountains.

"Is that everything?" said Torrance VIII.

"Until dawn, perhaps," said Westergaard.

"If you'll excuse me," said Verbunko, who left quickly. He didn't like Westergaard's attitude. He didn't like this situation. He was cut off from his machines. Lighting a cigarette, he popped the hatch out of the bunker proper, into an anteroom. The cigarette was bitter. He needed sleep. He needed a bracer. He grabbed a poncho. It was horrible out-side, but he was in a horrible mood. "I am corporation coun-sel," he reminded himself. He knew that he should be as anxious as Happy about Justine and Christine having come to Craven Castle, that he should be rushing to control the parties. His theretofore compulsion to soothe the Means just wasn't there. All these years, he thought—how many? twenty-five plus—maybe Justine and Christine should be told more of the truth. Woman goes mad. Divorce follows. Commitment to asylum follows. Discretion unto silence fol-lows. It happened every year among the very rich and the very poor. Verbunko's staff maintained a special section to deal with breakdown by employees and their families. There was a sanitorium in Tripoli for the cases that could not be corrected. This had been an extraordinary case. There was no one to fault. Why should the Means family be any more ready to admit incontinence in its blood than lesser folk? She'd been well cared for, almost indulged—these obscene costumes—and the child, well, he was provided for as long as he lived, regardless of his competency. The best doctors money could silence said he'd live out the century: the two of them, the mad woman of Craven Castle and the shame of the Means, content, if not loved, within these walls. Ver-bunko had not been present at the initial decision to mislead the Twins as well as the public about them. He'd often thought of pressing the Chairman to reverse his rash re-sponse to blood tragedy. Now there was an opportunity to amend without the Chairman's approval. Why not more of the truth, Happy? thought Verbunko, stamping out of the anteroom, up the stairwell to the first level of the castle's lower gallery.

He strode into the courtyard. He was soaked within five paces. He stopped in the middle of the bailey. He looked directly up. The rain was intense and icy. The dome of the sky was black and elemental. He sucked on his smoke to keep it lit. A gust blew him sideways. It was enough to ready him for debate with Justine. He could guess why they'd come, carrying portfolio cases, all secrecy and intrigue.

Justine was a Gnostic Princess. She would not be denied news. Jesus, I'm tired, he thought, reminding himself once again he didn't believe in the Son of God. He turned to march by the Landrovers and a baker's shabby delivery truck (the "Wonder" van).

"Psst!" came a voice.

Verbunko moved to the rear door of the van, open a crack. Swinyard had his head out enough to get wet.

"Hello, Swinyard," said Verbunko.

"Hello, Mr. Verbunko," said Swinyard, swinging the door open. Verbunko could see another figure in the van—a dwarf. "We'd like to deal," continued Swinyard. "Come on in."

"If we make it quick," said Verbunko, amused. Verbunko stepped up and in, crunching over stale popcorn and discarded junk-food wrappers, sitting on a speaker. The roof leaked. The walls were covered with the usual childish memorabilia. Verbunko lit another cigarette and tried to relax in the cramped space.

"This is Aaron Verbunko, Laddy," said Swinyard. "And Mr. Verbunko, this is the Count Wladyslaw Wrathnitski, Lord of Dominoes, Ringer of the Bell, and First Councillor to His Majesty, *Voluntas Hallei.*"

"Make more sense, Swinyard," said Verbunko. "Considering your predicament, I can't help you unless you make sense."

"You are Swiss?" said Laddy in French.

"I'm an American citizen," answered Verbunko in French. He recognized an accent there, Eastern European. He guessed, "And you are Polish?"

"Once," said Laddy. "I understand you are First Councillor to the Means and their allies."

"I am Vice-President of the Means Corporation," said Verbunko impatiently. "I don't think there's any point in characterizing my position as if I served an oligarchy. How is it that you are a Count? Do you serve a King? *Voluntas Hallei,* is it?"

"I was once a Count," said Laddy. "These titles do not

matter, as you know. The heart, Monsieur Verbunko, is the truth."

"A refugee, then," said Verbunko, "from the Germans? The Russians?"

"The Swedes," said Laddy. "My family's lands bordered the primeval forest, Bialowiecz. Do you know it? Similar to the forest surrounding this fortress."

"The Swedes?" said Verbunko. "But that was . . ."

"Monsieur Verbunko, it does not matter," said Laddy.

"Right on!" said Swinyard, who understood Laddy's tone.

"Swinyard," began Verbunko calmly, "I assure you that you have enough trouble now without alienating the only person who can intercede for you. Mr. Means has turned your prank over to his security forces. It will not go well for you, especially if you continue this masquerade."

"Yeah, well, yeah," said Swinyard, who felt cowed. But he reminded himself this was 1986, not 1968, and he was in the company of the wonderful. He stood to a stoop and said, "In the name of Revolution and Justice, I denounce you, Aaron Verbunko! And I denounce those you serve as villains and fiends! If justice is impossible in this great land I love, it is not because of weak men like me who do their damnedest to preserve decency! It's because of men like you who've abandoned their souls to the Devil! You're a scourge, Verbunko! You hear me? We're not gonna take it anymore! And if you get me, there'll be another and another to take my place! Threaten me, starve me, corrupt me, kill me! I am one of millions! You cannot stop an idea whose truth is eternal! Righteousness! That's what I say! Righteousness! True religion for all men who love! Even in the nether reaches of Hell there will be no escape for you and your kind! The Lord will come to establish His Kingdom on this Earth! It will happen! But for now, a mighty servant of the Lord has come! Here and now! The comet has come! And you are doomed!"

The van shook with Swinyard's sermon. Swinyard shook with Swinyard's sermon. He banged the walls. He stomped the floor. He levitated. Finally, Laddy reached out to comfort his friend, stroking him to quiet. Verbunko watched them. He had two good clues now: *"Voluntas Hallei"* and "The comet has come." He guessed the rest, asking:

"What is it that you and your cult want, Count? Has the Means Corporation anything you require? I can help you. I cannot promise. But I can facilitate any request."

"Cult?" said Laddy.

"Your comet cult," said Verbunko. "I do not mean to offend. Your brethren, how do you say, the 'Comet Clubbe.'"

"Do you know what this is, Monsieur Verbunko?" said Laddy, opening a drawer to produce a charcoal rubbing Effert had made of Wavy Rufus's half of the Babylonian tablet.

"A gravestone rubbing?" said Verbunko lightly.

"A representation of a document," said Laddy. "Your master has the other half of the document. To answer your inquiry, this is one thing I would like from you."

"For your worship service no doubt," said Verbunko.

"I marvel at you, Monsieur Verbunko," said Laddy. "You are a twentieth-century man. Your contempt for belief seems total. This time, however, it has led you astray. No cult. There is no cult. I understand your thinking. There is no cult."

"I see," said Verbunko, who did not.

"More importantly, though," began Laddy, "I need you to tell me if 'Harold Starr' means to harm the comet. Please do not waste our time with coy interrogatories. I have learned much of Grimmen Aircraft's work on a space vehicle to overtake the comet, from the very men who built it, though you thought them insignificant wastrels. Does 'Harold Starr' threaten the comet?"

"I have no comment," said Verbunko.

"Understanding this as a 'yes,' I want to know if there is anything you can do to halt this threat? Can the space vehicle be redirected, detonated, recalled?" said Laddy.

"I have no comment," said Verbunko.

"Understanding this as a 'yes,' I want to know what it will take to convince you this must be done," said Laddy.

"I have no comment," said Verbunko.

"I want you to know that my purpose here is not to punish you," said Laddy. "That would be futile. My purpose is to avoid a disaster. The consequence of your master's actions would be horrible and sudden. War, Famine, and Death have not ridden as they would then ride. I am in earnest, Monsieur Verbunko. My brother here is a good man, so do not let his volatile speechifying lull you. I represent forces more profound than you, a compleat twentieth-century man, can adequately envision."

"My dear Count, I am not unfamiliar with the New Testament's Book of Revelation. You would seem to threaten the Apocalypse. Surely you must know this is typical of numerous self-destructive communities throughout Christianity. It leaves me compassionate, but skeptical. You mention the four horsemen, three of them anyway. I . . . am embarrassed to continue," said Verbunko, his condescension palpable.

"Then you are acquainted with the appropriate text," said Laddy, "which continues, 'the stars in the sky fell to the earth, like figs shaken down by a gale; the sky vanished, as a scroll is rolled up . . .'"

"'. . . and every mountain and island was moved from its place,'" finished Verbunko, eyes closed, rubbing his temple with his free hand. "I congratulate you. I am moved, and impressed with your logic, your seeming logic. But this talk of a comet. No."

"Yes, and yes again, and again, Monsieur Verbunko," said Laddy.

"You are not an easy man to confront, Count," said Verbunko.

"I am First Councillor," said Laddy. "His Majesty bade me explain matters to you in a manner you would respect. What more can I do? Must we proceed with the storming of this fortress? Would that convince you? It seems excessive."

"Even if I were to believe you." said Verbunko, "the matter is out of my hands. I am not 'First Councillor.' I have no 'masters.' And the Means Corporation is part of a larger enterprise."

"They wouldn't understand you?" said Laddy.

"Understand what?" said Verbunko.

"The comet . . ." started Laddy.

"Sir, I assure you that even if the comet were to land in the courtyard, there is nothing I can do for you. I could not begin to explain. We are in the final stages of a complex development. I am anxious to calm you. What would you have me do?" said Verbunko.

"Stop 'Harold Starr,' " said Laddy.

"Impossible," said Verbunko, too quickly.

Laddy rocked himself aright and bounced gingerly out the door. Swinyard followed, leaving Verbunko alone to review.

Typical zealots, thought Verbunko, they knew too much and not enough. Their concern for the comet was touching and mad. The dwarf was a fine bluffer. But that he'd asked Verbunko to "stop" the operation meant that he didn't know what was at issue. The project was titanic. Still, it was an amusing idea, that one man could ask another to stop it. Theoretically, of course, one man could stop a machine, no matter how large, no matter how powerful—even a machine like ORACLE. Particular data read into the machine could produce any result. At this late moment, though, Verbunko had no idea of what sort of data read into ORACLE could stop "Harold Starr." It was only theory. As such, it piqued him. He finished his cigarette, lit another, and relaxed against the van wall. This had been an amusing interlude. He would tell Westergaard to be lenient with them. They couldn't be completely responsible for their actions anymore. In a way, he felt responsible. The operatic rudeness of the kidnapping affair had pushed Swinyard & Schleppend over the edge and into a cult—what else could it be, quoting Revelation 6?

"Mr. Verbunko," called Swinyard.

"Right there," he said, gathering his poncho, stepping back out into the storm. They were standing near the center of the bailey. Verbunko walked over to them, saying:

"Could we pick this up later? I've got some trouble inside."

"Above the clouds, Monsieur Verbunko," said Laddy loudly, over the clatter of the rain on the pavement. "It is nearly dawn. Will you stop this?"

"Enough, Count, enough," said Verbunko, turning away.

"Then you must be convinced," called Laddy, pointing straight up with both arms. "It begins!"

"What begins?" said Verbunko. He heard a series of muffled pops, like firecrackers under mattresses, "pofp, pofp, pofp." Verbunko looked up, shielding his eyes to study the sky. It was not as black as before, with some gray above the horizon, as if the sunrise were trying to cut through the rain clouds. The muffled pops continued, singly and doubly. Now and again, through the clouds, there was a dim flash, there to the east, the south, now the north and the west. The flashes seemed like signals. It looked to Verbunko like a fireworks display high above the storm clouds.

"Stop 'Harold Starr'!" called Laddy.

"Impossible!" answered Verbunko, surprised to find himself intimidated by the dwarf's manner. But it wasn't only the dwarf. The pops continued, seemingly bunching overhead. They were joined by cracks—like hammer blows on stone, sharp, "whack, whack, whack!" The flashes were distinctly brighter. Just above the castle walls, the lights appeared green, yellow, even pink. Suddenly, a "boom!" sounded above the "pofp!" and "whack!" Verbunko spun around to the explosion, directly overhead, deep up into the clouds. Another explosion, and this time Verbunko saw the first streak of light. The fireworks display was strengthening into something more threatening. Lights flashing, clouds muffling explosions, streaks ending in bursts of light and sound. Verbunko didn't like it.

"Stop 'Harold Starr'!" said Laddy, waving in a trance.

"No!" said Verbunko, cringing beneath a cluster of explosions accompanied by flashes bright enough to penetrate the cloud layer and cast shadows in the courtyard, like lightning, but stronger, more varied in color. Verbunko started to straighten up when the sky let go. The clouds were shattered with crashing explosions atop whining cracks and tumbling lights. The broad streaks lengthened. It sounded like thunder. It looked like intense heat lightning. It wasn't either. There were terrifying detonations north, south, east, and west. Verbunko was frightened now. It seemed as if heaven had commenced a barrage, and the main target of the barrage was the castle.

"Stop 'Harold Starr'!" called Laddy.

"No! No! No!" cried Verbunko, but not in response. He cried for help. The salvos sailed left and right above the castle walls, above the five towers. The celestial artillery men were walking their shells down to their target. The center of the tumult, directly overhead, continued its drop through the clouds.

"Stop 'Harold Starr'!" called Laddy.

"What is this? What?" cried Verbunko, fighting off the rain and the noise. The possibility of Apocalypse touched him. He rejected it with the belligerence of a man who truly understands victory and defeat. So what was it! He answered his own question. He said, "Meteors!"

"The meteors of the comet! The meteors of *Voluntas Hallei!* Stop 'Harold Starr'!" called Laddy.

"Meteors!" repeated Verbunko, looking up. How could these be meteors? He'd seen meteors before. He'd even seen meteor showers. Meteors? The radiance lowered the more. The explosions neared. A fireball streaked across the castle, striking the two front towers. Another ricocheted off a battlement to smash against a side tower. Craven Castle was bracketed. Now the big guns went to work. Verbunko screamed. Swinyard screamed. Laddy threw his arms up and down, as if imploring the salvos to do their worst. There was the whining sound of ricochets throughout the castle. The fireballs overhead dripped molten metal colored red and

389

yellow through the black rain clouds. The bolides detonated in geometrical patterns. Another whining streak across the castle and "Boom!" the fifth tower was afire. The castle's fire alarms—deafening klaxons—sounded. The meteors continued to tumble, to streak, to dance around the castle walls. The night was all but gone now, not with a sunrise, but with fireball glare.

"Stop 'Harold Starr'!" called Laddy one more time as he disappeared in a shower of sparks pouring onto the bailey. Verbunko fell to the pavement, on his hands and knees, then on his belly, burying his head in his arms, trying to breathe in the sea of fire.

"Come the Revolution!" called Swinyard, standing madly amid the bouncing micrometeorites, looking elected in the smoke and flame. He mimicked Laddy, thrusting his hands high above his head. A gust of rain momentarily cleared the bailey of smoke. The Count Wladyslaw Wrathnitski, Lord of Dominoes, Ringer of the Bell, and First Councillor to His Majesty, *Voluntas Hallei,* stood over the prostrate Verbunko and shouted:

"Of the comet!"

PARABLE PAUSE

THE BIRTH, THE CRIME, THE PEACE, AND THE TRIUMPH OF THE STRAW PEOPLE (1968–1978)

PART THE THIRD
THE PEACE

BY LEVIATHAN
STRAUSS
AS TOLD BY
SCHLEPPEND

IT was late September 1972, and the hippies hadn't yet applied to law school. Instead, they cluttered the urban romances of the West—San Francisco, New York, London, Rome, Athens, and most especially Paris, wherein they gathered along the Boulevard St.-Germain from the Hôtel de Cluny near the Sorbonne to the Place St.-Thomas d'Aquin near the Ministry of Works. No one was working. One might opine that Thomas Aquinas would have approved of their leisure. The flower children had come to Paris to loaf and to philosophize, to seduce and to realize their haphazardly informed prejudice that peace of mind could be had if "Peace on Earth" was established. Dressed in buckskin and in beads, in fantasy and in heat, they carried many different passports, many more different futures, but they held in common a single, self-deluding chant, "Peace Now!" The world was at war with itself on a jungle battlefield in distant Southeast Asia. Peacenik ideologues argued that every major world government contributed to the savagery with either weapons, words, or, worst of all, silent indifference. And here in Paris, argued the peaceniks, capital of the *colons* who had first perpetrated imperialism in fey Indochina, the silence was most contemptible of all; for the French government had seen fit to host the "Peace Talks" between the Capitalists and the Communists in a feudal palace near the Arc de Triomphe, and yet had not seen fit to tell the Americans the secret to Indochina. That it was headless. It couldn't perceive the Western flap about Reason and Honor. The French had guillotined Indochina in 1954, an often overlooked codicil in the Geneva Conference agreements.

So the flower children gathered to exchange melancholy. Some were draft dodgers. Some were despair dodgers. Most were on vacation from family, school, and numb selfishness. A few were on the run from the sinister inevitability of the Committee to Re-elect the President (CREEP) now barnstorming America with a campaign that would sweep, if the polls were right, every state in the Republic for the Republican ticket and the "One" Himself, Richard Milhous Nixon. These were hard times. The hippies knew it. They were about to make rock'n'roll illegal back in the home-of-the-free-if-you-can-pay-for-it.

See the hippies there in the Latin Quarter (where devils drink with saints, and pretenders pick up the check), the Citroëns and mopeds rushing by the modern shops and the medieval abbey. See the hippies in packs, playing guitars and chess, blowing mouth organs and dope, with their dirty Greek sandals, dirty American denims, and overloaded aluminum pack frames dangling mildewing bedrolls. Only Daumier could have done justice to a scene soon to become apocryphal forevermore.

Two of this hippie pack were not cheered by the resident bard's Doors medleys (there was a lurid rumor that the Doors' lead singer, Jim "Lizard King" Morrison, missing in action fourteen months now, had been found dead at the Hôtel du Rascal with needle tracks on his arm spelling "Means," though another version had it just "Mean"). These two dissidents ambled up Boul' Mich' toward the Luxembourg Gardens, panhandling enough *sous* to score some cous-cous at the Algerian PX at sundown. He was Passel Serf, from the Ohio River Valley, a skinny, animated young man of opinions he could not support with credit cards. She was Agnes Glory, a voluptuous Malibu girl (Piuma Road) with the blue light of five babies in her eyes, though she had yet to marry, yet to conceive, yet to deal for American bliss. They'd been together since Labor Day, when they'd met while selling their charter tickets home in order to finance another season in the Old World. Their romance had blossomed until the week before, when Agnes, hysterical about the

Bois de Boulogne dust in her strawberry hair, had left her pack in one corner while showering in another. Gone with their money was their dope stash as well. They'd been straight for a week, save for the occasional pass of a joint by slumming English royalty. Agnes was so straight that she'd been thinking aloud of calling her mother collect and ending her summer abroad with a flight home on the goat god's airline, Pan Am 747 Orly to Kennedy to L.A., *tout de suite*. This wouldn't have been total surrender to parental authority, since they'd blessed her trip in March —anything to get her to quit her subsistence job in the circulation department of that "horrid" Manhattan alternative weekly, *Kong*, and go to law school. Passel, who'd abandoned parental propriety the previous year when he'd dumped a prestigious New England university's prestigious graduate school for a life on the road (always a quick step ahead of his draft board, he having drawn a fat 100 in the Lottery of Death), was not unaware of Agnes's erosion. This was true love, however, not causative sex, so he wasn't going to ruin their last days together by anticipating her infidelity with his own pouting impotence. Besides, their hunger brought them closer and made their highs cosmic.

They turned left up Rue Soufflot, past the Pantheon, past the Lycée Henri Quatre, onto Rue Descartes, stopping at a scruffy sidewalk café:

ECRASEZ L'INFAME
Prop.: La Revolution
founded 1789

where they crashed in rickety chairs along the curb, unhooked their backpacks, ordered one franc's (a tenth of their wealth) worth of the house wine, and settled back to study the headlines of an international edition of the *Crimes:*

394

PEACE HINT IN PARIS
FRENCH FOREIGN MINISTER
ADMITS ACCORD NEAR
DRVN TALKING TO USA

"Another rumor of peace," said Passel, reading quickly aloud down the column, names such as Nixon, Kissinger, Rogers, Laird, Thieu, Thuouy, Thuy, Thi Binh— ah, yes, Madame Nguyen Thi Binh, the Viet Cong mouthpiece (Victoria Charlotte Herself).

"I'm ignoring your macho information games," said Agnes. "Do we spend our swag now, or go for more and feast tonight?"

"I'm for delayed highs," said Passel, looking past Agnes's eyes to discover a dark limousine awkwardly rounding the corner onto Rue Descartes. There was a stiff American flag on its hood. "Don't look now, Aggie, but they've come for us."

"Don't tease me," said Agnes, flipping for the astrology section.

"Look! Look!" said Passel, half serious now. He spied a face in the limo. He recognized the face. The limo stopped, its doors opening.

"Excuse me," said a burly American man jumping from the limo. "Are you kids Americans? Excellent. I represent your government."

Passel didn't dare look past the man's waist. This was Federal Heat. The Secret Service Agent confirmed as much by flashing a wallet before Passel's face. The eagle looked to have two heads and other embellishments of empire.

"Would you permit a high government official to lunch with you just now? A quiet repast? We're paying," said the Agent.

"Good afternoon," said K. before Passel could answer, K. emerging from behind the Agent to offer his dry right hand to Passel, who pressed it weakly. K. looked fit, tanned, and sated with foods not grown by Mother Nature. Taking Agnes's hand, K. continued, "This is generous of you. A romantic day, isn't it? And let me introduce my companions. This charming young woman is Christine Means. And this equally charming young woman is Justine Means. Christy and Justy, may I introduce, uh . . . ?"

"I'm Agnes," said Agnes, nudging Passel.

"Passel's the name," said Passel. He was stunned, not only because this was K., the National Security Adviser of the United States of America, a.k.a. the President of the Republic's de facto Minister of Fear, but also because these were the two most dazzlingly beautiful women he'd ever seen this close, let alone touched, which he did just then, first Christine's perfect hand, then Justine's perfect hand. Twins, thought Passel, else he really did see everything twice—crazy as Yossarian. They wore bright bonnets. They carried bright parasols. Passel could swear their slippers were emerald-covered. Before them, Agnes, at twenty-three, appeared fat and faded.

They sat in a semicircle, K. between Christine and Justine, Passel and Agnes opposite. K. ordered champagne and caviar and snail omelets from the Aussie waiter, who grimaced, knowing this was (the Commandant of the) Bad Company in pinstripes. K. beamed at his guests, saying:

"I have asked you to lunch because others have brought to my attention, for one reason or another, that I have been without input from the younger citizens for some time." K. paused while the Aussie waiter served the wine and appetizers. "As I am now involved in sensitive negotiations whose outcome have a considerable, not to say profound, bearing, on the younger generation, I felt that it was time I sounded young men and women such as you charming people on your opinions of the recent conduct of American foreign policy."

"I don't have any politics," said Agnes, eating as fast as she could before Passel's temper lost them their free lunch.

"You mean the rumor of peace?" said Passel.

"Among other things," said K.

"I ain't no draft dodger. Not officially," said Passel.

"What Henri means, Passel," said Christine, "is what do you think of winning the peace?"

"What do I think? He wants to know what I think?" squealed Passel.

Agnes deliberately soaked Passel's lap with champagne in an attempt to maintain this particular luncheon's peace. They fussed with repairs. K. sipped from his glass and asked:

"You don't believe in peace, is that it, young man?"

Passel stared right into K.'s smile. The man flabbergasted Passel to the point that he couldn't speak. Where, after all, should one begin to denounce K.? Passel opened his mouth, sucking in air to launch his attack, but, seeing Agnes readying another champagne salvo to keep him in line, decided to eat first and to pound the pulpit later. Passel said, "Sure, sure, peace, peace, uh, peace."

The food arrived amid more small talk, everyone aware that the central issue had been avoided for the sake of digestion. This was Paris. They ate without relish. Agnes gulped her omelet and ate half of Passel's, while chatting with Justine about wet-suit surfing. K. and Christine discussed an auction they'd attended that morning, where Christine had bid heavily for, but not acquired, a guillotine blade from the Revolution of 1848.

"Listen," said Justine finally, plates cleared for espresso, "We're having a party next Saturday. You two will love it. Can we expect you? Henri is the guest of honor."

397

"If we're in town," said Agnes, looking at Passel.

"It would be choice," said K. "There will be some people there who I know would regard it a rare opportunity to converse with younger citizens."

"Who's that?" said Passel.

"Why, the PRG, of course," said Christine.

"Who?" said Agnes.

"Victor Charles," said Passel, truly impressed.

Pleasantries and farewells were smoothly exchanged as the luncheon broke up with smiles, sighs, and the etiquette of the ruling class when it favors certain exotic members of the petit bourgeoisie. K. and his party were in the limousine and away faster than Passel could think to ask Agnes if this meant she'd be staying on in Paris another week, maybe with him, nice soft fern bed in the Bois de Boulogne, pillow of kisses? It did. They endured a vigorous week, dividing their time between panhandling, loafing, lovemaking, and studying daily *Crimes* and back issues of *Kong Weekly* (available for browsing in the lobby of the Left Bank's Hôtel du Rascal) concerning the current status of the conflict betwixt the Democratic Republic of Vietnam (DRVN) and the Provisional Revolutionary Government (PRG) and the Republic (USA). The salient points were these: the Capitalists hated the Communists very much; the Communists hated the Capitalists very much; bombs fall when dropped; men and women in black pajamas do not know enough to come in out of the storm; Senator George McGovern, challenging the President of the Republic with a platform largely informed by "Peace Now!" philosophies, was so far behind in the polls that a not-too-fanciful interpretation of the mood in the U.S.A. might have been that the family that kills together, votes together. These were complex doings. This was the Vietnam War. One heard all about it, read all about it, and forgot all about it. So had Passel and Agnes, as

398

completely as possible, given that it then bombed on—their Forever War. They had to relearn the vocabulary. It was educational but depressing, like apprenticing to a shroud-maker. Still they did their homework, hoping to know the bad from the real bad at the upcoming fete, the invitation (and two boxes containing costumes) to which arrived Wednesday at the Ecrasez l' Infâme café:

The Misses Christine and Justine Means
Cordially Invite You to a
Fancy Dress Ball
In Honor of
A Very Important Person
Nine O'Clock
Saturday, Seven October
In the Year of Our Lord
Nineteen Hundred and Seventy-two
Pavillon de Means
Place de Means
Paris
R.S.V.P./Cable MEANS

And so Passel and Agnes arrived at the Place de Means just past 9 P.M., Agnes dressed as a curvaceous duplicate of the Marquis Marie Joseph Paul Yves Roch Gilbert du Motier de Lafayette as he stood before the Estates-General as it convened at Versailles on 4 May 1789, ten weeks before the storm heard around the world at the (now) Place de la Bastille. Passel, who'd given Agnes his costume and decided against wearing hers, was less anachronistically done up. He wore his usual scruffiness, the exact duplicate of Citizen Passel Serf as he stood amid the Peace Moratorium as it convened on the Capitol Mall, 15 November 1969. He'd made one concession to the evening's masquerade. Courtesy of his comrades on Boul' Mich', he wore his Cincinnati Reds cap with a "McCarthy" button, blue and white, over the *C*.

"*Bonsoir, Messieurs-dames Serf,*" said the

doorman, ushering them into the Pavillon de Means, a palace with a million windows and twice as many chambers, stretching long and splendid about one-third of the Place de Means. He further ushered them down portrait-lined galleries to staircases, anterooms, more galleries, and, finally, a gem-studded ballroom, more dazzling than anything Passel had ever encountered, save the Twin Sisters Means.

"Are we too early?" said Agnes, for they were the first to arrive.

"Not for eats," said Passel, marching toward heaped tables. Agnes didn't follow, her elitism reemerging now that she'd emerged from her blue jeans and T-shirt. She retired to the powder room, or so Passel supposed when he turned to offer her snails only to find himself alone with the servants. He considered chatting with them, but they were better dressed than his father ever had been. Alone in that grand room, Passel suddenly (not surprisingly) had a persecution attack. It was a fierce one, chills and shakes. He dropped his plate and backed away from the dance floor. He grabbed the first door handle he found and yanked, letting himself through glass doors onto a large, torch-lit veranda, decorated this evening with an immense crimson awning patterned with astrological signs. The servants there also spooked him, so he continued to back away, down marble steps, onto a garden path. He edged the lily pond, deciding to feed the birds with the pastry he'd stuffed into his vest pocket. He found a marble bench with a good view of the veranda above, an equally good view of the garden wall close behind, ten feet high, over which Passel presumed there was escape if his fears worsened. They did, especially when the rhododendrons behind him started shaking.

"Who's there?" said Passel.

"Peace is at hand," said the bush.

"What?" said Passel, staring at the (not fiery) bush.

"Peace is at hand," repeated the bush.

"Okay, okay," said Passel, realizing as the bush shook again, then stopped, that there'd been a man in the bush. Passel had been taken as a sentry. He'd received the password. Passel stood to get out of here, but the bush shook again.

"Peace is at hand," whispered the bush.

"Okay, leave me alone," said Passel, dropping behind the marble bench. The bush talked three more times before Passel decided to quit this place regardless of jeopardy. The Means' ball clearly had been overrun with sappers. Passel knew that sappers carried satchel charges, rockets, and other articles of terrorist death. The Pavillon de Means was targeted by somebody's suicide squad. Passel circled the veranda, intending to grab Agnes and run. As he spotted the orchestra leader stepping to the microphone to commence the serenade, Passel thought about warning the lot to flee. He thought about being a hero. Then he thought about what sort of people were likely to attend a fancy dress ball in honor of K. Go sappers, he thought, ducking behind a statue till a servant had passed, then leaping over the marble balcony to scale a vine-covered wall to a second-story terrace, pushing open the doors to slink into a luxuriously appointed dressing room, white on white, a mirror on every third closet door. Passel was lost. Should he go back to the veranda? Not that crazy, he thought, expecting detonations and shrapnel slaughter any moment. He pulled at door after door, until he found one that led to a bedroom. The scent of perfume hit him with a rush, staggering him so that he had to grab for a bedpost.

"Hello, Passel, could you do me up, please?" said Justine, seated at her vanity table, her back to him.

"What? Hey! Listen! There're sappers out there! Rain's gonna fall! We gotta run!" said Passel.

"Passel, don't shout so. I can't follow you. Now, please, the hooks on my costume. Two of them," said Justine.

"Jesus God! Will you listen!" said Passel.

"I'm listening, dear. The hooks first, though," she said.

Passel surrendered to her freewill. Her beautiful, naked back won him over. She was dressed in swan feathers. A swan beak mask lay on her vanity table. As he hooked her, he couldn't help saying, "That's an outrageous dress."

"Thank you, Passel. Let me guess your costume," she said.

"I don't have one," said Passel, withdrawing his hands from her back. She was warm, soft, and humming. His hands shook. "I wore a good-guy button," he added.

"You have a costume," said Justine, turning to smile at him. "You're an Honest Man."

"You think?" said Passel, a part of his heart forever hers.

"Yes, and I think it was dashing of you to slip into my bedroom to help me dress," said Justine. "Shall we join the dancing?"

"Wait! The sappers. We can't! They've got tanks and bayonets. Ruthless," said Passel, giddy from her perfume.

"What a sweet imagination," said Justine.

"They were in the bushes. I swear. They had a password. I saw them, I think," said Passel. "Black pajamas!"

"Peace is at hand?" said Justine.

"How did you know?" said Passel.

"They're guests. Henri's idea. Or maybe it was Christy's. Trying to make the PRG feel more relaxed at a capitalist fete," said Justine, taking Passel by the arm and leading him out the door, down the grand staircase, and into the ballroom. The guests had gathered in force. There were generals, courtesans, usurpers, panderers, liars, goats, and several hunchbacks. Most were masked. Passel assumed all were in costumes other than those they wore elsewhere, but as midnight, and unmasking, approached, Passel sampling one too many punch bowls, he realized it didn't matter. The ruling class has the means to be whoever it wishes, he knew; and it was folly for embittered intellectuals like himself to believe anyone, even history, could sort the victims from the victimized. This crowd might be the bane of the earth. They might be earnest servants of the will of the people. Who could tell? Justine introduced him to French deputies, American sheriffs, North Vietnamese liaisons, South Vietnamese speculators, and more murderous-eyed colonels than he could count from every warring nation East and West: Poland to Cuba, Israel to Indonesia. Passel told everyone he was dressed as an "Honest Man." At that, their smiles sank and they turned away. Who wanted to meet an "Honest Man" in 1972? Too late for Greek sophistry! Too late for Truth, Justice, Mercy, and Beauty as well. Their smug hostility toward him left Passel dizzy—though it might have been the punch, or Justine's perfume—so disoriented, in fact, that after the unmasking at midnight, when every guest was revealed as a puzzle to which there would be no solution in the twentieth century (the Revolution—*écrasez l'infâme*—notwithstanding), Justine led him to a canopied table on the veranda to make him eat for sobriety. Passel dove into a school of shrimp just as he was reminded how irresponsible an escort he'd been:

"There you are," said Agnes. "Henri says his field marshals are jealous. You've kept Justine all to yourself."

"Say what?" said Passel, looking up to discover a

voluptuous Marquis de Lafayette hugging the arm of a short gorilla wearing black-framed glasses.

"Join us," said Justine. "You look smashing, Agnes. It seems you've stolen Henri from Christy. Congratulations."

"Good evening, young man," said the gorilla.

"Isn't Henri darling, Passel?" said Agnes.

"Uh, uh, who?" said Passel, watching the gorilla sit.

"He gives you credit for his inspiration. In the Age of the Guerrilla, he says, only a gorilla will do," giggled Agnes.

"Christy says you've dubbed him Kitsch Kong," said Justine.

"That was her idea," said Agnes, looking jealous.

"Where is she? Or did she give up?" said Justine.

"She's about," said Agnes, "a swan talking with a firebrand."

"Who's that?" said Passel.

"Madame Binh," said Justine.

"Victoria Charlotte? She's here?" said Passel.

"Of course, I'll get them," said Justine, away with a peck on his cheek. Passel saw Agnes wince at that, she saying:

"Having fun?"

"Don't give me that," said Passel.

"Henri says you helped her with her feathers," said Agnes.

"That's a great spy system you got, man," said Passel.

"I welcome the chance to comment," said the gorilla, "because I do not want you to succumb to misconceptions. One of Miss Christine Means's handmaidens observed you leaving Miss Justine Means's bedroom shortly before ten P.M. this evening. I repeated as much to my charming companion, Agnes."

"He got the hots for you?" said Passel to Agnes.

"Don't you dare!" said Agnes, reaching for a glass.

"Already get into your pants?" said Passel.

"Passel!" yelled Agnes, flinging the punch at him.

"Oh, Henri, here's another dispute for you to arbitrate," said Christine, arriving just then on the arm of the aforementioned firebrand, Madame Nguyen Thi Binh, chief Viet Cong delegate to the Paris Peace Talks, dressed this evening in black silk pajamas, a black orchid on her collar. Justine sat next to Passel. Christine and Madame Binh sat by the gorilla.

"Trouble, sweetie?" said Justine to Passel.

"Nothing homicide can't handle," said Passel, sitting quietly by, fuming, as he watched the two swans, the firebrand, the gorilla, and the Marquis titter in French. Snaked by the Minister of Fear!

"Passel," said Christine, "Madame Binh would like to know your impressions of her people's struggle for liberation."

"I think she's got a great infield, plenty of speed, and a solid bench. She needs the long ball," said Passel.

Christine translated as best she could, listening to Madame Binh's reply, then saying, "She would like to know where she might acquire this 'long ball.' "

"Trade is the usual way," said Passel, pausing while this was translated, "but tell her my friends are in the mountains. She might advertise in the personal columns of the underground papers."

"Young man," began the gorilla, "do you seriously maintain your romantic impertinence? I would say the one great tragedy is that our objective and the objective of our critics is quite similar. We both want to get out of the war. The problem is that we came into office with five hundred fifty thousand American troops in combat ten thousand miles away—in a war that had already taken

405

over thirty thousand lives. From our first day in office, we attempted to disengage from the war. We withdrew troops unilaterally. We made proposal after proposal. Our critics ought to ask themselves whether they do not have some responsibility for prolonging the war by the constant doubts they create. Should our policy in Indochina fail, the fate of the people there under Communist rule will suggest that those who tried to prevent defeat were not guided by ignoble purposes."

Passel swallowed his impatience. Christine translated K.'s speech for Madame Binh. The six of them fell into an awkward silence.

Passel finally asked, "Do you know baseball?"

"I'm familiar with the terminology," said the gorilla.

"Management always blames the players for a slump," said Passel.

"We are discussing international politics," said the gorilla, "and there is nothing to be gained by coloring our talk with the language of boys' games."

"You blow me away, you really do," said Passel.

"Go ahead," said Justine, patting his hand.

"All right, here it is," said Passel. "You guys called that doped-up mob of yours in Nam an army? You brag about withdrawing that mob? Cut the planes out, and they'd fly home on their own. You got the most mind-corrupt gang of officers since Rome leading, excuse me, hassling a pathetic bunch of losers, most of whom regard the fact they are in Nam as a curse. You know what the really heavy dudes said at Attica right before Rockefeller launched his legions at them? They said, what worse can they do to us, send us to Nam? That's it. You think that stoned mob in Nam's gonna fight for you? They wouldn't dig a latrine for you. Forget it. Victoria Charlotte here represents a peasant tyranny that is the product of a century of European colonial abuse. They're tyrants, sure, but

406

that's the mind-set that survives colonial policies. Regardless, the VC are ill equipped, ill trained, ill fed, and, all things considered, a lousy army. But you and your boss have made them, and their NVA allies, look like bloody military geniuses. Listen to me, the VC ain't shit, but there ain't no way that army of yours over there is gonna take 'em. They won't even shoot at 'em. Nobody cares. And I'm not talking pacifism. I'm no pacifist, and you know it. That's why you're so scared of me and my friends. We're American boys. We kill our breakfast and have enough left over for lunch and dinner, but we go out and shoot some more anyway. We like to kill. You dig? I got friends that would make you shudder. Hostile! You think candy-asses resist the richest empire the world has ever seen? You think your 'critics' have any respect for you? Shit! Those grunts in Nam, who are the pits, not even they respect you. And the flakiest little mental case you got over there, he'd learn to use his bayonet if he had something worth fighting for, like good old American pie. But Nam is not it. Nam is nowhere. You want colonies, you go blow it out your ear. And your boss calls us bums! Bums! My daddy fought the Nazis, and my granddaddy fought the Depression, and my great-granddaddy fought the railroads. You hear me? Bums, he said. I'd walk right through you if you were worth getting blood on my tracks. You're not. I know how to play the game. Me and my friends are in the mountains, as the Latinos say. Go defend yourself to history. I am history. I was here."

Ever the temperamental child, Passel threw his half-empty plate of rich food on the ground and stamped on it with his boots to the beat of the music from inside. It made him feel better. It also served, like guerrilla theater, to punctuate his diatribe. They all got the message. Passel had put his heel to the folk who fed him. In 1972, America came very close to internecine warfare in a subtle way—

in the theater of the mind, we slaughtered each other without mercy.

"Passel," said Christine, who'd translated Passel's speech for Madame Binh as best she could, given his idiosyncratic style. "Madame Binh would like to, uh . . ." Christine paused oddly. Her voice faltered as she continued, "Would like to know if you would welcome . . . peace. She is confused by your passions. Are you, or are you not, for, uh . . ."

"Peace," finished Justine.

"Why do you keep asking me that?" said Passel.

"Because you are murky on the subject," said the gorilla.

"Are you for peace, Passel?" said Justine.

"Peace of what?" said Passel.

"You're evading the issue," said Christine softly.

"You tell Victoria Charlotte that I don't believe in peace till the Promised Land," said Passel. "And you tell her that his kind of peace is my kind of sword. You tell her any peace treaty she signs with him is gonna explode in her mouth. And you can mention that I don't have any faith in her friends either. They're too wasted now to go for anything but more of the same."

Christine did so, listening to Madame Binh's monotone reply with a pained look on her face. Christine seemed to be shaking as she said, "Madame Binh thinks you are the toughest American negotiator she has met. She would like to know how you would bring, uh . . ."

"Peace," finished Justine.

"Stand still, it'll fall on you," said Passel.

"I cannot permit this to continue," said the gorilla.

"I get to you, man? The truth," said Passel.

"On the contrary, young man," said the gorilla, "though your manners are unrivaled by any in my experience, I feel that we have indulged you beyond your limits.

408

I cannot imagine any further advantages to this meeting. You clearly need a straw man of your own making to vilify. I remind you that foreign policy is built upon compromise and reconciliation, not upon vindictiveness, and, in your apparent case, weak bowels. It would be best if you, and this illusion of camaraderie you represent, limit your analyses to poetry. There, I believe, you will find the exaggerated states of being you require."

"Henri?" said Christine. She was very pale.

"Yes?" said the gorilla, reaching out.

"Christy, are you all right?" said Justine.

"Big Daddy wants me to get lost now?" said Passel.

The gorilla snorted in reply. Christine stood with Madame Binh. She wavered slightly, held upright by Madame Binh and the gorilla. Agnes went after the gorilla. She did not look back at Passel.

"Rumor of peace," said Passel, lighting up a joint, offering it to Justine.

"Don't joke, Passel," said Justine, who dabbed at her wet eyes with a swan feather. "Christy's really upset."

"No stuff?" said Passel, toking deep.

"I don't think it was such a good idea to have you here tonight," said Justine. "In your way, you've ruined the party."

"How did this hippie do that? Nobody listens to me. I was just blowing hot air in his face," said Passel.

"I can't bear to explain it to you," said Justine. "Accept what I say. You've been pure at heart in an otherwise uniformly tainted group. You've been honest. That's impolite. There is no way to say it. You don't understand, do you?"

"Nope," said Passel. The hint of tears was gone. The quiver in her voice was gone. This was a daughter of the ruling class.

"It's the peace," said Justine.

"Peace is at hand," said Passel, laughing ha ha ha.

"Yes, it is," said Justine, not laughing, "and there's nothing we can do anymore."

"I'm not following," said Passel.

"Do you believe in America?" said Justine.

"Sure, I go for that New Jerusalem stuff," said Passel.

"Then you should understand me when I say that we are losing America," said Justine.

"Who's winning?" said Passel.

"We're losing," said Justine. "We're slipping away. My sister and I, we had big dreams. We dream too, people like us. And now we're losing. Have you ever heard of the Straw People? I suppose not. You see, we can't take the burden of guilt much longer. It's crushing us. I see our grasp on this world slipping away. I don't really know what's to become of us. It hurts me to guess. You won't understand me, but I shall confide to you anyway that Christine and I are not entirely of this world, or of your world. Your friends in the mountains. The Straw People was our attempt to get into that world. To involve ourselves. And I think we've failed. Or maybe it's that we're not allowed in. I'm not sure. Failure, prohibition, rejection, much the same thing. We are the Means, you see, and . . . oh, it isn't worth the talk. I know Christine can't handle much more of this uncertainty, this realness. But, oh, Passel, what big dreams we had." She made an odd sweeping motion as she finished.

"Who's winning America, if you're losing?" said Passel, confused by, so passing by, most of what Justine had said.

"The peace," she said.

"What kind of peace?" said Passel, toking deeply on his funny cigarette and, in the (seemed like) clarity of his high, catching himself. He suddenly saw the light. This

fancy-dress ball on the Right Bank of Paris; these indifferently wealthy people; the war so far away it didn't seem
to exist save as a way of maintaining qualified pleasure for
the privileged and misconstrued pain for the under-
privileged; the very nature of the election year 1972,
when a candidate for the highest elective office of the
world's most powerful democracy could safely campaign
on a platform that promised to eliminate life, liberty, and
the pursuit of Reason within thirty days of the inauguration: all of this added up to the concept that Christine and
Justine, and now Passel, not to list the hundreds of thousands of other cousins who were on the run from the
approaching idiom, truly believed was corrupting them
along with the rest of America into slothful, greedy, vain,
and inadvertently cruel fools: all of it added up to the
concept that Passel then leaned forward and described to
Justine's swan tail as she floated away:

"The peace of the dead, huh? Rest in peace," said
Passel.

"Peace is at hand," called Justine, already far away.

"Peace is at hand," repeated Passel, settling back
into his chair, toking deeper, stoning himself from the
horror of it all. He surrendered to the peace. He could feel
it ooze over his soul, just as it oozed over all who had
thought that by promoting peace they were promoting
America. But something had gone wrong. What? Was it
perhaps that "peace" was not a rigorous enough argument, that to yearn simply for "peace" can too easily
become resignation before hate-mongers rather than an
effective arrest of vice? Is it not likely that the only true
"peace" is death, and that while there is yet life and hope,
one must fight for Virtue? It made a certain amount of
sense. It smelled of some cheap ironies, but then, thought
Passel, one can only philosophize as grandly as the times
live, and there wasn't much to work with on that account.

411

Passel, sighing, ripped his "McCarthy" button from his cap. He'd got fooled again. He resigned himself inside himself. K. (who not only would declare "Peace is at hand" at a news conference three weeks hence, but also would win the peace by advising his President to terrorize the reluctant DRVN to the peace table with the infamous Christmas "Peace on Earth" Bombing two months later, being rewarded for his peaceful efforts with one-half of the Nobel Peace Prize one year later) missed his finest diplomatic achievement that evening at the Pavillon de Means. K. missed witnessing Passel Serf at peace.

(to be continued)

Underground Maneuvers

BIANCA STUMBLED along in pursuit of the Means
women. The secret passageway led her to the depths
of Craven Castle; and, as she rushed downward, she
felt the dread of imminent disaster. Without a light, she
might have panicked in the dark confines of narrow halls,
low portals, rotten staircases, and cobweb-covered corners,
if not for her single obsession—that Vernal Means must be
rescued from any further desecration by her family. Europa
Stupefacenta's uncritical maternity for the unloved of this
world had passed on intact to her only child. In this peculiar
fashion, Bianca had become her mother. She could not help
herself from wanting to help others. The more wretched
Vernal Means seemed, the more Bianca needed to comfort
her. The more powerful Happy Means seemed, the more
Bianca needed to combat her. Bianca had heard the call of
sainthood. Bianca answered with her total being, crashing
down an earthen ramp, following her heart and the whispering of the twins ahead, their white-golden hair flashing now

and again from torchlight through air vents. And far, far ahead, Bianca could hear:

"Kee-kee-kee!" from Vernal Means.

"You! You! You!" from Happy Means.

The chase led to a low-ceilinged cave. Bianca had to double over, to support herself on her hands. She heard scraping sounds, the click of a lock, a crash. The cave was suddenly awash in dim green light from an opened door yards ahead. Bianca saw four silhouettes slip through the door in succession. Bianca hunched on, seeing now, in the dim green light, dark wet smears on the floor. It was Vernal Means' blood. Bianca followed the trail. At the door, she was able to stand upright. There was a ledge. She stepped through, making for a ladder's top rung to the left. Below her was a vast, subterranean chamber bathed in dim green light. The chamber seemed strewn with scientific equipment. There was a horseshoe-shaped structure along one stone wall with heavy black cables shooting out from all sides. And to the far end of the chamber, there was a two-story-high metal sphere, with ladders and catwalks attached, with the words

DANGER

POSITIVISM

printed in blue-black on its side. The chamber smelled of alcohol, asbestos, ozone, new plastic, and stale air. There was an ominous humming. There were no Means women to be seen. Bianca descended the ladder quickly. Now she was lost. She despaired of Vernal's fate. Angry with herself for lagging so far behind—she was not nearly so acrobatic as the larger American women—she lashed out at a table of glassware. She wanted to call out for Vernal, but was afraid. She spied a small door at the end of an aisle and moved toward it. It opened slowly.

"Peace in our time," said Monarch Means, in the lotus position in the middle of his apartment, adding, "Atoms for peace."

"Did you see them?" demanded Bianca.

"You must be one of the guests," said Monarch. "My name is Monarch, as in the butterfly, not the regent. Welcome, little sister. Would you take some tea? Biting jasmine tea?"

"Please help me," said Bianca, leaning against the wall.

"I am not of your world," said Monarch, standing to reach out to comfort Bianca.

"They're trying to kill her," said Bianca.

"The true path is inward," said Monarch.

"Accidenti! Listen to me, little one," said Bianca, taking his tiny wrist. "There are four women trying to hurt each other. We must stop them. I followed them here. Is there any other way out?"

"There is no escape," said Monarch.

"Have you got a light? A lantern?" said Bianca.

"Would you like to see my laboratory? I smash atoms, culture bacteria, and listen to my mother," said Monarch.

"One moment," said Bianca, studying Monarch's features. Yes, there it was, Means. "Come with me, little one," said Bianca, "we must help your mother."

"My mother?" said Monarch.

"She needs our help," said Bianca. Monarch fetched a candelabrum, lit it, and strode out into the chamber. Bianca followed him closely. They snaked left and right between the tables and crates, Monarch calling, "Mother? Mother?"

"They came in here. Are you certain there is no other way out?" asked Bianca.

"Mother?! Mother?!" cried Monarch, much louder. A crate tumbled over to the side. Footsteps approached. A voice:

"Mother?"

"Mother?" said Monarch Means, holding up his candelabrum.

"Mother?" replied the voice. It was Justine, leading Christine by the arm. Bianca squinted to see them. They looked terrible—their haughtiness gone to reveal frightened children.

"Come over here," said Bianca to them.

"Mother?" said Justine again.

"Where is my mother? Have you hurt her?" said Monarch.

"Your mother? My mother," said Justine.

"My mother," said Christine.

The four of them closed in an open space between the black cables and the two-story-high sphere. Justine touched Monarch's face. Christine, much more disoriented than her sister, tried to touch his face, but failed.

"This is your brother. See what you Means have done for him," said Bianca coldly, taking Monarch's arm and turning him about.

"No," said Justine.

"Witch," said Christine weakly.

"Tell them your name, little one," said Bianca.

"My name is Monarch Means, as in the butterfly, not the regent. Welcome, little sisters. My house is your house . . ."

"No!" cried Justine, cringing back with Christine.

"You are pathetic. Where has Vernal gone?" said Bianca. "Your mother," she corrected.

"My mother!" said Monarch.

"Mine!" said Justine.

Another crash from the right, and the four turned defensively. A figure emerged into the candlelight, saying: "Shut up, all of you."

"A fine gathering, Mrs. Means," said Bianca, who forced herself not to be afraid of Happy. "I have introduced your stepdaughters to their brother. This is their burden now. What have you done to her?"

"She crawled into a hole," said Happy.

"Mother?" said Monarch.

"Dig her out, if you care," said Happy.

"That creature was our mother?" asked Justine.

"Look what you've done to me, Jewess," said Happy, holding up her arm to poke at the burn in her shoulder.

"My mother!" said Monarch, looking toward Happy.

"No, little one," said Bianca, restraining him. Happy was not to be trusted. Happy still held that club in her right hand. "Come with me," said Bianca, urging Monarch back away from the Means women.

"What have they done to my mother?" whispered Monarch.

The Twin Sisters Means leaned against each other, grasping each other, weeping openly. Through their tears, they spoke, to each other, to themselves alone, to their fates. They sang a melancholy duet, their swan song:

Justine said, "How could that thing be our mother? I don't want this to be true. Someone must stop this. I deserve more. Haven't I, we . . . what did we ever do to come to this? I'm so afraid. Did you see her eyes, and her face? And why is she all twisted like that? Mother was so beautiful. She can't be that creature. Was that a human being? Am I going to change into something like that? What's to become of us, Christy? Why isn't there anyone here to help me? It's not fair. I tried, we tried. I loved our mother. How can I love that? It was she, wasn't it? Tell me that wasn't our mother. Where is Daddy? Why isn't Daddy here? Where're Tory and Aaron? I don't want to die. Hold me. This isn't fair. We're special."

Christine said, "It wasn't our mother. Mother was beautiful and willowy. We shouldn't be afraid. Daddy won't let anything happen to us. We've been so good, for a long time. I have a child, yes? He'll protect us forever. It wasn't our mother! Mother is with the angels. Remember how she used to say that we made the angels envious? Don't cry. Tory will save us. You're perfect, Justy, and you will always be perfect. We've lived good and happy lives. Daddy won't let them hurt us. I love you, Justy, and Tory, and my baby. It wasn't what we think. That's what will happen to Happy. Don't be afraid. What bad things could ever happen to us? Just hold me tight, and don't say those things. Love me, trust me. We're special."

Bianca, calming Monarch in her arms, watched Justine and Christine carefully, at the same time measuring the threat of Happy's madness. All three seemed to gorge themselves on self-pity and accusations. Bianca felt drained of pity, yet not sufficiently strong to generate hatred for them. She was honestly indifferent to their fates.

Bianca gasped for her breath. From somewhere far above, she thought she could hear explosions and the blare of a klaxon. It sounded like war. Bianca wondered if it was the rescue Cedric had spoken of. It could not have come at a more appropriate time, she thought. The rescuers could do as they wished. The irony of the drama seemed complete to Bianca: a great American family, wealthy and beautiful beyond any means, golden or otherwise, brought low by its own bad blood. The pure-at-heart were sure to triumph, she thought, and those who'd thought themselves well born were sure to fall. For their wickedness, the Means were to be visited with a terrible vengeance.

(Yet, Bianca should have looked more to herself. She was too quick to dismiss the Means. She erred in a way that displayed her rarefied European nature. She anticipated her American opponents. Great American families, like the Means, are not done until they are dead past resurrection by gossip. And when great American families, like the Means, go down, they suck friend and foe into the vortex. It is true that whom God the Father would utterly destroy for his sins, God the Father first raises up in his pride. But it is also true that when God the Father utterly destroys, the disaster knows no bounds. Look to yourself, Bianca.)

Indeed: for then the subterranean chamber burst into a withering heat. Bianca and Monarch were thrown back against the lab table by a whipping white wind. Bianca heard hysterical screams. Bianca heard an inhuman roar. Bianca fought her vertigo. Her stomach churned. Her breast contracted. She bent over the lab table and retched onto the broken glass tubing. She looked into the withering heat, but it was impossible to focus, her eyes swelling and tearing. At best, she gathered an impression of action and reaction. The stone walls of the chamber seemed to throb in the queer glow emanating from the base of the two-story-high sphere. There, a portal had opened, like a wound, and through it poured terrifying sights and sounds. Bianca could not look directly at the portal. She shielded her eyes, feeling the heat on her palms. A bloated figure emerged from the portal, advancing swiftly to the center of the chamber.

"Mother! No!" cried Monarch, breaking from Bianca. Bianca lunged for him, but the white wind was too much for her. She collapsed against the lab table, watching as Monarch struggled toward the center of the tempest. The withering heat and its diffuse glow seemed to pass through his body. He seemed transparent. He crawled against the white wind, tearing at the air before him, crying:

"Mother! No! What have you done? Mother!"

Bianca sobbed. She couldn't help Vernal. She couldn't help Monarch. She couldn't help herself. But she would not surrender to panic. She prayed:

"Father, forgive. Father, forgive me."

By now, Monarch—physicist, naturalist, brother— had reached the blazing portal. He reached inside and, grabbing a handlebar, pulled the hatch shut. The white wind died. The monstrous roar ceased. The subterranean chamber was once again bathed in dim green light, except, Bianca noticed, a glowing from off to the left. The glowing cried out, "My children!" It was Vernal Means. She radiated a smoking fire from within. She launched into her swirling dance, laughing, "Kee-kee-kee!" If anything, thought Bianca, her dance was faster, more vertiginous, more final. The dance of death, thought Bianca.

"You!" screamed Happy, dashing toward Vernal with the club raised high over her head.

"Mother!" cried Monarch, leaping like a wraith before his mother, blocking Happy's charge. It was over instantly.

"Father, forgive," said Bianca, seeing the crumpled figure of Monarch at Happy's feet. Happy had slain him with one blow. She had crushed his skull. Dead is dead, Bianca knew; and Monarch Means, so brave a breath before, looked as useless now as the positivistic machines filling his laboratory. Bianca staggered again, worse than before, for the slaughter of innocence overwhelmed her heart as no personal danger ever could. The chamber spun around her. She started to fall. She made one final effort to hold herself up. She thought she saw, though she couldn't be sure, Vernal Means spin to a halt and leap across the body of her baby, pressing his broken face against her smoking breast. Bianca thought she saw, though she couldn't be sure, the twins rush up behind Happy in an ambiguous manner, either for attack or for protection. And Bianca thought she saw, though she couldn't be sure, Vernal raise her corrupted eyes to stare murderously toward Happy and, because they were in nearly direct line, the twins. The eyes of death, thought Bianca. A howl pierced the subterranean chamber. It was Bianca's last sensation as she fell into the merciful release of unconsciousness.

The Battle of Craven Castle

THE PURE-AT-HEART were sure to triumph," dreamed Effert Broadsword, "and those who'd thought themselves well born were sure to fall." Then a crash woke him completely. He flung himself out of bed. There were explosions, sirens, screams. He pulled on his Nam surplus, laced his boots, and jumped into the common room. Through the windows he could see the rear of the castle in flames, the bailey below a sea of sparks and glowing embers. He pounded on Europa's door, calling, "Signora!" just as the tower was struck by projectiles.

"Wham!" crashed one wall, dust and debris down.

"Ker-wham!" crashed another wall, beams and bricks down.

"Bimbo mio!" cried Europa, throwing open her door.

"Look out!" said Effert, tearing her out of the way of a falling beam. He swept her up into his arms, called for the guard to open up, then, hearing no response, kicked at the door. Still nothing, so he set Europa down and threw his two hundred pounds into it four times. On the fifth, not only the door gave way, but also the door jamb and most of the wall. The tower was disintegrating. Effert again picked up Europa and charged into the hall, down to the stairwell, before he'd thought what to do next. Providentially, Europa, who'd snared their coats while Effert had destroyed the door, did have a plan. She told him to put her down, calm down, put on his coat, and listen—the other prisoners were trapped in their towers too.

"Aye," said Effert, taking Europa's hand and leading her down the stairwell. The deeper they descended into the castle, the less dust and debris there were. The barrage had just begun to wear away the ramparts, and Craven Castle was big enough to withstand several hours of shelling—if that's what it was, thought Effert. At the bottom of the stairs, Effert shouted ahead. He saw guards running down the gallery toward the Great Hall. They veered through the double doors at the corner and scrambled out into the courtyard, where they were covered in smoke immediately. The scene out there was stupefying. Effert grabbed Europa, deciding to brave the Great Hall rather than risk the bailey. They dove under the horseshoe-shaped table as another patrol of guards trotted past. Effert didn't think they were looking for him. The castle was under attack, and they were running to their defense posts. Effert tapped Europa, saying, "The two stairwells there are to Gracie and Bianca, I think. I don't know which is which. Shall we split up?"

Europa was out from beneath the table and racing for the nearest stairwell before Effert could restrain her. She collided with two burly guards. All three went down,

Europa sliding away on the stone floor. Effert was at the guards immediately, kicking one in the head, flopping down on the other. As he rose up, a blow from behind doubled him backwards. Dazed, he dove for the table. Shots popped around him. Effert rolled underneath and inspected for holes.

"Now I aim. Come out!" called a guard.

"What's happening?" said Effert, stalling. He watched Europa, forgotten in the melee, crawl to a column and disappear. Another shot at his feet, and Effert said, "Okay," standing up.

"Let's take him to the captain," said the other guard. They pushed Effert before them as they trotted down the hall, across the courtyard in a rush, dodging sparks and shrapnel, and into a hatchway down to the command bunker. Effert was presented to Westergaard in the TOC. Torrance VIII stood next to him.

"What do you know?" said Westergaard.

"The sky is falling," said Effert. "I was hiding."

"Alone?" said Westergaard.

"Sure," lied Effert. They seemed unnerved.

"Captain!" said a sergeant, bursting into the room.

"Well," said Westergaard.

"There's a party of archers, with ladders, sir! Ladders. Approaching the front gate. At the bridge now, sir," he said.

"Lieutenant, are the men in place?" said Westergaard.

"What's left, sir," said Murtrux, looking grim.

"And the fires?" said Westergaard.

"With the rain, holding our own, sir," said Murtrux.

"Bring him along," said Westergaard, striding through the hatchway, followed by Torrance VIII, Murtrux, and two guards shoving Effert between them. They ascended quickly, bypassing the bailey, using the gatehouse stairwell. They continued up several levels to emerge onto a battlement running atop the gatehouse. Below them was the earthen ramp down to the roadway and the pine wood bridge. The storm raged. The barrage raged. But the dawn high above the storm had brightened the scene to a wet gray. The five towers of the castle were like flaming fingers.

Effert spun away from his guards to inspect the sky. So, he thought, a meteor storm. Effert called, "Come the Revolution of the comet!"

"What's that?" said Torrance VIII, grabbing Effert roughly.

"You messed with the comet, didn't you? The comet!" said Effert, wanting to tear at his face. But Torrance VIII looked beyond scarring. He knows, thought Effert. He knows what he's done. A meteor whistled over them, digging out a piece of the toothed outwork. They ducked below the battlement's wall and moved to the most forward position. There, they rose up to observe the scene. Twelve or so men, carrying longbows and two long scaling ladders, walked slowly across the bridge. They seemed unaffected by the barrage. They seemed unaware of the guns aimed at them from the castle's bartizans. They seemed cinematic, thought Effert. This reminded him of a scene from a flick— Errol Flynn? No, but yes, but no.

"Now hear this!" called Westergaard, spacing his words between explosions. "Lay down your arms! You are outnumbered! I have one of your comrades here! Surrender now!"

"Effert Broadsword!" called someone from below with a loud and authoritative voice. It seemed to come from one of two cowled figures.

"Crush this infamy!" replied Effert, who'd rehearsed this line for twenty years, just in case.

"Aye!" boomed another figure from below.

"Father!" said Effert, lunging forward. Murtrux took it as an escape attempt. He raised his pistol to knock Effert down. It was his last act. A cloth-yard shaft, no, three, pierced his neck and torso. He screamed as he fell backwards, over the edge, onto a rooftop below. Effert did not apologize, kicking the guards away, leaping over the toothed wall, swinging down to wend along a narrow ledge. The two guards grabbed for him and, exposing themselves, paid their lives for their zeal, a hail of arrows tearing them back.

"Open fire!" called Westergaard.

"Father!" called Effert, fearing for the men below as the marksmen in the castle's bartizans opened up with their automatic weapons. Initially, the cracking was sporadic as the riflemen sought line and range. Effert nearly lost his balance turning his head to see several of the archers fall wounded or dead. The others tramped onward. A massacre, thought Effert, regretting his temper. The cracking intensified. The archers spread out along the rocks along the ramp. The castle was built in such a way that there was no easy line of fire at the front gate. Still, Effert could see the archers would never make the cover of the walls. He edged to a gargoyle-headed drainpipe, grabbed hold, spun around, shouting, "Stop! Stop! Go back!"

"Effert Broadsword!" called that loud and authoritative figure again, reaching up to his hood to let down his hair. A glaring light filled the scene. Effert averted his eyes. The whole of the front of Craven Castle was lit up with a burst like a solar flare. The gunfire slackened, then became aimless, crack, crack. Effert pressed his head against the drainpipe, trying to clear his thoughts in the dazzling light. A ladder slammed against the wall next to him.

"Grace! We must get Grace!" said Cedric, climbing up the ladder to pull at his son's cuffs. Effert turned to see his father pass him and slip over the battlement like an acrobat. Three more men, wearing green tunics, with longbows over their shoulders, followed him. They were middle-aged, with paunches and gray whiskers, but they moved nimbly. Effert caught hold of the ladder and pulled himself up. He shouted to his new companions to exit through the barbican to the left. Quickly down the stairwell, Effert found the slit to the gatehouse proper, in the space between the inner wooden gate and the portcullis. They searched for levers and gears to raise the portcullis, but it was unnecessary. Effert turned to see a giant cowled man lift the porticullis with relative ease. The first man through was the other cowled figure. The foresters followed, carrying their wounded on the other scaling ladder.

"Effert Broadsword?" said Freewill.

"That's me," said Effert. The giant dropped the portcullis, whomp!

"Have we come in time?" said Freewill.

"Majesty," said Effert, after one look into the cosmic face. Effert went to one knee and bowed his head, saying, "At your service, Majesty."

"No need, pilgrim," said Freewill.

"I believed. I always believed," said Effert, lowering his gaze. Sure, it was corny, but Effert didn't care. To what end had Science ever led him? Science had alienated him from his native culture. Science had reduced him to such an extent that, at thirty-eight years of age, when most of his peers had turned their attentions from corporate advancement to winning yacht races, procuring giggling mistresses, and accumulating the trappings of folly, Effert was yet boyish, idealistic, and a believer in God the Father Almighty, Maker of Heaven and Earth (and Hairy Stars). On his knee, then, Effert set Science aside and chose, instead, another product of the Enlightenment, Romance. Embrace the imaginary, the remote, the heroic, the adventurous, and the mysterious, he thought; indulge sensibility, autobiography, and passion; most of all, celebrate the primitive, the natural, and the melancholy. In short, boy blue, regard fate as a calling. Chivalry, love, and wonder were sure to follow just as, in Newtonian mechanics, down follows up. Aye, thought Effert, for all my failures have led me here, on my knee— for this figure is surely a heavenly sign. Only a Comet Incarnate could have let down his hair to such an effect—a hairy star indeed.

"For your faith, and for your action in defense of liberty and for the promotion of Revolution," said Freewill, "rise, Effert Broadsword, a brother and true sword in my realm."

"Grace! We must hurry!" cried Cedric, pounding the stone walls, looking for the sally port. A stone gave way.

Cedric threw himself against it, disappearing inside the wall. Effert and the rest followed, down the narrow passageway to the Great Hall. The Great Hall was lit smokily with torches held high by mercenaries.

"Hold!" said Westergaard, standing stiffly before the table.

Effert held up his hand, stopping his party. The archers filed in along the rear wall, their weapons drawn and ready. Cedric moved to Effert's right. The cowled figures remained in the shadow of the passageway. Effert studied Westergaard and his two dozen or so men. It seemed inexplicable that Westergaard, the most professional and aggressive of soldiers, should choose to expose himself to attack rather than use the myriad blinds of the castle to cut down the attackers singly. This seemed a ruse. But why?

"Enough of this!" said Westergaard, pounding the table with his pistol butt. His men positioned themselves in a double volley line. From the right, four more guards marched out a party of bound prisoners. Among them Effert could see Europa, Abbott, Schleppend, and Bonaventuro Pellegrino.

"Grace!" called Cedric.

"No, Father," said Effert, yelling at Westergaard, "hand them over and . . ." A terrifying meteor salvo struck above them, sending beams crashing, ripping armor suits and displays of swords and trebuchets from the walls. A dust cloud swept through the room, obscuring Westergaard as he replied:

"I do not threaten! I do what I must!"

"Grandtour, what do you say?" said Cedric.

"Who?" said Effert, turning sideways to see a bounder in a green tunic and brown breeches, high black boots, with a quill of cloth-yard shafts on his back, a longbow at the ready. *Someone* had shot Murtrux in the rain at an incredible distance.

"This is Grandtour, Captain of the Comet Clubbe," said Cedric. "This is my son, Effert."

"Hiya," said Effert, smiling at the "Comet Clubbe."

"A fellow brother of the realm," said Grandtour, winking, saying to Westergaard, "You are captain here?"

"Do you yield?" said Westergaard.

"Give us our friends and we will go. Before the castle falls on us, copy?" said Grandtour.

"I do what I must," said Westergaard, waving to his men. They threw Europa to her knees. But before they could finish, Bonaventuro Pellegrino jumped down before her, yelling, "Me!" With that, Squelk drew his pistol and fired twice at his head. Bonaventuro Pellegrino fell forward heavily, silently.

"God!" said Effert, about to spring to the attack. Grandtour held him back, holding up his arm to signal to his men to prepare to shoot. Westergaard's men readied their automatic weapons. Squelk pulled Abbott forward and threw him to his knees also.

"Surrender!" said Westergaard.

"Villain!" said Grandtour.

"Remember me!" cried Abbott. The pistol cracked twice. Abbott fell forward heavily, silently. The shafts came up. The automatic weapons came up. There could be no reconciliation. The two companies would kill each other as the barrage pulverized the walls around them. There would be no escape. Effert straightened up. He could die as well as Abbott had.

Crash!

The twin doors from the bailey blew inward, torn from their hinges. Before Effert could think to dodge, a piece of one door slid across the stone floor to sweep him off his feet. As he went down, he saw the "Wonder" van bump up the two steps into the Great Hall and steer recklessly to the right, bearing down on Westergaard's men in the double volley line. They scattered left and right.

"Shoot!" cried Westergaard, but there was only a wild crack-crack from the fleeing guards.

"Shoot!" cried Grandtour, to more effect. Grandtour's men made short work of the scattering mercenaries. There was no return fire, such was the efficiency of medieval weaponry: one cloth-yard shaft, one downed adversary. The Comet Clubbe pressed the attack. Effert, up again, hopped to the "Wonder" van, which had crashed to a stop against the remains of the horseshoe-shaped table. Effert ripped back the driver's door.

"Did I do it?" said Swinyard, slumped over the wheel, breathless, but grinning.

"Herr Swinyard!" called Schleppend, released. "You nearly ran me down! Look what you've done to Effert's truck." He pulled his partner down and hugged him hard.

"Sorry about the truck, Effert," said Swinyard.

"Grace! Where are you?" said Cedric, searching the fallen.

"She's here, Mr. Broadsword," said Swinyard, pointing to the "Wonder" van. The curtain separating the driver's seat from the living quarters fell down. Gracie dove through into Effert's embrace, saying, "Oh, Effert, Effert," kissing and squeezing until they tumbled to the ground.

"Easy, Gracie, this is a battle," said Effert, holding her back enough so they could get to their feet. "Are you okay?"

"Am I? Oh, Effert!" said Gracie, jumping him again.

"Grace, Grace!" said Cedric, limping over to hug son and ward.

"You're hurt," said Gracie.

"My foot. Broken, I think," said Cedric.

"Oh, Uncle Cedric," said Gracie, holding him upright.

"Abbott," sobbed Cedric, leaning on Gracie.

"Look who's here," said Schleppend.

"We've got ourselves a prisoner," said Swinyard, pointing to Aaron Verbunko, now stepping cautiously from the van. Laddy followed him.

"Who's that?" said Effert.

"It's Verbunko, the Means' mouthpiece," said Schleppend.

"Oh," said Effert, having only seen Verbunko up close once before, at the Jousting Contest. He looked wan and weasely to Effert, albeit relaxed for a prisoner of war. Effert disliked him immediately. He reminded him of the wicked court ministers of fairy tales. "What do we do with him?" added Effert, picking up a genuine broadsword from the floor.

"His Majesty would appreciate an interview with Monsieur Verbunko," said Laddy.

"Sure," said Effert, wondering who the hooded dwarf could be, though only a brother of the realm could look so fabulous.

"What have you got to say for yourself?" said Cedric.

"I have no comment," said Verbunko.

"My son is dead. My friend, an Italian diplomat, is dead. Many are dead. You are responsible," said Cedric.

"I have no comment," said Verbunko.

Laddy spoke to Verbunko in French. The two of them walked over to the shadows of the passageway. Two of the cowled figures joined them. Effert had no idea what they were discussing, but it was obviously important to them. He turned to attending the dead and wounded. Grandtour and his men made stretchers of the planks of the shattered table. The Great Hall was a shambles and getting worse as the barrage continued. This interview couldn't go on too long. No victory was complete, Effert knew, until withdrawal was complete. He saw that Grandtour had joined the conference. There was shouting now. Schleppend went over, then Swinyard. Effert heard snatches:

"Repeat, space vehicle!" said Grandtour.

"It can't be done!" said Verbunko.

"A supercomputer, that's all!" said Schleppend.

"You know nothing!" said Verbunko.

A direct hit overhead sent timbers into the balconies, debris cascading down to bury half the table. Dust wafted up to sweep over the living and the dead like a wave. More explosions in the courtyard sent debris crashing through the stained-glass windows. Effert rushed to the conference, saying:

"We've got to go, Majesty!"

"Grandtour?" said Laddy, not ignoring Effert, just

concentrating on the issue at hand. Grandtour waved to a pixyish forester, saying:

"Orbiter can clear what he jammed. Affirmative."

"There is nothing you can say," whined Verbunko.

"Stop 'Harold Starr'!" said Swinyard.

"Stop 'Harold Starr'!" said Schleppend.

"No! No! No!" said Verbunko, who then had to protect his face from wild blows by Swinyard & Schleppend. Management had once too often refused labor's demands. Laddy stopped the thuggery with a gesture. Verbunko was not given further opportunity to resist. Orbiter grabbed him by his suit jacket and jerked him away. Verbunko pointed weakly toward a hallway to the far right. Off they went, the three cowled figures close behind. Their mission, Effert now understood, was to stop "Harold Starr." More of the puzzle fell into place for Effert; yet what was the Means Corporation doing messing with the comet? Was "Harold Starr" simply a spacecraft? If it was, that would explain that second point in space discovered by Swinyard & Schleppend on the Means' machine, ORACLE, the night they broke into Torrance VIII's study: spacecraft closing on the comet. The more he knew, the more confused he grew, shaking it all off with the thought, confirmed once again, that Big Business makes No Sense.

"What can they say?" said Schleppend to Swinyard.

"Comet talk," said Swinyard, laughing a little madly, picking up a mace, and skipping over the rubble to join Laddy.

"What was that?" said Effert to Schleppend.

"Well, roomie," said Schleppend, "I think the Proto Industrial Trust has met its match."

Effert might have pursued Schleppend's coyness, and Swinyard's obtuseness, if more salvos hadn't just then ripped part of the roof away. Flames shot through the superstructure. Grandtour and the Comet Clubbe leaped to their tasks. Effert organized the column and was about to order retreat when he was reminded that the first thing a leader of an expedition must do before quitting the scene is to count heads. Europa, having been buried by debris from the "Wonder" van's ramming, having been knocked senseless by a blow from Squelk following Bonaventuro's execution, struggled off the makeshift stretcher, straightened herself with heroic determination and, wiping off her blood-and-plaster-smeared mouth, yelled:

"Bianca!"

Effert looked to Cedric. Cedric looked to Gracie. Gracie looked to Effert. They looked to each other and withered a little inside themselves. How could they have been so selfish? Effert could see his destiny now, chivalry lighting a fire in his heart. Schleppend stepped up to offer his legal expertise, Grandtour stepped up to offer his longbow, and those of Gemini, Apollo, and Viking, the others being enough to get the casualties back to the forest hideout. Gracie stepped up to offer the fact that only she knew where Bianca had last been seen. Cedric stepped up to offer that his children never again go anywhere he didn't. And Europa stepped up to offer the theme of their quest, *"Presto!"*

"You had Abbott and the Florentine shot?" said Torrance VIII, truly shocked.

"No, no, they fainted. We only pretended to execute them," said Westergaard.

"And then?" said Torrance VIII.

"We were outflanked, forced to withdraw," said Westergaard.

"I won't waste our time demanding an explanation as to why you didn't kill them all. You will answer for your failure later. What are you doing about it now?" said Torrance VIII.

"We expect relief momentarily. We can hold here until we get this chopper off, or until another arrives," said Westergaard. "Unless you have additional orders, sir?"

"No, no, it's that Happy and my sisters are very ill," said Torrance VIII.

"We must wait, sir," said Westergaard.

431

"I expect you to do something! If there is any more combat, shoot to kill! Do you hear me?" said Torrance VIII.

"Yes, sir," said Westergaard, spinning away to check his perimeter again. He had two dozen men left, out of eighty—two dozen! And Means threatened him with review of his conduct, because like a good field commander, he'd not opened fire before he could assess the size and ordnance of the opposition. Means expected him to do something. The hangar behind him was on fire. Five of the six helicopters were broken in half. The control tower was flattened. He had no radio communications. He had no retreat, his defensive line was strung fifty yards across the ridge of the heliport landing pad, one hundred yards uphill from the postern gate, with only the cliff to his rear. He was facing an unknown, arguably deranged adversary—bows and arrows, scaling ladders, and, if his hunch was right, meteors. The castle was being pulverized to a ruin. The rain and wind made visibility minimal. And, worst of all, he had seen the Means women. They were ill, all right, and he recognized their affliction. He'd fought every sort of battle but that. Theoretically, they'd have a warning. Westergaard crouched by Squelk. "Give me a white flare if they rush us, a red flare for the relief choppers."

"Yes, sir," said Squelk. "Who are they, sir?"

"I only begin to understand," said Westergaard, which was, coincidentally, the very same thing Effert said just then:

"I only begin to understand," when asked by Gracie, as they crawled into the vestibule leading to the postern gate, who those three men in robes were.

"But," said Gracie.

"I believe in the comet, I believe," said Effert.

"But," said Gracie.

"Ya gotta believe," said Schleppend.

"But," said Gracie.

"Faith, Grace, above all else," said Cedric.

Grandtour bounded back with his scouting report. Westergaard and his men held the airfield, standard

432

operating procedure in event of overrun. Obviously, Westergaard had made his stand in the Great Hall to buy time for the Means to get off the high rock. But something had gone awry. The last whole "dragon" (helicopter) was in trouble, two technicians tinkering with its wiring. Nearby, said Grandtour, under a tarp, were several yellow-haired women on stretchers. Among them was a slight, dark-haired woman.

"Bianca," said Gracie.

"Aye," said Effert, issuing orders. Cedric was to remain back here, out of the line of fire, with Gracie and Europa. He, Grandtour, and Schleppend joined Gemini, Apollo, and Viking at the ground-level port in the postern gate's left bartizan. Effert could see Westergaard running in a crouch from man to man. He could see the tarpaulin covering the Means women and Bianca. He could see the remaining Huey's blade spin once, choke, spin twice, choke. He could see the one hundred yards of killing ground from the postern gate to the landing pad. He could see that a charge would be stupid.

"Could it be worse?" said Schleppend, peering out.

"You had to ask," said Effert, waving at the horizon. Below the black rain clouds, just above the mountain peaks and the tips of the pine trees, three helicopters bobbed in tight formation, blue and green landing lights lit, their searchlights sweeping in arcs before them. Westergaard's reinforcements had come. The relief pilots veered back and forth between streaking meteors. They were brave men, Effert knew. Old Westergaard was the bravest. Once relieved of the Means' safety, he would counterattack mercilessly. And, as if things weren't perilous enough, the meteor storm was slackening. The bolides had all but ceased. The fireballs streaked intermittently now. The micrometeorites fell in bunches. The barrage was lifting of its own accord, or, if Romance is to be believed, of the accord of higher players in this adventure. Still, all this considered together, the course of action seemed clear to Effert, who turned to Grandtour, saying:

"Save what we can."

"Affirmative," said Grandtour.

"What about Bianca?" said Gracie.

"I told you to stay back!" said Effert.

"You can't leave her," said Gracie, joined by Europa and Cedric. The three of them looked wildly to Effert.

"You don't know what you're saying," said Effert. "Let's get out of here. Grandtour, we two in the rearguard. You two on the point. Schlep, get moving with Gracie. Father, take Europa."

"Non! Bimba mia! Non, Eeefert!" said Europa, hugging Gracie.

"Effert, you can't do this! You can't leave Bee with those people. Where's this faith of yours?" said Gracie.

"Oh, Gracie, Gracie," said Effert. The roar of the relief helicopters neared. A red flare shot skyward. Searchlights swept over the heliport pad, against the walls of the castle, lighting up the postern gate. Effert felt he could see into everyone's heart. They understood his dilemma, but they wanted him to change fate, to reach into history and force it to give Bianca her freedom, the Means their due, and this whole episode a happy conclusion. How could he deny such a request? Of course it was unfair; of course it was what folk always asked knights in bright armor whose righteousness was, to their minds, sufficient to best the wicked. How could he not try? Effert said to Grandtour, "Shall we give it a go?"

"A Go situation," beamed Grandtour, jumping down to the portal of the postern gate. Gemini, Apollo, Viking followed. Effert's last remark to Schleppend and Cedric was to get the women back if they didn't come back.

"My Effert," said Gracie.

"My son," said Cedric.

"My roommate," said Schleppend.

"Oh, Schleppend, tell me, I can't look," said Gracie, burying her head in Europa's bosom.

"Okay," said Schleppend, stepping cautiously to the port of the bartizan, Cedric stepping up behind him, his hand on Schleppend's shoulder. "I can see Grandtour,"

434

continued Schleppend, "and the rest. Westergaard's stood straight up. He shakes his fist. There they go. They spread out in separate directions. A guard shoots a white flare! Another is up with flags. He waves to the choppers. One circles the tower. Effert doesn't see it. He runs to a bunch of rocks. Westergaard yells to his men. They fix bayonets. Effert still doesn't see the chopper. Grandtour sees it. Grandtour and Viking stop. They shoot! Again! They're shooting arrows at the chopper. It swerves away from Effert. It has arrows in its runners. Grandtour shoots again."

Ker-wham!

"Grandtour shot the chopper down," said Schleppend. "It's in flames. He did it!"

"A meteor," said Cedric.

"It fell on Westergaard and his men! Right on top. They are on fire. No, not Westergaard. There's another guard. Eight more. They've set up again. Viking got one. Viking and Apollo keep it up. Effert is up. Fifty yards to go. Look out! Westergaard waves his hands. Here comes another chopper. It's got a machine gun. Effert and Grandtour are down!"

"Come the Revolution," said Swinyard, suddenly beside Schleppend.

"Of the comet," said Schleppend reflexively, turning to find his bosom buddy grinning broadly, mace over his shoulder. "Did it go down?" asked Schleppend.

"ORACLE sure did. Tilt. Laddy asked it the true nature of revolution," said Swinyard.

"The ball went down?" said Schleppend incredulously.

"Schleppend!" screamed Gracie.

"Oh, yeah," said Schleppend, back to the port.

"It's finished," said Cedric, who'd been watching.

"Effert, Grandtour, and Gemini are surrounded," said Schleppend. "The chopper is over 'em. Let's go, Herr Swinyard!"

"Take another look," said Swinyard casually.

"His Majesty!" said Schleppend. "There they go,

435

across the field. Westergaard sees them. Rollo's got his robes off. Damn! He really is a Viking. He is big. Big! Rollo's got his battle-ax. Viking and Apollo are up. More arrows into the chopper. There's Orbiter. He's with them. The chopper backs off. His Majesty points to the Means. The other chopper has landed. The Means get in. Effert sees them. He's up again. Westergaard's got a pistol. Effert and Westergaard run for the chopper. It starts to lift off. It stops. Means is out. He points to someone. Verbunko!"

"What?" said Swinyard, jumping down to where he'd left Verbunko, who'd given his word of honor he wouldn't escape. (The faithless are without honor, remembered Swinyard, too late.)

"Verbunko is near the Means' chopper," continued Schleppend. "Westergaard sees him. He backs away from Effert. Effert is hit. No! He's down. Westergaard signals his men. They fall back. They form around the Means' chopper. The other chopper is over them. Herr Swinyard, come back! He's after Verbunko. Verbunko falls down. He's up. He won't make it. Here come Grandtour and Gemini. His Majesty, Rollo, and Laddy are halfway to the pad. His Majesty points. The other chopper dips down. It shoots! Look out! Rollo!"

"My dear God!" said Cedric.

"I don't believe this. This is not happening," said Schleppend. "Rollo buried his ax in the helicopter's cabin. He stood right up in front and chopped the chopper. The pilot can't believe it. He's in trouble. He spins. The trees!"

Ker-wham!

"That's two down. The trees reached up and pulled it down! Two down. Verbunko is at the chopper. Westergaard and his men shoot. Verbunko is inside their semicircle. Means has the cabin door open. The Contessa is out of the chopper. She runs away. Run this way, Bianca!"

"Bimba mia!" cried Europa.

"Verbunko's got her," continued Schleppend. "The villian! By the wrist. She shouts at him. He shouts at her. In

436

the middle of this, they're having a debate? What could they say?"

("I've come," said Verbunko, "for I intend to share my life and love with you regardless. There's one way to go now. I've risked fifty dangers to take you there. Up, and quickly, with me!")

"Go, Blue," shouted Cedric (Yale '40), hammering the wall.

"Effert is up," said Schleppend. "Verbunko and Means have the Contessa. The chopper is shut. Verbunko waves to the pilot. Westergaard raises his pistol. Well shot! Grandtour shot Westergaard through the wrist with an arrow. Westergaard changes hands. Another arrow. Westergaard is down. No! He charges Effert with his head. Effert tackles him. The guards are up. They aim. Look out, Grandtour! Look out, Viking!"

Errrrrrrrrrrrrrrrrrrr . . .

"What's that horn?" said Cedric.

"Got me," said Schleppend.

. . . rrrrrrrrrrrrrrrrrrrr . . .

"They point toward us, up above us," said Schleppend. "The chopper is up. It hovers. They point from the chopper. Westergaard and Effert stop. They all stop. Everyone points up. I can't see what they're pointing at. The guards throw down their guns. They jump over the cliff. Westergaard shouts. The chopper is higher. There it goes!"

"Non!" cried Europa, breaking free from Gracie.

"Signora!" called Gracie, to the chase.

"Grace!" called Cedric, limping after her.

"Wait for me," said Schleppend, following. As soon as he'd cleared the postern gate, he turned to see what had transfixed the combatants enough to transform a defeat for the attackers into a draw—the Means escaped, but Craven Castle fallen to the Comet Clubbe. He could see a pillar of flame surrounding the fifth, tallest tower, licking higher and higher at the winding staircase. He could hear the screeching horn from deep within the castle. He studied the high tower itself. He squinted into the red and orange flames dancing about the highest ramparts. What was that? An arm? Two arms? Was there someone up there, flailing through the flames? For an awful moment, Schleppend thought he saw a human being, an old and ugly woman, dancing on the tower's ramparts as the flames enveloped her like jaws closing on prey. Then she was gone. The horn continued . . . rrrrrrrrrrrrrrrrrrrr. Schleppend, shaken by the sight, put it out of his mind, like all the rest of this strangeness, and turned to trot toward his allies, now gathered in several different groups on the heliport pad. Effert had Westergaard prisoner to the left. Europa stood nearby shrieking, flapping her hands futilely at the helicopter disappearing over the horizon. Gracie tried to comfort her while restraining Cedric from attacking Westergaard. To the center, Apollo, Gemini, and Orbiter had set themselves to work on the last whole helicopter, abandoned by the Means when the relief chopper landed. And to the right, Grandtour, Viking, and Swinyard were huddled with His Majesty, Rollo, and Laddy. Schleppend walked toward them. Laddy was kneeling, drawing in the mud:

"That's the 'Macho Project,' " said Schleppend as the rain obliterated the symbol.

"That's what I told them," said Swinyard.

"Are you sure that's what it means?" said Viking.

"So?" said Laddy.

They were distracted by Westergaard's bellowing. Cedric had jumped him, dragged him to the ground, and was throttling him with both hands. Westergaard lay there, not resisting in any way.

"For Abbott! Murderer! For Abbott!" screamed Cedric.

"Do your worst," said Westergaard.

Which Cedric might have done had not Effert pulled him off, saying, "Father, he's wounded. Stop."

"He murdered Abbott," said Cedric.

"We're all dead," said Westergaard as Effert helped him up. "The pile, you fools. The pile. Why else did my men run?"

"What's a pile?" said Gracie.

"I can guess. Radiation," said Effert.

"So they've got us after all," said Cedric.

"You fools," said Westergaard, "It already got the Means and the Contessa. All dead men. There's nowhere to run."

"Oh, please, God, no," said Gracie.

"Captain Westergaard," said Laddy, splashing over to them, "please desist from alarming these good people."

"The pile!" said Westergaard.

"Desist!" said Laddy, turning to Grandtour and Viking, who'd followed him over. "Sirs, I advise you and your friends to make your escape in that flying vehicle. Can it be done?"

"Apollo is a space mechanic. Gemini is an astronaut. Affirmative, Laddy," said Grandtour.

"Away then," said Laddy. "Effert Broadsword, His Majesty would have a final word."

"The pile, you fools!" screamed Westergaard as Viking grabbed him, dragging him to the awaiting helicopter, already whirling to life—Apollo the spacemonkey, Gemini the spacejockey. Westergaard bellowed the more at the idea of escape. "Minutes at most. That's it. The end!"

"Is that true?" said Effert to Laddy as they walked over to Freewill and Rollo.

"I think it easiest to explain to you," said Laddy, "that we have some knowledge of what is called 'radiation.' His Majesty is, after all . . ."

"A comet," finished Effert. They reached Freewill and Rollo.

"Well struck, Effert Broadsword," said Freewill, as

Effert went to one knee in the mud, holding his genuine broadsword before him, handle up.

"Your servant, Majesty," said Effert.

"Your labor is far from complete," said Freewill.

"I've got the Means' address," said Effert.

"I thought as much. I advise you to await a sign," said Freewill.

"What kind of sign?" said Effert.

"You will know it," said Freewill. "Events are confused by passions now. Speak with your mentor, the mathematician. He will help explain. We have not determined all that we sought. The Means and their overlords are powerful and shrewd despots. They are adept at the politics of falsehood. You will have to combat them the rest of your days. The same will be true for your son, and his son, whom I hope to meet, in my time."

"I understand," said Effert.

"Remain diligent and defiant, Effert Broadsword. The time is fragile, as before. Is this a clear English?" said Freewill.

"Storm warning," said Effert.

"The rain will pass with me," said Freewill.

"Storm, Majesty," said Laddy. "As a revolutionary tempest."

"Yes, I understand now," said Freewill. "Is this what Errol Flynn says?"

"Errol Flynn?" said Effert.

"Captain Blood, The Adventures of Robin Hood, The Sea Hawk, Elizabeth and Essex, The Prince and the Pauper, Virginia City, The Charge of the Light Brigade, Dodge City . . ." said Freewill. "Sublime philosophical achievements."

"Oh," said Effert. "Errol Flynn. He keeps the faith."

"Keep the faith also, Effert Broadsword," said Freewill, reaching out with his right hand, "and away with you, bold one."

Effert bounded up and away, racing across the heliport pad, a genuine broadsword held high in one hand, the touch of a Comet Incarnate held tight in the other, bound for the waiting helicopter loaded now with the rescuers and the rescued, bound for a life of diligent defiance in the service of cosmic revolutionaries, and bound for the love of a woman and the children she'd give him, to continue, as before, awaiting the coming of the comet. Effert dove through the cabin door. The helicopter was immediately away from the high rock, swooping toward the Comet Clubbe and auxiliary (Lyra, Yella, and Wavy Rufus) sheltered within this enchanted Everpine Forest: a forest that had, when it was most crucial to the safety of good men and true, reached out to aid the cause of liberty, love, and wonder.

The helicopter passed. The meteors passed. The fire passed. The pile (Danger/Positivism) passed. The storm passed. The comet passed. All passed, which is to say that all that's passed is, if not exactly prologue, an introduction to the flight of Wavy Rufus's imagination a night and a day and a night later as he sat once again in his tower room atop Broadsword Hall, with his pupils gathered at his feet to hear several surprising aspects of the further adventures of Halley's Comet, with one particular pupil, Effert, keeping one eye on Wavy Rufus and the other on the skylight for a promised sign.

Book VII

*Wherein the Means Suffer
Unhappy Ends*

"Harold Starr" Stopped

1 A comet is a celestial body.

1.01 A comet is a celestial body defined as a member of mankind's solar system, in that all known comets (in over fifty comet groups) display characteristics that indicate they have originated not from interstellar space but from a belt-like distribution at the near limit of the solar system's gravitational reach, and that this belt probably derives from a comet cloud located at the far limit of the solar system's gravitational reach.

1.02 A comet is a celestial body dating from the primitive solar system, a nearly pristine object (very little altered by subsequent chemical processes) which could have transported the ingredients of life soup to the planets and planetoids.

1.1 A comet is a celestial body that can be spoken of as having three parts: the nucleus, the coma, and the tail.

1.11 The nucleus is a dense conglomeration of particles (in the form of solids, including water ice, more volatile ices, siliceous rocks, and other ingredients associated with the mysterious carbonaceous chondrite meteorites).

1.12 The coma is a loose conglomeration of particles (in the form of dust and gas) streaming off from the nucleus.

1.13 The tail is a still looser conglomeration of particles (in the form of dust and gas) swept back by the solar wind as the comet approaches the Bright One.

1.2 A comet is a celestial body with a periodic orbit, attaining aphelion, perihelion, and comet-Earth minimum separation once each revolution.

1.21 So-called short-period comets are denoted by attaining aphelion, perihelion, and comet-Earth minimum separation every century or less—Halley's Comet being the premier "short-period."

1.22 So-called long-period comets are denoted by attaining aphelion, perihelion, and comet-Earth minimum separation once every one thousand to one million years—long enough to have come once in history.

2 A space vehicle is a manmade body.

2.01 A space vehicle is a manmade body defined as a physical and statutory extension of its builders, in that it is launched into space to perform tasks beyond the boundaries of their territorial jurisdiction but within the purview of what can be understood as legal liability.

2.02 A space vehicle is a manmade body with a limited history, in that, as of 1986, approximately a dozen nation-states have constructed and/or launched space vehicles, and only two of these states have constructed and launched space vehicles that consequently rendezvoused with and landed upon a celestial body other than the Earth.

2.1 A space vehicle is a manmade object that can be spoken of as having three parts: the guidance system, the payload, and the propulsion system.

2.11 The guidance system can be either Earthbound or on-board.

2.111 If the guidance system is Earthbound, the space vehicle is said to be a mechanical robot.

2.112 If the guidance system is on-board, it can be an astronaut, or it can be an on-board computer (linked or not linked to an Earthbound computer).

2.113 If the guidance system is an astronaut, the space vehicle is said to be manned.

2.114 If the guidance system is an on-board computer linked to an Earthbound computer, the space vehicle is said to be a cybernetic robot, introducing the dangerous philosophical issue "What is a man?" Philosophically speaking, there is no difference between a manned space vehicle and a cybernetic robot-equipped space vehicle.

2.12 The payload can be instrumentation, additional astronauts, weaponry, or simply an artifact, like a crest.

2.13 The propulsion system can be chemical, nuclear, ion drive, solar sail, a combination of these (primary and secondary systems), or simply one supplanted by gravity in extraterrestrial free fall (noting that there is no space or time where or when there is no gravity).

2.2 A space vehicle is a manmade body that can be injected into Earth orbit, and from Earth orbit into solar orbit, and from solar orbit into the gravitational field of any other celestial body, especially that of the planets and planetoids, though even so small (in mass) a body as a comet can capture a space vehicle.

2.3 Statutorily speaking, there is only one international treaty addressing the claims made by a space vehicle (manned or other): "Treaty on Principles Governing the Activity of States in the Exploration and Use of Outer Space, Including the Moon and Other Celestial Bodies."

2.31 This treaty was signed in January 1967 by interested parties in Washington, London, and Moscow, including many, but not all, of the approximately a dozen nation-states capable, as of 1986, of space flight.

2.32 This treaty cites the international character of space (a vague concept), forbids weapons in space (a vaguer concept), and requires signatories to aid and to protect distressed space vehicles (a still vaguer concept).

2.33 The section of the treaty relevant to the claims made by a space vehicle (manned or other) is Article II, which reads, "Outer Space, including the moon and other celestial objects, is not subject to national appropriation by claim of sovereignty, by means of use or occupation, or by any other means."

2.4 "A treaty is only as bad as the men who make it."— Anon.

3 Halley's Comet is a celestial body.

3.01 Halley's Comet is said to belong to the Neptune group of comets, in that it reaches aphelion beyond the planet Neptune; it is also said to have originated, at some undeterminable date, not from interstellar space but from a beltlike distribution of comets at the edge of the solar system.

3.02 Halley's Comet may be one of the oldest members of the solar system, possibly predating the major planets, as close to the Creation as mankind can yet reach, given that the proto-solar cloud condensed with materials drawn from the masses of first-generation stars.

3.1 Halley's Comet can be spoken of as having three parts: the nucleus, the coma, and the tail.

3.11 Halley's Comet's nucleus is said to display the following physical properties: diameter, 3.5 miles; mass, 70 million tons; rotation, 4/Earth day; shape and structure, irregular and unknown; composition, H, He, C, N, O, Ne, Na,

Si, S, Ar, K, Ca, Mn, Fe, Co, Ni, Cu, Kr, variously arranged into parent molecules, including the range of organic molecules discovered in the profoundly mysterious carbonaceous chondrite meteorites (comet as cosmic spermatozoon).

3.12 Halley's Comet's coma is said to be formed when the nucleus's parent molecules are heated by solar radiation to release, through violent and unpredictable processes (jets and halos), an enormous atmosphere of neutral molecules and ionized molecules (dust and gas), expanding upward of a million miles from the nucleus.

3.13 Halley's Comet's tail is said to be formed when, as the comet approaches the Bright One, the solar wind sweeps the neutral and ionized molecules (dust and gas) of the coma back away from the nucleus.

3.2 Halley's Comet is a celestial body with a periodic orbit, attaining aphelion, perihelion, and comet-Earth minimum separation once every seventy-four to seventy-nine years (ellipse altered by Saturn and Jupiter and "sshh!" et cetera).

3.21 On New Year's Eve 1984, Halley's Comet was 4.3 A.U. (400 million miles) from Earth and 5.3 A.U. (500 million miles) from the Bright One, totally beyond observation (retrieval) from Earth, with an apparent magnitude of 18.0.

3.22 On Woodstock Eve 1985, Halley's Comet was retrieved by the large reflecting telescopes in the People's Republics of Chile, Russia, and California, with an apparent magnitude of 15.0.

3.23 On Guy Fawkes Eve 1985, Halley's Comet was retrieved by naked eyes in both the northern and southern latitudes, with an apparent magnitude of 7.0.

3.24 On Christmas Eve 1985, Halley's Comet, passing southward through the Earth's equatorial plane, appeared to have a faint, 1/2-degree tail, retrievable by the naked eye in New York City and Rio de Janeiro, Peking and Melbourne.

3.25 On Martin Luther King Eve 1986, Halley's Comet, passing temporarily out of sight of observers in both latitudes, had a clear tail of 1 degree.

3.26 On the Ides of March Eve 1986, Halley's Comet, now one month after perihelion, had a faint tail of 20 degrees, visible to all observers worldwide.

3.27 On April Fool's Eve 1986, Halley's Comet reached comet-Earth minimum separation at .4 A.U. (37 million miles), with an apparent magnitude of 4.0 and a tail stretching 40 degrees across the night sky.

3.28 On the first of June 1986, Halley's Comet, passing out of sight of any naked eye on the Earth, crossed the orbit of the planet Mars.

3.3 Halley's Comet is a celestial body that was the subject of a proposal by the National Aeronautics and Space Administration to launch a space vehicle (mechanical robot) either to fly by, or to rendezvous with, or to land upon and return from the comet during its apparition in 1985/1986.

3.31 Owing to political and philosophical vagaries then extant in the most honest, most confused democracy on the face of Creation (the nation-state most hospitable to unfettered positivism since Auguste Comte, that heretical Cartesian, first dared to flout metaphysics by proposing that scientific knowledge is the *sine qua non* of Creation), NASA's proposal to intercept Halley's Comet with a mechanical robot was proposed, then rejected, then reproposed, then mysteriously lost in the mails. The FBI did not investigate. The *Crimes* did not investigate. *Kong* did. PIT does not return phone calls.

4 "Harold Starr" is a space vehicle.

4.01 "Harold Starr" is a space vehicle that is defined as a physical and statutory extension of its builders, in that it was designed, built, and launched to perform a task beyond the boundaries of their territorial jurisdiction but within the purview of what can be understood as legal liability.

4.02 "Harold Starr" is a space vehicle built by Grimmen Aircraft Corporation for its parent, the Means Corporation, which itself built "Harold Starr" for its parent, the Proto Industrial Trust (PIT).

4.1 "Harold Starr" is a space vehicle that can be spoken of as having three parts: the guidance system, the payload, and the propulsion system.

4.11 "Harold Starr" 's guidance system is said to be an on-board computer linked to an Earthbound computer (ORACLE), supplemented with on-board optical navigational equipment.

4.111 It is important to note that the presence of an on-board computer linked to ORACLE qualifies "Harold Starr" as a cybernetic robot—meaning that, philosophically, there is no difference between "Harold Starr" and a manned spacecraft.

4.12 "Harold Starr" 's payload is said to be a crest showing a five-towered pentagonal castle atop a sinister rock, all encircled with the Latin motto *Omnino Omnino Omnino* (By All Means By All Means By All Means).

4.13 "Harold Starr" 's secondary propulsion system is said to be the highly maneuverable ion drive, which system provides the capability of reducing "Harold Starr" 's velocity to near zero (facilitating rendezvous).

4.131 "Harold Starr" 's primary propulsion system (transporting "Harold Starr" from Earth into Earth orbit) is said to be chemical, meaning that "Harold Starr" was launched from a rocket base somewhere on Earth owned or controlled by the Means Corporation (likely leased from a nation-state not a member of the United Nations General Assembly, though it could be any nation not a signatory of the exclusivist "Treaty on Principles Governing the Activity of States in the Exploration and Use of Outer Space, Including the Moon and Other Celestial Bodies").

4.2 "Harold Starr" is a space vehicle that was injected into Earth orbit in the early fall of 1985, and then injected into solar orbit in the late fall of 1985, reaching perihelion in the winter of 1986, and vehicle-Earth minimum separation in the spring of 1986.

5 "Harold Starr" is a space vehicle that was designed, built, and launched with the mission of rendezvousing with and landing upon a celestial body, Halley's Comet.

5.01 The hazards of a rendezvous with a comet evidencing the active phenomena precipitated by solar radiation (coma and tail) necessitate that the rendezvous in anticipation of a landing be performed at a distance greater than 1 A.U. from the Bright One (pre-perihelion for Halley's Comet: before November 1985; post-perihelion for Halley's Comet: after April 1986); this is all the more important to ensure optimum conditions for communication between the on-board computer and ORACLE in consideration of the unpredictable dust and gas activity (jets and halos) within one million miles of the nucleus.

5.011 A post-perihelion rendezvous (after April 1986) in anticipation of a landing is preferred because the rate of approach could be adjusted optimistically with regard to the accordingly decreasing cometary activity (coma and tail).

5.02 The hazards of an actual landing upon a comet evidencing the active phenomena precipitated by solar radiation (coma and tail) require that the landing be performed when the comet is at a distance from the Bright One greater than 1.5 A.U. (pre-perihelion for Halley's Comet: before October 1985; post-perihelion for Halley's Comet: after May 1986).

5.021 A post-perihelion landing (after May 1986) is preferred because the rate of descent to the (unknown) surface could be adjusted optimistically with regard to the accordingly decreasing cometary activity (coma and tail).

5.1 "Harold Starr" on the surface of Halley's Comet would occupy and claim the comet for itself (a cybernetic robot), for its builder, the Grimmen Aircraft Corporation, for its builder's owner, the Means Corporation, and for its builder's owner's governor, the Proto Industrial Trust (PIT).

5.2 Statutorily speaking, the only document addressing the claims made by a space vehicle landed on celestial bodies is the aforementioned 1967 international treaty. This treaty is worth the pinewood it's printed upon. What is more, this treaty does not apply to the private sector, especially when the space vehicle in question is owned and operated by a multinational corporation which is itself governed by an international consortium of unknown origins.

5.21 Furthermore, the complicated histories of the East India Companies of Britain (chartered by Parliament 1600), of Holland (chartered by States-General 1602), and of France (chartered by the King 1604) suggest that private-sector exploitation of a "New Frontier" offers enough advantages for all concerned parties, and also enough difficulties for any opposing parties, that the Means Corporation's claim on Halley's Comet not only could be argued (by Verbunko, et cetera) analogous, statutorily, to European colonial expansion, but also could be argued (by Verbunko, et cetera) advantageous for mankind.

5.22 Nevertheless, statutorily speaking, the Means Corporation's claims of ownership (by occupation by a cybernetic robot) of Halley's Comet would mark the first recorded instance of the private ownership of a celestial body other than the Earth and objects fallen to the Earth. (Who, after all, owns the 'Allende Meteorite, 1973'?)

5.3 The Means Corporation's occupation of Halley's Comet would give the Means Corporation exclusive access to the second deepest interplanetary probe in history (after *Pioneer 10*).

5.4 Philosophically speaking, if the private sector can own (by possession) mankind's iconography—hence the vast private collections of art that fill the so-called public museums —it would seem that the private sector can also own (by occupation) one of mankind's icons.

The Passing of Wavy Rufus

BUT WHY?" said Swinyard. "Why should the Means want to own Halley's Comet? What can they do with it? I mean, really, why?"

"Sadly," said Wavy Rufus, rocking on his sorcerer's stool, "I can't even begin to speculate."

"Aw, come on," said Effert.

"You said it was all speculation anyway," said Schleppend.

"True," said Wavy Rufus, "but, my children, even in speculative history, there must be a sensible warrant for another statement. There is none. Not one."

"The Means must've said or done something," said Swinyard.

"Beyond 'Harold Starr,' they were a model of silent discretion," said Wavy Rufus. "Nothing was revealed. Their secret remained, profoundly, a secret. Humbling, when you consider what must be the size of the conspiracy."

Effert and Swinyard & Schleppend shifted their legs carefully, so as not to disturb Gracie, Lyra, and Yella Kissl asleep in each of their respective laps. They listened while Wavy Rufus answered several questions in Italian from

Bonaventuro Pellegrino. After several contemplative moments, listening to some rock on the radio, Schleppend said:

"Precedent?"—his legal brain trying to think as Verbunko might've thought—"Could that be why they wanted Halley's Comet?"

"Yes, please continue," said Wavy Rufus.

"I can't," said Schleppend. "But I feel we've missed something obvious. We're thinking too hard. Verbunko is a genius. He knows how to make the simple appear complex, and vice versa. 'Harold Starr' seems complex, which means there is probably something very simple about it, and its purpose, that we should examine from another direction. A simple warrant. For example, what does it mean that ORACLE indicated that 'Harold Starr' is part of the 'Macho Project.' What *is* PIT's 'Macho Project'? And for heaven's sake, what is PIT? We don't even know that, and they pay us twice a month. Oh, I don't know."

Bonaventuro Pellegrino asked Wavy Rufus several more questions, and then Wavy Rufus turned to them all to say:

"The Commissar sympathizes with your dilemma, children. He says to tell you, 'Tyrants define themselves.' Meaning that to ask for an explanation from tyrants is to give them more than their due. They are without reasons. A Roman concept."

"What he also means," said Swinyard, his SDS rhetoric spilling up from forgotten parts, "is that the true masters of the Earth—and I say masters, understanding that we are slaves—can't help themselves from craving to become the masters of space. What begins so badly can only get worse."

"No!" said Effert. "There must be a reason. Twisted, perhaps, but a reason. If we find it, we can fight."

"My Christian knight," said Schleppend. "There are turns that have no reason. As a Jew, I acknowledge this. Perhaps you must also, Effert, in this century of unsurpassed blasphemy. Even a true sword might not be enough."

"No surrender," said Bonaventuro Pellegrino in Italian, nodding to the Americans. He didn't understand

453

them. He thought they were either foolhardy men or dead men. But he owed them. What is more, he liked them. They were compelled. He turned to Wavy Rufus, saying, "Tell them, ancient Professor, that their anxiety must not be permitted to turn to despair. Tell them that what they feel about 'Harold Starr' is the same frustration all revolutionaries experience when they must fight despotism with limited resources, limited information, and limited time, but with a rich and abiding spirit. Tell them they must not permit their ignorance to be used by the despots against them. That they must answer the oppression of miseducation with the exuberance of violence. Tell them the Revolution demands of them their whole beings, regardless of their personal desires, for we have nothing to lose in our fight against tyranny but the chains of tyranny. We must fight on, blinded, wounded, widowed, and deprived, for the future belongs to the strong-willed."

Wavy Rufus translated, adding, "Yet the question of violence remains open in my heart of hearts. It has caused much suffering for us, hasn't it?"

"The Contessa?" said Bonaventuro Pellegrino. "An unfortunate casualty in a great victory." Wavy Rufus translated.

"That's where we part company on this trail, Mr. Commissar," said Effert. "My friends are my life. Where would I be without those I love? No party, no state, no philosophy is more important to me."

Swinyard & Schleppend nodded in agreement, but Bonaventuro Pellegrino, once Wavy Rufus had translated, said, "You Americans had your New Jerusalem handed to you. You don't know what it is to have to steal food from tyrants in order to feed your children. Your naive sense of honor and decency will betray you. Your land is now as corrupt as Europe ever was. You must make sacrifices for the Revolution. The Contessa. It's a hard lesson. It is best learned quickly. But this is academic. I am exhausted. I bid you good night."

Wavy Rufus translated as Bonaventuro Pellegrino waved good night and went down to his rooms to check on

Europa, who'd taken to crying herself to sleep. Swinyard & Schleppend said good night as well, getting Lyra and Yella Kissl up gently, escorting them downstairs to the guest rooms. Effert sat quietly for a while, then said to Wavy Rufus, "Imagine me academic."

"He didn't mean it harshly," said Wavy Rufus. "We're all tired. Perhaps I went on too long tonight. I wanted you to hear it through, though. An old man can't count on tomorrow."

"You'll live forever, Wavy Rufus," said Effert, stroking Gracie's sleepy head in his lap. She looked to be dreaming of the promises she'd secured from him the night and day before, their first moments together in the same bed (sleeping off the effects of the battle of Craven Castle) in fourteen years. She was growing up, and so was he—a little late, but steady. Effert kissed her on her forehead. He decided to spend the rest of the night here, meditating, like a "Christian Knight," upon what Wavy Rufus had said was his heart: *Credo, ergo sum,* or "I have faith, therefore I am."

What do I have faith in? thought Effert. He had no faith in courts. For crucial example, he had no faith in Cedric's, Abbott's, and Swinyard & Schleppend's legal maneuvers against the Means. If Effert awaited the courts, Bianca would spend the rest of her life the subject of a sensational but futile legal battle. He had no faith in politics. For crucial example, he had no faith in Europa's diplomatic maneuvers against the Means. If Effert awaited politics, Bianca would spend the rest of her life the subject of a sensational but futile international dispute. He had no faith in schools. For crucial example, he had no faith in Swinyard & Schleppend's renovated SDS rhetoric, or in Yella Kissl's renovated Weatherwoman tactics ("firebomb the Great Monoliths!"), or in Lyra's astrology (though he would never again slight star-talk, however starry-eyed). If Effert awaited the schools, Bianca would perish a lengthy appendix. And he had no faith in the et cetera weighty institutions of the land, like the military, the church, or the Yale Alumni Association.

No! He had faith only in his loved ones and in one

more thing. He believed in Halley's Comet. He believed the comet had come, as promised; had done, as promised; and had gone, as promised, leaving behind the promise of a sign. And that sign would best the Means and free Bianca. For if there was one lesson more than any other to be learned from the history of Halley's Comet, it was this: "Don't f—— with the comet," which was what Effert supposed His Majesty had said to tilt ORACLE and to stop 'Harold Starr.'

Gracie stirred, then settled again. Dream deeper, thought Effert, suspecting this was the time of night—the time of man—for second sight. And so, with visions of steel and steed, of lances and leather, of broadswords and baby Broadswords, Effert locked in again on his meditation on faith, keeping his mind off his thighs, his eyes on the skies.

For his part, Wavy Rufus sat absolutely still above his great-granddaughter and great-grandnephew. He was pleased to have them near. But their questions nagged him. And the bitterest fact was that time was against him. The strain of imagining the who, what, when, and where of "Harold Starr" had drained him. He'd need weeks, months, to develop what Schleppend had properly identified as clues that required different approaches. Time, time, time, thought Wavy Rufus, knowing he could no more ask for more of it than he could ask positivists for an equation for Virtue. Tick, tick, tick, thought Wavy Rufus, suddenly feeling a "tock."

He sat straight up on his stool. He clutched his chest. Ah, yes, he thought, here it is at last, that Distinguished Thing. He felt tired and airborne all at once. Not yet, he begged, for I have not done yet. Then another gust of destiny swept through him, sending his thoughts higher still. He heard music. He saw a staircase. He spoke up:

"I dislike sloppy endings, don't you? How about it? I go quietly, in exchange for a hint. Maybe more. I make the offer." He relaxed, and then spoke his dying words. They were two. They sounded drily and airily above Broadsword Hall. Effert didn't hear them, lost in his knightly prayers.

Gracie didn't hear them, lost in her (almost) maidenly dreams. The ghost of Landrover didn't hear them, lost in his obsession with fetching a javelin for Rollo. Only the Angel of Death heard them, and, graciously, at the behest of the Lord God Almighty, Maker of Heaven and Earth (and Hairy Stars), agreed to answer Wavy Rufus's last request: "But why?"

And this is what Wavy Rufus believed he learned about the purpose of "Harold Starr" and the purpose of the "Macho Project" and the purpose of PIT as he climbed the Stairway to Heaven:

This celestial body, in elliptical orbit about a G-type star, is said to be formed from the same interstellar gas and dust cloud that birthed the whole of the solar system, and is said to be four point five billion years old, having experienced intense meteor bombardment three point five billion years ago.

> That celestial body, in elliptical orbit about a G-type star, is said to be formed from the interstellar gas and dust cloud that birthed the whole of the solar system, and is said to be four point five billion years old, having experienced intense meteor bombardment three point five billion years ago.

This celestial body has a hot interior, a well-differentiated surface predominantly of flowing water supplemented by a mineralogically homogeneous regolith crust, a thick and well-mixed atmosphere, an ionosphere, a magnetosphere, a radiation belt, a magnetic field, and one seismically inactive (dead) satellite.

457

That celestial body has a hot interior, a well-differentiated surface predominantly of a mineralogically homogeneous regolith crust supplemented by frozen water, a thin and well-mixed atmosphere, an ionosphere, a radiation belt, a magnetic field, and two seismically inactive (dead) satellites.

This celestial body's interior is well differentiated and can be measured by seismic disturbances (quakes), which indicate a solid metal inner core, a molten metal outer core, and a three-part mantle, the upper level of which is a nonuniform crust composed of igneous rocks (volcanism), metamorphic rocks (tectonics), and sedimentary rocks (erosion) varying between five and fifty kilometers thick.

That celestial body's interior is well differentiated and can be measured by seismic disturbances (quakes), which indicate a molten interior, and a three-part mantle, the upper level of which is a nonuniform crust composed of igneous rocks (volcanism), metamorphic rocks (tectonics), and hypothesized sedimentary rocks (erosion), varying between ten and seventy-five kilometers thick.

This celestial body's surface is over eighty percent flowing water (with enough water ice in two permanent polar caps, if melted, to cover the remainder of the surface); the remainder is a continental crust that has undergone radical changes in size and location in the last point twenty-five billion years.

That celestial body's surface is over ninety percent continental crust (with major surface features over one billion years old); the remainder is one permanent water ice cap and one permanent carbon dioxide ice cap; however, it is indisputable that water has flowed abundantly on the surface in several periods between three point five billion years and point five billion years ago, and that this was possible only with profoundly different atmospheric conditions than now exist.

This celestial body's neutral atmosphere was once composed predominantly of hydrogen and helium, with smaller amounts of methane and ammonia, and trace amounts of lighter gases, but without oxygen; and it is believed that this atmosphere was totally lost (by an unknown process) to be replaced by the present one, which is itself a result of volcanic outgasing from the interior, with all the oxygen produced by organics over the last point five billion years.

That celestial body's neutral atmosphere is said to have once been thick, composed predominantly of nitrogen, and to have been capable of supporting copious amounts of water (vapor, liquid, and ice); and it is believed that this atmosphere was lost, perhaps through radical alterations of the axis tilt, and perhaps because of periodic changes in the G-type star's luminosity.

This celestial body's neutral atmosphere is thick, composed predominantly of nitrogen (seventy-eight percent) and oxygen (twenty-one percent) with traces of argon, carbon dioxide, neon, helium, and methane, in that order, arranged in five discriminated regions in such a way that the mean surface temperature (depending upon solar radiation penetrating the atmosphere and being reflected by water vapor and CO_2—the Greenhouse Effect) is approximately two hundred ninety-seven degrees Kelvin.

> That celestial body's neutral atmosphere is thin, composed predominantly of carbon dioxide (ninety-five percent) with small amounts of nitrogen (two point five percent), argon (one point five percent), and traces of oxygen, carbon monoxide, neon, krypton, and xenon, in that order, arranged in two discriminated regions in such a way that the mean surface temperature (depending upon solar radiation penetrating the atmosphere, but without a Greenhouse Effect) is approximately two hundred thirty degrees Kelvin.

This celestial body's lithosphere, hydrosphere, and atmosphere are a biosphere supporting variegated organics (wholly dependent upon abundant water supplies), which are said to have a history of at least three point two billion years (from fossils)—dating from a hypothesized contamination of inorganic tidal pools by amino acids and nucleotides, perhaps by nonunique chemical reactions, and perhaps by nonunique introduction of such by extraterrestrial objects, i.e., comets, meteors, and et cetera cosmological phenomena.

> That celestial body's lithosphere, hydrosphere, and atmosphere are said, *ambiguously,* not to be a biosphere, supporting no identifiable organics at the present time—though the ambiguous nature of the evidence, combined with the hypothesis that organics thrive in

abundant flowing water, makes it probable that during the periods of freely flowing water (three point five billion years to point five billion years ago) organics existed (now fossils); and these organics of course dated from hypothesized contamination of inorganic tidal pools by amino acids and nucleotides, perhaps by nonunique chemical reactions, and perhaps by nonunique introduction of such by extraterrestrial objects, i.e., comets, meteors, and et cetera cosmological phenomena.

This celestial body's biosphere has a long (three million years) history of nonironic sentient beings and a short (ten thousand years since the waning of the last ice age) history of ironic sentient beings, meaning Civilization—the result of which is that this celestial body is markedly depleted of natural resources, heavily polluted by carcinogenic agents, and dangerously overcrowded by increasingly intractable, irrational beings, especially in the fertile temperate zones.

That celestial body's lithosphere, hydrosphere, and atmosphere have an unknown history—the result of which, upon evidence (interplanetary probes) is that that celestial body is laden with natural resources, without pollution, and without a single factor in the interior, on the surface, or in the air, to preclude relatively simple introduction of controlled organics, that is, colonization.

This celestial body has an inclination of equator to orbit of twenty-three point five degrees, a sidereal rotation period of twenty-three hours, fifty-six minutes, a distance from the G-type star of one A.U., and an astrological sign written thus:

⊕

That celestial body has an inclination of equator to orbit of twenty-four degrees, a sidereal rotation period of twenty-four hours, thirty-seven minutes, a distance from the G-type star of one point five A.U., and an astrological sign written thus:

♂

Clearing the final step, Wavy Rufus turned around, looked back down the winding staircase, and said:

"Well! Mars, then. Not 'Harold Starr,' but hairy star. And not the 'Macho Project,' but the Mars Project. It was all just silly camouflage. Like the lad Schleppend said, it was so obvious we couldn't see it. The Means want Halley's Comet to establish a precedent for claiming the planet Mars. For themselves, and for their masters, PIT. A whole planet, privately owned. The megalomania of those pirates is their best weapon. What dare! Mars!"

"¿Che pasa?" said Pedro (St. Peter), sitting up in his hammock.

"They're after Mars, fourth planet from the Bright One, that one just there, ruddy," said Wavy Rufus, pointing down to the right, pausing as he sniffed Pedro's suntan butter.

"Who's after Mars?" said Pedro, reaching for his reading glasses.

"Oh, 'They.' The usual lot," said Wavy Rufus. "They're now calling themselves the Proto Industrial Trust. PIT."

"Is that right? Well, the pit's in the other direction. This here is the pearly gate. You don't have any call to hassle that other now," said Pedro, flipping open the guest book.

"There never was," said Wavy Rufus, admiring the scale of the gate, "it's just that . . ."

"Yer home free, brother. Relax," said Pedro.

"I wish Effert, that's my great-grandnephew, and his friends, I wish they knew what I know," said Wavy Rufus.

"Believe me," said Pedro, closing his guest book, passing a folder of orientation papers and bicycling maps to Wavy Rufus, "it's more fun for them not knowing."

"Figuring it out for themselves, you mean?" said Wavy Rufus.

"We used to interfere," confided Pedro. "Had a whole department to intercede, interrogate, interrelate, you name it. It was revelation here, miracle there. It got out of hand. We were misunderstood. People got lazy, reticent. We changed our policy. This is better. Not great. But better. Any other questions?"

"Amen," said Wavy Rufus.

"That's the spirit," said Pedro.

And with that, it seems neatest to leave Wavy Rufus looking over heavenly meal plans while chuckling about mankind's appetite. For it was true, he knew, that man's hunger, working in conjunction with his bizarre yen for profit, had moved him from a fire in a cave on an antediluvian river shore eight millennia before the birth of the Savior, to a fire on a volcanic plain on the moon two millennia after the birth of the Savior, and that once Neil Armstrong had placed his silver bootie on the Sea of Tranquillity, 20 July 1969, mankind's nature changed profoundly and forevermore.

The change was philosophically staggering. It could not be ignored. It had to be confronted. American capitalism's finest moment, the Apollo Space Program, altered Thought with space change in analogous proportion to the manner in which the Holy Roman Empire's finest moment, Christopher Columbus, altered Thought with sea change.

This is primary. The instant in time that *Homo sapiens*

touched lunar soil, Earthman became Spaceman, from which there is no turning back. Good riddance to all that. Hello to high, wide, and hairy.

In specific application, Wavy Rufus knew, since the People's Republic of Russia had retrieved evidence from Venus that that planet would be instantly fatal to even a protected astronaut, the relatively hospitable surface of Mars had become the most seductive distant shore in history. Columbus Again has sailed. Columbus Again has returned evidence of a charming New World. It hangs there in the night sky, nine months from the Manhattan Island by chemical rocket ship. To not walk the "Indies," once it was known it could be walked, was unthinkable to every bounder in Christendom. To not walk Mars, now that it is known it can be walked, is also unthinkable to every bounder in Christendom.

The only column of data that remains blank in the Book of Bounderism is who will do Mars, and what they will do with Mars once it's theirs to walk. If one pshaws and says, "Who would want Mars?" then one is likely of the same (small) mind-set that pshawed and said, "Who would want *Nueva España?*" Man is by reputation and design an explorer, a conqueror, and an owner. From the brackish waters of Babylon to the volatile ices of Halley's Comet, this is the irrefutable case. And so it will be with interplanetary space. Earthman has not known colonial hubris as he will know it as Spaceman. This is so obvious, it seems trite. And one should not balk at the idea of colonization, for a payload of viruses, bacteria, and nominally protected algae and fungi would commence the kingdom of Mars with a busy irreversibility.

As for the existential dimensions of "Harold Starr" and et cetera Great Schemes, like the "Mars (not Macho) Project," it seems best to consider that some men can look at the dome of the sky and see only daylight and darkness. Others can look at the dome of the sky and see the atmosphere's life-support system and, beyond, the cosmos' twenty-billion-year-old H and He cloud. What is more, to be fair to those who function better when relieved of positivism's jargon, it also seems best to consider that some men can look at a comet and see an irregular clump of ice, dust, and gas. Other men can look at a comet and see a Revolutionary.

And what do you see when you look at the Phantom of Liberty yet burning patiently off the Manhattan Island's Wall Street, up which motor the plushly upholstered sedan chairs bearing the fabulously wealthy children of industrial largess past the impossibly poor victims of industrial rapine? And what do you see when you look at the G-type star called "Sun," when you look at the glitter of the planet called "Venus," when you look at the ruddiness of the planet called "Mars," when you look at the rest of the celestial bodies that comprise our (arguably unique) solar system?

Do you see, as the Means Corporation and its overlord, the Proto Industrial Trust (PIT), that Creation is a primary industrial trust to be plundered (one celestial body after another) at will for self-aggrandizement? Or do you see, as Effert Broadsword and his compatriots—true swords and brothers & sisters of the realm—that Creation is a primary sacred trust to be celebrated for the wonder of it all?

PARABLE PAUSE

THE BIRTH, THE CRIME, THE PEACE AND THE TRIUMPH OF THE STRAW PEOPLE (1968-1978)

PART THE FOURTH

THE TRIUMPH

BY LEVIATHAN STRAUSS AS TOLD BY SCHLEPPEND

AFTER

AFTER the concert, the socialites, celebrities, record company executives, and coke dealers fled the child mob outside the Garden for their private crimes about the Manhattan Island, and for one private crime in particular, the infamous prizefight club—

STUDIO BEEFCAKE
Prop.: Dead Souls
founded now

—they all sweeping from their limos past the secret police force hefting aluminum baseball bats to beat back the child mob, and into the cool, perfumed confines of the most exclusive fad of 1978. Studio Beefcake was the place. It was it, now, and happening. To get inside, a soul had to pass more pedigree tests than were ever administered by any Falling Empire in history: not only rich, not only pass-for-Apollonian, not only young, drugged, bedecked, it was also necessary to be a Someone, e.g., Johnny Someone B. Goode.

The strobes pulsed and the searchlights found and the mechanized music throbbed as the celebrants wedged down the four narrow staircases (all lined with musclemen in brass breastplates, hence "Beefcake") to the balconies lipping Studio Beefcake's most popular feature—a translucent dance arena, with diamond earrings still attached to detached ears and diamond wedding rings still attached to detached fingers embedded in the Plexiglas floor, so that as the colored lights played off the gems, they showed with a sinister sparkle.

So much cold ice hooked on decayed flesh appealed to the crude of the crowd, especially the coke dealers and record company executives, who were interchangeable and ex-felons. And that it appealed to so unsavory a group excited the celebrities (flick, tube, and rock),

467

who were ill educated, mean-spirited, and ex-delinquents who'd never had the smarts to steal big before they found the Show Business. And that it excited the celebrities amused the socialites, who were mostly the younger children of America's financial empires, slumming in Manhattan in the same manner that their cultural ancestors had slummed in Paris's Place Pigalle, in London's Soho, or in Rome's Spanish Quarter: smell the freaks, tell your grandchildren how rude they could be, asking you to dance, just-like-that.

The music blared. The dance floor was soon draped with undulating female skeletons and their shorter male partners, all couples trying to outdo each other in graceless idiocy. Those not exhibiting their groins on the dance floor moved around the balconies out of sync with the mechanized music, so wasted they couldn't find the bar with their elbows. The syphilitic waiters and Latin busboys kept the food and drink circulating the giant chamber evenly, while the midget dealers (with large heads) and their goonish bodyguards (with small heads) skulked in shadowy corners, hustling chemistry sets. And above it all the dance music—that muck out of every recording studio from New York to California to the Caribbean, without heart, without meaning, just mind-numbing duochord, sounds to hump yourself by, the product of all those people who knew better, from superstar to sessions man, having sold out rock'n'roll to the panderers, slanderers, and wall-eyed fat men with law degrees who crawled out every time one rolled a rock these days. (After Nixon, they thought to save it they had to deal. God forgive them; no one else will.)

By 2 A.M., Virtue safely in eclipse for the night, Studio Beefcake smelled of sweat, guilt, desire, whiskey, and perfume, a mixture guaranteed to twist the nose of the intrepid young man just then squeezing through the child

468

mob on the curb and up to the secret police at the front door, he waving his press credentials high, screaming to the Someone-spotter named Ernst:

"Press! *Kong Weekly!* I called ahead!"

"What's yer name, boy?" said Ernst, checking his clipboard.

"Leviathan Strauss! Strauss! *Kong!*" called Levi.

"Like the pants?" said Ernst, checking off the name.

"The composer," said Levi, shoving through the bouncers, straightening his bow tie as he cleared the last step, popping off his Panama as he popped the glass doors. He inhaled, toking especially deep on the dope mixed with deep-sea products. Properly inspired, Leviathan Strauss, ace alternative news journalist, Counterculture archivist for America's only living underground newspaper (the *Voice, Barb, Phoenix,* and et cetera long since stuffed), charged into this den of Lotus Eaters.

Levi, ordinarily the most temperate of men, had come tonight on a dare by his censorious editor-in-chief, Molly Beagle, that he couldn't make it through the prizefight, that he was so out of sympathy with modern sensibility that he would flee gagging rather than accept Studio Beefcake's complex version of hip. Levi was something of a sentimental joke about *Kong's* expensive new offices (having moved from a subbasement of the Empire State Building to a lower Manhattan neighborhood so bizarrely avant-garde it was called HoHo), because he still used expressions like "running dog" and "up against the wall" in his copy, and not infrequently ended his cynical barrages with that comforting but tiresome chant, "Come the Revolution . . ."

"What's yer thing?" said the hostess, of indeterminate sex, taking Levi's arm as he reached the top level of balconies.

"I'm here to cover the fight," said Levi.

"A sports columnist?" said the hostess.

"A cultural essayist," said Levi.

"No camera?" said the hostess.

"A poet has need only of his eyes," said Levi.

"My dear, how sweet," said the hostess, guiding Levi to the bottom level of tables, nearest the dance floor. He handed her a silver dollar, but she refused, saying she didn't have any children of her own. Levi tucked himself into his seat and yanked out his notebook. The others at the table were agog.

"What is that?" said a soap-box starlet.

"It looks like a journalist," said a Queen of the Body Wave.

"Maybe even a columnist?" said a designer label.

"Press, folks. *Kong Weekly,*" said Levi, flashing his card. That dulled them down, as they'd never heard of *Kong.* Levi checked his Agnew—fifteen minutes to fight time. He halfheartedly examined the dancers. He played celebrity games. He overheard conversations that would have made the French Surrealists weep. The genius of modern times included the concept of clone-after-birth: born unique, live photocopied. Accordingly, there were only about twelve different people in a crowd of five hundred. Groan, thought Levi, sorry he'd come, but hanging in there. He ducked lower in his seat to avoid the waiter, and, as he did, he spied two golden statues across the floor. Whammo! Levi didn't immediately believe it, sitting upright, rubbing his eyes free of the carbon cloud. Yep, there they were, as if they'd just stepped out of the enhanced color of the television specials featuring their arrival at White House dinners, Academy Award ceremonies, and Super Bowls. Levi bounced over the railing, dodging and shoving to the opposite rail. He had eyes only for those four perfect ankles. He didn't see the burly bodyguard appear from the shadows to hoist him by the

470

collar, hold him at eye level with the Twin Sisters Means.

"Press! You know me! Cambodia breakdown! May of '70! I was on your chopper!" choked Levi.

"Wait," said Justine to the bodyguard.

"Leviathan Strauss is the name, Counterculture's the game," said Levi, easier now, as the bodyguard lowered him atop the railing. *"Kong Weekly.* You know me. At least, I remember you two."

"I don't recall the face," said Justine, brushing back the manicured hands of her escorts, leaning forward through an opium haze to look closely at Levi. "The voice either."

"Oh, gee, I had a beard then. Thinner. Bushmaster first class," said Levi. "Cleaned up my act since then. New York press corps, you know. Call me Levi. Ever read your clips? I was putting them together last month."

"I'm sorry," said Justine, who seemed dopey. It was the music.

"Not important," said Levi. "May I sit? A few questions?" He slipped onto half a chair, the other half held by one of Justine's pretty escorts. Levi gave a quick look to Christine, though he didn't know which was who. Her tummy showed a bit beneath her satin gown. What was this?

"What about Cambodia?" said Justine.

"Right," said Levi, "uh, Iz Christine, remember? I sure do. We came in with a platoon of skytroopers. The looie who picked flowers for you? Was it you, Justine?"

"Yes, for me," said Justine, "and for Christy."

"Mmh," said Christine. Levi studied her. Eight years ago, she'd seemed sharp, as connected as one could be. Now, though her eyes were still that dazzling azure, her posture seemed watery, her manner blasé. She'd been a goddess then; she was a goddess now, but a tarnished icon. And she was showing a lot of tummy.

"I heard later he got wasted by some of our boys who went native," said Levi. "That so?"

"That might be true," said Justine.

"Justy, no!" said Christine.

"Maybe I got my stories mixed," said Levi, realizing he'd touched something deep. He watched the sisters lean together to confer, Christine bobbing her head as she talked, Justine shaking hers as she listened. For a moment, Levi saw the old Christine emerge, but then she slipped back into indifference. Levi debated, while waiting for the current high-energy blaring to ebb, if he should broach a tip he'd heard recently about a hot manuscript. It was loose and dirty stuff, but if even one of the details were true, it was thermonuclear. Levi decided he owed it to the good old days of radical rumor.

"Perhaps you did," said Justine, turning back to Levi.

"Dizzy me, I saw a lot of weird stuff back then," said Levi. "It was stormy weather. Speaking of which, Miss Means, would you comment, please, on a report I've received that you and your sister have completed a book entitled *The Annals of the Straw*, uh, *Men*? Nonfiction. Tapes, photos, and correspondence, I think."

"You're not sure?" said Justine.

"Just a tip," said Levi, bearing down. "Were you, or were you not, the leaders of an urban guerrilla faction called the Straw Men?"

"It's so romantic when you say it," said Justine.

"Excuse me?" said Levi.

"Your hard-nosed query," said Justine, giggling.

"Oh, gee," said Levi, charmed by her manner. She glowed.

"Wonderful!" said Justine, touching Levi on the cheek with the smoothest hand he'd felt since the crib. "Such an old-fashioned flair, Levi. Doesn't he, Christy?

Those righteous eyes. How do you keep your naiveté, your youth?"

"I'm not getting this," said Levi.

"It's gone, Levi," said Christine of a sudden, patting her tummy, saying in a tired voice, "done and gone. Only this is real."

"My sister puts our case succinctly and dramatically," said Justine, patting Christine's tummy, "don't you agree?"

"She's pregnant, huh?" said Levi.

"Penetrating. You've discovered our secret. Our only secret. The rest was fantasy," said Justine.

"Cambodia wasn't fantasy," said Levi. "Neither was that skytrooper who bought it saving your ass."

"Very well then, if you insist, look about you, Levi," said Justine. "Do you see anything left? Is there anything in this spinning to suggest there was a 1968? A Parrot's Peak or a Paris Peace Talk? I tell you it was fantasy. The Christmas Bombing was a television special. Really, Levi, our younger friends think the *Mare Tranquillitatis* won the Derby."

Levi smiled sincerely. She was sly and bitter. Her ideals were gone. She was less dangerous now than she'd been in 1970, but crueler. Levi was no dogmatic scold. He extended to the rich the same possibility he extended to the poor—the opportunity to live justly. Justine had had the same ideological childhood as he, or as any member of the educated bourgeoisie. She had made her choice, then, mysteriously, abandoned the Revolution. It was not a novel tale these days.

"You won't be publishing your story?" said Levi.

"Dear, dear Levi," said Justine.

"Would you like me to look it over?" said Levi.

"Are you having fun tonight?" said Justine. "Have you enough money? What do you want from life?

473

Personality? Power? Freedom? Ha-ha-happiness? Three addresses, two women, one child, and no memory? It's yours! I pronounce you possessed! Why aren't you grabbing? Is it me you want? Oh, my, how easy, I'm yours. Thirty-two years of the best of all possible worlds, and my tits don't sag."

"Miss Means, no," said Levi. "We didn't lose. We didn't win. But we didn't lose."

"Since you introduce summary positions, Levi," answered Justine sharply, "suppose you help me with a box score."

"Excuse me, a box score, like in sports?" said Levi.

"Martin Luther King?" said Justine.

"He's dead," said Levi, "but . . ."

"Eugene McCarthy?" said Justine.

"Exile," said Levi.

"Bobby Kennedy?" said Justine.

"Myth," said Levi.

"Johnson, McNamara, Westmoreland, Abrams, Nixon, Laird, Rockefeller, Ford, Kissinger, Helms, Wallace, Thieu? Thieu!"

"Expelled, all expelled," said Levi.

"Hoover and Hendrix. Humphrey and hippies?" said Justine.

"Gone with the wind," said Levi.

"As if they never were. Fantasy," said Justine.

"What of the book?" pressed Levi. "The Straw Men, is it? And that skytrooper, Caw? You remember all that."

"Yes, we were the Straw People," said Justine.

"It's true then, there is a book," said Levi.

"We never dreamed that a whole generation would want to become Straw People as well," continued Justine. "There's the conundrum, my crusader, there's the true conundrum. What they reviled most—greed, luxury, indifference—that is what they are becoming."

"Not everyone. If you look hard, there is resistance. No surrender," said Levi.

"Don't think so much, Levi," smiled Justine. "You'll turn a girl's head. I worry for you."

"The manuscript. The Straw People," said Levi.

"No more," said Justine dismissively.

Levi was airborne again, dangled by his collar above the dance floor, just as it began to change, by trapdoor and by floating stage, into a prizefight ring. Levi rolled his head back to give Justine an open-mouthed expression of longing. He wanted more from her. She knew more, that Gnostic Princess. He wanted confirmation that a manuscript existed. If he was going to pursue it like an unholy grail, he wanted a hint that it was not a chimera. For his trouble, he took a mean blow as the bodyguard dropped him, his extended head cracking against the marble wall beneath the balcony. He saw lights. He lay there weakened, his brain scrambled for the rest of the night. In his daze, through the haze, Levi watched Studio Beefcake's patrons and matrons gather at ringside to witness the weekend's erotic centerpiece, a bare-knuckled (not Queensbury) bout between two mock gladiators, rented from a recently developed service called

HAVE MEAT WILL TRAVEL
Wire CUT
New York City

What distinguished HMWT from other sadomasochistic circuses, like funny-car racing, roller derby, or the National Football League, was that its athletes were paid for winning, not performing. Death was possible; maiming suspected; beatings commonplace. The kinds of men who opted for bare-knuckle, winner-take-all exhibitionism were in it for the cash, not for headlines. Indeed, there were no names given. Masks were policy. The police were not invited.

"Ladies, gentlemen, and groupies!" began the mistress of ceremonies at the center of the pink ring. "Studio Beefcake is pleased to welcome you to the main event!"

"Hooray!" screamed the crowd as two ordinary-looking, pathetically scarred, desperately drugged-up young men leaped into the ring, stripping down to pasties, heating themselves up the more for their blooding by pogoing about in circles, displaying and splaying their ends to the cheers of the groupies.

Levi needed air. He needed to escape from these wretched libertines oohing and aahing as, the bell sounding, the two fighters closed sloppily on each other, kicking, spitting, and gouging. Levi was as confused as he was disgusted. He gagged. Okay, Molly Beagle, he thought, you win, I can't take it anymore. The culture has changed and I haven't.

Levi reached the elevator in a crouch and spun to sit as he was raised toward the exit. His seat inadvertently gave him an excellent view of the ring. He could see one fighter twisting a small crucifix in his hand. There was blood on that cross.

Later that night, back in his apartment, Levi pulled on his robe and flopped down before his typewriter. He had in him tonight that rage that harries martyrs to pull down the temple on their own heads; so Levi tapped out the first draft of his next piece for *Kong,* in which he vowed to track down, no matter how long it took, no matter how much he'd have to make up, the true story of Justine and Christine Means and their co-conspirators, *The Annals of the Straw People.* See above.

The End

476

Death of a Champion

AT MEANS Manor, Happy Means lay dying grotesquely, drugged by the surgeons into a stupor that was no escape from the pain that tore at her body from without and the demons that tore at her mind from within.

Abandoning all hope by the Ides of June, the surgeons had permitted her removal from the hospital quarters they'd established in the bowels of the Manor to her own rooms at the pinnacle of the rear wing. Her handmaidens had arranged her swathed body in the center of her enormous canopied bed; then, on Happy's whispered instructions, had draped the bed in layers of black lace, with wreaths of blood-red roses hooked from post to post, dangling down to heap several feet deep about the bed's platform. The effect was a gaudy bier, of course, with an emaciated figure buried beneath gold coverlets, the only sign she was yet alive the plastic tubes running from various orifices to canisters, sleekly paneled machines, and towering life-support systems arranged discreetly to one side of the sumptuous, cloying bedchamber.

Following her death sentence, her family kept a vigil at her bedside as best they could, given they suffered from wounds as well. Torrance VII scraped his face and throat in despair until he broke all his overlong fingernails, leaving his fingertips swollen with infection. Torrance VIII tortured himself with guilt for not preventing his Happy's murder, salving his conscience with quantities of drink and drug that left him perpetually awake and morbid. Torrance IX suffered from the neglect of his mother, who refused to see him; for the Twin Sisters Means, once the most beautiful of earthly creatures, suffered from a malady similar in kind, though not in degree, to the one that was slowly killing Happy. The surgeons said the Twins would not die. The surgeons said the Twins would live out the century. The surgeons said there was no reason why, with time and surgery, they couldn't repair the external damage. Yet the surgeons said they were unable to predict whether the Twins would look as before, since, as one knows, beauty is more than skin deep. There was no knife that could reverse history.

"Radiation sickness," said the surgeons.

"Operable," said the surgeons.

"Mind sickness," said the surgeons.

"Inoperable," said the surgeons.

In his way, Aaron Verbunko served the Means more passionately than ever before. Always the Prime Minister, he now became the prime confessor also. It was Verbunko, not the corporation, not the money, not even the civilization, who kept the family from disintegrating as Happy lay dying grotesquely. He managed pastoral feats that betrayed his churchly learning. He comforted Torrance VII, fending off the inquiries of the emissaries of the Proto Industrial Trust (PIT) demanding an explanation for the last-minute abortion of "Harold Starr." He comforted Torrance VIII, fending off the lawsuits and diplomatic protests from the Broadswords and the Florentines. He comforted Torrance IX, dispatching the heir apparent to exile in a Swiss Calvinist academy, ensuring that, whatever happened, the family's twisted spermatozoa would continue. And he tried to comfort the Twin Sisters Means, especially Justine, though there was little he could to do to reconcile them to their alteration. Yet, if the truth be told in complete, Verbunko scurried, manipulated, dangled, cajoled, urged, counseled, and juggled, not because he was loyal (which he was not), and not because he was generous (which he was), but because, if he did not, all his years of work would likely go to waste, or worse, to PIT. Matters had nearly escaped him. The battle at Craven Castle had been more than seemed understandable. However, Verbunko had understood, as he watched the battle unfold, that even if "Harold Starr" was stopped, and that even if this stopping weakened the Means in relation to PIT, he, Verbunko, being loyal to appropriate calculation and nothing else, could compensate for the Means' failure and, in doing so, assert his own rule. But he'd not anticipated that the failure of "Harold Starr" would go so far. There were aspects of the battle that made Verbunko shiver. Worst of all, the physical damage to the women exacerbated everything; and Happy's lingering made nonsense of any timetable he might construct. In many tiresome ways, Verbunko acknowledged, the Means Family Empire smacked of disaster. Some circumstances were desperate. It was all Verbunko could do to keep himself steeled for his moment to wrest control from the Means, which was not yet, not yet. He must wait. It was Verbunko's final opinion that if he could hold the family together until Happy was dead, gone, worm-worried, a portrait on the wall, he could then strike. Until her death, he would get no cooperation, even for maintenance work, from the Chairman, Torrance VII, or from the President, Torrance VIII. Indeed, father and son, husband and lover, had become irrational in their gloom. They would not leave the Manor. They would not take calls or messages from the Great Monolith Southeast. They would acknowledge no one other than the servants. They would sign nothing. They nearly said nothing. Means Manor took on the atmosphere of a palatial tomb prowled by two melancholy lords more concerned with death than with life. It certainly became as quiet as a tomb, smelling of the damp, and everywhere the aroma of Happy's cut roses. Though it was one of the hottest, driest Junes in years, following that freakish rain torrent throughout May, the Manor became dreadfully chill. Not even the uncountable fireplaces, which Verbunko ordered roaring with wood fires, could warm and dry the rooms.

This cold should explain why, on Summer Solstice Eve (the first weekend of summer) 1986, Aaron Verbunko, having spent another three straight days at his offices at the Monolith fending off the hounds of PIT, having decided to devote his Saturday night to ministering to the Means, and, perhaps, to further conversation with the Contessa, reached behind him to pull on his suit coat as he stepped from his air-cooled sedan chair into the oppressive evening's heat to the front doors of Means Manor. His aides, both Ivy League toadies, tapped on the doors in tandem. There was an unusual delay. They tapped again. The doors opened slowly, a servant bowing as he saw Verbunko. Verbunko cringed as a rush of blizzardy air swept over him. He moved inside a few steps, then shivered as the chill penetrated his clothes. The only light came from the fires roaring about the foyer. Something was profoundly wrong. It was cold as Hell.

"What's happened?" said Verbunko.

"Oh, Mr. Verbunko!" said the servant. He sobbed.

"Tell me now!" said Verbunko. The servant fell to his knees, pointing to the rear of the Manor. Verbunko ordered his aides to get to the phones in his sedan chair and call the chief surgeon and his staff. He walked quickly to the main staircase, taking one step before he paused, pounded on the banister, then jumped down to race to the elevator bank to the hospital quarters in the bowels of the Manor. He kicked at the wall of the elevator car as it descended the two levels, then kicked at the door until it slid open. He sprinted the corridor. He grabbed for his key, inserted it, and crashed through the room door, calling, "Contessa! My Contessa!"

She wasn't in her sitting room. She wasn't in her bedroom. He called her again. No response. He popped the door to the treatment center, pounded on the door to the whirlpool, then opened it—nothing. He bypassed the common room to Justine's door. It was locked. Locked! He pounded. No response. He doubled back, this time through the common room. There was one tiny handmaiden on duty at her desk, stiff and vacant-looking.

"Don't be alarmed," said Verbunko. "Tell me what's happened."

"They took her!" gasped the handmaiden.

"No! No!" cried Verbunko. He feared the worst. Yet, as he discovered—reversing his path, mounting the main staircase two floors up to the immense gallery leading to the rear wing, flinging open the glass doors to pass into the outer reception rooms of Happy Means' suite, crossing her anteroom (where there should have been handmaidens and nurses), and finally arriving at the delicate twin doors to her bedchamber, where stood a lone handmaiden sobbing uncontrollably in the firelight—it was much, much worse than that.

"Will you tell me what has happened, please? Where has everyone gone, dear? Calmly, please. What?" said Verbunko. She jumped at his legs, pawing at his feet, jerking in her grief. Shaken, Verbunko stepped carefully away from her and tried the doors. They were locked. Locked again! He called, "It's Verbunko! Please open up. Please?" He did not wait for a reply, throwing his weight against the doors. He surprised himself with his strength. The locks gave way.

Verbunko fell to the floor, pricking himself on several discarded bouquets of roses. The air reeked of dead flowers. The fires had burned to embers. The drapes had been ripped into tatters. The whole wall of windows behind them had been brutally removed. The surgeon's machines lay smashed on their sides. The room was empty. There was no bed, no Happy, no sense. Verbunko scrambled to his feet. It seemed to him as if a fantastic beast had shoved its head through the wall to suck out the room's contents. Verbunko walked over the broken glass, through the shattered wall of windows, onto the balcony, to the balcony's edge, where he found scaffolding, winches, pulleys, ropes. He stared into the dark. He saw it. Out there, in the mist of the Great Meadow, lit by a ring of servant-held torches, he saw it.

"No!" cried Verbunko, flinging himself over the balcony, searing his hands as he slid three stories on a line, landing in a heap at the edge of the marble terrace. Dazed, he forced himself aright. He staggered across the terrace. He jogged down into the gardens to the lip of the Great Meadow, where he paused to catch his breath and to scream, "Stop this thing! You must not do this thing!" A man possessed, Aaron Verbunko walked stiff-legged onto the Great Meadow.

The scene was more bizarre than it had seemed from the balcony. The silk-draped stage, theretofore used only for the "Rites of Spring," had been raised again at the center of the gentle ridge forming one entire side of the field. Burly servants (Westergaard's command had been replaced immediately, of course, for there is always more Bad Company to serve the masters of Earth) stood in a line before it, around it, holding oil torches on long staves stuck in the ground. On stage, the center throne chair was gone, replaced by Happy's bier. Happy's emaciated figure lay still as death in the center, beneath heaped roses and cold coverlets. To the left of the bed, Torrance VII, in formal attire, knelt in mourning, his head buried in the coverlets, his hands thrown out before him. To the right of the bed, Torrance VIII, also in formal attire, knelt in mourning, but his head was up, his lips moving, as if talking to Happy. To Torrance VIII's rear, in their customary chairs, sat Justine and Christine. They wore their usually lovely silk and satin gowns, but beneath was bandaging, not flesh. Indeed, their skin was covered completely to their necks. The bandaging on their faces was patchier. The surgeons had removed some from their profiles to reveal reddened cheeks, scabrous noses, gouged lips, and the retreat of their hairlines. They would lose all of their hair before the process was done. Once white-golden and as soft and full as an angel's, their hair had become dry, brittle, orangish, and as dead-looking as last year's straw. In this unexpected way, Justine and Christine had truly become Straw People. Profoundly more sad, though, was the fact that the azure light in their eyes was gone forever.

Yet what sickened Verbunko was not on the stage. Ten yards in front of the stage, there was a stake, surrounded by a pile of wood. And seated in a chair beside the wood was the Contessa, in a green hospital frock, with bandaging on her arms, legs, and neck. Her face was damaged, but she was not as altered as the Twin Sisters Means. She'd loosed her black hair from braids, and it swept over her shoulders, covering the worst of the scars on her cheek. She'd never looked more fey to Verbunko. Her eyes shone with drugs and fear.

The cordon of servants opened to let Verbunko through. He veered toward the Contessa, but a bodyguard grabbed him and pointed to the stage. Verbunko rubbed his arm as he backed off. Was he a prisoner or a jailer?

"We've been waiting for you, Verbunko," said Torrance VIII.

"What is this?" said Verbunko, ascending the stage.

"She's gone!" howled Torrance VIII, flinging himself closer to Happy. Verbunko walked to the bedside. He looked from the Chairman of the Board to the Chairman's second wife. Happy Means was dead. Her corpse lay rigid. They'd removed the bandaging from her face. It was burned to the bone—black and crusty. How had she lived so long? Her mouth was twisted, her eyes fixed and wide, as if she'd died with a final scream.

"Mercifully," said Verbunko.

"My stepmother is dead, Verbunko," said Torrance VIII.

"I'm sorry. Why wasn't I called?" said Verbunko.

"Because we knew you'd come," said Torrance VIII.

"What is going on here, sir?" said Verbunko.

"She was a great lady," said Torrance VIII. "She was everything to me. I never told her how much I loved her. I can't understand why she had to die like this. Do you know how much pain she had? Can you imagine? She fought it, though. She was my empress."

"She's at peace now, sir. The pain is gone," said Verbunko.

"Before she left us," continued Torrance VIII, reaching out to grasp Happy's bandaged hand, "she revealed to us that it was our responsibility to avenge her murder."

"She was delirious," said Verbunko.

"She revealed to us the witch among us," said Torrance VIII.

"Oh, my dear boy," said Verbunko. "Tory, listen, please? I'm sorry for you. She was magnificent. But not this. There aren't any witches. Tory, listen to yourself. You're not thinking clearly. You need a long sleep. Whatever she said to you, she didn't mean it. She wasn't herself at the end. She died in great agony. I'm sure she meant to forgive, not condemn." Verbunko didn't believe a word he said. He tried to disguise his false tone by asserting, "Not this, Tory. No."

"A witch trial," said Torrance VIII.

"You can't do it," said Verbunko.

"It is done," said Torrance VIII.

"You can't mean it," said Verbunko.

"We waited for you before we passed verdict," said Torrance VIII.

"Mr. Means, tell your son this can't be," said Verbunko to Torrance VII.

"She's gone!" howled Torrance VII, pawing at the bed as thorns tore his wrists and face.

"My father is in accord with Happy's last request," said Torrance VIII. "We are as one, my family."

"You must get some rest, Tory," said Verbunko, realizing, for the first time, that mad as this scene seemed, the Means were capable of playing it. He must not panic. He must think. "There are funeral arrangements. We'll need you."

"Ample evidence of her witchery was presented," continued Torrance VIII. "She refused to speak in her own behalf. Her silence is her guilt."

"Yes, I see," said Verbunko, taking a turn about the stage to clear his mind. It was pointless to argue with father and son. Studying the dull gaze of the Twin Sisters Means, he could see they seemed as drugged as when he'd last visited. He walked to the edge of the stage. If he'd been a younger man, he might have tried bolting for the Contessa, then away. But with the guards, the dark, his aching bones, that was folly. He had only one weapon with which to rescue the Contessa, and that was the only real tool he'd ever had to make his way in a world usually as mad as Tory seemed tonight. He had his tongue. Verbunko conceived his plan with one cluck of that tongue. He would neither attack nor flee. He would stall, until either the chief surgeon arrived or Torrance VIII sunk so far into his grief that he no longer cared for revenge.

"You say the accused offered no defense?" said Verbunko, turning, loosening, readying. "Is that so, sir?"

"None. There is but one verdict," said Torrance VIII.

"Perhaps," said Verbunko. "Yet it would be more proper if she were to offer a defense. Since she chooses not to speak for herself, I would like to speak in her stead."

"The defense attorney, is that it?" said Torrance VIII.

"Yes, sir. If she'll have me," said Verbunko, walking down the steps, crossing to Bianca. As he did, he scribbled in his notebook, tore off the page, folded it, and palmed it.

"Will you permit me to defend you?" asked Verbunko.

"At what cost?" said Bianca with drugged resignation.

"Would you pay such a cost?" said Verbunko.

"Oh, Aaron," said Bianca, looking down.

"Would you, my dearest love?" said Verbunko, slipping the note to her as he patted her right hand.

"No," said Bianca.

"No matter. There will be no charge," said Aaron Verbunko with a smile, never more pleased with himself, as he turned toward the stage. He walked to a midpoint between Bianca and the Means. He looked up to the family that had been his passion for too many years to forgive. He looked back to the woman who'd been his passion for such a short time. With one broad gesture, Verbunko began his finest night on Earth. He began his defense of the Contessa Bianca Stupefacenta Capricciosa, accused, this day, of witchcraft. Yet Verbunko's defense was no ordinary plea. He didn't speak of magic, superstition, and the irrationality of those who trust in gossip, slander, and last requests. Instead, he spoke of himself, of his birth in Switzerland, his mother and father and brothers, his first memories, his schooling. Then he spoke of the Church, of his own faith, of his first communion, of his wonder at the priests and the bishop when he had visited their canton. He spoke of his training for the priesthood, of the ambivalence of a young man faced with abandoning his lust for the ways of the world. He spoke further of his entry into the Church, of his successes, few, and of his failures, many. He spoke grimly of his loss of faith, of quitting the Church and turning to his career as an expert not of God's law but of man's law. He spoke of his awakening to his gifts of rhetoric and reason, of how quickly he'd risen in the material world to his present eminence. His voice lightened as he spoke of his relationship with the Means, of his meeting with the Twin Sisters Means in Paris when first he'd joined the Means Corporation in Europe. He spoke lovingly of Justine. Removing his coat, rolling up his silk sleeves in the heat, he continued, speaking of the events of the last few years, of "Harold Starr," of his many doubts about the Proto Industrial Trust, of his gradual realization he could use the success of "Harold Starr" for his own aggrandizement. He spoke bitterly of the last few weeks, of his consternation at the battle at Craven Castle, of his attempt to use the abortion of "Harold Starr" to further his ambitions. Finally, he spoke of the Contessa, of his love for her, of how it had grown from their first meeting last fall till now, when she meant everything to him: the sun, the moon, the stars, his life, everything.

One hour, two, then three, quickly four, Verbunko sang on and on. At first, he talked haltingly, anticipating the chief surgeon; but soon he forgot all but the sound of his own voice as he immersed himself in his monologue, which was, from his first "I was born . . . " to the incessant "I confess . . . ," the autobiography of Aaron Verbunko. Verbunko described himself. Verbunko criticized himself. Verbunko accused himself. Verbunko cursed himself. Verbunko condemned himself. After five hours of talk, he said:

"You must understand, then, Mr. Means, that the Contessa did not kill Mrs. Means. It was Aaron Verbunko. If there is a demon, it must be me. I thought that I had put such things behind me when I lost my faith, but I see now that good and evil are not things one can choose or not choose. They are always present. Like the Lord and the Devil. I understand this now. I am your murderer. Take me. The demon is in me. Take me."

And with that, Verbunko sank to his knees, exhausted but charged as he had not felt since he'd left the Church. He clasped his hands before him.

"Attention! Attention!" said Torrance VIII, leaping up from Happy's side. "Attention!" His cry startled the assembled. Verbunko had mesmerized them. They shuffled in their places. "Attention! Does the defense rest?"

"God, yes," said Verbunko.

"The verdict! We must have the verdict," said Torrance VIII.

"She is innocent, sir. Innocent!" cried Verbunko.

"So you vote," said Torrance VIII. "I vote guilty."

"No!" cried Verbunko.

"That's one to one," said Torrance VIII. "Father?"

"Guilty," said Torrance VII, face still in the thorns.

"That's two to one," said Torrance VIII. "Now Christy?"

"Not guilty," said Christine, her dulled eyes straight ahead.

"That's two to two," said Torrance VIII. "It's up to the tie-breaker. Your beloved Justine, Verbunko. How does she vote?"

"Guilty," said Justine.

"No, God, no!" cried Verbunko, falling forward on his face. He prayed for strength. He raised his head. He turned back to the Contessa, saying, "The note."

Bianca shook her head free of fear. Verbunko had reserved her a final line of defense. She opened the paper and read. Of all the sentences Verbunko could have written her, this seemed to Bianca the most incredible. She'd expected a tender sentiment, perhaps an expression of his love. Instead, Verbunko had written:

"Demand a champion."

Bianca looked to Verbunko. The drugs the surgeons had given her had numbed her to many of the day's events. She'd felt in a nightmare right up to the moment Verbunko had asked to defend her. She'd awakened from her daze well enough to listen to his confession. By the finish, when he'd offered to exchange himself for her at the stake, she'd wept. She hadn't realized how dear he'd become to her. If not for the circumstances, she might have loved him. She might have. Oh, Aaron, she thought, oh, Aaron, at least I trust you. Bianca said, "I demand a champion."

"You what?" said Torrance VIII.

"She demands a champion!" said Verbunko, standing again, pointing accusingly at Torrance VIII. "You heard her. A champion. If she is to burn, she deserves a champion to come forward and fight for her. Trial by combat!"

"This is the way you want it?" said Grandtour.

"Aye," said Effert, adjusting his seat amount Come Home Effert (All Is Forgiven).

"You got the floor plan straight?" said Westergaard (now become a stalwart of the Comet Clubbe).

"Aye," said Effert, adjusting his genuine broadsword.

"Give 'em what-for," said Westergaard, slapping Effert's boot with his bandaged hand.

"God's will be done," said Grandtour, slapping Come.

"With a little luck," said Effert, reining Come forward, away from the Comet Clubbe's encampment and toward the Manor. He didn't look back. Grandtour, Westergaard, and the rest had prepared him as best they could for the combat ahead. The doing of Bianca's rescue was up to him. He'd wasted three weeks puzzling as to what His Majesty had meant in asking him to await a sign. He'd developed a pain in his neck from studying the sky, and still there was nothing. What would a sign promised by a Comet Incarnate look like? Since a comet itself is generally considered a sign, what could a sign for a sign be? And then, the night before, while reading over Wavy Rufus's diary from the day he'd lost his eyesight midcentury tracking the comet Mar'zi'pan, Effert had experienced the revelation he'd awaited. Perhaps it was his grief over Wavy Rufus, perhaps it was the diary, perhaps it was there inside him all the while: he'd had his sign. Wasting little time on the mechanics of quitting Broadsword Hall, traveling to the Comet Clubbe's encampment (where they'd dutifully maintained a close watch over Bianca while Effert dallied for his sign), and setting the rescue plans in motion, Effert rode convinced of his quest. With such a sign, no true sword could falter. Effert knew now that the most profound sign of all is that which rests in every man's breast. Effert knew now that it was idle to look to the sky, or to entrails, or to other superstitious claptrap, or even—and this was subtle—to the signs of the times laid out like so much doom each morning in the *Crimes*, for a sign certifying this or that quest. Effert knew now that one acts when one must act. A sign was required, but a sign from the heart. Effert Broadsword knew now that the sign he'd awaited was his own freewill. When he'd willed to go, he'd done so, reaching down to pat Come's mane, reining his horse from the cover of the woods to the edge of the clearing leading toward Means Manor. The air was hot and dry. The sky was gray, the first rays of a new day shooting from the east. What was that? Down there in the Great Meadow? A cordon of torches? A stake surrounded by a wood pile?

Effert studied the figures. He recognized enough. Kicking at Come just a little, Effert Broadsword flew across the field.

"Get on with it," said Torrance VIII to his bodyguards.

"You must grant her request," said Verbunko.

"What champion, then?" said Torrance VIII.

"Well," said Verbunko.

"You, Verbunko? You'd fight me?" said Torrance VIII.

"Well," said Verbunko. That wasn't his preference. He'd intended this as a stalling tactic.

"Get my horse and harness, man," said Torrance VIII to a bodyguard, who raced toward the stables.

"Aaron!" said Justine through her stupor.

"Aaron!" said Bianca through her stupor.

Verbunko turned from his past to his present, from his present to his past. Neither would have him. Neither would let him go. Perhaps, thought Verbunko, letting Tory ride me down would be the easiest escape from my crimes.

"You've charmed them both," said Torrance VIII.

"I've cursed them both," said Verbunko.

Then came a clamber of hooves, a flutter of wings, the heavy breathing of animals rushing pell-mell, and shouts from servants and bodyguards. A cry: "Means!"

"Look there, Verbunko," said Torrance VIII, "the witch has her champion after all."

"I've come for her, Means. I've come alone," said Effert.

"Will you fight for her?" said Torrance VIII.

"Anytime, anyplace, any way," said Effert.

"I've wanted this," said Torrance VIII, seeing his horse and harness approach. He stripped off his coat.

"Wait, Tory," said Justine, fighting the drugs. She crooked her finger. He bent down to her. She whispered.

"Ridiculous, Justy," said Torrance VIII, annoyed.

Justine nodded her head. She was in pain, but she

nodded on and on, watching Verbunko, nodding on and on, until Tory said:

"It seems that I am not to be the family's champion."

"Yes," said Verbunko.

"Justine has chosen you. I'm obliged to obey her," said Torrance VIII.

"I understand, Mr. Means," said Verbunko. Justine had waited until events could not be reversed, and then she had revenged herself on Verbunko for the Contessa. She had called in Tory's debt to her, one of "absolute obedience" for his failure to sully Grace Thyme. Verbunko was to be sacrificed after all, not as he'd intended it, nor as Torrance VIII had intended it, but as Justine wanted it.

"Means!" cried Effert, not understanding this grotesque scene, but sickened by it: that corpse, the Contessa by the stake.

"You are Effert Broadsword?" said Verbunko, walking over.

"I am," said Effert, reining Come over to the small, thin, tired-looking man with the silvery accent.

"I am Aaron Verbunko."

"I remember."

"You must believe that I have only one desire now, and that is to save the Contessa's life."

"What's happened here?"

"The Means intend the Contessa harm. That is all you need to know. You are familiar with the medieval concept of trial by combat?"

"Victory means innocence. Defeat guilt."

"Correct. You are the Contessa's champion. I am the Means'. You must kill me. No. Don't quibble. It is much too late. Do as I say. There is no other way. Believe me."

"I'm not gonna fight you like that."

"Set aside your naive sense of fair play. I am totally serious. A man usually is about his own death. If you can, make it a clean blow. But kill me, grab the girl, and run for your life. That, at least, is jargon for you Americans."

"Your steed, Verbunko," called Torrance VIII from the stage.

"Thank you, Mr. Means," said Verbunko, walking away.

"Hey!" said Effert, but Verbunko did not look back, marching to a pale Arabian by the stage, asking the bodyguard for assistance. He was boosted into the saddle. He wobbled, as the mount, unsure of its rider, skittered to the side, threatening to topple Verbunko. He yanked the reins, and the horse steadied. He reached down to the bodyguard for the genuine broadsword. It was heavy, and Verbunko had to balance it across the saddle, finally saying:

"Aaron Verbunko is prepared to defend the Means Family."

"Is he?" said Torrance VIII.

"I won't fight that little guy. I want you," said Effert.

"In time," said Torrance VIII. "Are you sure you can manage this, champion?"

"Aaron Verbunko is prepared to defend the Means Family."

"Away then," said Torrance VIII, throwing high his arms.

Verbunko kicked and pulled and pushed his mount, urging it into a jerky trot, panicked as it was by its inexperienced rider. Verbunko guided the horse in the general direction of Effert, who, peeved by this nonsense, sat arms folded atop Come, not making a move to fight. Come, however, was spooked by Verbunko's desperate mishandling of the other horse. Come bounced back and forth in place as Verbunko's mount bounced close to Effert. Verbunko raised the genuine broadsword as high as he could.

"Give it up," said Effert.

"Forgive me!" cried Verbunko in hope and despair, kicking his horse once more, lurching close enough to Effert to make one awkward pass with his sword. His swing missed harmlessly, of course, but his follow-through unseated him. His Arabian bucked and veered from Come's snorting. Verbunko flew a dozen feet in the air to crash to the ground gracelessly, twisted in a pathetic and still heap.

Effert reined Come over to Verbunko. That seemed a broken man. Effert dismounted. He reached under Verbunko's back to hold him up. Verbunko's head rolled back limply.

Aaron Verbunko was dead. He had died a victim to the violence of his own contending passions. At the last, he had discovered a grand thing in his heart to believe in, the love of a woman who might have loved him; and he had pursued true love unto the sacrifice of his own life, a gesture that seems a final and humble repentance.

"Get him up. He can defend us better than that," said Torrance VIII.

"Your champion is dead," said Effert. He did not lay Verbunko's corpse down gently. He did not close its eyes. He did not whisper from *Julius Caesar:* "When beggars die, there are no comets seen. . . . " He did not await another empty threat from the stage. Verbunko's last expression told Effert all he'd ever need to know about the worthlessness of vainglory and the pricelessness of love, of even the possibility of love. Leading Come, Effert moved directly to Bianca. He lifted her into the saddle. He mounted behind her. He urged Come forward. No one dared block him. Under the gray and starless dawn of the first day of summer—the longest day of the Year of Our Lord 1986, and the last day of Aaron Verbunko and the power of the great American family Means—Effert Broadsword rode to freedom with the Contessa Bianca Stupefacenta Capricciosa weeping quietly against his breast.

VOLUME THREE

Going

"Enjoy."
—The Famous Serpent

Book VIII

Wherein the Reign of Revenge
Visits the Manhattan Island

Europa's Dream

A N APPENDIX to this romance, if you will: For three weeks after the above events, Europa Stupefacenta was on her way back, on foot, to Broadsword Hall, from visiting her daughter in the hospital on the Upper East Side of the Manhattan Island, when she was overcome with her relief at Bianca's improving condition. The surgeons promised full recovery from the effects of capitalism and positivism.

Europa suddenly found herself crying copiously. She rested on a wooden bench along the Central Park, to the north of the Grand Army of the Republic Plaza at Fifty-ninth Street and Fifth Avenue. She relaxed in her seat, watching the snake dances of the syphilitic flagellants and the caravans of plushly upholstered sedan chairs until she fell into an exhausted sleep. It so happens that it was sundown of the fourteenth of July, which is also known, especially by Europa and other perpetual revolutionaries, as Bastille Day. Perhaps that explains Europa's dream.

Europa opened her eyes to find herself pressed to the edge of the bench by an fat old woman dressed in greasy rags. Europa realized she was surrounded on all sides by rotund old women dressed in greasy rags, some seated along the wall, or squatting on the grass, or huddled along the curbstone, only a few fortunate enough to have a seat on a bench. They chattered incessantly. Some few of them knitted. Their smell was fetid. Their mood was festive.

"Good uns tonight, eh?" said the rag woman.

"Che?" said Europa.

"I say, good uns tonight!" shouted the rag woman.

"Non parlo inglese," said Europa.

"Tha's awright. Don't bother me none. Them don't mind," she said, gesturing toward the plaza.

It was dusk, the air grown cooler, and heavy, as if before an approaching summer storm. There seemed a transformation. Indeed, when Europa looked up, as best she could through the crowd so thick and restless that it only intermittently parted to permit an unobstructed view, she discovered the scene was changed totally. As Europa studied the transformation, sirens sounded in the far distance. Then a clap of thunder, no, that was cannon fire, a lengthy salvo ripping the evening. The effect on the crowd was as if a chairperson had gaveled them to order. The dozens, tens of dozens, thousands of women in greasy rags immediately sought their places, not as if they were being corraled unexpectedly, rather as if they'd done this many times before. The congress of rags came to order. A whispery quiet fell from one side of the crowd to the other. And, as they settled, Europa assessed what had become of the Grand Army Plaza.

The pavement was shattered. Chunks of concrete and tarmac were heaped into islands in the sea of rags. The streetlights were torn down, poles dangling wires, a few truncated poles used as props for torches. Otherwise, the electric lights of the imperial city were dark.

To the west of the plaza, the Plaza Hotel had been gutted by fire above the twelfth floor, a dark smoke stain across both its northern and eastern faces. Below the twelfth oor, most of the windows had been smashed out. Human faces shone eager and expectant from every portal. And large, multicolored banners flapped across several of the floors, bearing crudely printed slogans. The largest banner hung over the first floor entranceway, facing east, a billowing red field reading:

LIBERTY! FRATERNITY! REVENGE!

To the east of the plaza, the Sherry-Netherlands Hotel seemed a total hulk, with more dark smoke stains across its western and southern faces. Across the rubble pile that was once Fifty-ninth Street, the General Motors building seemed untouched by fire. The windows on the western face had been smashed out, however, with small banners draped at random. More human faces peered through the portals. There also seemed heavy sacks suspended by ropes from the roof. The sacks had arms and legs. And on the first floor, the large picture windows had been savaged, revealing tents and makeshift shelters in the lobby and display rooms. The GM building was a steel and concrete cave for squatters.

To the south of the plaza, the Bergdorf Goodman department store was gone, as if it had never been there, replaced by a foreboding, eastern-winged, five-storied mansion of brick and gray stone slabs, which was, though Europa could not know it, the Vanderbilt Family mansion resurrected. Candlelight blazed in the open windows, especially from the gables and spiral towers, illuminating slouching men in dark cloaks bustling back and forth as if burdened with ponderous decision making. The mansion was ringed by an iron grillework fence with two towering gates, open now toward the plaza, another billowing red banner strung between them, reading:

COURT OF REVENGE!
New York Committee of Public Safety

And atop each upright iron bar in the fence there seemed a different-colored and different-sized ball, or were those heads?

The plaza itself was filled with the spillover from the congress of rags and with platoons of surly young men in red shirts. Some of the men were armed with sinister pikes, others balanced tapered clubs on their shoulders, all of them lounged on low wooden bleachers arranged at random in the plaza. Curiously, the plaza fountain (a cakelike affair, with five tiers of pools, the outer three squarish, the inner two roundish, about a pedestal supporting a marble dish) bubbled ferociously, but it had been unmistakably altered. The central golden statute of "Abundance" was gone, replaced by a wooden superstructure. The platform overhung the bowl by several yards, and had a wooden staircase off to the right, a dozen or so steps down to the first tier of the fountain. Atop the wooden platform stood several half-naked men wearing hoods. Atop the wooden platform stood the towering arch of a guillotine. And atop the wooden platform stood a pole displaying a flapping flag with a red field, reading:

REVENGE!

Europa was spellbound by the guillotine's blade. It reflected an eerie reddish-gray light. It occurred to Europa that the whole scene was virtually without lights—electric or otherwise—and yet all seemed well lit with that eerie reddish-gray light. Europa looked up from the blade, up and up, past papers swirling overhead like vultures, up and up, past black smoke clouds from fires burning uncontrollably in the lower city, up and up, to the dome of the night sky. There, above the city, was a brilliant ball of reddish-gray fire with two tails, like swords. One tail flared off to the east in a scimitar shape to disappear behind the Plaza Hotel. The other tail flared off to the west in a saber shape to disappear behind the General Motors building.

"La cometa," said Europa.

"Ain't she somethin' tonite?" said the rag woman.

"Favolosa," said Europa.

The rag woman chuckled, elbowing another rag woman next to her on the bench. They exchanged sentences

...intelligible to Europa. The second rag woman leaned over to Europa, saying:

"Where ya been, honey?"

"Che?" said Europa.

"You feelin' poorly?" said the rag woman.

Europa shrugged in her ignorance, afraid she'd invite abuse if she persisted. She turned back to the plaza. A scarred, balding man in a dark cloak with a booming voice was making a speech atop the wooden platform. Europa watched him, understanding little. He gestured broadly to the crowd, now and again throwing his arms skyward, toward the comet, in a motion of servile supplication. Near the end of his shouting, he held up a yellow sheet of paper. Each time he pointed to it, the congress of rags reacted with gasps and whistling. He finished his harangue with chest-pounding and yellow-paper-slapping, reaching down to heave a loose bundle of yellow sheets into the crowd. The hooded men helped him. The plaza filled with swirling yellow papers. The crowd lost its relative composure, coming to its feet, not simply to grab for the papers, but also to crane to the far right, up Central Park South. Europa heard drum rolls, more cannon fire, and sirens sounding in celebration. The rag women squealed and shouted, a few dancing in tight circles, arm in arm. Europa half expected, as she pushed herself to her feet, then up onto the bench, to see a parade of saints.

Instead, she witnessed a parade of a thousand devils. As far as she could see, there were two-wheeled wooden carts, each jammed with ashen-looking men and women in greasy rags. There was little to distinguish the people in the carts from the crowd, save for the opinion that the former were leaner and prouder-looking. But then, one man in rags is another man in rags. Whoever these unfortunates were, they suffered. The throng pelted them with stones. A few young men in the crowd ran to the tumbrels to rip at the women. It was uniformly merciless. Worse, the tumbrels were not pulled by oxen, or by horses, or even by large dogs, but by small children. Red-shirted men with pikes marched alongside, poking at the children if they lagged or stumbled, snatching the collapsed to heave them up to the prisoners. From the way the prisoners comforted the exhausted children, the dynamics of the scene were clear. The children of the ruling class hauled it to the blade.

Europa was stunned by the cruelty. But there was another aspect that appalled her more. As the scene unfolded, an undeniable tempo emerged. The evening was not extraordinary. The evening was like many before. The congress of rags was a season ticket holder. The summer was just begun.

As soon as the first tumbrel had pushed through to the fountain, the red shirts fell upon the children, heaving them into the fountain's pools. Other red shirts pulled the prisoners from the tumbrel, dragging them up the steps to the guillotine. There, the scarred, balding man read off a name from the yellow sheet. Invariably, the prisoner would not cry out, would rather sink in a faint, held up only by the hooded men, who deftly tossed the victim to the block. A drum roll and then, "God have mercy!" screamed the crowd (a phrase Europa understood perfectly). The blade fell—whop—quickly to be drawn back up. The hooded men passed the corpse over the side to be laid back in the empty tumbrel. As for the amputated head, it depended upon the crowd. An executioner would hold each head high. If the crowd jeered, the head was dropped into a barrel of flames. If the crowd cheered, the head was tossed to the mob, to be batted around like a toy balloon.

The blade cut its way through the tumbrels. Europa lost sense of time. And now she could see why they'd left the fountain bubbling. As the water pushed through the planks of the platform, it washed the guillotine clean. As the Court of Revenge ran wild, as the congress of rags ran riot, the plaza's fountain ran red.

Europa swooned when a woman's head—its eyes wide in disbelief—flew dripping over her own head. But the press of the crowd was such that Europa couldn't fall. She slipped down slowly to her bench seat, suffocating on the

..ell and the bloodlust of the crowd. She sagged forward, head between her knees. As she sat this way, she spied one of those yellow sheets. Europa pulled it over. She puzzled. Most of it was impossible for her. It was a list. Across the top it said, "No. 40." There were four columns of names. They were still in the *B*'s. Each patronym was followed by an "& et cetera." And across the bottom of the sheet was a line drawing of the comet overhead, twin-tailed, one to the east like a scimitar, the other to the west, like a saber. Oddly, the comet's portrait had been sketched so that it appeared like a signature to the death list. Accordingly, below the comet's "signature," the publisher had printed, as an author might supplement his own signature with his name in type-face, the word "REVENGE!"

This, then, thought Europa, losing (regaining?) consciousness, this, then, was another sort of revolution in the days of a comet.

Book IX

Wherein the Elect
Go Off on a Comet

Aphelion

ND A final appendix to this romance, if you will; for nearly thirty-eight years after the above, most players long since gone, if not forgotten, Mrs. Grace Thyme Broadsword chanced to turn to her husband, Effert Broadsword, to ask him, "What do you think it's like there, on the comet?"

"Gosh, Gracie," said Effert, "I've always told the children it was philosophical, like a Greek island."

"You really think so?" said Gracie, setting down the letter she was writing to her eldest granddaughter, little Bee.

"Why not?" said Effert. "Except, you know, talkier. Blue sky, blue sea, red clay, gray rock, white sand, and some light green ravines. Maybe a laid-back town with an amphitheater and a good Greek restaurant."

"A Greek restaurant on a comet?" said Gracie.

"Olives, lots of black olives. And goat's cheese," said Effert.

"Oh, Effert," said Gracie.

"Oh, Gracie," said Effert.

A debate continued aimlessly elsewhere as well, this one well past the planet Neptune in space, and, to Wavy Rufus's thinking, well past boring in quality, the Englightenment panel having suffered several setbacks by permitting Rous-seau, who was well read but long-winded, to define "Virtue" at length. And so Wavy Rufus slipped off the end of the bench and crept out of the amphitheater. It was nearly suppertime anyway. Yet what most interested him was securing a place in the domino contest tonight. The Italians had challenged the English, and Wavy Rufus had secured special permission from Laddy to play for the English team, with Grandtour as his partner. The prize was a revolution's worth of Virginia tobacco, always hard to obtain this far away, thirty-eight Earth years from the Virginia fields.

As usual, Wavy Rufus took the long way down to the market square, swinging over the ridge above the shoreline. Ever since he'd gotten his eyes back—it was considered tasteless to think of it as "ever since he'd died"—he'd preferred the long way on any journey. There was always something to see—goats, chickens, sea gulls, and, of course, the tide, which was ever-changing, depending upon the comet's proximity to which celestial body. Like so many of his fellow "revolutionaries," Wavy Rufus chose to spend the bulk of his days down by the seashore. When he'd been alive, there'd never been enough time truly to enjoy a swell sea swell. It was a point of debate among the "revolutionaries" as to why a man or woman should keep his or her fascination with the sea so long after his or her passing from Earth. Wavy Rufus's opinion was that of the four available essences—earth, air, fire, and water—the only choice that made aesthetic sense was the sea. That positivist rubbish about a body craving the primeval tide pool seemed trite. But then, Wavy Rufus had experienced considerable erosion of his positivism since first he'd cleared the pearly gates to find his soul ticket stamped through for the realm of the comet calling himself *Voluntas Hallei*, where he'd existed happily this past aphelion.

Speaking of which, thought Wavy Rufus, looking one

ᴜre time out to sea, turning to pick his way down to the domino table, that bell sounding now should be it. "Dong, dong, dong," went the bell, very unobtrusive. Without time at all other than good times, the only events that mattered enough on the comet to mark were perihelion and aphelion. His Majesty didn't fuss with either, just a simple bell tolling the evening of the day they swung around to begin the 3.3-billion-mile fall to perihelion. Indeed, His Majesty lorded over a remarkably mellow domain. The most ostentatious display Wavy Rufus had witnessed since his arrival had been the red wine (claret) party Laddy had given for the French author Jules Verne (passing through on a speaking tour), marking an anniversary of the publication of his novel *To The Sun!* and its sequel, *Off On A Comet.* Monsieur Verne, a charming dilettante, had remarked at the time, a trifle high on the wine:

"Who could have guessed that a comet was philosophical, like a Greek island?"

About the Author

John Calvin Batchelor was born in Bryn Mawr, Pennsylvania, in 1948. He is the author of seven novels: *The Further Adventures of Halley's Comet* (1981), *The Birth of the People's Republic of Antarctica* (1983), *American Falls* (1985), *Gordon Liddy Is My Muse, by Tommy "Tip" Paine* (1990), *Walking the Cat, by Tommy "Tip" Paine: Gordon Liddy Is My Muse II* (1991), *Peter Nevsky and the True Story of the Russian Moon Landing* (1993), and *Father's Day* (1994). He lives in New York City with his wife, son, and daughter.